7-16

FANTASY IN DEATH

FANTASY IN DEATH

J. D. ROBB

G. P. Putnam's Sons

New York

PUTNAM

G. P. PUTNAM'S SONS
Publishers Since 1838
Published by the Penguin Group
Penguin Group (USA) Inc., 375 Hudson Street, New York, New York 10014, USA •
Penguin Group (Canada), 90 Eglinton Avenue East, Suite 700, Toronto, Ontario M4P 2Y3,
Canada (a division of Pearson Penguin Canada Inc.) • Penguin Books Ltd, 80 Strand,
London WC2R 0RL, England • Penguin Ireland, 25 St Stephen's Green, Dublin 2,
Ireland (a division of Penguin Books Ltd) • Penguin Group (Australia), 250 Camberwell Road,
Camberwell, Victoria 3124, Australia (a division of Pearson Australia Group Pty Ltd) •
Penguin Books India Pvt Ltd, 11 Community Centre, Panchsheel Park,
New Delhi–110 017, India • Penguin Group (NZ), 67 Apollo Drive, Rosedale,
North Shore 0632, New Zealand (a division of Pearson New Zealand Ltd) •
Penguin Books (South Africa) (Pty) Ltd, 24 Sturdee Avenue,
Rosebank, Johannesburg 2196, South Africa

Penguin Books Ltd, Registered Offices: 80 Strand, London WC2R 0RL, England

Library of Congress Cataloging-in-Publication Data

Robb, J. D., date.
Fantasy in death / J. D. Robb.
  p.   cm.
ISBN 978-0-399-15624-3
1. Dallas, Eve (Fictitious character)—Fiction.   2. Policewomen—Fiction.   3. Women detectives—Fiction.
4. Virtual reality—Fiction.   5. Electronic games industry—Fiction.   6. New York (N.Y.)—Fiction.   I. Title.
PS3568.O243F36   2010   2009041114
813'.54—dc22

Printed in the United States of America
10 9 8 7 6 5 4 3 2 1

BOOK DESIGN BY MEIGHAN CAVANAUGH

This is a work of fiction. Names, characters, places, and incidents either are the product of the author's imagination or are used fictitiously, and any resemblance to actual persons, living or dead, businesses, companies, events, or locales is entirely coincidental.

While the author has made every effort to provide accurate telephone numbers and Internet addresses at the time of publication, neither the publisher nor the author assumes any responsibility for errors, or for changes that occur after publication. Further, the publisher does not have any control over and does not assume any responsibility for author or third-party websites or their content.

Which would you rather be—
A conqueror in the Olympic games,
Or the crier who proclaims who are conquerors?
—PLUTARCH

True, I talk of dreams,
Which are the children of an idle brain,
Begot of nothing but vain fantasy.
—WILLIAM SHAKESPEARE

FANTASY IN DEATH

WHILE SWORDS OF LIGHTNING SLASHED AND
stabbed murderously across the scarred shield of sky,
Bart Minnock whistled his way home for the last time.
Despite the battering rain, Bart's mood bounced along with his
cheerful tune as he shot his doorman a snappy salute.

"Howzit going, Mr. Minnock?"

"It's going up, Jackie. Going way uptown."

"This rain could do the same, if you ask me."

"What rain?" With a laugh, Bart sloshed his way in soaked skids to
the elevator.

Thunder exploded across the island of Manhattan, midday com-
muters sulked under overpriced umbrellas bought from enterprising
sidewalk hawkers and maxibuses spewed up walls of wet. But in Bart's
world the sun beamed in golden rays.

He had a hot date with the sexy CeeCee, which in itself was nothing to sneeze at for a self-proclaimed nerd who'd been a virgin until the somewhat embarrassing age of twenty-four.

Five years later, and largely because of the success of U-Play, he could have his pick from a bevy of eager women—even if the eager was mostly due to the money and media his company generated.

He didn't mind.

He knew he wasn't especially good-looking and accepted his own awkwardness in romantic situations. (Except for sexy CeeCee.) He didn't know art or literature, didn't know a good vintage from a bottle of home brew. What he knew were computers and games and the seduction of technology.

Still, CeeCee was different, he thought as he turned off the locks and security on his trilevel apartment with its four-star view of downtown. She liked gaming, and didn't care about vintage wine or art galleries.

But even the evening with the sweet and sexy CeeCee wasn't the reason for the whistling or the big, bright grin on his face as he reset the door locks.

He had the latest version of Fantastical in his briefcase, and until he tested it, played it, approved it, it was all his.

His in-house intercom greeted him with a cheery *Welcome home, Bart,* and his server droid—custom-made to replicate Princess Leia, classic *Star Wars,* slave-girl mode (he was a nerd, but he was still a guy)—strolled out to offer him his favorite orange fizzy with crushed ice.

"You're home early today."

"I've got some work to do in the holo-room."

"Don't work too hard. You need to leave in two hours and twelve minutes to arrive at CeeCee's apartment on time. You're scheduled to pick up flowers on the way. Will you be staying the night?"

"That's the plan."

"Enjoy. Your shoes are very wet. Would you like me to get you a fresh pair?"

"No, that's okay. I'll grab some on the way up."

"Don't forget," she said with the quick Leia smirk that always tickled him. "Should I give you a reminder about your date closer to departure time?"

He set his briefcase aside, shook back the light brown hair that forever fell into his eyes. "That's okay. I'll set up a buzz in holo. You can just shut down for the night."

"All right. I'm here if you need me."

Normally, he'd have used his personal Leia for some conversational practice, might have had her keep him company while he unwound from the day and talked about current projects. There was nothing like a droid as far as Bart was concerned. They never judged, unless you programmed them to.

But Fantastical called him. He opened his briefcase, took out the disc, gave it a friendly kiss as he started up the stairs.

He'd decorated his spaces to his own whim and taste, so toys abounded. Props, weapons, costumes, and art from vids and games served as decor and amusement with every room on every level outfitted with various game systems, vid systems, screens, and comps.

It was, for Bart, a dream realized. He lived, as he worked, in a big e-playroom.

His second-floor office was a to-scale reproduction of the bridge of the galactic warship *The Valiant,* from the vid of the same name. His work on the gaming discs for the vid had given his fledgling U-Play its true start.

He forgot about changing his shoes, or changing his wet shirt, and went straight to the third floor.

Security on the holo-room required his thumbprint, voiceprint, and a retinal scan. Overkill, he knew, but it was more fun that way, and fun was always the name of the game. He might have opened up the space regularly for friends and guests, but he liked having the superspy aspects in place.

He reactivated them on entering, then shut down all outside coms. For the hour—okay maybe ninety minutes—he intended to play, he wanted no interruptions.

The whole point of gaming, to Bart's mind, was the immersion of self in the fantasy, or the competition, or just the fun. And Fantastical would take that immersion of self several steps beyond what was on the market in mid-2060.

If the latest adjustments and enhancements worked, the businessman inside the gamer reminded him.

"They'll work. It'll be mag to the nth," he muttered as he inserted the disc and ran through the startup. Once again he used his voiceprint, then his password. The new version was totally top secret. He and his partners hadn't built U-Play on geek alone. He understood, very well, the cutthroat business in the gaming field, and actually found the corporate espionage kind of a rush.

He was a player, he thought. Not just in games but in the *business* of games. U-Play's success provided everything he and his friends, his partner, had talked about, dreamed about, worked for.

With Fantastical, they'd be kicking it all up—and—fingers crossed—become *major* players.

He'd already decided on the scenario, a favorite, and the level. He'd practiced, studied, refined, and reworked this fantasy, the elements of it countless times during development, and now set for the game he code-named K2BK. He'd take the role of the battered and cynical hero, battling the evil forces of the beleaguered kingdom of Juno on the endangered planet of Gort.

The mirrored walls of the holo-room reflected him as the light began to swirl and dim, as his damp and wrinkled khakis and Captain Zee's T-shirt, his wet skids transformed into the scarred battle gear and boots of the warrior king.

In his hand he felt the hilt, and the weight of the broadsword. And that rush, yes, that new rush of his embodiment of the hero, and the battle to come.

Excellent, he thought. *Excellente primo.* He could smell as well as see the smoke of battle, and the blood already spilled. He reached up, felt the bulge of biceps, the pucker of an old scar.

Twinges and aches throughout his body spoke of wounds barely healed, a lifetime of combat.

Best, he *felt* strong, bold, brave, *fierce.* He became the courageous warrior king about to lead his exhausted, wounded, and unnumbered people into battle.

He let out a war cry—because he could—and heard the power of his voice shake the air.

It rocked completely.

A scruff of beard covered his face, and a tangle of hair tickled his neck and shoulders.

He *was* Tor, the warrior, the protector and rightly King of Juno.

He mounted his warhorse—on the second try, which wasn't bad— and charged into battle. He heard the cries of friend and foe as swords clashed and fire lances spewed death. His beloved Juno burned so he hacked his way through the lines while blood splattered and sweat streamed down his skin.

At his partner Benny's suggestion they'd added an optional love inter-

est. In order to reach his woman, a brave and beautiful warrior coura-
geously defending the castle walls, he had to fight his way to the front and
engage in the ultimate battle—*mano a mano* with the evil Lord Manx.

He'd reached this level countless times during development, had
gone beyond it only a handful as he programmed the challenge to the
top of the scale. It took skill, timing, agility to fight through, to dodge
the flames from lance and arrow, to deflect the slash of sword—or what
was the point?

Any hit would lower his score, potentially send him into humiliat-
ing retreat, or a valiant death. This time he wasn't looking just to beat
the level, but to hit a new record.

His horse screamed in challenge as they galloped through the stink
of smoke, leaped over bodies of the fallen. He braced and clung when
the horse reared, and still was nearly unseated.

Every time that happened, he met Manx on foot, and every time he
met Manx on foot, he lost Juno, the woman, and the game.

Not this time, he swore, and gave another booming cry as he broke
through the smoke.

And there, the walls of home where the brave fought those who tried
to destroy it. And there, the dark, fearful visage of Lord Manx, sword
red with the blood of innocents.

He felt a pang—for loss, for the happier times of his childhood before murder and deceit had sullied it.

"Your trap failed," Bart called out.

"I would have been disappointed otherwise." Manx grinned, his
black eyes shining with death. "It was always my wish to meet you
here, to end you and your line on this ground."

"It will end here, and with your blood."

The men charged; swords met. A snap of lightning Bart had added
for drama spurted and sizzled from the cross of the blades.

Bart felt the impact race up his arm, and the bolt of pain in his shoulder had him making a mental note to lower the levels on the default. Realism was important, but he didn't want gamers bitching because they'd programmed it too hot.

He turned into the next strike, blocking it, and he felt a wrenching *pop* in his shoulder. He nearly called for a pause in the program, but was too busy dodging a swipe.

What the hell, he thought as he struck out and nearly got by Manx's guard, winning wasn't winning until you worked for it.

"Your woman will be mine before nightfall," Manx snarled.

"She'll dance on your—hey!" His sword slipped, and his enemy's blade sliced his arm. Instead of the quick jolt to mark the hit, the pain seared. "What the hell. Pause—"

But for Bart, it was game over.

Lieutenant Eve Dallas badged the shell-shocked doorman and breezed by. The sun and sultry heat left over from the night's storms boosted her mood. At her side, her partner, Peabody, wilted.

"A couple months ago all you did was bitch about the cold. Now you bitch about the heat. Never satisfied."

Peabody, her dark hair pulled back in a stubby tail, continued to bitch. "Why can't they regulate the temperature?"

"Who are they?"

"The weather people. We must have the technology. Why not give us at least a couple weeks of steady mid-seventies? It's not too much to ask. You could get Roarke to work on it."

"Oh yeah, I'll tell him to get on that, right after he buys up the last ten percent of the universe." Eve rocked back on her heels as they took the elevator up, and thought of her husband of almost two years.

Actually, he probably could figure something. "If you want regulated temps, get a job where you work inside with climate control."

"June's supposed to be daisies and wafty breezes." Peabody waved a hand in the air. "Instead we're getting thunder boomers and humiture to kill."

"I like the boomers."

Peabody's dark eyes narrowed as she studied Eve's angular face. "You probably had lots of sex last night. You're almost perky."

"Shut up. I'm never perky."

"Almost. You're verging on perk."

"You're verging on a boot up the ass."

"That's better anyway."

Amused despite herself, Eve straightened her long, lean frame, then strode out the elevator when the doors whisked open.

The uniforms in the hallway came to attention. "Lieutenant."

"Officer. What have we got?"

"Victim's Bart Minnock, the U-Play guy."

"You play what?"

"U-Play, sir, it's the comp and holo-game company. The girlfriend found him this morning. He stood her up last night, she says, and she came to read him the riot act. House droid let her in, and when she got here he was locked in his holo-room, got the droid to open it up." The uniform paused. "I think you're going to want to see for yourself."

"Where's the girlfriend?"

"CeeCee Rove. We've got her inside, and an officer's with her. Got the droid on hold."

"We'll take the scene first."

She stepped inside, scanned. What she could see of the first level struck her as a clubhouse for a very rich, very indulgent adolescent boy.

Bright, primary colors with more cushion than structure, walls of screens, games, and more games, toys—heavy on the war toys. Not a living area so much as a big playroom. She supposed, given his profession, it fit.

"Third floor, LT. There's an elevator."

"We'll take the stairs."

"It's like a personal fun park," Peabody commented as they started up. "McNab would weep with joy and envy," she added, thinking of her main man. "I've got to say, it's pretty frosty."

"He might live like a kid, but he had very grown-up security on the door." She detoured on the second level long enough to determine the master bedroom was another playground, the guest rooms equipped for plenty of entertainment. He kept a home office that reminded her of a small version of Roarke's home computer lab, but with more fanciful touches.

"Serious about his work," she murmured. "Lived his work."

She backtracked to the stairs and up to the officer on the door of the holo-room.

"This door was secured?"

"The girlfriend states it was, sir, and the coms shut down. The droid confirms. It had emergency bypass clearance. The log shows the victim entering, then securing the room at sixteen thirty-three. No other entry or attempted entry until nine-eighteen this morning."

"Okay." Both Eve and Peabody opened their field kits, sealed up. "Record on," she said and stepped to the doorway.

She wasn't often surprised. She'd been a cop nearly a dozen years, and though she knew she hadn't seen it all—you never did—she'd seen plenty.

But her long brown eyes widened briefly as she took in the scene. "Now, this is something you don't see every day."

"Man. Oh, man." Peabody sucked in a sharp breath.

"Don't even think about booting."

"Have to think about it." Peabody swallowed hard. "Won't do it."

The body lay sprawled, arms and legs splayed in the bloody pool that spread over the floor. The head sat several feet away, the filmed eyes wide, the mouth in a gaping O.

"It must be said the victim lost his head, which is a pretty good guess for cause of death. Alone in a secured holo-room, no weapons. Interesting. Well, let's have a look."

She heard Peabody swallow again.

"Take the play board, see what he programmed," she ordered. "And I want all security discs and logs, building and for this unit."

"On that," Peabody said, grateful for the reprieve as Eve crossed to the body.

For the record, Eve verified the fingerprints. "Victim is identified as Bart Minnock of this address, age twenty-nine." She pulled out a pair of microgoggles. "From the on-scene exam, it appears the head was severed with a single, powerful blow. No signs of sawing or hacking." She ignored the discreet gagging sound from Peabody's direction. "In addition, the victim incurred a six-inch gash on his left forearm. There's some bruising, but none of those wounds would've been fatal. ME to confirm. Morris is going to love this one," she added, then rose to examine the head.

"Had to be a hell of a blade—big, sharp bastard, to decapitate this clean. A lot of force behind it. The secondary gash could've come from the same weapon. Glancing blow sort of thing. Defensive wound. The bruising's pretty minor."

She sat back on her heels, the head at her feet. "There's nothing in here that could've caused these wounds. No way he could've cut his own head off, deliberately or by accident with what he had to work with."

"I can't get it to run," Peabody told her. "The program. The disc won't even eject without the proper security sequence. All I've got is the log-in time and program end time. It ran for just over thirty minutes, and ended at seventeen-eleven."

"So he came home, came up here almost directly, programmed the game. It looks like it, and he, ran for the thirty minutes. We need an e-team and the sweepers in here. I want the ME to red-flag the tox screen. Maybe somebody slipped him something, influenced him to by-pass his own security, somehow keep it off the logs. Set it up, then take the droid. I'll take the girlfriend."

Eve found CeeCee in the media room on the first level. A pretty blond with an explosion of curls, she sat in one of the roomy chairs. It dwarfed her, even with her legs tucked up, and her hands clasped in her lap. Her eyes—big, bright, and blue—were red-rimmed, puffy, and still carried the glassiness of shock.

Eve dismissed the officer with a nod, then crossed over to sit. "Ms. Rove?"

"Yes. I'm supposed to stay here. Somebody took my 'link. I should tag somebody, shouldn't I? Somebody."

"We'll get that back to you. I'm Lieutenant Dallas. Why don't you tell me what happened?"

"I told somebody." CeeCee looked around vaguely. "The other police. I've been thinking. Is Bart playing a joke? He does that sometimes. Plays jokes. He likes to pretend. Is this all pretend?"

"No, it's not." Eve took the chair facing so her gaze would be level with CeeCee's. "You were supposed to meet him last night?"

"At my place. At eight. I made dinner. We were going to have dinner at my place because I like to cook. Well, sometimes. But he didn't come."

"What did you do?"

"He can be late. It's okay. He gets caught up. Sometimes I'm late, so it's okay. But he didn't come, and he didn't answer the 'link. I tried his office, too, but Benny said he left a little after four to work at home for a bit."

"Benny?"

"Benny Leman. He works with Bart, and he was still there. They work late, a lot. They like to."

"Did you come over here to find out what he was doing?"

"No. I almost did. I got pretty steamed because I went to a lot of trouble, you know? I mean I *cooked,* and I got wine and candles, everything." She drew in a breath that hitched and stuttered. "And he didn't come or let me know he'd be late. He forgets, and that's okay, but he always answers his 'link, or remembers before it's really late. He sets reminders. But I was pretty steamed, and it was storming. I thought, 'I'm not going out in this.' So I drank some wine and I ate dinner, and I went to bed. Screw it."

She covered her face, keening a little, rocking herself while Eve stayed silent. "I just said screw it, screw you, Bart, because I'd made a really nice dinner. But this morning, I was really, *really* steamed because he never came or tried to reach me, and I didn't have to be to work till ten, so I came by. I thought, okay, that's okay, we're going to have our first big fight because that's no way to treat somebody. Is it?"

"No. How long have you been seeing each other?"

"Almost six months."

"And this would've been your first big fight? Seriously?"

CeeCee smiled a little even as tears continued to drip. "I got a little bit steamed once in a while, but you can't stay mad at Bart. He's such a sweetie. But this time, I was laying it down. Leia let me in."

"Who's Leia?"

"Oh, his house droid. He had her designed to look like the *Star Wars* character. From *Return of the Jedi.*"

"Okay."

"Anyway, she said he was in the holo-room, fully secured, and had the coms down. DO NOT DISTURB. That according to her morning log, he'd been in there since about four-thirty or something the day before. So I got worried. Like maybe he'd gotten sick in there, or passed out, and I convinced her to bypass."

"You convinced a droid?"

"Bart programmed her to listen to me after we'd been tight for a few months. Plus he'd been in over his twelve-hour limit. Then she opened the room, and . . ."

Her lips trembled; her eyes welled anew. "How can it be real? First I thought it was, and I screamed. Then I thought it was a joke, or a droid, and I almost got steamed again. Then I saw it was Bart. It was Bart. And it was horrible."

"What did you do?"

"I think I kind of fainted. But, like, on my feet. I don't know, for a second or a minute everything went black and swirly, and when it wasn't, I ran." Tears streamed down her cheeks even as she flushed. "I ran downstairs. I almost fell, but I got downstairs and I called nine-one-one. Leia made me sit down, and she made me tea. She said there'd been an accident and we had to wait for the police. That would be in her programming, I guess. But it can't be an accident. How can it be an accident? But it has to be."

"Do you know anyone who'd want to hurt Bart?"

"How could anyone want to hurt Bart? He's just a big kid. A really smart big kid."

"How about family?"

"His parents live in North Carolina. He bought them a house on the beach because they always wanted one, once U-Play took off. Oh God, oh God, his parents! Somebody has to tell them."

"I'll take care of that."

"Okay, okay." She shut her eyes tight. "Good. Because I don't think I could. I don't know how. I don't know how to do any of this."

"What about you? Old boyfriends?"

Her eyes popped open. "Oh God, no. I mean, yes, I had boyfriends before Bart, but nobody who'd . . . I never had the kind of breakup that would . . . I wasn't seeing anybody special or regular before I hooked up with Bart."

"How about at his business? Did he have to let anyone go recently, or reprimand anyone?"

"I don't think so." She swiped at her cheeks now as her brow furrowed in thought. "He never said anything to me, and he would've. I think. He hated confrontations, except in a game. He'd have told me if he'd had trouble with anyone at work, I really think. He's a happy guy, you know? He makes other people happy, too. How could it happen? I don't know how this could happen. Do you?"

"Not yet."

She had CeeCee escorted home, then began her own room-by-room. Plenty of them, she thought, and each designed so the occupants could play in comfort. Roomy chairs, oversized sofas shouted out in their bright colors. Nothing dull for Bart. The menus of the AutoChefs and Friggies ran to those adolescent tastes again—pizza, burgers, dogs, chips, candy. Fizzies and soft drinks outnumbered wine and beer and liquor.

She found no illegals, and only the mildest of over-the-counter chemical aids.

She'd nearly completed her initial search of the master bedroom when Peabody came in.

"No illegals that I've come across," Eve began. "No sex toys either, though he's got some porn on vid and on game discs. Most of the comps throughout are passcoded, and those that aren't are game-only. No data, no com."

"The droid confirms the girlfriend's statement to the first-on-scene," Peabody told her. "The vic told her to shut down for the night after he got home, and her log confirms she did. She has an auto-wake for nine, which activated as the vic didn't start her up prior. She's a little spooky."

"How?"

"Efficient. Plus she doesn't look like a droid. She doesn't have any of the tells, like the occasional stuttering, the blank stare while it processes data. Definitely cutting-edge there. I know she didn't actually *feel* shock and grief, but it seemed like she did. It did. She asked me if someone would contact his parents. That's active thinking. It's not droidlike."

"Or it's careful and thorough programming. Let's find out more about U-Play. You don't get a trilevel in this neighborhood for chump change. Let's find out who gets the money, and who's lined up to take over the company. We need to know what he was working on. And who was as good as he was."

She paused, looked around the room again. "Somebody got in here, got past the droid, got into that holo-room without leaving a discernable trace."

She only knew one person who'd be able to pull that off—and she was married to him. Maybe Roarke would know another.

"Priority is to get that disc out of the holo-room unit, run it."

"E-team's on the way, and so are the sweepers. One of the uniforms got all security discs for the last twenty-four."

"You keep on the room-by-room. I'm going to notify next of kin via 'link. We'll see what EDD can do for us, then we'll pay a visit to U-Play."

She took a few moments after the notification to let it all settle. She'd just crushed the lives of two people she hadn't known existed less than an hour before, Eve thought as she sat on the side of Bart Minnock's bed. They would never really be the same, nothing would ever be as it had been for them.

Murder did that. Took lives, crushed others, changed still others forever.

So why had someone needed or wanted to end Bart Minnock's existence? And why had they chosen the method used?

Money. Jealousy. Revenge. Secrets. Passion.

From all appearances, he had money, she thought, and ran a quick, standard financial. Okay, he had money, and U-Play was a strong, young company. Her first instinct was to take CeeCee at her word. No jealous exes. But money often generated jealousy. Revenge might come through a competitor, or an employee who felt shafted or underappreciated. Secrets, everyone had a few. Passion? Gaming had certainly been the victim's.

Method . . . Murder during game play. Kind of poetic in a sick way. Decapitation. Sever the head—the brain—and the body falls. Minnock was the brains of U-Play it seemed from her quick run. Would the body fall without him? Or was someone ready and waiting to slip in and take over?

Whatever the answers, the method had been bold, purposeful, and complex. God knew there were easier ways to kill. It was very likely the killer was just as serious and devoted to gaming as his victim.

**2**

EVE HEARD MCNAB BEFORE SHE SAW HIM. IF he'd been a teenaged girl instead of a grown man she'd have called the sound he made a squeal.

"Holy jumping Jesus! This place is iced to the cube!"

"Settle down, boy. This is a crime scene."

She caught Feeney's reprimand, but she recognized the edge of excitement in his tone. The EDD captain and her former partner wasn't just a grown man, she thought, but a freaking grandfather.

Still, maybe e-geeks were always kids under the skin.

"Somebody should say something. Like a prayer."

And they'd brought Callendar. The reverential whisper made Eve shake her head. Maybe she'd expected more from that source as Callendar was female.

She went to the stairs, looked down at the three of them. She saw Feeney's grizzled head—the ginger and silver—McNab's eye-searing orange cargo pants, and the sunburst pattern of Callendar's shirt.

"When you've finished being awed and gooey, maybe you could mosey on up here. We've got a pesky little murder to deal with."

Feeney looked up, and Eve saw she'd been right, there was a flush of excitement on his usually mopey face. McNab just grinned, and the little bounce in his step had his shining blond ponytail swaying. Callendar at least had the grace to look slightly sheepish as she hunched her shoulders in a shrug.

"This place is a cathedral to all that is E and Game," McNab called up.

"I'm sure the dead guy up here would be thrilled with your approval. Holo-room, third floor."

She headed up herself, then paused a moment when she saw Chief Medical Examiner Morris hadn't sent one of his team for the on-scene, but had come himself.

He looked good, but then he always did. His slick black suit missed being funereal by the touches of silver in the cord braided through his long queue and the subtle pattern of his tie. Still, he seemed to wear black more often these days, and she understood it was a subtle symbol of mourning for his lost lover.

It had been his life Eve had crushed one morning in the spring, his life she knew would never be quite the same because of that loss.

He must have sensed her for even as he continued to examine the body, he spoke. "This is something you don't see every day, even when you're us."

"That's what I said."

He looked up then, and his exotic face softened, just a little, with a smile. "But then people often lose their heads over murder. When the data came in, I wanted to see for myself, on-scene." He nodded toward the head. "From the spatter and pool, it appears that part of him left this part of him in a hurry, went splat—"

"Is that a medical term?"

"Of course. Splat and roll. It's fate's little jab in the ribs that the face landed up and toward the door. It looks like the poor bastard died before he knew his head took wing, but we'll take all of him in and see what we see."

"A lot of force to decapitate that clean, and a damn sharp blade."

"I'd agree."

"The girlfriend's about five-two, maybe a hundred and ten fully dressed. She wouldn't have the muscle. A droid could do it."

"Possibly, if the programming was altered and enhanced."

"I haven't come across anything that says self-termination, but a logical theory, given the circumstance, might be he wanted out, wanted out in a flashy way. Programs the droid. It does the job, disposes of the weapon, resets the security. It feels like bullshit, but it's an angle."

"People often do the incomprehensible. It's what makes them so fascinating. Was he in play?"

"Apparently. Whatever disc he had going is fail-safed, still in the unit." She gestured to the controls. "EDD's heading upstairs. Maybe he had the droid in play, too, and something went very wrong." But she shook her head, slid her hands into her pockets. "And that wouldn't explain the droid reprogramming itself. It's cutting-edge—ha-ha—according to Peabody, but that's beyond any edge. Droids require a human operator to alter programming."

"As far as I know, but then I don't know much about this sort of thing. In general, human-replicate droids strike me as mildly creepy and just a little pitiable."

"Yes!" She pulled her hand out of her pocket to point at him. "Exactly."

"And since they don't do the incomprehensible without that human operator programming it, they're just not that interesting." Morris shrugged as he got to his feet. "You should ask your expert consultant, civilian. He'd know whatever there would be to know, I'd think."

"I'll see what the department geeks have to say before I tap Roarke."

"Whoa."

She turned to see the aforesaid geeks step in.

"Big whoa," McNab repeated. "Now that's a large fucking shame. Bart Minnock, boy genius."

"I always figured he'd come out ahead." Callendar winced. "Sorry."

"It's inevitable. That's Morris's." Eve jerked a thumb toward the two pieces of Minnock, then the control panel. "That's yours. It appears the vic came in to play or maybe to test a new program. Whatever he put in is still in there. It's passcoded and fail-safed. I need it out without damaging it or the unit. I need the security on this door and the entrance door fine-toothed. The logs say nobody went in or out once he locked in, but since he didn't do that to himself with his fingernails, the logs are off. Peabody and I will be in the field. Since everyone here has a good head on their shoulders—see? Inevitable. I'll expect some progress by the time we get back to Central."

She left them to it, signaled to Peabody.

"Uniforms did the knock-on-doors," Peabody told her as they started out. "Since his place takes up the top three floors of the building, we didn't get anything. The doorman on duty last night came in when contacted. He confirms time of arrival, and swears no one came in for Minnock or accessed any of the three floors until the girlfriend went up this morning."

"A smart e-geek employs, works with, and knows other smart e-geeks. Let's go find out who didn't like good old Bart."

U-Play sprawled and spread over the converted warehouse. Activity, and what struck Eve as a manic energy, buzzed and beeped in the air. From the countless comps and screens, the open labs and offices came the sounds of vehicle crashes, space wars, maniacal laughter, booming threats, and the cheers of the victorious.

Little worlds, complex fantasies, endless competition, Eve thought. How did anyone keep it straight?

People, some who looked barely old enough to buy a brew and all clad in wild colors or the sag and bag of lounge wear, bounced over the four open floors. To her ear, they seemed to all talk at once in their incomprehensible e-shorthand as they operated handhelds, communicated on headsets, played with smart screens, and slurped down a variety of bottled go-drinks.

It was like EDD on Zeus, Eve thought.

"It's Nerd World," Peabody said. "Or Geek Galaxy. I can't decide which because it's full of nerds and geeks."

"It's Nerd World in the Geek Galaxy. How can they hear themselves think? Why doesn't anybody close a door?"

"As someone who lives with a geek with aspects of nerd, I can tell you they claim the noise, the movement, the basic chaos keeps them up, keeps them sharp."

"Their heads should all explode." Eve watched people ride up and down old freight elevators cased with glass or jog up and down iron stairs in clunky airboots or skinny skids. Others lounged in reclining chairs and sofas playing games with the glassy and focused stare of marathon runners.

Eve grabbed one, a young woman wearing what looked to be a pair of overalls that had been splattered with paint by a crazed three-year-old.

"Who's in charge?"

The woman, who had multiple rings in her ears, nose, eyebrows, blinked. "Of what?"

"Of this." Eve raised an arm to encompass the madness.

"Oh, Bart. But he's not in yet. I don't think."

"Who's next? Down the chain?"

"Um."

"Let's try this." Eve pulled out her badge.

"Oh, gosh. We're all legal and stuff. Maybe if you want to talk about licenses and all that, you want Cill or Benny or Var."

"Where do I find Cill or Benny or Var?"

"Um." She pointed up. "Probably on three." She turned a circle, looking up. "There's Benny, on three. Really tall guy, red dreads? I got work, okay. So . . . cha."

Benny Leman topped out at about six foot eight, by Eve's gauge, and ran about two hundred after soaking in a lake for a few hours. He was a walking stick figure with skin the depth and gloss of ebony and a fiery headful of floppy dreadlocks.

By the time they'd climbed to the third floor, her eardrums throbbed from the noise, her eyes twitched from the assault of color and image, and she'd decided U-Play was in reality the seventh circle of hell.

She found Benny doing the typical e-geek prance as he shouted strange terms into his headset, operated a palm unit with one hand, and bapped his fingers on a smart screen with the other.

Still, he managed to send her a blinding white smile and hold up a hand in a "just a sec" gesture. His words hit her in one long buzz about nano, mothers, terabytes and CGI.

The 'link on his loaded work counter beeped, and when his pocket began to chime, Eve assumed he had a 'link in there, too. Someone came to the doorway, lifted the thumb of one hand, gave a back-and-forth move with the other. Benny answered with a nod, shrug, and shuffle, which seemed to satisfy his coworker, who dashed away.

"Sorry." In a pretty voice with just a hint of island breezes, Benny ignored the chimes and beeps to offer another smile. "We're a little busy around here this morning. If you're here for the interview, you really want Cill. I can—"

"Mr. Leman." Eve held up her badge. "I'm Lieutenant Dallas, NYPSD. This is my partner, Detective Peabody."

"Golly." Though the smile remained, it edged toward puzzled. "Is somebody in trouble about something?"

"You could say that." She gestured to Peabody to close the door. Like the walls, it was glass, but at least it cut some of the noise. "Would you turn off that screen?"

"Okay. Am I in trouble about something? Oh shit, did Mongo get on the 'link? I didn't get home last night, but my droid's supposed to look after him. I—"

"Who's Mongo?"

"My parrot. He's a good boy, but he likes to access the 'link for cranks."

"It's not about your parrot. It concerns Bart Minnock."

"Bart? Bart's in trouble? That explains why I can't reach him. But Bart wouldn't do anything illegal. Does he need a lawyer? Should I . . ." Something crossed his face—a new kind of puzzlement, and the first shadows of fear. "Is he hurt? Was there an accident?"

"I'm sorry to have to tell you Mr. Minnock was murdered yesterday."

"Oh come on!" Quicksilver anger replaced the fear. "He was here yesterday. This isn't funny. Bart knows I cruise a joke as much as anybody, but this isn't chuckle."

"It's not a joke, Mr. Leman," Peabody said gently. "Mr. Minnock was killed late yesterday afternoon in his home."

"Nuh-uh." The childish denial came out poignantly as tears sheened deep, dark eyes. Benny took one stumbling step back, then simply sat on the floor. "No. Not Bart. No."

To keep their faces level, Eve crouched. "I'm very sorry for your loss, and I understand this is a shock, but we need to ask you some questions."

"In his apartment? But he has security. He has good security. He's too trusting. Did he let someone in? I don't understand." He looked at her pleadingly as tears streamed down his cheeks. "Are you sure? Are you positive?"

"Yes. Do you know someone who'd want to hurt him?"

"Not Bart." Benny shook his head. "Not Bart. How? How is he dead?"

She wanted to wait on the details. "When did you last see him or have contact with him?"

"He left early yesterday. I'm not sure. About four, maybe. He had a date with CeeCee. His girl. And he had some things he wanted to do at home. He was really happy." He grabbed Eve's hand. "CeeCee? Is she hurt? Is she okay?"

"Yes, she's fine. She wasn't there."

On a ragged breath, Benny closed his eyes. "No, that's right. He was going to her place, for dinner." He scrubbed his hands over his cheeks, then just left his face buried in them. "I don't know what to do."

"Was he having any trouble here, with the company, with employees?"

"No. No. Things are good. Really good. It's a happy place. Bart runs a happy place."

"What about competitors?"

"Nothing, really. Some try to hack in, or try to get a weasel inside. That's just the way it is. It's kind of like another game. Bart's careful. We're all careful. We have good security. We screen and delouse and realign regularly."

The door opened. Eve glanced back to see a stunning Asian woman with black hair tied at her nape to fall straight to her waist. Her eyes glowed cat green in her fine-boned face.

"Bens, what the hell? I'm piled up by six, and you're . . . What's wrong?" She rushed in to drop by his side. "What happened?"

"It's Bart, Cilly, it's Bart. He's dead."

"Oh, don't be stupid." She slapped his arm, started to rise again, but he grabbed her hand.

"Cilly, it's true. These are the police."

"What are you talking about?" Her reaction Eve gauged as insult as she pushed fluidly to her feet. "Let me see some badges."

She snatched Eve's then yanked a miniscanner out of her pocket. "Okay, maybe it reads genuine, but—" She broke off, and her hand trembled slightly as she stared at the name on the badge, then at Eve's face. "Dallas," she whispered. "You're Roarke's cop."

"I'm New York's cop," Eve corrected, then took back the badge.

"Roarke's cop doesn't bullshit." Cill knelt down, wrapped an arm tight around Benny's bony shoulders. "What happened to Bart? Oh God, oh crap, what happened to Bart?"

"Is there somewhere we can talk, privately, that's not the floor?" Eve asked.

"Ah." Cill passed a hand over her face. "Break room. It's up a level. I can clear it. But we need Var. We need to hear it together before we . . . before we tell the others." She turned, laid her brow against Benny's. "I'll clear it and get Var. Just give me a minute. Benny'll bring you up." She leaned back, took another breath before meeting Eve's eyes again. "You do murders. I know that, and it means Bart was . . . Did they hurt him? Just tell me if they hurt him."

"I can tell you I believe it was very quick."

"Okay. Okay. You take them upstairs, Bens, and don't say anything to anybody until we know what happened." She cupped his face briefly. "Just hang on now."

She rose, dashed out.

"What's your function here, Benny?" Eve asked. "Yours, Cill's, Var's. What's the pecking order?"

"On, ah, paper we're like co-VPs. But Cill's GID—Get It Done. I'm GTB—Go To Benny, and Var's BS—Brainstorm. Everybody knows they can come to one of us or—or Bart if they have an idea or a problem."

"And what was Bart's unofficial title?"

"Triple B. Big Brain Boss." His smile wobbled. "He's always the smartest one in the room. I guess I should take you up."

When they arrived, the wall screens were blank, the comps quiet, and the scatter of seats empty. Cill stood staring at one of the several vending machines. They offered fancy coffees, what appeared to be every soft drink on the planet, and a 24/7's stock of snacks. Eve imagined the AutoChefs were as primed as Bart's home units had been, and had a low-grade urge for pizza.

"I thought I wanted a power drink, because I always want a power drink," Cill murmured. "But I don't." She turned around. "Var's coming right up. I didn't tell him why. I thought . . . anyway, do you want something? I can just use my pass."

"We're good, thanks," Eve told her.

"You sit down, Benny." Cill swiped her pass then selected a bottle of water. She pushed it on Benny. "Drink a little."

She tended him, Eve thought. Not like a lover but a doting sister.

Cill went back to Vending, ordered up a coffee. "For Var," she said. "He'll want coffee."

He came in fast, a stocky man of about thirty wearing the maxi-cargos McNab favored in an eye-friendly khaki, but his well-worn skids were the same stoplight red as his shirt. His brown hair capped short around a face hovering between pleasant and homely.

"Jeez, Cill, I told you I'm buried today. No time for breaks. And with Bart still off-line I've got five shitloads to shovel before I—"

"Var." Cill passed him the coffee. "You need to sit down."

"I need to move. Seriously. So make it quick and . . ." He noticed Eve and Peabody for the first time. "Sorry." His face edged slightly closer to pleasant with his smile. "Didn't know we had company. Are you the reps from Gameland? I wasn't expecting you until this afternoon. I'd have been a little more organized by then. Probably."

"This is Lieutenant Dallas and . . ."

"Detective Peabody."

"Yeah." Cill took a deep breath, then closed the glass door. "They're here about Bart."

"Bart?" A quick laugh exploded. "What'd he do? Get drunk and jaywalk? Do we need to post bail?"

"Sit down, Var," Cill murmured.

"Why? What?" Amusement faded. "Oh hell, oh shit, did he get mugged or something? Is he hurt? Is he okay?"

"We're Homicide," Eve said. "Bart Minnock's been murdered."

The coffee slipped out of Var's hand and splashed over his bright red shoes. "What do you mean? What does that mean?"

"Sit down, Var." Cill pulled him to a chair. "Just sit down. We'll clean that up later."

"But this is crazy. Bart can't be . . . When? How?"

"Sometime between four-thirty and five yesterday afternoon, in his apartment a few blocks from here. He was found by CeeCee Rove earlier this morning, in his holo-room. He'd been decapitated."

After Benny's strangled gasp, there was utter silence. Beside him, Cill went deathly white. Her hand flayed out, and Var gripped it.

"Someone cut his head off?" As Cill began to shake, Benny put an arm around her so the three of them sat on the sofa as one unit. "Someone cut Bart's *head* off?"

"That's correct. It appears he was in the holo-room at the time of the attack, and had programmed a game by disc. EDD is working on re-moving the disc from the holo-unit. I'm going to need to verify the whereabouts of all of you from three to six yesterday."

"We were here," Cill said quietly. "We were all here. Well, I left just before six. I had a yoga class, and it starts at six. It's just down the street at Blossom. Benny and Var were still here when I left."

"I think I was here until about six-thirty." Var cleared his throat. "I-I went home. My group's got a game—a virtual game—of Warlord going, and we played from about seven to ten. Benny was still here when I left, and he was already in when I got here at eight-thirty this morning."

"I worked late and bunked here. Some of us were around until seven or eight—I don't remember, but we can check the logs. I shut the place up, and worked until about one, then I crashed. None of us would hurt Bart. We're family. We're family."

"They have to know." Cill leaned her head on his shoulder a moment. "It's one of the steps. You have to take the steps to get to the next level. If Bart let somebody into his holo, he trusted them, or . . ."

"Or," Eve prompted.

"He was showing off." Var's voice broke, and once again he cleared his throat.

"What might he want to show off? What was he working on he'd want to take home, play with, show off?"

"We've got a lot of things in development," Var told her. "A lot ready to roll out, others we're fine-tuning. Bart took hard copies home a lot, to play them out, look for kinks and glitches and ways to pump it up. We all did."

"Then he'd have logged it out?"

"He should have, yeah." Var stared blankly. "Oh, I could check. I can go check."

"I'll go with you, Peabody," Eve said with a nod, then followed Var out while her partner continued to interview.

They took one of the elevators down, with Var waving people off. His pockets sent out chirps and beeps and buzzes. She saw him start to reach in—an instinctive move—then let his hand drop away.

"They'll know something's up, something's wrong," he said to Eve. "What do we tell them? I don't know what to tell them."

"We'll need to interview all the employees. How many are there?"

"On-site? Seventy or so. We have a couple dozen nationally who work virtually—in sales, in testing, that kind of thing." He gestured her into an office that looked like the bridge of a starship.

"This is Bart's space. It's, ah, a replica of Galactica's CIC. Bart works—worked—best when he had fun with it."

"Okay. We'll need to go through his things here, and take his comps and com units in."

"Don't you need a warrant or something?"

She aimed a cool look. "Do you want me to get one?"

"No. Sorry." He raked a hand through his hair and sent the short ends into tiny tufts. "No. I just . . . His stuff. It's all his stuff. He'd have logged anything he took with him on this unit. It's inventory. The four of us have the same password here, so we can check what's in and out. There's a secondary, different for each of us, that's required on our own units to edit. So we can't mess around, you know?"

"All right."

He entered the password manually, his back to Eve. "Var," he said and held his pass up for verification.

Var is cleared, the computer announced.

"Show any log-outs for off-site use by Bart for June twenty-third."

"Make it a week," Eve told him.

"Oh. Amend to June seventeenth to June twenty-third."

One moment, please. How are you, Var?

"I've been better."

I'm sorry to hear that. Here's your list. Can I help?

"Not right now, thanks. There's nothing for yesterday." He gestured at the screen. "He's got a couple of in-developments off-site through the week, but he logged them back in. He didn't have anything out yesterday."

"I'll take a copy of that list, and a copy of any of the programs he took out this week."

"Oh wow, Jeez. I can't. I mean, I really can't just give you copies of stuff we've got in development." His face went from shocked, to pained, to worried. "It's, like, secret. Nobody but the four of us is cleared to take anything off-site. Benny won't even do that until we're about ready to rock it. It's why he ends up working all-nighters here. He's nervous about taking something that's not in the jump out of the building."

"I'll just get a warrant."

"Oh, man. I don't know what to do. I can't think straight." Tears swirled into his eyes before he turned away. "I have to protect the company, but I don't want to do anything that messes things up. I don't even know if I can say yes or no. We have to vote on it. The three of us. We'd need to figure it out. Can you let us try to figure it out first?"

"I'll give you some time. How long did you know Bart?"

"Since college. He was already hooked with Cill and Benny. They hit in, like, elementary, and then we all just . . . See the logo." He pointed to the logo of U-Play on the screen. "He'd come up with a lot of fancier ones, really rocking ones, but he wanted this. The words in a square. He said that was us, the square, because it took four of us to make it happen. Can I be excused for a minute? Please. I just want to, um, take a minute."

"Go ahead."

As he fled, Eve's 'link signaled. "Dallas."

"I've got good news and bad news," Feeney told her.

"Good first, it's been a crap morning."

"We were able to dig some of the program details out of the unit. The name's Fantastical, and it's coded SID.12—still in development, I'd say twelfth version. It's got the U-Play copyright, and the date of last edit as of two days ago."

"Was he playing solo, or was somebody in it with him?"

"The unit's set for solo, but that's part of the bad. No way to tell from the disc. No way to tell what the hell Fantastical is as the disc self-destructed when we bypassed the last fail-safe."

"Shit."

"It's pretty toasted. We might be able to get something off it, given a miracle or two. They have to have a copy. No way this is the only one."

"I'll get on that from here. I'm going to need a team to pick up the vic's work equipment. Try not to blow it up."

"That hurts, kid."

"Well, it might as well be a crap day for you, too," Eve said and signed off before signaling Peabody. "I need you to come to the vic's office, start a prelim search, and keep everybody else out. I'm on my way there."

"Copy that. I've got the salients on these two, and I'll do runs on the three of them. Are we going to interview the rest of the place today?"

"Better now than later. We'll keep it to whereabouts at the time of until we do more runs."

"There's over seventy of them, Dallas."

She sighed. "Contact Feeney again. He and McNab and Callendar can come down. They speak geek anyway."

"Copy that, too. McNab's going to wet his pants when he sees this place."

"And won't that be fun? You here, me there. Now." Eve clicked off again.

Eve took her time going back. She saw that Var was right—people knew something was up, something was off. Heads turned in her direction, whispers followed her. The place reeked of guilt and worry and just a hint of excitement.

What's going on, what did they do? Are we in trouble?

She spotted Var coming back from the opposite direction, looking wrecked, and the whispers pumped up to murmurs.

She let him go in ahead of her, then closed the door behind her.

"What's Fantastical?"

The question was answered with shocked silence.

"I'LL GET A WARRANT." EVE TRACKED HER GAZE from face to face, looking for the weak spot. "And the department e-team goes through every byte of every file. And I shut you down while they do. It could take weeks."

"But you can't, you can't shut us down," Benny protested. "We have more than seventy people on-site, and all the others online depending on us. And the distributors, the accounts. Everything that's in development."

"Yeah, that's a shame. Murder trumps all."

"They have bills, they have families," Cill began.

"And I've got the two parts of Bart."

"That's low," Var mumbled. "That's low."

"Murder usually is. Your choice." She held up her 'link.

"We can get the lawyers on it." Cill glanced at Benny, then Var. "But—"

"Murder trumps all," Eve repeated. "I'll get my warrant, and I'll get my answers. It'll just take longer. Meanwhile, your friend's in the morgue. But maybe a game means more to you than that."

"It's not just a game." Passion rose in Benny's voice. "It's the ult for Bart, for us, for the company. The top of top secret—and we swore. We all swore an oath not to talk about it with anyone not directly assigned. And even then, it's only need-to-know."

"I need to know. He was playing it when he was killed."

"But . . . but that's not possible," Cill began. "You said he was killed at home."

"That's right. With a disc copy of Fantastical in his holo-unit."

"That's wrong, that's got to be wrong." Paler now, Var shook his head. "He wouldn't have taken a development copy off-site without telling us, not without logging it out. It breaks protocol."

"He had it at home? He took it off-site, without telling any of us?" Benny stared at Eve with eyes that read betrayal as much as shock.

"She's just trying to get us to tell her—"

"For God's sake, Var, use your head," Cill snapped. "She wouldn't know about it if they hadn't found it at Bart's." As she pressed her fingers to her eyes, a half-dozen rings glittered and gleamed in the light. "He was so juiced up about it, we nearly had it down. Nearly. I don't understand why he'd have taken it out without letting us know, and why he didn't log it. He's pretty fierce on logging, but he was so juiced over it."

"What is it?"

"An interactive holo fantasy game. Multi-function," Benny continued. "The player or players choose from a menu of settings, levels, story lines, worlds, eras—or they can create their own through the personalize feature. The game will read the player or players' choices, actions, reactions, movements, and adjust the scenario accordingly.

It's nearly impossible to play any scenario through exactly the same way twice. It's always going to give the player a new challenge, a new direction."

"Okay, high-end on the fun and price scale, but not staggering new ground."

"The sensory features are off the scale," Var told her. "More real than real, and the operator has the option of adding in more features as they go. There's reward and punishment."

"Punishment?" Eve repeated.

"Say you're a treasure hunter," Cill explained. "You'd maybe collect clues or gems, artifacts, whatever, depending on the level and the scene. But you screw up, you get tossed into another challenge, and lose points. Maybe you're attacked by rival forces, or you fall and break your ankle, or lose your equipment in a raging river. Screw up enough, game over, and you need to start the level again."

"The program reads *you*," Benny went on. "Your pulse rate, your BP, your body temp. Just like a medi-unit. It tailors the challenges to your specific physicality. It combines the sensations of top-flight VR with the reality-based imagery of high-end holo. Fight the dragon to save the princess? You'll feel the heat, the weight of the sword. Slay the dragon, and the princess is grateful. You'll, ah, feel that, too. The full experience."

"If the dragon wins?"

"You get a jolt. Nothing painful, just a buzz, and like Cill said, the game ends at that point. You can start it up again, from that point or back at the beginning, or change any factors. But the program will also change. It morphs and calculates," he added, obviously warming to the topic. "The characters in each program are enhanced with the same AI technology used in droids. Friend or foe, they're programmed to want to win as much as the player."

"It's a leap," Cill said. "A true leap in merged techs. We're working out some kinks, and we've projected we can have it on the market in time for the holiday blast. When it hits, U-Play's going to go through the roof. Bart wanted it more user-friendly, and to keep the price point down. So we've been working on home and arcade and . . . it's complicated."

"We've got a lot invested, in the technology, the application, the programming, the simulations. If any of it leaks before we're ready to launch . . ." Var's mouth tightened.

"It could take us under," Cill finished. "It's a make or break."

"In six months, a year, we'd be up there with SimUlate. We'd be global, and seriously ding in off-planet," Benny told her. "Not just the up-and-comer, not just the wonder kids of gaming. We'd *be* gaming. But without Bart . . ."

"I don't know if we can do it. I don't know how we can do it," Cill said.

"We have to." Var took her hand. "We can't lose this. Bart started it, and we have to finish it. You have to keep the game under wraps," Var told Eve. "You have to. If anybody gets their hands on that development disc—"

"It self-destructed when the e-team tried to remove it."

"Seriously?" Benny blinked. "Frosty. Sorry," he said instantly. "Sorry. It's just . . . Bart must have added the security. That's why he's Bart."

"How many copies are there?"

"There were four. One for each of us to work with. It's what I was working on last night," Benny added. "I had it in sim, playing operator, and working with a droid. Mostly we work on it after the rest of the crew leaves."

"Only the four of you know about it?"

"Not exactly. Everybody knows we're working on something big. We've got a lot of good brains in here," Cill commented. "We use them. But nobody knows exactly what we've got. Just pieces. And yeah, some of those brains are smart enough to put a lot of the pieces together. But we've been careful to keep it on the low. Leaks are death in gaming."

She seemed to realize what she'd said, and shivered. "Do you think somebody found out, and . . ."

"It's an angle. I'm going to need a copy of the game."

The three of them stared at her, miserably.

"Look, if it's what you say it is, and anything leaks on my end, you're going to sue the department and possibly the city of New York for a big-ass bundle. If I'm culpable, you can probably sue me, too. I'll lose my rep and very likely my badge—and those are every bit as important to me as the game is to you. My only interest in the game is how it pertains to Bart's murder."

"She's Roarke's cop," Cill said.

"What? Shit."

Cill shoved around, burned Var with a look. "Roarke's not going to steal from us. He wouldn't rob Bart's grave, goddamn it." Tears flowed again. "He helped us get started. He *liked* Bart."

"Roarke knew Bart?" Eve asked, and tried not to let her stomach sink.

"He wanted to recruit us." Cill swiped at tears with the backs of her hands while her eyes shimmered in green pools. "All of us, but I think especially Bart. But we wanted to start our own. He helped us out, gave us advice, let us play off him for ideas on how to set it all up. We've all got an open offer from Roarke Industries, SimUlate, or any of the arms. He wouldn't steal from us. If we've got to give over a copy, I'd want it to be to Roarke's cop, and Roarke. He'll make sure nobody gets their hands on it. He'd do that for Bart."

She rose, still swiping at tears. "We'll need to talk to the lawyer. We'd need to cover that much, and maybe get some sort of documentation on producing a copy for you. It'll take a while to make a copy anyway. We've got a lot of security levels on it, and it's dense, so it could take a while. Maybe a day to get it handled. But I'll take care of it. Bart's dead," she said before either of her friends could speak. "Nobody's going to put anything in the way of finding out who hurt him. Not even us."

"I'm sorry," Var said as Cill left the room. "I didn't mean anything about Roarke, that way."

"No problem." Eve's 'link signaled, told her the e-team had arrived. "My team's here. You're going to want to tell your people what's going on."

She sent them out, and brought Peabody in. "I've got some details on the game the vic had in, and I'll fill you in on that later. For now, I want to divide everyone on-site between the five of us. Pick five locations for the interviews, get the full list of employees, divvy them up. We'll follow up with anyone who didn't report to work today. Get statements, impressions, salients, and alibis. We're going to run them all, then run their families and known associates. And we're going to check financials. Maybe we've got somebody passing on data to a competitor for a little extra scratch."

"You think this is about the game?"

"It's more than a game," Eve said with a thin smile. "It's an adventure. I need to take care of something. You can send my share up here when you've set up."

"You get the cool room."

"Yes, I do. Move."

Had to be done, Eve thought. She'd have filled him in when she got home in any case. And the murder would leak to the media before much longer. He'd know when it did as he made a point to monitor the crime beat. Just a way to keep up with her.

If she'd had the head for it, she supposed she'd have monitored the stock market and business news. Good thing for him she didn't have a clue.

She opted for his personal 'link, figuring he'd be too busy wheeling to answer, and she could leave him a v-mail.

But his face flickered on-screen, and those bold blue eyes fixed on hers. "Lieutenant, nice to hear from you."

The combination of those eyes, the faint lilt of the green hills and valleys of Ireland in his voice, might have turned a weaker woman into a gooey puddle. As it was she couldn't stop the quick jump of her heart.

"Sorry to interrupt whatever."

"I'm on my way back from a lunch meeting, so you caught me at a good time."

Her eyes narrowed. "Where?"

"Florence. The pasta was exceptional. What can I do for you?"

"I caught a case."

"You often do."

Better quick, she thought. It somehow always was. "It's Bart Minnock."

It changed—the easy good humor, the innate flirtation dropped away. The hard lines of anger didn't diminish that striking face, but instead made the compelling the dangerous.

"What happened to him?"

"I can't get into all the details now, but I just found out you knew him. I didn't want you to hear about it on a media report."

"Has it to do with his work or was it personal?"

"It's too soon to say, but his work's involved."

"Where are you?"

"U-Play."

"I'll be landing in about twenty minutes. I'll be there within forty."

"Roarke—"

"If it's to do with his work, I'll be helpful. If it doesn't . . . We'll see. He was a sweet boy, Eve. A sweet, brilliant, and harmless boy. I want to do what I can for him."

She'd expected as much. "Find Feeney when you get here. I'm sorry, Roarke."

"So am I. How did he die?" When she said nothing, sorrow clouded over the anger. "That bad, was it?"

"I'll talk to you when you get here. It's complicated."

"All right then. It's good he has you. I'll be there soon."

Eve took a breath. He would be helpful, she thought as she stared at the blank screen of her 'link. Not only with the e-work, but with the business. Feeney and his crew knew their e, but they didn't know the business. Roarke would.

She checked the time, then tried for Morris.

"Dallas."

"Give me what you can," she asked. "I don't know when I'm going to get in there."

"My house is always open for you. I can tell you he had no drugs or alcohol in his system. Your vic was a healthy twenty-nine—despite, it seems, an appetite for cheese and onion soy chips and orange fizzies. There's some minor bruising, and the more serious gash on his arm, all peri-mortem. His head was severed with one blow, with a broad, sharp blade." Morris used the flat of his hand to demonstrate.

"Like an axe?"

"I don't think so. An axe is generally thicker on the backside. A wedge shape. I'd say a sword—a very large, very strong sword used with considerable force, and from slightly above. A clean stroke." Again he demonstrated, fisting his hands as if on a hilt, then swinging like a batter at the plate, and cleaving forward. "The anomaly—"

"Other than some guy getting his head cut off with a sword?"

"Yes, other than. There are slight burns in all the wounds. I'm still working on it, but my feeling is electrical. Even the bruising shows them."

"An electrified sword?"

Humor warmed his eyes. "Our jobs are never tedious, are they? I'll be with him for a while yet. He's a very interesting young man."

"Yeah. I'll get back to you."

She pocketed her 'link and began to pace.

A victim secured, alone, in his own holo-room, beheaded by a sword, potentially with electric properties.

Which made no sense.

He couldn't have been alone because it took two—murderer and victim. So there'd been a breach in his security. Or he'd paused the game, opened up, and let his killer inside. It would have to be someone he trusted with his big secret project.

Which meant his three best pals were top of the suspect list. All alibied, she mused, but how hard was it for an e-geek to slip through building security, head over a few blocks, slip through apartment security, and ask their good pal Bart to open up and play?

Which didn't explain how they'd managed to get the weapon inside, but again, it could be done.

It had been done.

Reset everything, go back to work.

Less than an hour, even with cleanup time.

Someone at U-Play or someone outside who'd earned the vic's trust.

Possibly a side dish. Someone he snuck in himself, after he'd told his droid to shut down. He liked to show off. Guys tended to show off for sex, especially illicit sex.

The murder wasn't about sex, but part of the means might be.

She shuffled the thoughts back at the timid knock on the glass door. Overall Girl, she thought as she came in, who'd added red, weepy eyes to her ensemble.

"They said I had to come up and talk with you 'cause somebody killed Bart. I wanna go home."

"Yeah, me, too. Sit down."

Halfway through her complement of interviews, Eve got her first buzz.

Twenty-three-year-old Roland Chadwick couldn't keep still—but e-jocks were notoriously jittery. His wet hazel eyes kept skittering away from hers. But it was a hard day, and some in the e-game had very limited social skills.

Still, most of them didn't have guilt rolling off their skin in thick, smelly waves.

"How long have you worked here, Roland?"

He scratched the long blade of his noise, bounced his knees. "Like I said, I interned for two summers in college, then I came on the roll when I graduated. So, like, a year on the roll, then the two summers before that. Altogether."

"And what do you do, exactly?"

"Mostly research, like Benny. Like what's out there, how can we twist it, jump it up. Or, like, if somebody's got a zip on something, I cruise before we step so, like, we're not hitting somebody else's deal."

"So you see everything in development, or on the slate for development."

"Mostly, yeah." He jiggled his shoulders, tapped both feet. "Bits and bytes anyhow, or, like, outlines. And you gotta check the titles, the character and place names and that jazz 'cause you don't want repeats or crossovers. Unless you do, 'cause you're, like, homage or sequel or series."

"And yesterday? Where were you?"

"I was, like, here. Clocked at nine-three-oh, out at five. Or close. Maybe five-thirty? 'Cause I was buzzing with Jingle for a while after outs."

"Did you go out, for a break, for lunch, leave the building before you finished for the day?"

"Not yesterday. Full plate. Yeah, full plate with second helpings."

"But you took breaks, had some lunch?"

"Yeah, sure. Sure. Gotta fuel it up, charge it up. Sure."

"So, did you contact anybody? Tag a pal to pass the time with on a break?"

"Ah . . ." His gaze skidded left. "I don't know."

"Sure you do. And you can tell me or I'll just find out when we check your comp, your 'links."

"Maybe I tagged Milt a couple times."

"And Milt is?"

"Milt's my . . . you know."

"Okay. Does Milt your You Know have a last name?"

"Dubrosky. He's Milton Dubrosky. It's no big." A little sweat popped out above his upper lip. "We're allowed."

"Uh-huh." She pulled out her PPC and started a run on Milton Dubrosky. "So you and Milt live together?"

"Kinda. I mean, he still has a place but we're mostly at mine. Mostly."

"And what does Milt do?"

"He's an actor. He's really good. He's working on his big break."

"I bet you help him with that? Help him study lines."

"Sure." Shoulders jiggled again; toes tapped. "It's fun. Kinda like working up a game."

"Being an actor, he probably has some good ideas, too. Does he help you out there?"

"Maybe."

"Been together long?"

"Nine months. Almost ten."

"How much have you told him about Fantastical?"

Every ounce of color dropped out of his face, and for an instant, he was absolutely still. "What?"

"How much, Roland? Those little bits and bytes, or more than that?"

"I don't know about anything like that."

"The new project? The big top secret? I think you know something about it. You're in research."

"I just know what they tell me. We're not allowed to talk about it. We had to sign the gag."

Eve kept an easy smile on her face, and a hard hammer in her heart. "But you and Milt are, you know, and you help each other out. He's interested in what you do, right?"

"Sure, but—"

"And a big project like this, it's exciting. Anybody'd mention it to their partner."

"He doesn't understand e-work."

"Really? That's odd, seeing as he's done time, twice, for e-theft."

"No, he hasn't!"

"You're either an idiot, Roland, or a very slick operator." She angled her head. "I vote idiot."

She had the protesting and now actively weeping Roland escorted to Central, then sent a team of officers to scoop up Dubrosky and take him in.

His criminal didn't show any violent crimes, she mused, but there was always a first time.

She finished her interviews, calculating it would give Roland time to stop crying and Dubrosky time to stew. She found two more who admitted they'd talked about the project to a friend or spouse or cohab, but the Chadwick-Dubrosky connection seemed the best angle.

She broke open a tube of Pepsi while she checked in with the sweepers and added to her notes. She looked up as the door opened, and Roarke stepped in.

He changed the room, she thought, just by being in it. Not just for her, but she imagined for most. The change came from the look of him, certainly, long and lean with that sweep of dark hair, the laser blue eyes that could smolder or frost. But the control, the power under it demanded attention be paid.

Even now, she thought, when she could see the sorrow on that wonderful face, he changed the room.

"They said you'd finished with your share of the interviews. Do you have a minute now?"

He wouldn't have always asked, she remembered. And she wouldn't have always known to get up, to go to him, to offer a moment of comfort.

"Sorry about your friend," she said when her arms were around him.

She kept the embrace brief—after all, the walls were glass—but she felt some of the tension seep out of him before she drew back.

"I didn't know him well, not really. I can't say we were friends, though we were friendly. It's such a bloody waste."

He paced away to the wall, looked out through the glass. "He and his mates were building something here. Too many holes in it yet, but they've done well for themselves. Creative and bright, and young enough to pour it all in."

"What kind of holes?"

He glanced back, smiled a little. "You'd pull that one thing out of the rest. And I imagine though e-work's not your strongest suit, you've seen some of those holes already."

"More than one person knows a secret, it's not a secret anymore."

"There's that. Electronically it looks as though he covered the bases, and very well. It'll take some doing to get through all of it, and I'm told you've already lost a key piece of evidence."

"Self-destructed, but they got enough to give me the springboard. How much do you know about this game, this Fantastical?"

"Virtual/holo combo, fantasy role-playing, varied scenarios at player's choice. Heightened sensory levels, keyed through readouts of the player's nervous system and brain waves."

That pretty much summed up the big top secret project, she thought. "And when did you know that much?"

"Oh, some time ago. Which is one of the holes here. Too many of his people knew too much, and people will talk."

"Do you know Milt Dubrosky?"

"No, should I?"

"No. It just erases a possible complication. If the technology developed for this game is so cutting-edge, why don't you have it?"

"Actually, we've something I suspect is quite similar in development." He wandered over to Vending, scanned, walked away again. "But my people don't talk."

"Because they're paid very well, and because they're afraid of you."

"Yes. I'm sure Bart paid his people as well as he could, but there wouldn't have been any fear." He touched her arm, just a brush of fingertips, as he wandered the room. "They'd like him, and quite a bit. He'd be one of them. It's a mistake to be too much one of your own as they'll never see you as fully in charge."

"When did you last see or speak with him?"

"Oh, four or five months back anyway. I was down this way for a meeting and ran into him on the street. I bought him a beer, and we caught up a bit."

Restless, Eve thought. Pacing was normally her deal. Then he sighed once, and seemed to settle.

"One of my scouts brought him to my attention when Bart was still in college. After I'd read the report and done a little checking myself, I arranged a meeting. I guess he was twenty. God. So fresh, so earnest. I offered him a job, a paid internship until he got his degree, and a full-time position thereafter."

"That's a hell of an offer," Eve commented.

"He'd have been a hell of a recruit. But he told me he had plans to start up his own company, with three friends. He outlined his business model for me there and then, and asked for my advice." Roarke smiled a little, just a slight curve of those wonderfully carved lips. "He disarmed me, I have to say. I ended up meeting with the four of them a few times, and doing what I could to help them avoid some pitfalls. I don't suppose this one any of us could have anticipated."

"If he was that open with you, right off the jump, he might have been equally talkative with others."

"Possibly, though that was one of the pitfalls I warned them of. He—they—wanted their own, and I know what it is, that want, that need. That, and well, the boy appealed to me, so it was easy to give them a little boost."

"Money?"

"No." His shoulder lifted, a careless gesture. "I might have done so if they'd asked. But they had some seed money, and you'll work harder if it doesn't come too easy. I had this property—"

"*This?* This is your building?"

"Was, so relax yourself," he told her with the slightest hint of impatience. "I'm not involved here. I rented them space here for a time, and when they'd gotten off the ground, he asked me to sell it to them. As I said, the boy appealed to me, so I did. I made mine; they had theirs. Good business all around."

"And the business is worth considerable."

"Relatively."

"Compared to you it's a nit on a grizzly, but the money's a motive, as is the technology they're working on. Can they keep this place afloat without Bart?"

"No one's indispensable. Except you to me."

"Aww." But she rolled her eyes with the sound and made him laugh a little. "They'll split three ways instead of four."

"And take a hit for the loss of the fourth. From a business standpoint, eliminating Bart's a foolish move. He was the point man," Roarke explained, "the public face, the big picture man. And he was good at it."

"This kind of murder? Sensational, and tied in with the business. It's going to get whopping truckloads of media. Free media of the sort that generates sales out of sheer curiosity."

"You're right about that." He considered. "Yes, but that's a temporary boost, and still poor business sense. Added to it, unless their dynamics have changed, it's hard to see any of the other three hurting Bart."

"People do the damnedest things. I have another angle to check out. Feeney will keep you busy if you want to be. I need a copy of the game disc. They'll hand it over, but they're going to drag their feet some. If they trust you, you might be able to nudge that along."

"I'll see what I can do."

"I'll be in the field."

He took her hand as she walked to the door. "Take care of my wife."

"She takes care of herself."

"When she remembers."

She went out, started down. She glanced back once to see him at that glass wall, hands in his pockets, and that sorrow that perhaps only she could see, still shadowing his face.

4

BACK IN THE BUSY HIVE OF COP CENTRAL, Eve studied Roland Chadwick through the glass of Observation. He continued to sweat, just a bit, and his tear-swollen eyes tended to dart and dash around the room, as if he expected something to materialize in a corner and take a nice big bite out of him.

Perfect.

"We'll take him together to start," Eve told Peabody. "I'm going hard. He expects it from me now."

"And you'd give him herbal tea and a fluffy pillow otherwise."

"I'll leave the fluffy to you, after I storm out of the room in disgust, leaving dire threats in my wake."

"And I 'there-there' him until he spills his guts."

"That's the plan."

Eve watched as Roland laid his head on the table as if to sleep. It wouldn't have surprised her in the least if he'd popped his thumb in his mouth.

"While you're doing that, I'll start on Dubrosky. He's been around the block a few times, and he has to know his dupe in there is a very weak sister. I believe his guts will also spill."

Peabody smiled as Roland cushioned his face on his folded arms. "My guy will spill first."

"Maybe. Let's find out."

She strode in, a tough, impatient woman who seemed capable of taking that nice big bite and enjoying it. Roland's head popped up even as he shrank in his chair.

"Record on. Dallas, Lieutenant Eve, and Peabody, Detective Delia, in Interview with Chadwick, Roland, on the matter of the murder of Minnock, Bart. Roland Chadwick," she continued, using both names to add a little more intimidation, "have you been read your rights?"

"Yeah, but—"

"Do you understand your rights and obligations in this matter?"

"Okay, yeah, but—"

She dropped her file on the table between them with a force that echoed like a slap. It shut him up.

"You worked for Bart Minnock, correct?"

"Yes, ma'am, I told you how I—"

"Can you account for your whereabouts yesterday?"

"I was at home, I mean, I was at work, and then—"

"Which is it?" She snapped the words out, leaned on the table, deep into his space. "Home or work? It's an easy question, Roland."

"I-I-I-I was at work all day, until I went home." Like the words off his tongue, color stammered in his face, pink then white, pink then white. "I logged out and everything. It was after five. You can check. You can see."

"And you log out, Roland, *every* time you leave the building? Every single time?"

"Well, mostly. For sure at the end of the day. For sure then. I didn't do anything. I don't understand why you're so mad at me." His voice pitched into a whine threatening to reach dog-ears-only territory. "I didn't do anything."

"Is that so? Maybe Bart would disagree. Maybe he'd have a little something to say about that. If he wasn't dead." She flipped open the file, spilled the crime scene photos out. "But it's a little hard to get the words out when your head's across the room from the rest of you."

Roland took one look at the photos, went a very pale green. He said, fairly clearly: *"Gah."* Then his eyes rolled up white as he slid to the floor.

"Well, shit." Eve blew out a breath and fisted her hands on her hips. "Better get him some water, Peabody."

"It was kind of graceful, the way he went down." Peabody got a cup of water while Eve crouched down to pat Roland's cheeks.

"Out cold. He's not faking. Okay, Roland, come on back. Better get a medic in case . . . wait, here he comes. Roland!" She spoke sharply as his eyes twitched, then blinked. Then she gave a head jerk to Peabody so her partner would be the one playing nursemaid.

"Are you all right, Mr. Chadwick?" Peabody knelt down, eased his head up. "Try a little water. Take a sip, that's the way. Take a breath. Do you need medical attention?"

"I don't . . . what happened?"

"You fainted. Do you want me to call a medic?"

"No. No, I don't think . . . I just need to—" His eyes popped wide now, and he grabbed Peabody's arm like a drowning man. "Don't make me look again. Don't make me look."

"Tougher to look than to be part of causing it?" Eve said coldly.

"I didn't. I swear." He all but crawled into Peabody's lap, and Eve knew her work was done. "I *swear*! Don't make me look."

"Okay, it's okay. You don't have to look. Have some more water. We'll wait until you're feeling steady again."

"Fine, that's fine." Eve pushed the photos back in the file. "You want to coddle him, he's all yours. I can't stand being in the same room with him. Dallas, Lieutenant Eve, exiting Interview."

She slammed the door behind her, but not before she heard Roland's breathless thank-you to her partner.

Satisfied with Part A, she headed to the next interview room for Part B.

Milt Dubrosky had the buffed and polished looks of a spa rat. She imagined he devoted a good part of his day to the gym, and a good part of his week to treatments. His hair—too perfectly streaked to be nature's gift—lay in subtle waves around a smooth, fine-boned face. His eyes, a soft, shimmering blue flashed out of long, dark lashes as he beamed out a high-wattage smile.

"Officer, I don't know why I'm here, but at least the view just got a whole lot better."

"Lieutenant."

His smile flashed along with his eyes as he executed a snappy salute. "Sir, yes, sir."

"Record on. Dallas, Lieutenant Eve, in Interview with Dubrosky, Milton, on the matter of the murder of Minnock, Bart."

"What?" Those bold eyes widened as he sucked in a breath. "Bart's been murdered? When? What happened?"

"You've been in Interview before, Dubrosky." She tapped the file that held his record. "So you know I'm the one who asks questions, and you're the one who answers them. Have you been read your rights?"

"Yeah, the cops who brought me in. But they didn't tell me anything."

"Can you verify your whereabouts from between three P.M. and eight P.M. yesterday?"

"Sure. Sure. I was at my salon—that's Urban Meadows—from about one to three-thirty, then I met a friend for coffee. I did some shopping and went to another friend's place about five-thirty. Roland, Roland Chadwick. He works for Bart at U-Play. He got in shortly after I did, and we stayed in the rest of the night. He can vouch."

"The name and contact information for your coffee date."

"No problem. Britt Casey." He rattled off a 'link number and an Upper West Side address. "We're in a workshop together. Acting workshop. So we get together now and then to discuss craft."

He was good, Eve decided, but not that good. Poor Roland, she thought, just how many ways can you be duped? "And what time did you leave your acting pal and head out on your own?"

"Sometime around five, I guess."

"Coffee and shopping date. Where did you have coffee? Where did you shop? Do you have receipts?"

"I don't actually remember the name of the coffee shop. And I didn't actually buy anything. It was more window-shopping."

Eve said nothing, just stared at him.

"Okay, look. I was at the salon like I said. My consultant's name is Nanette. You can ask her. And I met Britt after, but it wasn't for coffee, if you get me." He tried the smile again, one that said *I'm a scamp, but you gotta love me.* "We went to the Oaks Hotel for a couple hours. See, the thing is, she's married and I'm sort of living with someone."

"Chadwick?"

"Ah, no. But my roommate and Britt? They don't know about each other. I'd really appreciate it if they could keep not knowing about each other."

"Name of the roommate?"

"Chelsea Saxton."

Eve lifted her brows. "And where, exactly, does Roland Chadwick fit in?"

Dubrosky lifted his shoulders, let them fall in an *oops* gesture. "You could say I'm sort of semi-living with him, too."

"With him also unaware of the other two, and they of him?"

"What can I say? I'm a people person."

"That's a lot of juggling. A man that adept at juggling would be able to juggle enough time in for a stopover at Bart's apartment."

"Never been there." He added an easy, cheerful wave. "No reason to. I knew him a little, sure, because Roland works for him at U-Play. Seemed like a nice guy. Ro sure thought the world of him. I don't know why anyone would kill the poor bastard."

"You're adept at e-work, too."

"A hobby, really. Acting's my real passion."

"And combining hobby with passion you can make some cash selling inside information to interested parties. Especially when you're stringing along a love-sick puppy with a bullshit IQ of zero, like Roland."

"Aw, now, Ro's a sweet kid. Maybe a little dim when it comes to anything outside of tech or gaming, but a sweet kid. And me? I've got a need to be admired, I admit it. He admires me." Dubrosky turned up his hands as if to say, "Just look at me? Who wouldn't admire all this?"

"Enough to leak data on Fantastical."

Dubrosky tried looking blank, but didn't quite pull it off. "Sorry, never heard of it."

"Save the bullshit, Dubrosky. My IQ in that area's tuned and toned. And, Admiring Roland's already spilled it." She leaned back. "Admiring you doesn't mean taking the fall for you. He's not quite as dumb as you think."

"Ro's not dumb." Dubrosky didn't miss a beat. "He just gets confused sometimes when it comes to reality. He's wired to games, and a lot outside his bubble gets past him."

"Like you have two side pieces, and a penchant for e-spying?"

"It's not illegal to spread yourself around. Believe me, all my lovers are happy." He wrapped an arm around the back of his chair, posed. "What's the harm?"

"It tells me you've got no scruples, and a man with no scruples doesn't think twice about cheating, stealing, lying. It's a short step over to murder."

"I don't kill people, sweetheart. I seduce them."

"Call me sweetheart again." She leaned in, eyes flat. "Go ahead."

"No offense, no offense." He held up his hands for peace. "I'm not denying I've taken my hobby too far a couple times. I get caught up, like anyone else. But if you've got my sheet, you know I don't do violence. The fact is, sweet—Lieutenant," he corrected quickly, "I don't need to. And sure, Ro's told me some things about the big secret project. He's excited about it, and he likes to talk. Part of a good seduction is listening. I listen. Not a crime."

"Try listening to this," Eve suggested. "Do you know what else I have besides your sheet? Your financials. It's pretty interesting reading, too. All these nice deposits, which I'd say keeps you in salon time with Nanette. More interesting as your employment records indicate you haven't had a paying job in close to a year."

"People give me money as gifts. It's part of the admiring."

"I'm going to bet Bart didn't admire you. I'm going to bet when you went to him asking for payment to keep the information your sap passed you, he'd have threatened to go to the cops."

"I don't do blackmail." He glanced down at his nails. "It's too messy."

"Here's something really messy." Once again she took out the crime scene photos.

Dubrosky didn't turn green; he didn't faint, but he did go stark white. "Oh my Jesus. Oh my Christ. Somebody cut off his head."

"I bet you practice swordfights in those workshops. Action roles, period pieces." Eve cocked her head as she gave him a cool up-and-down study. "You're in good shape. I bet you can handle a heavy sword without much trouble."

"Listen. Listen to me." Suave vanished in sober. "I make a living sleeping with people who can afford to slip me some cash, buy me nice things. I make more by selling information when I've got it. I don't hurt people. I sure as hell don't kill them. Roland's a mark, sure. He's easy. But the fact is, I'd just about tapped that out, which is why I'm easing over to Britt. She's got a rich husband who lets her play at acting and spend all the money she wants. He's out of town a lot—financial consultant. I figure I can tap that for a while, maybe get in the house, hack one of his comps, see what I see. I'm laying groundwork there, so why would I do something like this? I don't do this. I didn't do this."

"Who'd you sell the information to?"

"Ah hell." He pushed a hand through his hair, ruining its perfection and telling Eve he was sincerely frightened. "If I roll there, you've got to cut me a deal."

"I don't have to do squat. You've already confessed, on record, to corporate espionage. And here's the thing, Milt. I really, really don't admire you. Names. Now."

He sat back, closed his soft, shimmering eyes, and spilled his guts.

When she'd finished with Dubrosky, she had him escorted back to a cell. She would do what she could do to make sure he spent the next few years as a guest of the fine state of New York. And she hoped he sorely missed his salon appointments.

"I got mine," Peabody told her when they met in Eve's office.

"Then we're two for two." Eve programmed coffee, waved Peabody to the AutoChef so she could get her own.

"I didn't know half of what he was talking about. The more upset he got, the more he babbled, and the babble got pretty technical. I figure to ask McNab to look over the interview and interpret, but . . ." Peabody paused to give the coffee a couple of little blows before taking the first sip. "But what I got was he gave Dubrosky the details of his research and whatever work he did on the Fantastical project, and anything else he had a hand in or knew about. The guy's a walking mouth. They couldn't be screening as well as they seem to think they are."

"One of the holes," Eve murmured, thinking of Roarke's comment. She walked over to her narrow window, looked out at a passing airtram as she considered. "My guy's so slimy if I stepped on him I wouldn't wipe him off my shoe, I'd just incinerate the shoe. He lives off sex and what passes for charm, targeting marks, juggling them. He claims he was having sex with a new target when Bart lost his head. In the Oaks Hotel."

"That's pretty uptown for a sex con."

"The mark's got a rich husband. So, we'll check it out, but it rings. He's also living with yet another mark when he's not doing the walking mouth. They pay his freight, and he digs into their business, and sells the data to interested parties. I've got the interested party on this one."

She sipped coffee, thinking of the young, stupid Roland, the young, naive Bart. "I don't think Dubrosky got into Bart's and sliced him up. He might snag a fingernail or get spatter in his perfect hair. But he's going over for the rest. And if we pin the murder on the buyer, we may be able to slap him with accessory. He's earned a nice long stretch in a very small cage."

"You really didn't like him."

"I really didn't. But the point is, if he hadn't used the lovestruck Roland for gain, maybe Bart Minnock would still be in one piece. You take the two women he was juggling along with Roland. I want to get some data on Lane DuVaugne of Synch Entertainment before we talk to him."

Peabody looked into her coffee mug. "They're going to be pissed."

"Oh yeah. You get the fun stuff." She gave Peabody the names and contact information. "Be discreet," she added. "Britt Casey's married. She probably deserves a kick in the ass, but if she's as dumb as Roland, I'm inclined to cut her a break and try to keep her husband out of it."

"I'll be the soul. If this guy was banging three marks, how'd he have time for anything else?"

"Apparently, it's just a matter of good time management."

"I wonder what supplements he takes, or if he has a special diet."

"I'll be sure to ask next time we speak. Out."

Eve sat to begin runs on both DuVaugne and the company, and while the data began to screen, followed a hunch.

Once again Roarke answered directly. "Lieutenant."

"Are you in the house?"

"I am, yes. In EDD."

"What can you tell me, off the top, about a Lane DuVaugne and Synch Entertainment."

"I'll come down."

"You don't have to—" she began, but she was talking to empty air.

"Okay then."

She started with DuVaugne. The fifty-nine-year-old vice president was on wife two, who—no surprise—clocked in at twenty-eight years younger. They based their three-year marriage on the Upper East Side, with additional housing in Belize and the Italian Riviera. The current wife was a former lingerie model.

Men were so simple, really.

He'd held his position at Synch for sixteen years, and pulled in a hefty twenty-two million, before bonuses, annually.

He had no criminal record.

"We're about to change that."

What change do you wish to implement? the computer asked.

"Nothing. None. A person can't even talk to herself around here."

She did a quick scan on the company. It had been around nearly as long as DuVaugne had been alive, developing, manufacturing, and distributing games and game systems. Offices and plants worldwide. She frowned as she read the cities, backtracked through company history, tried to wade her way through the official financial and employment data.

She hated to admit it, but she felt some relief when Roarke walked in. Then he shut the door.

"Uh-oh."

"I simply prefer not to broadcast my business."

"Your business crosses with Synch?"

"Not at the moment. Where's your candy?"

"What candy?"

He gave her a look. "I know very well you hide candy in here. I need a boost. Give it over."

Her frown deepened, and she tracked her gaze toward the door. "Don't let anybody come in. It's a damn good hiding place."

"You know, you could easily rig a cam in here, and catch whoever's lifting your stash in the act."

"One day I'll catch the candy thief, but it'll be by guile and wit, not technology. It's a matter of pride and principle now."

She took a tool from her desk, then squatted in front of her recycler. After a few twists, she removed the facing and pulled an evidence bag from the back.

"Your guile and wit contest causes you to keep candy in the recycler, with the trash?"

"It's sealed." She broke the seal with a little pop and whoosh to prove it, then took out one of three chocolate bars. She tossed it to him, then bagged the remaining two with a fresh seal before hiding them again. She glanced back to see him studying the candy.

"If you're going to be so dainty give it back."

"There was a time I rooted through alley garbage for food, without a thought. Things change." He unwrapped the candy, took a bite. "But apparently not that much."

She replaced the tool, then stood, hands on hips, studying the recycler for any signs of tampering. "Okay. Still good."

"And a demonstration of true love if I ever saw one." He brushed a hand over her tousled cap of brown hair, then tapped a finger on the dent of her chin before touching his lips to hers. "Better than chocolate."

The shadows had lifted, she noted. Work could do that—focus and channel grief and regret. "Synch Entertainment."

"Yes. About a year ago I looked into acquiring the corporation."

"Naturally. It exists, so you want it."

"On the contrary." He sat in her shabby visitor's chair. "After some research and vetting I decided I didn't want it, or not at this time."

"Because?"

"It's in trouble. The sort I have no need or desire to take on. Better to wait until it's either limping along then buy it cheap, or wait until they shake things out, fix the problems, and offer a good price for a healthy company."

"What kind of problems? Other than they've closed two on-planet plants in the last sixteen months—small ones, outside the U.S. They have no plants or offices off-planet, so they're either missing that market altogether, or the cost of distributing their products to that market would be prohibitive."

He arched his brows. "Well now, my heart swells with pride. Listen to the business acumen."

"Be a smartass, lose the candy."

"Why don't you come over here and try to take it?" Smiling now, he patted his knee in invitation.

Oh yeah, he was feeling better.

"I don't know anything about the game market, except it has to be almost no-fail. People want to play, all the damn time. In arcades, at home, at parties, in the office. So why can't a company that's been in the game of games for over half a century make it work?"

"Because they've invested more, at least in the last decade, in marketing and execs than in creative minds and new technology, and they've continued to ignore the off-planet market, considering it too small and cost prohibitive." He shrugged as he took another bite of the candy bar. "They're stuck in a certain mind-set, and if it doesn't change, and soon, they'll shortly be a generation behind."

"Okay, so they overpay the suits and figure if it was good enough ten years ago, it's good enough now."

"Basically. The two people who founded it fifty-odd years ago sold it off during its prime. It's had its ups and downs since, as companies will. At this point it's in a slow but steady downswing."

"Something like U-Play's Fantastical would change the swing."

"It could, absolutely, if developed and marketed well. Is this your motive?"

"Might be. DuVaugne paid a source nearly a hundred and fifty thousand, so far, for data on the program. He's a VP at Synch."

"In Development," Roarke added. "I looked him up on the way down. He'd be a hero if he brought the company this idea, and the means to create it. I imagine his contract with them includes bonus clauses. He'd rake in quite a bit, and for a very small investment."

"Which is a very nice motive for murder, or for making another investment and hiring it out. He's also got a fairly new and very young second wife. I bet she likes the high life."

He smiled at her. "Most do."

"Uh-huh. So, when down the road a couple decades if you think about ditching me for fresh? Remember who carries a weapon."

"Something I never forget. Or fail to appreciate."

"Okay. I need to have a little chat with DuVaugne."

"I'd be interested in chatting with him myself."

"Can't do it. Can't," she repeated, shaking her head. "You're a competitor, and it could sour my chances of shaking him out. Complicate them anyway."

"Fair enough."

"I should touch base with Morris, and I want another pass at the scene. Keep me updated on the e-work."

"I'll do that, but I want to go with you to Bart's."

She started to speak, stopped and reconsidered. "You might be handy there."

"I do what I can." He balled up the candy wrapper, two-pointed it into the recycler before he rose. "Thanks for the candy."

She smiled. "What candy?"

**5** "DO YOU THINK THE PENIS EVER GETS TIRED?"

As she drove, Eve turned her head toward Peabody, tipped down the shades she rarely remembered to wear. "Whose?"

"Anybody's. I mean anybody with one. Does the penis ever just think: For God's sake, pal, give it a rest? Or is it all: Woo-hoo! Here we go again!"

"Is this germane to the case, or have you lapsed into girl talk?"

"It springs from the case. I was thinking about that asshole Dubrosky. There he is banging away at Britt Casey yesterday afternoon. A triple-header, according to her. Floor," she said, ticking it off on her fingers, "bed, and against the door. Then last night he's bucking with Roland in fantasy game-play. Pirate captain and cabin boy."

"Stop."

"Wait. And this morning? He sneaks in a coffee and a quickie with Chelsea Saxton, then gets a follow-up bj in the shower."

"Jesus, Peabody."

"Well, I didn't *ask* for the dirty details, but all three of them just splurted it all out when they found out about the others. I really think most ginnies would say: Hey! Don't even think about putting anything in there for a while."

"Ginnies?"

"It's a nice name for vagina. And I really think after a couple rounds, under most circumstances, your average ginnie would say, okay, that'll hold me for a while. But does the penis just keep searching out the next orifice? I wonder since I don't have one."

"In case you're wondering, neither do I."

"I've seen you naked so I know this. I think even the most stalwart and energetic penis would, at some point, say enough's enough for today or tonight, and since, hey, I'm all relaxed now, I'm taking a little vacation. Or just a nap."

"See now I've got this image of some cock sitting at a swim-up bar at a resort, wearing sunshades and drinking one of those stupid drinks full of fruit and paper umbrellas."

"Aw, that's cute."

"It's not cute. It's mildly scary. Or disgusting. I'm not sure which. Both." Eve blew out a tired breath. "I think both."

"It should have a little straw hat, too. Anyway, I don't think it's about sex with Dubrosky's penis."

"Peabody, I can't stress how much I don't want to think about his penis."

"It's addiction," Peabody continued, unfazed. "I bet Mira'd agree," she added, referring to the departmental profiler and shrink. "He equates his worth with his penis, and also uses it as a weapon."

"Okay, now I see it wearing a gold chain and toting a blaster. Stop now."

Shifting, Peabody gave Eve a look of delight. "You get the best pictures in your head. It's why you're a good cop. Dubrosky said all that crap about needing to be admired. But see, he's probably talking about his looks, his manner, but subconsciously, he's talking about his penis."

"Okay, if I agree with you, because actually I do, will you stop?"

"I just think it's interesting. Now take this DuVaugne—"

Eve's jaw tightened. "Do *not* start on his penis."

"A man ditches his wife of about twenty years for a big rack and a fresh young ginnie."

"Oh my God."

"He does that because he's starting to think about his own mortality—and he really doesn't want to. He needs the big rack and fresh young ginnie so he can say: Hey look what I've got, look where my penis gets to go, and it proves I'm still vital and virile. Which circles right back to the penis, which, *yes,* demands to be admired. You know, we could consult with Charles about this."

Eve pulled in at the morgue, and indulged herself by resting her brow on the steering wheel for a minute. "We don't need a former licensed companion now sex therapist to investigate this case. Plus he and Louise are on their honeymoon."

"But they'll be back in a few days. I think gaining insight into the penis may help in investigations down the road."

"Fine, you go right ahead and consult with Charles. Write me a freaking report on same. But now, I don't want to hear the word *penis* for the rest of the day."

"There's really no nice word for . . . that particular thing," Peabody continued as they headed inside. "Everything's either too hard—get it?—or too silly. But when you think about it, it's pretty silly to have that particular thing swinging around down there. So—"

"I will kill you. Save the taxpayers' money by doing it right here in the morgue. It's efficient."

Eve used the cool air, the white walls to offset the images Peabody's theories etched in her brain. She spotted Morris in the tunneling corridor, speaking to one of the white-coated techs.

"I'll be in to check in a few minutes," he told the tech, then turned to Eve. "I wondered if you'd make it in today."

"I wanted to catch you before you left."

"I was heading to my office to send you a report. You'll want to see him again."

He began to walk with her.

"Tell me about the burns."

"Minor, but found along every wound, even the bruising." He pushed open the doors of his autopsy room where the body lay on a steel slab, with the head on a smaller tray. He offered them both microgoggles. "You'll see they occur with increasing severity. The bruising on his skin, left forearm, and here on the ankle? So minor he might not have felt the jolt. But here? On the shoulder, which shows slightly deeper bruising and inflammation—there'd been a good wrench in that area—it's more pronounced."

"The more severe the wound, the more severe the burns?"

"No, though I initially thought the same. But the shin shows more bruising than the ankle, the forearm, but the burns are very mild. The arm and the neck, the burns are virtually identical. And, we'd have to say the neck is a more serious wound."

"So . . . the jolts—whatever caused the burns—increased along with the game. The longer he played, the bigger the shock when he got tagged."

"It seems most likely."

"Challenges usually go up in gaming," Peabody commented. "As you move through a level, or head up to the next."

"Okay." Eve let that one simmer in her brain. "Power boost maybe. Roarke's got this virtual game. You use actual weapons—guns. If the bad guy makes a hit, you feel a little jolt. So you know you've been hit and where. Enough to register, but not to hurt. Somebody changed the rules on Bart. But that doesn't explain the internal burns. I get how he might have them on the skin, but the gash, the slice, those are inside, too, not just on the outside. Which means the weapon itself had to carry a charge. What's the point? Isn't a big, sharp sword enough?"

"It certainly would've been."

She stepped over to the head, examined the neck. "And do they match up?"

"Perfectly."

"Maybe the charge added to the thrust. Added power, so the killer didn't need to be particularly strong. Gave the killer more leverage, speed." She pulled off the goggles. "Face-to-face?"

"That's how it plays," Morris agreed.

"It would have to be fast, wouldn't it? Damn fast. He's not drugged, he's not restrained, and he's facing someone with a big sword. He'd run, try to get the hell away. He'd take it in the back, but I'm damned if he'd just stand there and get his head offed. The killer gives him a taste of it with the arm wound. Wants to see his reaction, wants to shock him. And then, one clean blow."

She shook her head. "I'm going back to the scene."

DuVaugne came first.

She had Peabody check with his office, and as she suspected, he'd left for the day. Corporate execs and cops had neither the same work hours nor pay scale.

She didn't begrudge him that part, but it was a pain in the ass to know she had to drive all the way uptown, then down again.

"You know," Peabody began and Eve snarled.

"If you mention any part of anyone's anatomy I'm shoving you out the window and into oncoming traffic."

"I wasn't going to, but know I'm thinking about it again. What I was going to say was about the sword. Not the euphemistic male sword, but the murder weapon. Last year I went to a con with McNab."

"Why would you go to a con?"

"A game con—convention—in New York at the convention center. A total geek-fest, which is actually a lot more fun than it might sound."

"Since it sounds like a nightmare in hell, it wouldn't have to come up much to be any fun at all."

"Well, people dress up like characters from the games, and vids and screen shows. Actors who play the characters come and sign stuff or do demos. They sell all kinds of stuff, even have auctions. High-dollar, too. There are parties and contests and seminars, and a lot of hands-on. You can play just about any game out there if you're willing to buck the crowds, stand in line. U-Play had a big presence there, I remember. Hey, I probably saw the vic before he was a vic. Anyway, it's three days of geekdom."

"Gee, sign me up."

"What I'm saying is they have weapons. Play weapons and prop weapons and virtual weapons. A big chunk of popular games deal with some sort of warfare."

"Yeah, people never get enough of killing each other." But, she thought, it was an interesting angle. "An electrified sword would go over big there."

"Bet your ass. We got a pass into one of the auctions, and there was a sword—not electrified—from Elda, Warrior Queen, and it went for over five million."

"Fucking dollars?"

"Yeah, fucking dollars. It was the one Elda used in the vid to defend her throne and all that. The games are the total. McNab and I play them."

"Who gets to be queen?"

"Ha-ha. They're holo-games, too, but since we don't have a holo we only play the comp. Anyway, there are weapons galore at these cons, and plenty of vendors and collectors. You've got blasters and magic maces and fire lances and light sabers and disintegrators. But from what I saw, swords are the biggest deal. They're sexier."

An interesting angle, she thought again. A good line to tug. "I bet Bart thought how sexy it was to have his head lopped off with one. Collectors, vendors, and cons. It's a good avenue to explore. But maybe we'll get lucky and DuVaugne will just whip out his magic sword, we'll blast him, and wrap this case up."

"I know a euphemism for the p-word when I hear one."

Eve slid to the curb in a no-parking zone and engaged her On Duty light. "If he whips out anything, we take him down."

Laughing, Peabody climbed out. "Some place."

If you went for steel and glass and sharp angles, Eve thought. The gold tone of the privacy window glass reflected the beam of sunlight, making her grateful for her shades. She wondered how many people had been blinded just walking by the three-story extravaganza of what was probably some post-post-modern designer's idea of city slick. She imagined there had once been a dignified brownstone or tidy brick townhouse in that spot, destroyed or mortally wounded during the

Urban Wars. In its place stood the gleam of brushed steel framing walls of that gold-toned glass.

Maybe the occupants felt lofty inside their glass box, or enjoyed their nearly unobstructed views of the streets and city.

She'd have felt exposed and creeped. But it took all kinds.

Rather than steps from the sidewalk to the entrance a sloped ramp led the way to a platform where a motion detector immediately sent out a low beep. She scanned the dual cameras, the palm plate.

"Open view, serious locks," she commented.

Voice recognition unaccepted. These premises do not accept solicitations. All deliveries must be cleared. No guests are expected at this time. Please identify yourself and state your business. Thank you.

"Well, it said *please*." Peabody shrugged. "And *thank you*."

"Yeah, real polite. I guess they don't much like the neighborly drop-in."

Identification is requested within ten seconds. These premises are protected by Secure-One. Identification failure will alert the authorities in ten seconds.

"Not so polite now." Eve pulled out her badge. "Dallas, Lieutenant Eve, NYPSD. We have business with Lane DuVaugne."

No appointment is scheduled.

"Scan the badge, and inform Mr. DuVaugne the cops are at the door. Failure to do so will result in a whole bunch more cops with a warrant arriving within thirty minutes."

Please place your identification on the palm plate for verification scan. Thank you.

"Got its manners back," Eve commented as she complied.

Identification verified, Dallas, Lieutenant Eve, of the New York Police and Security Department. Mr. DuVaugne will be informed of your arrival. One moment, please.

It took more than a moment, but the security cleared and the door opened.

The servant droid, all skinny dignity in a stark black suit, had Eve muffling a snort. He could have been Summerset's brother, not only in appearance, but by the derisive dismissal on his face as he peered down at her.

"Hey, he looks a lot like—"

"The biggest pain in my ass," Eve finished, and thinking of Roarke's majordomo smiled thinly. "Got a name, pal, or just a number?"

"I am Derby." He'd been programmed with a tony British accent. "If you'd inform me of the nature of your business with Mr. DuVaugne I will relate same to him. Your companion has not yet identified herself."

"Peabody, Detective Delia." Peabody held up her badge.

"Now that we're all nicely ID'd, you can *relate* to your owner that the NYPSD will speak with him here, in the comfort of his own home, or we'll escort him to our house for a chat. That would be the less comfortable and more public Cop Central. Our business with him is none of yours. Process that."

"I will so inform Mr. DuVaugne. You're requested to wait in the anteroom. I have engaged all internal security cameras. Your movements and conversation are being recorded."

"We'll resist scratching in inappropriate places."

He sniffed, turned his back, then led them across the open foyer with its central pool of Venus-blue water guarded by some sort of metal sculpture of a mostly naked female poised to dive in.

The glass-walled anteroom held twin gel sofas in glittery silver with murder-red cushions, chairs in a dizzying pattern of both colors. All the tables were clear glass. Some held gardens of strange blooms winding in their bases. From the ceiling a tangle of steel and glass formed chandeliers. The floors were the same tone and texture as the exterior steel.

Eve tried to think if she'd ever seen a more hyper-trendy and less comfortable room, but couldn't come up with one.

"Wait here," Derby ordered. When he left, Eve walked to the front wall.

Yes, it definitely made her feel exposed.

"Why would anybody want nothing but a sheet of fancy glass between them and the rest of the world?" She managed a shrug instead of a shudder, then turned away. "Impressions?"

Peabody circled her eyes as if to remind Eve they were being recorded. "Um. It's really clean? And quiet. You can't hear any street noises at all." She gestured to the window. "It's kind of like a vid with the audio muted."

"Or we've stepped into an alternate universe where the world outside this glass is soundless. And creepy."

"Well, it's creepy now." Then Peabody winced, circled her eyes again. "But really clean."

Eve turned again at the sound of footsteps—a man's, and from the click-click, a woman's heels.

She noted the woman first, and realized the new wife had modeled for the mostly naked sculpture in the foyer. Now she wore a short summer dress that matched the soft blue of her eyes and the current rage of footwear that left the top of the foot unshod. Her toes sported polish in various pastel shades. Her hair fell in a tumble of red with gilded highlights around a face dominated by full, pouty lips.

Beside her the man stood nondescript in a conservatively cut business suit. Still, his jaw held firm, and his burnished brown eyes matched his sweeping mane of hair.

His slightly crooked tie and the slumber-satisfied look in his wife's eyes gave Eve a solid clue what the couple had been up to during her arrival.

"Lieutenant Dallas, is it, and Detective Peabody." DuVaugne crossed the room to give them both a hearty handshake. "What can I do for you?"

"We're investigating the murder of Bart Minnock."

"Ah." He gave a wise nod, a regretful sigh. "Yes, I heard about that. The media doesn't have many details."

"You were acquainted with Mr. Minnock?"

"No, not really. I knew *of* him, of course, as we're in the same business."

"Geezy, honey, you gotta ask them to sit down. Tsk."

She actually said "Tsk," and with the heavy Bronx base struggling to affect the rounded tones of her droid, Eve found it rather remarkable.

"I'm Taija. Mrs. Lane DuVaugne. Please, won't you sit?" She gestured the way screen models did to showcase prizes on game shows. "I'd be happy to order some refreshments."

"Thanks." Eve accepted the invitation to sit. "We're fine. So you never met Bart Minnock?"

"Oh, I believe we met a time or two." DuVaugne took a seat on the red and silver sofa with his wife. "At conventions and events, that sort of thing. He seemed to be a bright and affable young man."

"Then why did somebody kill him?" Taija asked.

"Good question," Eve said, and made Taija beam like a student flattered by a favored teacher.

"If you don't ask questions, you don't find anything out."

"My philosophy. Let me apply that by asking you, Mr. DuVaugne, if you can verify your whereabouts yesterday between three and seven P.M."

"Mine? Are you implying I'm a *suspect*?" Outrage sprang out where,

Eve thought, puzzlement would have been a better lead. "Why, I barely knew the man."

"Geezy, Lane wouldn't kill anybody. He's gentle as a lamb."

"It's standard procedure. As you said, Mr. DuVaugne, you and the victim were in the same line of work."

"That's hardly a motive for murder! Countless people in this city alone are in the gaming business, but you come into my home and demand I answer your questions."

"Now, now, honey." Taija stroked his arm. "Don't get all worked up. You know it's not good for you. And she's being real polite. You're always saying people need to do the jobs they're paid to do and all that. Especially public servants. You're a public servant, right?" she asked Eve.

"That's right."

"Anyway, honey, you know you were at work until nearly four. He works so hard," she confided to Eve. "And then you came right home and we had our little lie-down before we got dressed for the dinner party at Rob and Sasha's. It was a really nice party."

"Taija, it's a matter of principle."

"There, there," she said, stroking. "Now, now."

DuVaugne took a slow, audible breath. "Taija, I think I'd like my evening martini."

"Sure, honey, I'll go tell Derby to mix you one right up. 'Scuze . . . I mean, please excuse me a minute."

After she'd clicked out, DuVaugne turned to Eve. "My wife is naive in certain areas."

Maybe, Eve thought, but she also came off as sincere, and absurdly likeable.

"Naive enough not to understand 'working hard' includes you paying a con man for confidential information on the workings and proj-

ects of U-Play? We have Dubrosky in custody," Eve said before he
could speak. "He rolled on you."

"I have no idea what or who you're talking about. Now, I'm going
to ask you to leave."

"Peabody, read Mr. DuVaugne his rights."

While he blustered, Peabody recited the Revised Miranda. "Do
you understand your rights and obligations in this matter?" Peabody
finished.

"This is beyond belief!" His face burned bright red as he shoved to
his feet. "I'm calling my lawyer."

"Fine. Tell him to meet us down at Cop Central." Cool and calm in
contrast, Eve rose. "Where you can chill in Holding until he arrives, at
which time we'll filter our questions through your representative on
both matters—your involvement in corporate espionage and your connection to Bart Minnock's murder."

"Just a minute, just one damn minute. I was nowhere near Minnock's
apartment yesterday. I've never *been* to his apartment."

"You've requested a lawyer, Mr. DuVaugne," Eve reminded him.
"We're obliged to wait until your representative meets with you before
we take any statements or continue this interview. We'll hold you at
Central prior to that, and prior to booking you on the pending charges."

"Arresting me? You're arresting me? Wait. Just wait." He didn't
sweat like Roland, but his hand trembled as he pushed it through his
glossy mane of hair. "We'll hold on the lawyer; we'll keep this here."

"That's your choice."

"Martinis!" Taija announced in a bright singsong as she preceded
Derby into the room. "Let's all sit down and have a nice drink. Oh,
honey, look at you! All red in the face." She walked over, patted
his cheeks. "Derby pour the drinks. Mr. DuVaugne needs a little
pick-me-up."

"Give me that." DuVaugne grabbed the oversized shaker, dumped the contents into a glass to the rim. Then downed it.

"Oops! You forgot the olives. Derby, pour our guests drinks."

"We're not allowed to drink on duty, Mrs. DuVaugne, but thanks."

Taija's mouth turned down in a sympathetic frown. "Geezy, that doesn't seem fair."

"Taija, go upstairs. I have business to discuss here."

"Oh." After shooting her husband a hurt glance, she turned to Eve and Peabody. "It was nice meeting you."

"Nice meeting you, too."

"Derby, leave us alone." DuVaugne sat, rubbed his fingers over his eyes. "I didn't have anything to do with Minnock's murder. I was at my office until four. My driver brought me home. I didn't leave the house again until seven. You can check all this."

"Can and will. But when a man pays someone to steal for him, it's a short step up to paying someone to kill for him."

DuVaugne dropped his hands. "I don't know what this Dubrosky character's told you, but he's a thief and a liar. He's not to be trusted."

"You trusted him with about a hundred and fifty thousand," Eve pointed out.

"That's business, just the price of doing business." He waved that away, then settled his hands on his knees. "And he came to me. He said he wanted to develop a game, and was working on some new technology, but needed backing. Normally, I'd have dismissed him, but he was persuasive, and the idea was interesting, so I gave him a few thousand to continue the work. And a bit more shortly after as I confess I was caught up. I should know better, of course, but poor judgment's no crime. Then, after I'd invested considerable time and money, he told me he'd stolen the data from U-Play."

On a huff of breath, DuVaugne poured a second martini—and

remembered the olives. "I was shocked, outraged, threatened to turn him in, but he blackmailed me. I'd paid him, you see, so it would look as if I'd hired him to access the information. I continued to pay him. I didn't know what else to do."

Eve sat for a moment. "Do you buy any of that, Peabody?"

"No, sir. Not a word."

Obviously stunned, he lowered the glass. "You'd believe a common criminal over me?"

"In this case," Eve considered, "oh yeah. You're not naive, DuVaugne. Not like your very nice wife. And you wouldn't take a big chunk of cash out of your own pocket to help some struggling programmer develop a game. You hired Dubrosky, and you paid him to do exactly what he did—use some silly sap to feed him the data you wanted. You bring the game and the technology to your company, which is downsizing rapidly, you get to be the hero. Your investment pays off several hundred times. The only hitch to pulling it off? Bart Minnock."

"I'm not a murderer!" DuVaugne downed half the second martini before slapping the glass down. "If Dubrosky killed that man, he did it on his own. I had nothing to do with it."

"You just paid him to steal?"

"It's business," DuVaugne insisted. "It's just business. My company's in some trouble, that's true. We need an infusion, some fresh ideas, a boost in the market. When information comes my way, I use it. That's good business. It's the way of the industry. It's very competitive."

"When you pay someone to steal and/or transfer proprietary information it's called theft. And guess what? You go to jail. And if that theft is linked to murder you get the bonus prize of accessory thereto."

"This is insane. I'm a businessman doing my job. I'd never hurt anyone or have a part in it."

"Stealing the results of someone else's sweat hurts, and we'll see what we add to that before we're done. You can call that lawyer on the way downtown. Lane DuVaugne, you're under arrest for the solicitation of theft of proprietary information, and for the receipt of same, for conspiracy to commit corporate espionage. Cuff him, Peabody."

"No. Please, please. My wife. You have to let me explain to my wife. Let me tell her I'm going with you to—to help you with your investigation. Please, I don't want to upset her."

"Call her down. Tell her whatever you want. But she's going to find out when she has to post bail—if you get it."

S he hadn't done it for him, Eve thought as she let Peabody handle the booking. She'd done it to give his wife a little more time to adjust to the coming change. DuVaugne could talk with his lawyer, could try to wheedle, but there was no way they'd have a bail hearing until morning.

She'd see what he had to say after a night in a cell.

In her office, she tagged Roarke to let him know she was back, then wrote and filed her report.

While waiting for him she did what she hadn't had time to do all day. She started her murder board.

When it was done, she sat, put her feet on the desk, sipped coffee, and studied it.

Bart Minnock, his pleasant face, slightly goofy smile, rode beside the grisly shots from the crime scene, the stills from the morgue, and the people she knew connected to him.

His friends and partners, his girlfriend, the sad sack Roland, Dubrosky, DuVaugne. She scanned the list of employees, of accounts, the financial data, the time line as she knew it and the sweepers' reports.

Competition, she thought, business, ego, money, money, money, passion, naivete, security. Games.

Games equaled big business, big egos, big money, big passions, and the development thereof, big security.

Somewhere along the line that security had failed and one or more of the other elements snuck through to kill Minnock.

"I heard you made an arrest," Roarke said from behind her.

"Not on the murder, not yet. But it may connect. They'll push this project through, this game, without him. Not just because it's what they do, but because they wouldn't want to let him down."

"Yes, it'll be bumpier, and there may be a delay, but they'll push it through."

"Then what's the point of killing him." She shook her head, dropped her feet back to the floor. "Let's go take a walk through the scene."

 SHE LET ROARKE DRIVE SO SHE COULD CON-
tinue to work on her notes, determine who among
those interviewed needed a second pass, and who she
still needed to contact.

"I've got a buzz out to his lawyer—on vacation. She's cutting it short
and I'm meeting with her in the morning. She was a friend," Eve added.
"She seems inclined to give me whatever I need, and already outlined
some basic terms of his partnership agreement and will. Nearly everything goes to his parents, but his share of U-Play is to be divided among
the three remaining partners. It's a chunk."

"Are you thinking one or more of them decided to eliminate him so
they'd have a bigger slice of the pie?"

"Can't write it off. But sometimes money isn't the whole deal."
Money, she thought, was often the easiest button to push but not the
only button. "Sometimes it's not even in the deal. Still, I can't write it
off. You said they'd probably have some bumps and some delay in

getting this new game out, but they're going to reap a whirlwind of publicity so it seems to me when it hits, it'll hit big. Would that be your take?"

"It would—and it will. Even though we have a similar game and system about to launch, it's a considerable leap in gaming tech. And they'll have a lot of media focused on them due to Bart's death, and the method. It'll give them a push, but for the long haul? Losing him is a serious blow."

"Yeah, but some don't think long haul. And conversely, from a competitive standpoint, if you cut off the head—literally and figuratively—you're banking that the delay's long enough to give you time to beat the jump. They may be partners, and all bright lights, but Bart was the head. That's how it strikes me."

"I'd agree. And, if it's business? It feels more like competition than any sort of bid for splashy media attention. I can't see that, Eve."

Maybe not, she thought, but it was a by-product. "What do you know about game weapons—the toys used in a game, vid props, replicas, collector's items."

"They can be and are intriguing, and certainly can command stiff prices, particularly at auction."

"You collect." She shifted to study his profile. "But you mostly collect real."

"Primarily, yes. Still, it's an area of interest for anyone in the field, or serious about gaming. Game weapons run from the basic and simple to the intricate and complex, and everything between. They can and do add an element of immediacy and realism, a hands-on."

He glanced at her. "You enjoy weapons."

"I like knowing I've got one. One that does what it needs to do when I need it to do it."

"You've played the games. You're a competitive soul."

"What's the point of playing if winning isn't the goal?"

"We stand on the same side there."

"But a game's still a game," she pointed out. "A toy's a toy. I don't understand the compulsion to live the fantasy. To outfit your office like the command center of some fictional starship."

"Well, for the fun or the escape, though no doubt some take it too far. We should go to an auction some time, just so you can experience it. Gaming and the collecting that's attached to it, it's an interesting world."

"I like toys." She shrugged. "What I don't get is why anyone would spend millions on some play sword wielded by some play warrior in a vid or interactive."

"Some might say the same about art. It's all a matter of interest. In any case, some pieces of interest to collectors would be based on those vid props, and used in various games, or simply displayed. Depending on the accessibility, the age, the use, the base, they can be valuable to collectors. We routinely issue special limited editions of some weapons and accessories, just for that reason."

"How about an electrified sword?"

He braked for a red light, then smiled at her. "You'd have your fire sword, your charged-by-lightning, your stunner sword and so on. They'd give off a light show, appropriate sound effects—glow, sizzle, vibrate, that sort of thing. But no game prop would do more than give an opponent a bit of a buzz. They're harmless."

"You could doctor one?"

"I could, and bottom out its value on any legitimate market. There are regulations, Eve, safety requirements—and very strict ones. You'd never get anything capable of being turned into an actual weapon through screening. It wasn't a game prop that killed Bart."

"A replica then, made specifically for the purpose. A killing blade that carries enough of an electric current to burn."

He cruised through the green, said nothing for a moment as he swung toward the curb in front of Bart's building. "Is that what did him?"

"That's what we have at this point." She got out after Roarke parked. "That tells me it wasn't enough to kill. There had to be gamesmanship, too. It had to be fun or exciting for the killer. Whoever did it had to be part of it, part of the game. And he played to win. I have to figure out what he took home as his prize."

"Lieutenant." The doorman stepped away from his post. "Is there any progress? Do you know who killed Bart—Mr. Minnock?"

"The investigation's ongoing. We're pursuing all leads. Has anyone tried to gain access to his apartment?"

"No. No one's been up there since your people left. He was a nice guy. Hardly older than my son."

"You were on duty when he got home yesterday." It had all been asked before, she knew, but sometimes details shook out in the repetition. "How was his mood?"

"He was whistling. Grinning. I remember how it made me grin right back. He looked so damn happy."

"And no one came in after him, or before him, who might have access to his apartment?"

"No one. Quiet yesterday. You remember the weather we had? People stayed in, mostly, if they didn't have to go anywhere. Hardly anyone in or out all day, and I knew all of them."

"Did he have any trouble with anyone in the building? Any complaints?"

"He was a friendly guy, easygoing, but maybe a little shy, a little quiet. I never heard him complain about anybody, or anybody complain about him."

She shifted angles. "Maybe he was particularly friendly with one of the other tenants?"

"Well, the kids, sure."

And there, she thought, a new detail. "What kids?"

"The Sing kids, and the Trevor boy. We don't have a lot of kids in the building. Couple of teenage girls, but they're not so into the game scene. But the younger boys, they were big for Bart."

"Is that so?"

"Yeah, he let them come up and play now and then, said they were his market research. Gave them some demos here and there, passed them new games before they hit the stores."

"Were the parents okay with that?"

"Sure. He wouldn't've done it otherwise. In fact, Dr. Sing joined in sometimes. He's more into strategy games and like that than the action stuff the kids like. Those kids are taking it hard, really hard, since the news got out. Well, the Sing kids. The Trevors are on vacation, so I don't know if they heard about it."

"What's the Sings' apartment?"

"They're in five-ten if you want the main. It's a nice two-level job. The whole family's up there now, if you want to talk to them. I can buzz up, let them know."

"Why don't you do that? After, we'll be working in Mr. Minnock's for a while."

"It's good you're keeping on it. That's good. Whoever hurt that boy . . ." His lips thinned as he looked away. "Well, I can't even say what I think about it. We get fired for that kind of language."

Roarke keyed up his PPC as they got in the elevator. "Sing,

Dr. David—neurologist. His wife's a pediatric surgeon. Susan. Boys, Steven and Michael, ages ten and eight respectively. Married twelve years. Both graduated from Harvard Medical School, and both are attendings at Mount Sinai. No criminal on either."

"Since when do you access criminal records on that?"

"Since I consult with my lovely wife." Roarke slipped the PPC back in his pocket.

"I've got a guy in a cage right now for accessing proprietary information."

Roarke merely smiled, held his hands out, wrists up. "Want to take me in, darling?"

The elevator doors opened and spared her from an answer. "I just want a look, a sense. Maybe the whole deal was some sort of accident. Everybody's playing, having fun, until somebody gets their head chopped off."

"And a couple of kids clean up after themselves, reset the security, reprogram a very sophisticated droid?"

"No, but they have really smart parents. I assume smart given the Harvard Medical. It's not likely, but—"

"You can't write it off," Roarke finished, and pressed the bell for 510 himself.

"Try to look like Peabody."

"Sorry?"

"Serious, official, yet approachable."

"You forgot adorable."

"Peabody is *not* adorable."

"She is from my perspective. Besides, I was talking about me."

She barely smothered the laugh before the door opened.

David Sing wore jeans and a spotless white shirt. In her boots Eve had an inch on him, and his weary eyes skimmed from her to Roarke.

He spoke with a precision that told her English wasn't his first language, but he'd learned it very well.

"You're the police. I'm David Sing. Please, come in."

There were touches of his Asian heritage in the decor—the pretty colors, the collection of carved dragons, the pattern of the silk throws. He ushered them to a bright blue sofa that showed both care and wear.

"We'll have tea," he said. "My sons' nanny is preparing it. She stayed late this evening as our children are very upset by what happened to our friend. Please sit. Tell me how I might help you."

He hadn't asked for ID, but Eve took out her badge. "I'm Lieutenant Dallas. I'm primary investigator in the matter of Bart Minnock's murder."

"Yes. Jackie explained when he called up. And I recognize you. Both of you. We heard of Bart's death this afternoon, and my wife and I took leave immediately. We didn't want our sons to hear of it before we could speak with them, prepare them. Ah, here is our tea. Min, this is Lieutenant Dallas and Roarke."

The woman who rolled in the tray was tiny and hadn't seen seventy for a number of years. She bowed slightly, then spoke in a quiet voice in a language Eve didn't understand. Then she laid a hand on Sing's shoulder in a gesture that spoke clearly of a long and deep connection.

"I'll pour, Min." He reached up, gave the hand on his shoulder a light squeeze. "Go, put your feet up awhile." He added something in their native language.

The woman kissed the top of his head, then left them.

"Min was my nanny when I was a boy. Now she helps take care of our boys." He poured pale gold tea into handleless cups. "My wife is upstairs with the children. We can speak freely."

"It would be helpful to speak to your wife, and your sons."

"Yes, they'll come down shortly. I thought, if you needed to give any details . . . I hope you can spare the children some of it. They're very young, and they were very fond of Bart."

She wished briefly for Peabody. Peabody was better than she was with kids. Well, anybody was, she decided, and considered Roarke.

"We'll be as sensitive as possible with your children, Dr. Sing."

"They understand death, as well as a child can. Their parents are doctors, after all. But it's difficult for them, for any of us to understand how their friend could be upstairs one day, and gone the next. Can you tell me if there are plans for any sort of service? I think attending would be helpful for them."

"I don't have that information at this time, but I'll see that you get the details when I do."

"Thank you. I understand you're very busy. I'll get my family."

When he left the room, Eve shifted to Roarke. "I think you should talk to the kids."

"Funny. I don't."

"They're boys. They'd probably relate better to you."

Face placid, body at ease, he sampled the tea. "Coward."

"Yes, but that doesn't mean I'm not right. Besides, I'm primary. I get to call the shots."

He smiled at her. "I'm just a civilian."

"Since when?" she retorted.

"Try the tea. It's very nice."

"I'll show you what you can do with the tea." But she postponed the demonstration as she watched the Sing family come in.

The woman had the dark skin, the ice-edged cheekbones, and regal bearing of an African princess. She must have topped out at six feet, and she carried it on a lush and admirable body. She and her husband flanked the boys, a hand on each shoulder indicating a united front.

Eve didn't know much about kids, but she was pretty sure she was looking at two of the most beautiful examples of the species. They had their father's black, almond-shaped eyes, their mother's cheekbones, and skin of an indescribable tone that somehow blended their parents to golden, glowing perfection.

The boys held hands, a gesture that gave her heart one hard wrench. Beside her, she heard Roarke sigh, and understood.

Such youth, such beauty should never have to face the senseless violence of murder.

"My wife, Susan, and our sons, Steven and Michael."

"Lieutenant. Sir. You're here to help Bart." Susan stroked a hand gently up and down Steven's back.

"Yes. Thank you for your time." Eve braced herself, looked at the children. "I'm very sorry you lost your friend."

"The police find the bad people," the younger boy, Michael, said. "And arrest them. Then they go to jail."

Someone, she thought, had given the kids the basic pecking order. "That's right."

"Sometimes they don't." Steven's jaw tightened. "Sometimes they don't find them and arrest them. And sometimes when they do they don't go to jail."

And, the reality. "That's right, too."

"Lieutenant Dallas always finds the bad people," Roarke told the boy, "because she never stops looking. She never stops looking because even though she didn't know Bart before, he's her friend now, too."

"How can she be his friend if she didn't know him?"

"Because after he died, she went to him, and looked at him, and promised him her help. That's what friends do. They help."

"He helped me with compu-science for school," Michael piped up.

"And he let us play his games and let us have fizzies . . ." He slanted a look up at his mother.

She smiled. "It's all right."

"We're not supposed to have too many fizzies," Michael explained. "They're not really good for you. How do you catch the bad people? Don't they hide and run away?"

Okay, Eve decided, she could handle this. "They try to. You might be able to help me find them."

"You need clues."

"Sure. Sometimes I get clues by talking to people. So why don't you tell me about the last time you saw Bart?"

"It wasn't yesterday or the day before, but the day before that." Michael looked at his brother for verification.

"It was raining a lot so we couldn't go to the park after our music lesson. We got to go up to Bart's and be a test study."

"What did you test?"

"Bases Loaded," Steven told her. "The new version that's not even out yet. It's total and almost as good as playing in the park for real."

"Was anyone else there?"

"It was just us, until Min came to get us. And Bart talked her into playing Scrabble before we left. She won. She always wins Scrabble."

"Maybe he talked to someone on the 'link."

"No, ma'am, he didn't. Oh, but Leia was there. I forgot."

"The droid."

"She made snacks. Healthy snacks," Michael added with another glance at his mother. "Sort of healthy."

"Did he show you any other new games? Something else that isn't out yet?"

"Not that day."

"How about Fantastical?"

Both boys angled their heads. "What is it?" Steven asked. "It sounds like a magic game. Linc likes magic games especially."

"Linc Trevor," Sing supplied. "He's a friend of the boys, and lives in the building. He and his family are on vacation."

"They've been gone *forever*," Michael complained.

"Less than two weeks." Susan glanced at Eve. "They'll be gone a month altogether."

"When he gets back and before school starts we're going to have a party. If it's okay," Steven added. "Bart said we'd all get together: Linc and Bart's friends from work, and there'd be a brand-new game. The best game ever. We'll all get to play, and. . . but we can't. We won't. Because Bart's dead now. I forgot. Bart's dead."

"You're helping me help him right now," Eve told him as the boy's eyes swam.

"How?"

"By talking to me. Did he tell you anything about the new game? The best game?"

"He said you got to be anyone or anything you wanted. Imagine your reality and go beyond. That's what he said. I remember because it made me laugh. It sounds funny."

Even Bart couldn't resist leaking a little of the project." Eve paused outside the crime scene apartment before breaking the seal. "Only a couple of kids who really didn't process any more than 'party' and 'new game.' But if he said something to them, he may have said something to someone who'd process a lot more."

"Killing him didn't get them the game," Roarke pointed out.

"We can't be sure of that. We can't know what he may or may not have told his killer. Dubrosky used sex to get data. The killer may have used the same, or some other type of seduction. Praise, interest, financial backing. It goes back to the game," she said as she closed and locked the door behind them. "It has to."

She stood a moment, taking in the living area, trying to see it through the victim's eyes. "However smart he is, he's simple. The colors in here, throughout the place. Stimulating, sure, but simple. Primary colors. Game and vid posters for art, reflecting his taste. What he likes, what he's comfortable with. Every room set up for games.

"He's loyal, but that's also a simplicity. You make friends, you keep friends. Playmates become workmates, and you know them, understand them, again relate—and it's comfortable. His current girlfriend, very comfortable relationship there, too. No drama, no kink. Just a nice girl hanging with a nice boy. Relatively new friends? Kids in the building. They're simple, too. A kid's going to play as long as you let him play. He's not going to want a fancy meal when pizza's on the menu. He gets kids because a big part of him still is one."

"I've nothing to argue about so far." Roarke watched her wander the room.

"Kids—unless you were you or me—are generally pretty trusting. He's got good security. He's not a fool. But he brings home a developmental disc, without logging it out. Their big project, and he carries a copy home, where again, sure he's got good security. But what if he got mugged on the street, hit by a maxibus, had his pocket picked? He doesn't think of that because he's simple, and because he wants to play the game. In his own place. His game. So . . ."

She walked back to the door. "He comes home, a little earlier than usual. He can't wait. The doorman's not lying, so he came in alone. EDD reports that his droid's programmed to bring him a fizzy when he comes in, remind him of any appointments or events. The memory log confirms that behavior, and the ordered shutdown. He drinks his fizzy, and the timing of the shutdown and the holo log-in indicates he went almost directly into the holo-room. Droid's log has it suggesting he change his shoes. They were wet from walking home in the rain. But he didn't. Security logs at the entrance show him wearing the same pair he died in."

"Young," Roarke commented, "eager to play. Not much thought about damp shoes."

"Yeah." She shook her head as they started up. "Maybe someone was already here. Maybe he let someone in after the shutdown, before he went up."

"Someone he knew and trusted," Roarke prompted.

"No sign of struggle, no defensive wounds except for arm gash, no chemicals in his system, no evidence of restraints. Maybe they freaking hypnotized him, but otherwise, he went into the holo-room with his killer."

"A playmate."

"Not a pint-sized one. Neither of those Sing kids could cover this."

"So you can write them off."

"If they'd been here and there'd been an accident, they'd have spilled it." She thought of those dark, liquid eyes again. The simplicity, the innocence. "The younger one spilled about the fizzies. You could say, Gee, that's cute, but what it is, under it, is honest. Still, possibly an accident with someone not as simple or honest as a couple of kids."

"They're a lovely family."

Her gaze tracked as they continued on, as she looked for anything out of place, anything she might have missed before. "I don't know why it always surprises me to see that sort of thing. Maybe I don't generally interview lovely families. Steady ones. My impression is Bart came from the same. Maybe it's a disadvantage in its own way."

"What way would that be?"

"You can end up too simple and too trusting." She glanced at him. "That's sure not our problem."

"The cop and the criminal?" He laid a stroke down her back. "I'd wager there's a good many of those from steady families as well. Is that what worries you, Eve, about starting one of our own? Not time yet," he added, helplessly amused by the quick panic in those canny cop's eyes. "But when it is, is that your worry? We'll either raise cops, criminals, or the too trusting?"

"I don't have a clue. But just a for instance, who'll remember to say, 'No more fizzies'? What if I want one? Or no pizza for dinner again, when come on, why the hell not? It's another endless set of rules to learn. I haven't worked my way through the marriage rules yet."

"And yet, here we are." He lowered his head to kiss her lightly. "I think there's a lot of on-the-job training involved in raising children."

"That's fine when it's consenting adults, but it ought to be a lot more solid when there's one of those little squirmy things involved, like Mavis's Bella. Anyway . . ." She'd let herself become distracted, and Bart deserved better.

"He goes in, alone or with a playmate. Alone doesn't make sense. His pocket 'link was still on him, and shut off—downtime corresponds to the holo-log entry. He came in, shut down his coms so he wouldn't be disturbed. Or someone shut them down for him. But alone would mean someone came in after him, which means that person or persons circumvented the security not only on the building, but the apartment and this room."

Blowing out a breath, she shook her head. "It's too much work, too much trouble. If you're that good, you minimize the risks."

"And come in with him."

"He had to have company in here. Maybe he'd planned it that way, though there's nothing on any of his 'links or comps to show he intended to meet anyone. An impulse. Someone from work, from the building, someone he ran into on the way home. And still an outsider had to get by the doorman unless they came in earlier or accessed another opening in the building. Delivery entrance, roof, an empty apartment. We know at least one apartment's vacant with the Trevors on vacation. Probably others, or others just empty during the day."

"They'd have to expect Bart to come home in order to cross paths."

"Exactly," she agreed. "Which goes right back to someone from U-Play. All it takes is one tag. He's on his way. Get in, arrange to run into him—knock on the door a couple minutes after he's inside. Time to have him shut down the droid so he's got everything set for game time. 'Hey, how's it going—I was just in the neighborhood, thought I saw you come in.' Bart's all whistling-a-tune happy, excited. He's nearly ready to launch his baby, just wants to play with it first, fine-tune. Here's someone he knows. Another game player. It virtually has to be or why bring them in?"

She paced the room, stopped, put her hands on her hips. "I don't like it. Too loose, too many variables." She closed her eyes a moment, tried to see another angle. "He takes the game disc, but doesn't log it. Or he did and someone doctored the log. Either way, it's a work thing. Someone from work, someone involved in the project, maybe someone he wants along to help with specifics. But on the down-low. They don't come in together, so maybe the killer arranges to meet him. 'I'll be right behind you' sort of thing. Gives him a chance to get in another way, before or after Bart leaves. Before's better. Got a couple things to do first, so I'll meet you. Access on the sly so nobody knows you're there. Disc's not logged out, and Bart's place is a short walking distance from the warehouse. Busy place. Is anyone really going to notice if someone's gone for an hour?

"It could work." Complicated, she thought again, but doable. And didn't gamers prefer the complex? "You're in, and the only person who knows you're in is going to be dead."

"And the weapon?" Roarke asked.

"Big shiny toy. Look what I've got. Just had to show you. Game's in, and they play because that's got to be part of it. The competition, the game. It wasn't a goddamn accident. It was premeditated. Otherwise there's no need to avoid coming in through security. No need to time it just so. Some sort of war fantasy, fight, sports—something to explain the minor bruising. Fight. Sword fight? Knights in shining freaking armor or warlords or whatever the fucking hell boys play."

She circled the room trying to see it, to get some sort of picture in her head. "Maybe Bart's getting the upper hand, racking up points. That just pisses you off, helps wind you up for the kill. Give him a taste first or maybe you just missed. First blood with that arm wound. See the shock on his face, smell the blood—it's like copper on the back of the throat. Then one vicious swing, and it's done. End of game. The blood's real though, so much of it now that copper taste is too strong. Clean up, change clothes, stuff the bloody ones in a bag. Get out the same way you got in."

"And leave the game disc behind?"

"If he knew Bart well enough to get in, he knew him well enough to know the security. Anybody tries to eject without all the codes, it self-destructs. It's just a copy. It's not about the disc, it's about the whole— the game, the company, the man, everything. Because to do what was done here, you were very, very pissed off. Passion," she murmured. "Passion and ego more than money, I think. Money'll play a part. It nearly always does, but it's not leading this charge."

She held up a hand as a new thought emerged. "He brought the disc home. Five-minute walk. I bet it's not the first time. Did EDD download the full log?"

"It goes back to the beginning of the year. It's archived prior. I only glanced at it as we're working on getting into his comps and trying to piece together what we can from the disc. And don't hope for much there. It's hardly more than ashes."

"But the log may give us a pattern. That, the building's security discs, and the security discs and logs from U-Play."

"It's going to be a long night," Roarke predicted.

**7** ON THE WAY HOME SHE CHECKED IN WITH
members of the team, logged the updates. She sent
copies of all reports to her commander, then requested
a consult with Mira for the next day.

"Two arrests today," she said, thinking of DuVaugne and Dubrosky.
"Both deserve the cage time, but neither of them killed my vic. Someone
closer than that. Someone more fun."

She remembered Peabody's angle. "These conventions—cons—
where people get all dressed up in weird outfits, play games, have contests, take seminars. I bet you'd meet a lot of fun people at those, if
that's what you're into."

"Shared interests, like minds. That's what you're after."

"And the weapons. Fancy magic sword. Maybe it was a bribe, or some
sort of payment. Let me play the game, let me be—what did Bart call it
with the Sing kids—your test study—and you can have the sword."

"Most auctions and shops have records of that sort of sale. I can try to find it." Roarke maneuvered around a maxibus, threaded the needle between a couple of Rapid Cabs while evening traffic spurted, snarled, or stalled. "But it's just as likely it was private, and no record exists."

"Worth a shot. Tie the sale to someone at U-Play. Someone he met at a con, and maybe hired. For the warehouse spot, for consulting. Someone he used before in test studies." She stared out the window where the warmth had tourists flooding the sidewalks, but she saw a secured holo-room where her victim died in shoes wet from a whistling walk in the rain.

"He knew his killer," she stated, "or whoever set him up for the kill."

She thought of DuVaugne again as they drove through the gates of home. Not in the killing sense, but in taste, in scope. The steel and glass box, she thought, so cold, so hard, so desperately trendy. And here was Roarke's taste and scope in the strong and graceful lines of home, the towers and turrets adding a little fancy, the streams and rivers of flowers, the warmth and color.

Yet the man who'd built it had lived in the cold and the hard for so long, as she had. When given the choice, he'd taken the strong and the warm.

And, in turn, had given them to her.

"We should eat."

He turned to look at her as he stopped the car. "Now you're stepping on my lines."

"You could start the search for the weapon, and I'll put something together."

"Will you now?"

She couldn't really fault his skepticism. "I won't program pizza."

He got out of the car, waited for her, took her hand. "What's the occasion?"

"You have good taste in houses."

"I have good taste in all manner of things. Especially wives." He lifted her hand to his lips as they walked up the steps and into the house.

She gave Summerset a good, long study as he stood exactly where she'd expected, like a harbinger of doom in the foyer with the chub of cat at his feet.

"I saw your evil twin today," she told him. "Wait, you're the evil twin. I think he has the same tailor, too. I. M. Funereal."

"Well, that was clever," Roarke said and pinched the hand he'd just kissed. "We'll be eating upstairs tonight," he told Summerset.

"Hardly breaking news. There's some very nice grilled swordfish, if the pair of you choose to eat like adults."

"Swordfish," Eve considered. "Might be lucky, considering. You didn't have to pinch me," she added as they continued up and the cat, his mind very likely on food, raced ahead of them. "I really did see his evil twin today. You can ask Peabody. Of the droid variety, and it had one of those fake-sounding upper-class Brit accents, but it was a ringer. I bet you could buy it cheap if you ever want to replace dour with droid."

"You're asking for another pinch."

"Probably a bad idea, about the switch. As much as I hate to say it, I think the droid's worse. Did Summerset ever tell you not to drink too many fizzies because they're not really good for you?"

"Possibly. Probably," Roarke said as they turned into the bedroom. "I want to change out of this suit."

"And while he was doing that, he taught you how to steal."

"I already knew how to steal. He taught me how to steal with a bit more finesse. Dinner," he said as she shed her own jacket. "And if it's the swordfish, open a 'fifty-seven Lautrec. It should be a nice complement."

"No pointers," she told him and changed her boots for skids. "Otherwise it doesn't count in my column."

She strolled out, still wearing her weapon harness, which he assumed she'd forgotten she had on as it was as much a part of her as the shallow dent in her chin.

Wanting the ease and comfort, he changed into jeans and a T-shirt before making the 'link calls he preferred to address in private. There had been too many eyes and ears on him throughout the day, he thought now. Cops' eyes, cops' ears. They might have been his wife's, his friends', but there were some matters easier done without the weight of the law on his shoulders.

Eve's law, he thought, could be particularly heavy at times, so he programmed a series of runs, scans, and searches by remote before continuing on to his office, which intersected with hers.

He could hear her talking to the cat, ordering her computer to run a variety of probabilities, then her movements around the room.

Setting up her murder board, he concluded while he programmed searches from different angles and apexes for a sword that may or may not exist.

A fairly typical evening for them, Roarke supposed, and he had no complaints. He would have to devote several hours of what might have been free time to his own business due to the interruption of the day—and likely days more. But he liked his work, so that wasn't a true sacrifice.

In any case, the interruption had been his call, his choice.

The boy had sparked something in him in life—all that enthusiasm and discovery. And the boy had touched something in him in death— the waste, the cruelty of the waste.

It had touched deep because Bart had trusted him—a competitor— and one with the means and experience to betray that trust and crush a young company like a hatching egg under a boot.

Perhaps that explained why he felt obligated to help find out who'd do so. Not to the company, but to the boy himself.

Eve had called Bart simple, Roarke recalled. He wasn't sure he agreed entirely, but certainly Bart had been uncomplicated. Open, eager, honest, brilliant, and making a mark doing what he loved with people he loved.

Life should be so uncomplicated for everyone, Roarke thought.

Maybe, at the base of it, Bart had sparked something in him due to their differences rather than their similarities. No one, Roarke admitted, would ever consider him open or honest. And he'd never, even as a boy, held that fresh eagerness or casual brilliance.

Still, he'd made his mark while Bart had only begun to scratch the surface of his own potential.

He left the search on auto and walked through the shared doorway to see Eve finishing her murder board. As they often did, he thought, they'd have the dead as company for dinner.

The cat watched her, sprawled over the back of her sleep chair like a fat, furry blanket. Galahad switched his tail as a casual wave of greeting as Roarke crossed over. He ran a hand over the cat, head to switching tail, and got a low, murmuring purr in response.

"You took a while, so I figured I'd set up. I already fed the cat," she added. "Don't let him tell you different."

Roarke picked up the wine she'd set on the table by the window— she'd taken his advice there—and poured two glasses. "The searches are running." He lifted one of the hot lids and noted she'd chosen the swordfish, married it with asparagus, and fries.

"The fries are a compromise since I'm eating fish." She turned from the completed board to take the wine he offered. "I thought about making yours with one of the rice deals you seem to like for no good reason I can think of. But then it's more like going out to a restaurant than fixing a meal at home. So you get what I get."

"You have the oddest thought patterns at times." Because what she'd done, how and why she'd done it, chased off some of the shadows, he touched his glass to hers. "It looks good."

"It ought to. I slaved over a cool AutoChef for a full five minutes." She sat, smiled at him. "Why does a fish have a sword?"

"Is this a riddle?"

"No, it's a question. Do they do the *en guard*, *touché* thing or just go around stabbing unarmed fish because they can?"

"Maybe they do battle with the hammerheads."

"Sword's got a longer reach than a hammer, but a hammer could break a sword. It might be interesting, but I think it's stupid to bring a hammer to a swordfight, unless it's all you've got."

"Use whatever weapon comes to hand, and anything that comes to hand is a potential weapon."

"Yeah. If Bart was gaming a swordfight, he wouldn't have brought a hammer."

Easier, Roarke realized, to consider the details of death than to sink into the philosophy of it. "Depending on the game, the level, the programming, he might have had to earn his weapons. They can also be lost or broken, jammed or simply run out of charge or ammunition, again depending."

"Did you ever play with him?"

"A couple of times. We never did holo, as it generally takes more time, and the facilities. But we played some VR, and some straight comp. He was very good, quick reflexes, and though he tended to take unnecessary risks, he made up for that with enthusiasm. But for the most part we talked technology, the business, marketing. We only had contact a handful of times the past two or three years."

"Did you ever have him over here?"

"No. I'm not as trusting, and there was never any reason or purpose to it. We didn't actively socialize, or have anything in common really but a common interest. He was very young, on several levels, and as many in their twenties do, he considered someone in their thirties as another generation."

"Jamie's younger," she pointed out, speaking of Feeney's godson and another e-wiz. "He's been around a lot. You've worked with him. So have I."

"Bart was nothing like Jamie. He hadn't that edge, the street savvy, and certainly not any aspirations to turn his considerable e-skills toward a career in EDD. Jamie's the next thing to family."

Roarke paused, sipped some wine. "And does this conversation help you justify bringing me, a competitor of your victim, into the investigation as a consultant?"

"I don't have to justify your participation, but it doesn't hurt given the business interests, and the fact you told me you have a similar project under development, to keep it all open."

"It's always pleasant not to be a suspect." He watched irritation cross her face, and honestly couldn't say why he'd pushed that particular button.

"Look, from a strictly objective view, you could have smashed U-Play before it ever got off the ground, and at any point since then. They don't threaten you. Hell, you've got the hammer *and* the sword, plus a couple of blasters and a pocketful of boomers. If you want to take down a company, and effectively, its brain, you use money, strategy, and guile, not a magic sword."

She stabbed a piece of fish. "You have another perspective on the victim—not a partner, not exactly a friend, not an enemy, and a competitor only in the most technical sense. So you add to my picture of him while laying out the basics and the extent of your association."

"That's a lot of explanation," he said mildly.

"Maybe."

"Then I suppose I should add my own, in the interest of full disclosure and openness. I've implemented level-three runs on any of my people involved in the development of the holo-game project, and those on the fringes of it. Their associations, financials, communications."

"That's not your job."

"I disagree. They're my people, and I will be bloody well sure no one in my employ is involved in this, on any level, in any way."

"The Privacy Act—"

"Be damned." And a hot thread of anger, he admitted, felt more comfortable than this inexplicable sorrow. "Anyone employed by me or seeking to be is routinely screened, and signs a waiver."

"Not for a level three, not without cause. That's cop or government level."

"Murder would be cause on my gauge." His tone was as crisp and chilly as the wine.

"It's a gray area."

"Your gray is broader and darker than mine. There are incentives attached to a project like this, bonuses that could be very lucrative." He stopped again, angled his head. "Which you know very well already as you've done or are doing your own level three, on my people."

"It's my job."

"You might have told me. You might have trusted me enough to get the information for you."

"You might have told *me*," she countered. "Trusted *me* enough to do my job. Dammit. I didn't tell you because you had a personal attachment to the victim, and I didn't see the point in adding to the upset by telling you or asking you to get the data. What's your excuse?"

"I don't need an excuse. They're my people. But the fact is once I have the data, and—whatever the results—pass it to you, you'd be able to contract or expand your suspect list."

"All you had to do was tell me."

"And the reverse holds just as true, so there's no point in you getting pissed off."

"I'm not pissed off. I'm . . . aggravated."

"You're aggravated? Consider, Eve, how aggravated I might be if it turns out that someone I trust, someone I pay had anything whatsoever to do with that."

He gestured to the board.

"You can't be or feel responsible for every person who pulls a check from Roarke Industries." She threw up her hands. "It's half the fucking world."

More than one hot thread of anger wound through him now. "Oh yes, I bloody well can, and it's nothing to do with numbers and everything to do with being in charge. You are and feel exactly the same about every cop in your division, in the whole shagging department come to that."

She started to argue, then stopped because he was right about that much. "Any data from your run has to coincide with mine, and officially come from mine whether it clears your whole crew or somebody bobs to the surface."

"I know how it works, Lieutenant. I'll just get back to it then, so you can have what you need and shift it back to your side of the line."

"That was low," she mumbled as he walked out.

"Maybe it was."

She sat, brooding into her wine. She didn't know, exactly, why they were at odds. They were doing basically the same thing for basically the same reason.

Basically.

But he should've let her do it, or waited until she'd assigned him to do it. And that probably grated. The *assign* portion. Couldn't be helped. She was the LT, she was the primary, she gave the damn orders.

Now she was passing aggravated and heading toward pissed, she realized.

She'd just been trying to shield him a little. Wasn't that her job, too? she thought in disgust as she rose. Part of the marriage deal? So why were they fighting when she'd done her job?

And now she had to do the damn dishes, which she'd fully intended to dump on him.

She gathered them up as she scowled at the door he'd closed between their offices, and the red light above it that indicated he'd gone private.

That was pattern, she thought as she carted the dishes into the kitchen. When he was seriously peeved he walked away, closed up until he cooled off. Which was probably for the best as it saved a serious bout. But it was . . . aggravating.

She wondered why two people who loved each other to the point of stupid managed to aggravate each other as often as they seemed to.

She couldn't think about it now, she decided as she dumped the dishes in the washer. She had work to do.

She programmed coffee and took it back to her desk.

Since he was doing the runs, whether she wanted him to or not, she'd let that part slide for now. No point in doubling the work.

Instead she studied the probabilities she'd set up before dinner.

With the available data, the computer calculated a more than ninety-two percent probability Bart Minnock had known his killer. It gave her just under sixty on premeditation, high nineties on the killer working in or involved in the gaming business, which dropped to middle seventies on personnel from U-Play.

"If it wasn't premeditated, how'd he manage to clean up and walk out without his clothes full of blood? Dammit."

Had the killer taken some of Bart's clothes? she wondered. Take a shirt, take some pants—Bart wasn't in a position to complain. That increased the possibility of accidental or violent impulse.

"Need the weapon. Need to ID the weapon. Who owned it."

She brought up Bart's financials again, scouring them for any sign of a major purchase from an individual or a vendor who might deal in gaming weapons.

She cross-referenced the financials with the inventory list of weapons, toys, props found in his apartment and his office.

"Light saber. That's a kind of electrified sword. Not a blade though, more like . . . a tube? Not a broad straight edge, not the weapon."

She picked her way through U-Play's financial records. Steady, she thought, gradual and healthy up-ticks since inception, with a lot of the profit rolled back in. That showed partners in for the long haul.

The four of them attended a lot of cons—individually or as a group, and sometimes sent other employees. The business picked up the freight, and paid the hefty fee for display and demo space, often sponsored contests and events.

A lot of money for that, she noted. Was that usual, practical, smart? She glanced toward the closed door. She'd just have to ask her expert consultant, civilian, when he was in a better mood.

Using the crime scene images, Morris's findings, the sweeper's reports she programmed a reconstruction of the murder. Eyes narrowed, she watched the two comp images stand face-to-face, watched the sword slice down so the tip ripped open the victim's forearm, then swing up, back before making that slightly downward and powerful beheading stroke.

"That had to hurt—the first gash. It had to hurt as well as shock.

What does someone usually do when something hurts, when they've been cut, when they're bleeding? Why didn't you, Bart?" she asked aloud. "Why didn't you press your hand to the wound? No blood on your palm, and there would've been. It cut, it burned, it bled, but you don't attempt to staunch it, feel it. It's instinctive. But you couldn't if you had something in your hand, like the hilt of a sword. Couldn't if you tried to defend, or if the killing blow came too fast."

She ran it again, changing variables, then dragged a hand through her hair. "What was the game? Why would you play with a fake sword if your opponent had a real one?

"Because you didn't know. But you damn well should have."

She rose, paced, then gave in and rapped a fist smartly on the closed door.

It took a moment. Did he do that on purpose? Make her wait? Then the light flipped green, and the door opened.

"I need to use the holo-room," she said. "I need a game that approximates what Bart might have been into at the time of the murder. I need you to set it up and go through it with me."

"All right. I'll meet you there."

"I don't suppose you have a couple of swords, of the nonlethal variety."

"Everything in the weapons room is authentic, so no. You'll have to make do with holo-weapons."

"Okay." She tried to think of something else, then simply shrugged and started to the holo-room.

Roarke's was bigger than the one in Bart's apartment—big surprise, she thought sourly. It probably met or exceeded the specs of anything Roarke had in any of his R&D operations.

But the size didn't matter.

A holo-reconstruct of a murder that took place during a holo-game would give her a better feel, she hoped, for what had happened. *What* often led to *why* and *why* to *who*.

She walked around the large, empty space, listening to her own footsteps echo. She wasn't much for games, not really. Training exercises, now, that was different, and she found the holo-room handy there.

More than once Roarke had used it to take her somewhere fantastic—a rainy night in Paris, a drifting boat on an empty sea. Romantic, seductive—well, the holo was handy there, too, though at the moment she doubted either of them felt particularly romantic.

He came in with a disc. "You're still wearing your weapon."

She'd forgotten, and now stripped off the harness to lay it and the weapon by the door.

"You wanted something close to U-Play's Fantastical. We've been dissecting what we have of it in EDD, but I don't have the data or components here. It seemed . . . a gray area to bring any of that home to continue the work here."

"Agreed."

"But I have our most current version of our game—no title as titles can leak. It's Program HC84-K."

"You have that at home? Isn't that shaky security?"

"First, someone would have to know it's here, then get through house security, into my private office, and find the vault, get through that security, then get through the passcodes and fail-safes on the disc. If they managed all that, they're likely good enough to have developed this themselves."

He slid it into a slot as he spoke, used both palm plate and retinal scan, added a voice command and several manual ones.

"In any case," he continued, "it's something I've been fine-tuning myself, and I prefer to do that here. So . . ."

He stepped back, studied her. "You want sword play, but you don't know the era, the setting, the mode, or the goal. We haven't managed to get anything off the disc Bart used to give you any of that. You'll have to pick."

"I don't know. Sword fight. Not foils," she added. "Broad blade. Strong, straight."

"Broadsword." He tilted his head, smiled a little.

"Don't put me in some dumbass girl costume." She jabbed a finger at him. "I mean it. I'm not doing this half naked for your perverted amusement."

"A shame, but fair enough. Let's try a few." He went manual again, she suspected to keep his little game a secret until she was sucked in.

The air shimmered, wavered, and in a moment she found herself standing in a shadowy forest—and dressed in some sort of ancient Asian garb. She had a sword in her hand and soft boots on her feet.

"When and where are . . ."

She broke off, eyes huge. While her thoughts were in English, her voice had come out in what she thought was Japanese.

"How the hell—"

"Translator feature. Adds to the realism," he said in the same language. "It's just slightly out of loop. We're working on that."

"I . . . No, it's too weird. I don't want to speak Japanese."

"All right, let's try another."

With barely a shimmer this time, she stood on a green hill, her hair long and tied back. She wore, as Roarke did, some sort of leather top that hit mid-thigh and snug pants that slid into the tops of boots.

She hesitated, then gave it another try. "Okay, now where . . . Gaelic. It's Gaelic, isn't it? I get the accent."

"Ireland, Tudor era."

"It . . . it smells green, and there's a hint of something earthy, smoky."

"Peat fires. All the sensory features have been enhanced. In the real-world scenarios, the language, the syntax, the clothing, well, every detail's been meticulously researched and replicated. There are any number of fantasy options already programmed in, or the players can program their own, either from an option menu or by going manual. There's no limit."

"Okay, frosty, because I'm hearing you speak Gaelic, but I'm processing English. Did Fantastical have this?"

"I don't know, but tend to doubt it from the data we have, from their setup at the warehouse. We'll offer a cheaper version without the translator, but I project the translator feature—which will be steep—will be a main selling point. And there's the added educational aspect."

"Sure. Educational." She tipped her head. "I hear . . ." She turned on the hill, and let out a stunned breath. A battle raged in the valley below. Hundreds of warriors, horses, fires. She was pretty sure she was watching a castle being sacked.

"More scope than I've seen in holo before, more range. It's more like being in a vid. A really well-produced vid."

"That's only limited by your skill and imagination. The program will adjust, follow your choices, your strategy."

"How do you stop it?"

"By simply telling the program to halt, pause, or change. In a multiplayer game, doing so would cost that player points or result in disqualification."

"Yeah?" She turned back to him and didn't he look amazing with all that black hair blowing in the wind, in that scarred leather and with a bright sword in his hand. "I won't be calling time-out." She lifted her sword. "Let's play."

8

SHE SET, PLANTING HER FEET AS SHE STRUCK
out. She heard the ring and clash as steel met steel, felt
the force of it sing up her arm.

They eyed each other over the deadly vee.

"I take it you've fancied we're enemies."

"More fun that way," she said, and spun back to return with another
thrust.

He blocked, then worked her back a few paces. "That would depend." He feinted, struck right, right again, then left. She repelled, a
kind of testing denial before thrusting forward to force him back.

He swept up, under her guard, but she danced aside, then whirled,
using the rotation to add speed and strength to the next attack.

"You've been practicing," he commented while their blades whistled
and sang.

"You, too."

"Part of my job." His blade clashed and shimmered against hers. "But you don't see many cops in sword fights."

"You never know."

She knew him, knew he held back a bit. Knew he was amused by the situation, and that gave her an advantage. Using it, she smiled at him. "Sword's got weight." She gripped the hilt in both hands as if to test it, and when he lowered his sword a fraction, charged in.

She caught his shoulder, just a quick bite before he slapped her blade aside.

And she saw blood well.

"Oh Jesus. Oh shit. I cut you. How—"

"It's not real." He held up a hand before she could rush forward. They both knew he could have taken her down, ended the game in that moment of shock. "Just part of the program." He inclined his head. "Your point, Lieutenant."

"It could've happened that way. Something like that. Come on." She used her free hand, wiggling her fingers in challenge. "Keep it going."

"It's your game. And I'd say that's enough of a warm-up."

He came in hard, driving her back. She nearly lost her footing, felt the rush of displaced air and adrenaline as his blade whooshed by her face.

This time when she gripped the hilt in both hands it was to gain the power necessary to repulse the attack.

She felt the sting, could have sworn she smelled her own blood, when he scored a glancing blow on her hip.

"Your point."

They circled each other while in the valley below the battle raged on. Her sword arm ached from the weight, the effort, her hip throbbed, and sweat coated her skin. She could hear her own breath, wheezing a little now, and see the blood staining the torn leather on Roarke's shoulder.

She was having the time of her life.

She lifted the sword high over her head, point toward her opponent, and once again planted her feet. "Tie breaker."

He smiled at her, baited her with a crook of his finger. Though her eyes narrowed she wasn't so easily caught. She pivoted, spun, met his thrust with a downward arc, then swiped up and barely missed that compelling face.

Sun eked through the clouds, shone on the biting blades as they whizzed, hacked, clashed. Her heart thundered in her chest, a drumbeat of battle pounding in the blood.

The wind and his own rapid movements had his hair dancing around a face damp with sweat. She thought his eyes brighter, bolder than the blades.

He gave no quarter; she wanted none. Thrust, strike, attack. Thrust, strike, defend. As they matched power against power, speed against guile, she felt the thrill of battle against a perfectly matched opponent.

Once more their swords crossed, held. They stared at each other, breath labored, sweat dripping.

"Screw the game," he said.

"Oh yeah."

They tossed their swords aside and leaped at each other.

They rolled over the thick, coarse grass, mouths meeting, clashing as their blades had. Breathless, desperate, she gripped his hair, used her teeth. Her breath came short and harsh as she tugged and yanked at leather.

"How the hell do you get this *off*?"

"How the devil do I know?"

"It's your game."

"Bloody hell." He rolled her over, shoved her facedown in the grass to attack the laces. "Bastard's knotted like steel." Inspired, he yanked the dagger from his belt and sliced them free. He flung the dagger point down in the grass.

Lowering to her, he gave himself the pleasure of her naked back, the lean length of it, the play of muscle under hot, smooth skin. When his hand passed over the wound in her hip, she flinched.

"How's the hip?"

"Hurts—just enough to let me know I took a hit." She flipped over, reared up, pulling the dagger out of the ground. "Shoulder?"

"I'll live."

She smiled. "Better hold still or I'll win by default." She sliced the dagger down the leather. Her eyes on his, she turned the blade. "Trust me?"

He gripped her wrist, shoved her arm down until her fingers opened on the hilt. "No."

With a laugh, she pulled him down to her.

His mouth warred with hers, quick bites, sliding tongues while their bodies, slick with sweat, stained with blood, moved over the rough grass.

Smoke plumed from the valley below, and on its edges echoed the endless combat. It seemed apt, she thought. No matter how in tune she and Roarke might be, there was always another battle brewing under the calm.

And always with it, always this need to take, to consume, to have, to be. Even now, in the midst of this violent fantasy, she wanted nothing more than his hands on her, then his body mated with hers.

She rolled again, straddled him. His hands closed possessively over her breasts before he pushed up so his mouth could do the same.

She tasted of the fight—hot, damp, hints of leather, and under his hungry mouth her heart thundered. For him. As her body trembled— all that strength, all that will trembling. For him. That was his miracle, his greatest treasure.

"Mine," he said. "My heart." And he felt the new thrill of hearing her answer him in the language of his blood. His hands tangled in her hair, the long, wild tumble of it—another new and oddly seductive sensation.

He overbalanced, taking her down to her back with the swords crossed just above her head. Now when he thrust, when she cried out, it was only in pleasure.

Power met power again, and with it speed while the new battle raged. When she closed around him, when she shuddered through her release, she dragged him with her through the violence, and into the peace.

She lay faceup, the wind washing over her, the determined beams of sun pulsing red against her closed eyes. The grass, all those rough tufts, made her skin twitch—but it didn't seem like a good enough reason to move. Particularly since Roarke lay beside her, nearly in the same position.

The clanging of her heart in her ears had slowed and quieted enough so she could hear the continuing war in the valley below them. Apparently, the hillside had come to a truce.

"Who won?" she asked.

"Let's call it a draw."

Seemed fair enough. "I guess we're still a little pissed at each other."

"I thought it was aggravated."

"Same thing. But between the fighting and the sex, I worked most of mine off."

"Then we'll call that a draw, too."

What was the point in arguing about it? she asked herself. They'd just start it all up again, and nothing would change what he did, who he was. Nothing would change what she did, who she was.

Sometimes that middle ground between them was narrow and slippery. The trick was figuring out how to navigate it.

"It's a good game," she told him. "Realistic, compelling, involving."

"We barely touched the surface."

"This." She touched a hand to her hip, examined the smear on her palm. It looked like blood, felt like it, smelled like it.

"Illusion. It involves sensory enhancement, the scan of your vitals, your physicality, the motions, reactions."

"What if you cut off a limb—or a head."

"End of game. Or in multiplayer, end for the player who lost the limb or head."

"I mean, would you actually feel it, see it?"

"Not the human players. If you were playing the comp, a fantasy figure, and got that kind of hit on it, you'd see it."

"What about a droid?"

"Well, you could program it to play against a droid. Same results. The droid is solid. Therefore, the game would treat it as it would a human. The weapons aren't real, Eve. They can't harm anyone."

"Which is what the vic would have assumed, whether he played against a human, a droid, or a fantasy character. Just a game. But it wasn't." She continued to study the blood on her palm. "I felt the hit— not like a cut, not like you'd just sliced me with a sword—"

"I'd hardly have done so if you would have."

"But I got a jolt. Like an electric shock. Mild, but strong enough to let me know I'd taken a hit. And it throbbed—when we fought. I was fighting wounded."

"Which would be the point."

"I get that. I get it. But the vic had those burns. Up the voltage, you'd get burns."

"Not without direct contact. The game reads the hit, registers it, transmits it."

"Okay, but if somebody reprogrammed the game, and used an actual weapon." She sat up, pushed her hair back—surprised and disconcerted by the length of it.

"It's different. Your hair." His gaze ran over it. "Interesting."

"It gets in the way."

When he smiled, she ran a long, loose lock between her fingers. "It feels real. If I tug it, I feel it, even though it's not really there. My weapon's over there. I can't see it, but it's there. It's real. So if his killer brought it in—like I did—oh yeah, forgot. Sets it down in a specific place. He's only got to remember where it is, pick it up, use it. But why do all that? Why go through the motions of the game first?"

"More sporting?"

"Maybe. Maybe. The bruises, the burns. If the game was sabotaged ahead of time, the levels bumped up beyond what they could be for code, for sale, that ups the competitive level, too, doesn't it? And if the killer used a droid, he wouldn't have to be here. Alibis, none of them would matter with that angle. Talk Bart into testing the game at home with a droid."

"The droid would have to be sabotaged as well, or built and programmed off code. The weapon would register as real, as lethal, so it would have to be programmed either not to register the weapon as lethal, or to discount it. Then to clean up and reset the security. Some of that would involve computer use, and that should have alerted CompuGuard."

"You could do it."

"Yes, I could do it. But I have unregistered equipment and the privacy to do the work without sending out flags. EDD combed the warehouse. There's no unregistered equipment there. And none in Bart's apartment."

"Which only means, potentially, someone else had a copy of the disc, and worked on it off-site. You know this whole thing is showy. Show-offy," she added and started to rise.

And remembered she was naked, and her illusionary clothes torn and bloody. "Ah, let's shut this down."

"If we must. Game end."

The hillside vanished, the sounds of war faded away. She watched the blood on her palm do the same. She picked up her shirt, studied the ragged tear down the back.

"There was no dagger," Roarke explained. "So essentially I tore the shirt you actually had on to remove the tunic you didn't."

"Different cause, different method, same result. That's what we've got here. Somehow. A mix of illusion and reality combined to murder." She held up the ruined shirt. "Essentially someone did this to Bart Minnock."

In the morning, because there seemed to be no point not to, she compared the results of her level three to Roarke's.

"There's nothing here that sends up any flags, not on this investigation."

"No," he agreed, but continued to study the data on-screen.

"Do you see something I don't?" she asked.

"No, not as applies to this. I can't decide if I'm relieved or frustrated."

"Well, it would be easier if something had popped here, or on the runs I've done on U-Play employees. DuVaugne was the big pop at Synch, but he's just a cheat."

She downed more coffee. "Whoever did this is a lot more tech-savvy and creative than DuVaugne. From what we know of the victim, considerably more to have been able to get past his guards. I've got meets with the lawyer and with Mira today. Maybe that'll shake something loose."

"I've meetings of my own. I'll do what I can to work with EDD when I'm clear."

"I'm going to try another angle. The sword. I'm going to send Peabody and McNab on that trail, figuring the team should include a geek and nongeek. McNab can talk the talk and pass for a collector. There's what they call a mini-con in East Washington."

"We have a booth there. I can easily arrange to get them in."

"Fine. Saves me the trouble." She crossed to the murder board, walked around it. "I'll be talking to his three partners today. Individually this time."

"Longtime friends suddenly turning murderous?"

She glanced over at him. "People get aggravated."

Roarke lifted an eyebrow. "Should I worry about losing my head?"

"Probably not. We tend to blow it off, fight it off, yell it off, so the aggravation or the serious piss doesn't dig in too deep. With other people, sometimes it festers. Maybe we've got a festerer here. These three have the means—the tech savvy, the creativity. They had the vic's trust, and easy access to his home, his office. They've got motive, in as far as they'll benefit from his death by upping their share of the company. And opportunity, as much as any."

"They loved each other."

"That's just one more motive. How many women and kids are in Dochas right now, because someone loves them?" she asked, referring to Roarke's abuse shelter.

"That's not love."

"The person doing the ass-kicking often thinks it is. Believes it is. It's an illusion, like the game, but it feels real. A lot of nasty things grow out of love if it isn't . . . tended right. Jealousy, hate, resentment, suspicion."

"A cynical, and unfortunately accurate assessment. I love you."

She managed a half-laugh. "That's kind of odd timing."

He crossed to her, cupped her face in his hands. "I love you, Eve. And however many mistakes either of us makes, I believe we'll do our best to tend it right."

She lifted her hands to cover his. "I know it. Anyway, any time something nasty crops up, we end up burning it off with some serious mad before it roots."

"I wasn't even mad at you, not really. I realize I'd hoped to find someone in that search, even if it was one of mine. It would be specific, you see, instead of this vague worry and wondering if I'd have a target."

He glanced toward her murder board. "I can't explain even to myself why his death strikes me, and where it does."

"He might've been you, if things had been different. He might have been you," she repeated when Roarke shook his head. "If you'd had a different scenario to play in childhood. Or some parts of you might've run along parts of him. We can both see it. So I guess that's why I went around you, and you went around me."

"And why, when confronted with that choice, we both got . . . aggravated?" Watching her face, he ran his hands up and down her arms. "It rings true enough, considering us."

"Considering us. We're okay."

He rested his brow on hers. "We're okay."

"Here's what you have to do." She eased him back so their eyes met. "You have to stop asking yourself if you'd done something different, said something else, pushed another button, if Bart would have come on board with you instead of starting his own company. And if he'd done that, he'd be alive. Life's not a program."

"I haven't been doing that. Very much," he qualified. "But I could have pushed other buttons, said considerably more, and done quite a bit

differently. I liked the idea of him striking out on his own, following
that jagged path. So I didn't. And I know perfectly well none of this is
on me, and now I can be relatively sure none of it's on any of mine. It
doesn't give me that specific target, but it helps clear my head."

"Okay, head's clear. And since I know you're going to poke around
on the magic sword angle whenever you get time today, make sure you
let me know anything you come up with."

"I'll do that."

"I've got to go. Lawyers and shrinks and suspects."

"Oh my." Her puzzled stare made him laugh and pull her to him for
a cheerful kiss. Then just hold on to her for a moment more. "Go on
then, be a cop. I'll let you know if and when I can get away to work with
Feeney."

He'd find a way, she thought. He always did.

She met Peabody in the offices of Felicity Lowenstien. The sharp-
looking reception area—small, efficient, and done in reds, blacks,
and silvers—was manned by a sharp-looking woman who, either by
design or preference, matched the decor with her short silver hair, black
suit, and large red fabric rose at the lapel.

She took them straight back—no fuss, no waiting—past a small
office, what looked to be a tidy law library, a closed door. The woman
knocked briefly on the next door, then opened it.

"Lieutenant Dallas and Detective Peabody."

Attorney Lowenstien rose from behind her desk. As she came
around it Eve noted that the woman had boosted her five feet of
height with three-inch scalpel-edged heels. She also wore black with just
a hint of white lace at the cross of her jacket. Her hair, rolled back in a
smooth twist, was a dense brown with gilded streaks.

She offered both Eve and Peabody a firm shake, then a chair.

"I appreciate you coming here. I've got everything I think you'll need or want." She paused, let out a breath. "Let me give you some personal background. I met Bart in college, through Cill. Cill and I got to be friendly, and she decided she'd fix me up with Bart."

"Romantically?"

"That was the idea. It didn't take, but Bart and I became friends. When we all established ourselves in New York, I became his attorney. I handled the partnership agreement, and I handled his estate. I don't do criminal law, but I dated an ADA once." She smiled, just a little, in a way that told Eve things hadn't taken there either. "I know there's little you can or will tell me, but I have to ask. Do you have any leads?"

"We're pursuing several avenues of investigation."

"That's what I figured you'd say." She sighed as she turned her gaze toward her window. "We didn't hang out often anymore. Cill and I, or Bart and the others. Different directions, work, that kind of thing. But he was a good guy. A sweet guy."

"When was the last time you had contact with him?"

"Only a few days ago, actually. He wanted to see about endowing a scholarship—or have the business do one—for the high school he, Cill, and Benny graduated from. We scheduled a meeting for next week—the four of them, me, and the financial adviser. We talked for a while, actually. Caught up since it had been several months since we'd actually talked. He was seeing a woman, seriously. He seemed really happy."

"Did he speak to you about any projects—work projects?"

"No, not really. I'm not especially e-savvy, certainly not on Bart's level, or the others. But I got the impression something was brewing. He was excited."

"Were the others on board about the scholarship?"

"Absolutely. As far as I know," she qualified. "They never did anything without all four agreeing."

"So he didn't seem concerned about anything or anyone?"

"On the contrary. He seemed on top of the world."

On top of the world," Eve said from the driver's seat. "Happy-go-lucky. Doesn't seem like the type who ends up on a slab at the morgue with his head on a tray."

"He was rich, relatively successful, content, and in a competitive business," Peabody pointed out. "Fertile ground for jealousy."

"Yeah, it is." She pulled out her 'link when it signaled, read a text from Roarke. "We're splitting off. I want you and McNab to go to East Washington. There's a mini-con at the Potomac Hotel."

"Road trip!" Peabody pumped her fists in the air.

"Before you break out the soy chips and go-cups, you're going as collectors. You're especially interested in swords."

"Undercover road trip!" And now executed a quick, happy dance.

"Jesus, Peabody, maintain some dignity."

"I've got to go home and change. I look too much like a cop."

Eve surveyed the breezy summer pants, the cheerfully striped skids. "You do?"

"I've got just the thing. Things," Peabody corrected. "I need a lot more sparkles, more color."

"Great, go get those, grab McNab, and take the first shuttle."

"Shuttle. Like one of Roarke's right?"

"No, like the shuttle regular people, including cops on undercover road trips take."

Peabody's acre of grin tumbled into a pouty "Aw."

"I want buzz on U-Play, any underground data that might've leaked on this game, info on the sword, or its type. And I want you to stay out of trouble."

"It all sounded like fun a minute ago."

"You want fun? Go to the circus. For now, get McNab, go there. Pick up your con passes at Central Information. They're under your name. And I don't want to see any toys or games on your expense chit."

"What if we have to buy something to maintain our cover?"

"Don't."

"Less and less fun all the time. Are we cleared for a hotel if we need to follow up a lead?"

Eve shot her a narrowed stare. "It better be a damn good lead and a cheap hotel or I take the expense out of your hide."

"If there's any rumors, innuendoes, or hard data on this sword, a con's the place to find them. Really."

"If I didn't believe that you wouldn't be going." She pulled over to the curb in front of Peabody's apartment. "Go get your geek on. Check in when you get there. Don't screw up."

"Your level of confidence brings a tear of joy to my eye."

"You'll be bawling tears if you screw this up," Eve warned, and, dumping Peabody on the sidewalk, swung back into traffic.

At Central she went straight to Homicide. No need to visit EDD as Peabody would've tagged McNab seconds after she hit the sidewalk. She'd go up, confer with Feeney after she had time to check in on her own division and read through more thoroughly the files she'd gotten from the lawyer.

She stepped in, stopped short when she saw her commander. "Sir."

Commander Whitney nodded, gestured toward her office. "A moment of your time, Lieutenant."

He was a big man who moved well, who still managed to move like a cop despite his years behind a desk. Command lined his dark, wide face and, she thought, had added the gray to his close-cropped hair.

She stepped in behind him, closed the door.

"Can you spare me some of that coffee?"

"Yes, sir." She programmed it for him. "I have a meeting with Doctor Mira shortly to consult her on the Minnock investigation."

"So I read in your report. You've come from the victim's lawyer."

"Yes, sir. Another college friend. She's been very cooperative. I have the terms of his estate, will, partnership. It seems very straightforward."

He nodded again, sat in her visitor's chair. Eve stayed on her feet.

"The circumstances are . . . bizarre is the word that comes to mind," he began, and sipped coffee like a man sipping a very fine wine. "And those circumstances are leaking to the media. Too many people knowing too much, and with the circumstances, very juicy fodder."

She glanced at her 'link, and the rapidly blinking light indicating numerous messages. "I don't believe we should issue anything but the standard media release at this time. Beyond bizarre there are a number of lines and angles to deal with. We can't deny the beheading, but I believe it's necessary to keep as much of the rest as possible under wraps for now."

"Agreed. If the public gets the idea that this happened as a result of a game, we'd have panic. Every mother's son and daughter in the city has a gaming system of some sort."

"I'm concentrating on identifying the weapon, or rather have Peabody and McNab on that. I'm sending them to a games convention in East Washington today."

"You've made two arrests. We'll use that for now to keep things quiet. I've spoken with Captain Feeney. You'll have as much from EDD as you need—including civilian consultants." He paused, sipped again.

"Roarke disclosed he knew the victim, and that his own company has a similar game under development."

"Yes, sir. I conducted a level three on those employees connected to that R&D. I found nothing."

"Keep it documented, Dallas, and be sure Roarke has clear documentation of when and how this game of his has been developed."

"Yes, sir."

He finished his coffee, set it aside. "I'm not here to tell you how to do your job," he said and rose. "But only to precede cautiously, and clearly, where the personal overlaps."

"Understood, Commander. I can ask Roarke to turn over the documentation, so that it's in our files."

"He's already done so, through Feeney." Now Whitney inclined his head. "He is consulting primarily with EDD, correct, Lieutenant?"

"Yes, sir. Yes, that would be proper procedure."

"I'll let you get back to work."

Alone, she stewed for a moment. It might have been proper procedure for Roarke to give Feeney the documentation, but he might have *told* her he'd done it. Of course, he would have told her if she'd asked. Or he probably assumed she'd known he would, or . . . screw it.

She couldn't stand here trying to decipher the workings of Roarke's brain when on this point she couldn't quite decipher her own.

She gave it up and walked out to keep her appointment with Mira.

**9** THERE WAS A CERTAIN RITUAL INVOLVED IN Eve's consults with Mira. Mira would offer—and Eve would feel obliged to accept—a fancy cup of flowery tea. They both knew Eve preferred coffee, just as they both knew the tea represented Mira's calming influence, a break from the pressure. At least for that initial few moments.

As Eve sat in one of Mira's blue scoop chairs she noted, as usual, the office was efficient and female, like the woman who ruled it. Apparently it didn't bother Mira in the least to discuss the criminal mind, and the horrors inflicted on victims while photos of her family looked on.

Maybe she chose calming colors in her decor and her wardrobe to counteract those horrors, and scattered those photos around to ground herself to her own reality.

It occurred to her that she herself placed no photographs in her office—not at Central, not at home. Maybe, she considered, they'd be a distraction from the work, or maybe she'd just find it disconcerting to be "watched" while she worked. Or . . .

Didn't matter, didn't apply. Such analyses and suppositions were Mira's territory. Eve needed the mind of the killer, needed to live inside it awhile—and her own sparse, uncluttered style suited her.

She considered her work outfit, one she'd chosen by simply grabbing what seemed easiest. Summer jacket, sleeveless tank, light-weight pants, boots. Work and weather related, period.

But Mira went for a breezy suit, sort of like a peppermint—white with tiny flecks of candy pink. The flecks matched the shiny shoes with the skinny heels that set off Mira's very nice legs. She wore her glossy brown hair in flattering waves around her soft and pretty face, and added a little bit of glitter and shine in earrings, necklace, a fancy girl's wrist unit.

Nothing overdone, Eve thought—at least not that her sense of style could discern. Everything just so, just right. And, yeah, she admitted, calming.

"You're quiet," Mira remarked as she handed Eve the ritual fancy cup of flowery tea.

"Sorry. I was thinking about wardrobe."

Mira's eyes, blue and as soft and pretty as the rest of her, widened in both humor and surprise. "Really?"

"As it applies to profession, or activity or personality. I don't know." See, she told herself, thinking about personal choices, personal style, *was* distracting.

"Peabody and McNab are heading to DC—a little undercover job at a game con," she continued. "She's all about needing to go home, shed what she thinks makes her look like a cop for what she thinks will make her look like a game buff. I figure she's still pretty much going to look like Peabody because whatever she puts on came out of her closet, right, and she has it there because she put it there."

"True. But there are different aspects to all of us, and often our choice of outfit for a particular occasion or duty reflects that aspect. You wouldn't wear what you're wearing now to accompany Roarke to a formal charity function, for instance, nor what you'd worn there here at work."

"I would if I was running late for the charity deal—or if I got tagged while I was at the deal to a scene." Eve shrugged. "But I get you. It'd be easier if we could wear whatever we want wherever we want."

"And this from a woman who greatly respects rules. Society and fashion have them as well. Added to that what we wear can put us in the mood for what we have to do."

She thought of the costume the game had programmed for her. She had to admit it had put her in the mood to fight, and made the sword feel familiar and right in her hand.

"The victim's wardrobe didn't have a lot of variety. He had some formal stuff and more traditional business attire mixed in, but primarily he went casual. Jeans, cargos, khakis, tees, and sweaters. And a lot of that—the shirts—was logoed and printed with game and vid stuff. He lived in his work."

"You understand that."

"The not just what he did but who he was, yeah. Everything I've got says he freaking loved it. He had toys and souvies all through his place. Games and game systems everywhere."

"He must have been a happy man, to be able to do what he loved, and what he excelled at, every day. To make his living doing what made him the happiest. And with longtime friends."

"Happy, normal, nice—these are the kinds of words I'm getting in statements from people who knew him."

"Yes, it fits. He had a good life, and what appears to me to be a very normal and healthy one. He had a relationship, one that mattered, kept contact with his family, maintained his friendships, had enough ambition to work to see his company succeed and grow, but not so much as to exclude those relationships and friendships."

She drank some tea, and Eve understood Mira took those moments to line up her thoughts.

"Your report says he enjoyed the company of children in his building, and was friendly with their parents. As much as he lived his work, he appeared to be well-rounded."

"How does a healthy, well-rounded, happy guy get his head cut off in his own secured holo-room? That's not really a question for you," Eve added. "That's something EDD and I have to figure out. But why, there's a question. The method's significant, and required a lot of trouble, a lot of work."

"And it's distracting."

"Yeah, which could be part of the point. We're puzzling over how the hell, why the hell, and maybe who the hell slips by. What kind of person uses this method, these circumstances?"

"Decapitation is certainly a form of mutilation, and would indicate a need or desire to defile—to conquer absolutely."

The pink drops at Mira's ears danced a little at the shake of her head. "But the extent of the other injuries don't jibe with that, nor does the care in accessing the victim and leaving the scene. Those are organized, layered details, studied and complex. Severing the head from the body may be symbolic as the weapon used, and the method. A game. The victim lived and breathed games, and used his head, if you will, to build his business from them."

"Which points to a competitor, or even some wack job who didn't like his score on the games. Wack job rings truer because there are easier ways, and less publicity generating ways, to off a rival. Or, more crazy, somebody who has some sort of violent objections to the games themselves. However whacked, he had to have superior e-skills to get in and out undetected. Unless he lives or works in the building. We're not getting a bump there, so far."

"The victim's company would hire those with superior e-skills."

"Yeah. Added to that whoever did this had to know the vic, the setup, had to know he'd be home and ready to play the game. The game disc itself would've been worth considerable to a competitor, a rival. If that was the case, why not kill Bart before he'd locked in the disc? You do that, you've got it all—dead guy and the development disc for his next big thing. But he leaves it behind, which tells me either he didn't need or want it, or it wasn't any part of the motive. And I don't like the second option. I think he just didn't need it."

"You're looking at his associates and employees."

"Top of the list," Eve confirmed. "He sure as hell wouldn't have played the game with someone who wasn't involved in it, who didn't know about it, and couldn't be trusted to keep it quiet. He used those kids for test studies on games, and my impression is he enjoyed playing with them. But he wasn't ready to take it to them yet."

"Because, at this point, it wasn't only a game. It was a project. An important one."

"Yeah. He told them he had something coming up, gave them a few vague details because, I think, he was too juiced not to. But they routinely play and test games in all stages of development at the U-Play offices."

"Where the details wouldn't have been so vague, even to those outside the inner circle."

"According to the log the vic played this one often—solo and multi. Various partners when he went multi. EDD's working on digging through that to see which fantasy scenarios, if any, he might've played repeatedly. And against whom. I'm going to push for a copy of the disc. The partners are being fairly cooperative, but they're dragging their heels on that."

Mira nodded, apparently enjoying her tea. "You have an organized, detail-oriented, e-skilled killer, one I believe, as you do, the victim knew and trusted. However, the method of the murder is violent and brutal—fast, efficient, and with a warrior's weapon. A fanciful one perhaps, but an old method. The decapitation is also warriorlike—the total defeat of an enemy, the severing of his head from his body. An execution method, and one that would take focus, skill, and strength."

"Not your typical e-geek."

"Not at all, the pathology diverges sharply. You may have two."

"Yeah, I thought of that. One to plan, one to execute the plan. I've even considered a droid. Someone who can reprogram, avoid alerting CompuGuard, and could convince Bart to try out the game against a droid. But how did he get the droid in there, and when? How did he get the weapon in, and when?"

"A droid? That's interesting." Mira sat back, recrossed her fine legs as she considered. "Certainly you'd have that quick efficiency, the necessary strength. And if programmed for warrior, for sword skills, very effective. It would suit the killer's—speaking of the human element—pathology. The use of those clever e-skills. In a way, in his way, he would have pitted himself against the victim, thereby winning the game by his proxy, and eliminating his opponent with a method that spotlighted those skills. Droids have been used in combat and in assassinations before, which is why the laws and safeguards are so stringent. It would be a challenge to subvert those laws and safeguards. The killer enjoys a challenge."

"Maybe we need to take another look at the vic's house droid. It's had the once-over in EDD, and there was no sign of tampering or repro-gramming. But it was already inside, already trusted, and there was more than enough time between the murder and discovery to repro-gram, dispose of the weapon. Leave her just where she's supposed to be. Or . . . maybe she was replaced earlier with a duplicate."

The idea added another angle, more complications, and thinking of them Eve drank tea without realizing it. "Detail-oriented, organized, sure. But it's a kind of showing off. Plus, it's childishly risky. All of it. If Bart doesn't do precisely what he did, it falls apart. He doesn't go home early, doesn't take the disc home, isn't able to take the time to play the game then and there, it doesn't work."

"Calculated risks. Most game players take them, as do killers."

"Especially if the player knows his opponent's habits and style." It just kept circling back to that. To knowledge and to trust. "There's a lot of ego involved in game playing, especially if you take it seriously. A whole lot of ego. Nobody likes to lose. Some people practice obsessively, some cheat, some go off and sulk after a loss—and that can turn to festering obsession."

"The more seriously one takes the game," Mira commented, "the more real the game is to the player, the more frustrating the loss."

Eve nodded. "Fights break out in arcades regularly. This wasn't like that, not that passion and pissed at the moment. But it might have had its roots there, and what grew out of them turned entertainment and fantasy into something real."

"Some have difficulty separating the violence in a game from actual violent behavior. Most use it as a release, as a way to play hero or villain without crossing lines. But for some, gaming stirs up violent tendencies already in place, held back, controlled."

"If it wasn't games it would be something else. But yeah, I'd say the line's blurred between fantasy and reality. The killer's crossed it. Maybe he's done, he got what he wanted. He won. But it seems to me when the line's that blurred, and it gets crossed, it's easy to cross it again."

"Winning can be addictive," Mira agreed.

"So can murder."

Going from Mira's to EDD was something like leaving an elegant home where people engaged in quiet, intellectual discussion and being flung into an amusement park run by teenagers on a sugar rush.

Eve didn't suffer from culture shock; she was too used to it. But both her ears and eyes began to throb when she was still ten feet outside the division.

Those who walked and worked here favored colors and patterns that stunned the system and spoke in incomprehensible codes that jumbled in the mind like hieroglyphic tiles. No one stayed still in EDD. The techs, officers, detectives all pranced, paced, or paraded to some inner music that always seemed to be on maximum speed.

Even those who sat at desks or cubes jiggled and wiggled, tapped and trilled. Feeney ran what Eve saw as a madhouse with a steady hand, even thrilled at being at the controls. In his baggy pants and wrinkled shirt, he struck her as a sturdy, unpretentious island in a riotous sea.

In his office he stood in front of a screen, frowning, mussed, *normal* as he moved blocks of numbers and letters—those hieroglyphics again—from location to location.

"Got a minute?" she asked him.

"Yeah, yeah. You took my boy."

Since they were all his boys—regardless of gender—it took Eve a minute. "McNab? I asked you first."

"I hadn't had my coffee. You get these notions in the middle of the damn night it puts me at a disadvantage."

"It was after six this morning."

"Middle of the night when I didn't crash out until two. Now I'm doing his work."

She shoved her hands in her pockets. "I asked first," she muttered. "What is that?"

"It's bits and pieces we got off what's left of the game disc—which isn't a hell of a lot. We've got it running through the computer, but I thought I'd try it the old-fashioned way."

"Any luck?"

He sent her a weary glance. "Do I look lucky?"

"Take a break for a minute." Her fingers hit something in her pocket. She pulled it out. "Look. I have a sucking candy. It's yours."

He eyed it. Then shrugged and took it. "How long's it been in there?"

"It can't have been long. Summerset's always bitching about stuff I leave in my pockets. They're my pockets. Plus it's wrapped, isn't it?"

He unwrapped it, popped it in his mouth.

"I've got a couple new angles I want to try," she began. "I want another look at the vic's house droid."

"She's clean."

"Yeah, yeah, I know, but two possibles. One, the killer programmed and used her for the kill, then set her back to normal. Two, he shut her down and brought in a dupe for the kill."

"You're looking at a droid whacking the guy's head off?"

"I'm looking at the possibility. We've got two divergent styles—and Mira agrees."

While he sucked on the candy, she ran him through the high points of the consult.

"How'd he switch the droids?"

"One step at a time, Feeney. Plus I don't know they were switched.

It's a possibility. If you could run a second, deeper diagnostic on it, with those two possibilities in mind, we might be able to confirm or eliminate."

"Somebody's going to fuck around with a droid's programming, bypass the safeguards, they need time and privacy. And equipment."

"They have equipment at U-Play. Plenty of them work late, stay after hours. That's time and privacy."

He scratched his cheek. "Maybe."

"The second thing is going over the game logs, finding a pattern to the vic's play. What version did he favor, who'd he play with. I want to see who he beat routinely, and what he beat them playing."

"Now you figure somebody cut off his head because he beat them gaming?"

"It's a factor. It plays. Why kill him during a game unless playing the game mattered? It's showing off, isn't it? All of this is a kind of showing off. Look how good I am. I made it real. I won."

"Can't tell anybody though. That takes some shine off it. You don't play enough," Feeney decided. "A serious gamer? He wants his name on the board. He wants the cheers and applause. He wants the glory."

"Okay, okay, I get that." She paced the office. "So maybe he gets that applause, that glory another way. Like . . . people who steal art or have it stolen then stick it in a vault where nobody can see it. It's all theirs. It's a kind of glory, too. The big secret, the ownership. That takes control, willpower and a hell of an ego. It took all of that to set up this kill. It took precision, brutality, and cold violence to execute the kill. So, it takes me back to maybe we've got two involved. Maybe two people, maybe one and a droid. Or maybe a multiple personality type, but that's low on the list for now."

He sucked on the candy, scratched his cheek again. "The model's copyrighted on account it's a replica of a vid character and there's merchandising rights and all that. Then you gotta register a droid. There's some getting around all of that if you buy it black or gray market, but this one's the real deal. She's got her registration chip and the proper model number. We got the vic's registration and his authentication certificate. If she was messed with, she passed the standard diagnostic. We can run deeper. As for copies, well, it's a popular model. It's a classic for a reason. You can run a search for ownership on that, and maybe you'll get a pop."

"Unless it's black or gray market."

"If you were to run a probability, I'd bet it's going to be high the vic would spot a knockoff. Even a dupe would have to be the real deal to get by him, if you're asking me. Not to say they don't have the reals off the grid, but what's the point of going that way when it's no crime to buy the real through proper sources? Less risky that way. We'll go take a look at her."

He led the way out and through to Evidence. He coded in, pressed his thumb to the plate.

Feeney, Captain Ryan, is cleared.

He opened the door to an organized pirate's cave of electronics. Comps, 'links, screens, com and surveillance devices, all labeled, stood and sat on towering shelves. The droids were well represented as well—mechanical-looking household and yard droids, cheap mini-droids, and a number of the human replicas lined up like suspects.

Eve studied the victim's choice of house droid. "That outfit wasn't designed for fighting."

"Slave-girl version, episode six. But she handles herself. Girl's a rebel and holds her own. Helped kick the Empire's ass."

"Jesus, Feeney. It's a droid—a replication of a *fictional* character from a space opera."

"I'm just saying," he muttered. "This model's top of the line. She's designed to exactly replicate the character physically, and she has top-flight programming capabilities."

"Did he play with it?"

"Now it's my turn. Jesus, Dallas."

"Not that way. Ick. Gaming. Did he use it in the games?"

"She's programmed to participate. She'd interface with the game program, upload the scenario, the rules. She'd be a tough opponent."

Didn't look so tough in that outfit, Eve thought, but she'd take Feeney's word.

"It could handle a sword?" Eve asked.

"Damn right."

But Eve shook her head. "The vic was taller, considerably. Blow came from an upward angle, slicing down. It could've been standing on something, or it took the higher ground."

"If she or one like her was programmed to do this, they'll end up scrapping her. Damn shame. She's a real beauty."

She started to point out, again, it was a machine, but remembered who she was talking to. "Run it, and I'll do the search on the model."

"I'll run her myself. I'll put Callendar on analysis for the repeat scenarios and players."

"Appreciate it. I'll be in the field, at U-Play."

"Hell of a place," Feeney commented. "Too bad about the boy. He had a good thing going there."

It didn't surprise Eve to find the U-Play offices more subdued. The noise level remained high, but the bright, or slightly wild-eyed look of those who manned systems, cubes, offices, labs had been replaced by the solemn.

A great many wore black armbands along with their colorful attire, and she noted a great many who'd rushed around the day before weren't in attendance today.

"Lieutenant." Var came down the stairs from one of the upper levels. His shadowed eyes and unhealthy color showed signs of a hard, restless night. "Have you got any news?"

"We're working some angles. You seem to be understaffed today."

"After we . . . made the announcement, we gave everybody the option of staying home today. We talked about closing up, out of respect, for a couple days. But . . . we decided we'd all handle it better if we had the work. It's not helping much." He scrubbed his hands over his face. "Maybe it's worse, I don't know. Everything around here's Bart. It's like I'll be working on something, and I'll think of something I want to ask him or tell him. Then I remember I can't. We talked to his parents. God. God. That was hard. That was horrible. We're going to have a memorial here tomorrow afternoon, because . . . This is where he liked to be best. Do you think that's right? I mean, it's not a church or a bereavement center, but—"

"I think it's right."

"Okay. Well, we thought so, so . . . Okay."

"Are Cill and Benny in today?"

"Yeah. Do you need to talk to them? I can—"

"I'll get to that. Since you're here, why don't we talk first? How about your office?"

"I . . . sure." He looked flustered at the idea of going solo, but led the way upstairs to one of the glass-walled rooms.

"Don't you ever want some privacy?" she asked him.

"Um." He glanced around, as if surprised.

"Never mind." She scanned his office. Cluttered workstation, multiple comps and systems, plenty of toys, a barstool in the shape of a tentacled alien. "I'm not altogether clear on who does what around here. The four of you were partners, but you must have each had specific functions, duties, responsibilities."

"Well, we all worked on development. Depending on who came up with the concept, we each took different stages."

He took a seat, turned off his headset. "Benny's primarily research, Cill's the organizer and I guess you'd say the mom when it comes to the staff. I target the marketing. But we all overlap. It's loose. We like it loose."

"And Bart?"

"Development, sure. He could always take a concept and make it better. I guess you could say he had a better head for the business of the business. Accounts and clients and the money details. The profit margins, development costs, that kind of thing. We all got into it, but he could keep a lot of it up here." He tapped his forehead. "And he was sort of the public face of U-Play."

"He got most of the media attention."

"He liked to get out there, mix and mingle, talk it up." He let out a sigh, rubbed a hand over his short hair. "Benny, he gets jittery with that kind of attention. Cill gets self-conscious and uncomfortable."

"And you?"

"I like the quiet." He smiled. "You know, the behind-the-scenes stuff, the figuring out, the in-house stuff. Most people who do what we do aren't so good with outside. Bart was better at it. Do you want, like, a soda or something?"

"No, I'm good. Who'll be the public face now?"

"I . . . I don't know. We haven't talked about it. I guess we haven't really thought about it." He lowered his head, stared at his knees. "We have to get through today, and tomorrow, and the next."

"Maybe you'll bring in another partner."

"No." He said it quickly, firmly as his head jerked up again. "No, it's ours. We'll figure it out."

"And your plans to launch Fantastical?"

"We'll stick to the schedule. It was Bart's baby."

"I need that disc copy, Var."

"We're going to have it hand-delivered to Captain Feeney at EDD. It's nearly ready. Um. We have papers that need to be signed. Confidentiality and all that."

"Okay. Bart worked on the program quite a bit then. Testing it, playing various scenarios and levels."

"Sure. We all did. It's part of it." His pleasant face turned earnest. "If we don't have fun with it, why would anybody else? You really can't market what you don't believe in. Or you can't do it really well."

"Good point. So, did he have a favorite fantasy game, a scenario he liked to repeat?"

"He liked to mix it up. That's the beauty of the game, or one of them. You can do whatever you want, depending on your mood."

"Which ones did the two of you tend to play out?"

"Jeez, we've been at this for months now. A lot of them. Old West, Ancient Rome, Alternate Universe, Quests, Rescues, Gangsters, Wars. Name it, we probably played it at some point."

"Who won?"

He laughed. "It was hard to beat Bart, but I got my share of points." The laughter died. "It's going to be weird, not having him in the holo. Not having him when we launch Fantastical."

"I'm sure it will. Do you ever play with droids?"

"Droids?" Var blinked himself back. "Sure. We use them for testing, at different stages of development. Nobody keeps a secret like a droid. But in the final stages, it's got to be human competition. We're not selling to droids."

"Sorry." Cill stood in the doorway. "I saw you in here, Lieutenant. Is there anything . . . Is there news?"

"No, I'm sorry. Just a routine follow-up. It helps me get a clearer sense. I appreciate the time," she said to Var, then turned back to Cill. "Why don't we go to your office? I'll try not to take up too much of your time."

"That's okay. You can take as much as you need. Var, when the lieutenant's finished with me, I think I'm going home. I'm useless here today. I've screwed up everything I've worked on, and had to back out. I'm just making a mess of things."

"Do you want one of us to go with you?"

"No. No. I think I just need to be alone. I just need more time. You can let Benny know if you see him before I do. I'll come in tomorrow. I'll be better tomorrow."

"I'll tag you later and make sure you're okay." He went to her, gave her a hug that seemed both sincere and awkward to Eve. "Try to get some rest, okay?"

"Yeah. You, too." Her bold, bright eyes watered up before she turned away. "My space is down this way, Lieutenant."

Along the way, Eve glanced back to see Var standing behind the glass, watching them go, looking miserable.

"Do you want something?" Cill asked. "I've got power drinks, soft drinks, fizzies, diet and regular."

"No, but go ahead."

"I haven't got a taste for anything." Cill shoved her hands in her pockets, pulled them out again, twisted her fingers together. "You do this all the time. I mean, you talk to people who lost somebody. I was wondering if you know how long it takes before you stop forgetting you lost somebody, stop expecting to see them."

"It's hard," was all Eve said.

"I don't know if it's going to be worse to stop forgetting, stop expecting. If it's going to be worse when I remember all the time. It's like . . . You look down at your hand, you don't really think about it being there. It just is. And if you lost it, wouldn't you keep expecting to see it there?"

"I guess you would. Grief counseling can help. I can give you a couple of names of people you could talk to, who might be able to help."

"Maybe." She shoved her mass of dark hair behind her shoulders. "I've never done therapy or counseling or any of that. But maybe."

"You knew Bart a long time. The two of you must've worked on a lot of programming, a lot of games together."

"Tons. We brainstorm. Sit around, get some pizza or whatever and just make stuff up. Then we get down to it. How do we translate that into a program? Benny's point man on research. You dupe somebody's game, you've wasted time and money and resources."

"So you pitched ideas."

"I guess you could say. We knock them off each other, springboard them."

"Who came up with Fantastical?"

"Ah . . . gosh." She sat, brow knitted. "I'm not really sure. A lot of the concepts evolve through the brainstorming. I think . . . maybe Var had this idea for a fantasy game that offered user-controlled scenarios. Then I think . . . yeah, I think I said something about there being plenty of those already. What's the next level? How about we take it holo, refine, *seriously* refine the imagery, the lag time."

She looked away from Eve, stared through the glass wall of the office, where people zipped by. "Then, if I've got it right, Benny piped up with there were holo-games and programs along the lines already, and how Roarke's company had the juiciest imagery out there. So what's the next, next level?"

"Didn't Bart have anything to say?"

"Oh yeah, he hangs back sometimes because he's working on it in his head." She rose, got one of the power drinks.

Moved well, Eve thought, thinking of the yoga classes. Strong and fluid.

"You sure you don't want?"

"Yeah, thanks anyway."

Cracking the tube, Cill sat, then after one sip set the drink aside. "I guess I don't really want it either. I forgot where I was. Oh yeah, so we kept tossing stuff around, back and forth like, and Bart says not just juicier imagery. Full sensory load, smart tech. Military uses smart tech for training. We apply that to the game, add the full sensory, go full-out on imagery."

She picked up the drink, just held it. "It's a big investment, of time, energy, and money, but he really sold it to us. He was like, 'We don't just offer a menu of choices for mix and match. We open it up.' Not just user-controlled, but the user can literally program his fantasy, every element, or mix his elements in with default elements. We just kept kicking it until we had the basic outline. Then we had to do the roll-up-the-sleeves and figure out how the hell to do it all."

She nearly managed a smile. "And we did. It's going to be the ult of ults."

"You've been testing it, playing it."

"Oh hell yeah. The four of us, or whoever's around and up, worked on it mostly after hours. At least at first. Lowdown on this one because it's going to be big. That's why we wanted to get Felicity to draw up some paperwork before we duped it for you guys."

"Understood. What did Bart like to play best?"

"Oh, he mixes it up. But whatever he plays, he likes being the hero.

Who doesn't? He likes scenarios where he's fighting for a cause, or the girl, or his own soul. Best was that combo."

"The program puts you into the scene, makes you work for it, right?"

"Wouldn't be fun otherwise."

"So was he good at the fight?"

"Better than the rest of us most of the time. Bart likes to watch vids on gun battles, sword fights, knife fights. He studies instructional discs, talks to soldiers and cops and all that. It's important when you're programming to know the moves, the strategies, so you can offer them to the player."

She took another absent sip of the drink, stared out the glass again. "I guess most programmers aren't all that physical, but Bart works at it. He likes to win—and he likes to play. He's a hell of a gamer. Was," she said, in a voice that started to shake. "He was. He was my best friend in the world. I don't know what I'm going to do now. I don't know what any of us are going to do."

Eve took out a card, wrote down a couple of names and contacts. "Try one of these names. It can help to talk, and to have somebody listen."

"Yeah, okay. Yeah, I think I will. Is it a problem if I go home now?"

"No. Cill, do you know the Sing family?"

"Oh sure, sure. The kids are seriously sweet."

"Var mentioned you were having a service for Bart here tomorrow. They'd like to come. If you'd let them know."

"Yeah, I will. They're on my list already, but I'll take care of it right off. I'll do it from home. I just think I want to be home."

"Okay. Where can I find Benny?"

"He was in his office when I went by a little while ago. Mostly the three of us are just sitting around trying to get from one minute to the next. He's probably still there."

10 SHE DIDN'T FIND BENNY IN HIS OFFICE, WHICH offered her the perfect opportunity to study his space. Open door, she thought, glass walls, implicit permission. Like the others, he had an office Friggie and AutoChef, a range of comps, a collection of toys and games.

More files, more clutter than Var, less than Cill, she noted, with active memo cubes stacked on his workstation, a mound of discs beside them. More discs filed by number on a shelf—and, as in Mira's office, several photos.

She studied Benny with Cill and Bart as kids, all fresh faces and goofy smiles. Benny, tall and skinny even then, had an explosion of improbable red hair. He towered over his companions as Cill's sharp green eyes sent out a wickedly happy glint, and the doomed Bart stood in the middle. In another they were teenagers at what looked to be the Jersey shore, sunshades, geek tees, windblown hair, mugging for the camera.

Still another had them dressed in costumes, with Cill in a fancy wig that had big rounds of hair at both ears, and a white flowy dress—with some sort of blaster in her hand. Benny wore a kind of space soldier suit, a smirky smile, and held another blaster, while Bart wore a white tunic and carried a glowing tubular sword.

No, light saber, she corrected. Sure, sure, the Jedi deal, the *Star Wars* thing—like his droid.

She took a closer look at the light saber, shook her head. It just wasn't the murder weapon.

Other pictures included Var—older now, college time—shaggy hair, sloppy clothes, sleepy eyes. Then the four of them stood in front of the warehouse, with patchy snow on the ground. Each wore a U-Play T-shirt and mile-wide grins as they toasted the camera with glasses of what was likely champagne.

She filed it all away before wandering out. She scanned the area—the glass boxes, the open stairs, the clear cubes, and workstations. Not so much bustle today, but still plenty of movement.

She frowned as she watched the way the sun beamed down and flashed over all the glass—and threw certain areas into soft shadows.

That was interesting, she mused. Glass walls or not, at certain times of the day sections were glared to invisible by the slant of sunlight.

She stopped a guy with a half a million tiny braids before he could whiz by on airskates. "I'm looking for Benny."

"Um. His office?"

"No."

"Um. Maybe he went home. It's a crap day. Yo, Jessie? Benny?"

"Um. I think he was going to Lab Three. Maybe."

"Lab Three," Airskate said helpfully. "Maybe."

"And where is that?"

"Um. Third level." He pointed east. "That way."

"Thanks." She wondered how many "ums" were dropped in the air on any given day.

She took the long way around. No one stopped her, asked who she was, what she was doing. People went about their business, or gathered in little groups with the slash of those black armbands like wounds on their bright colors.

Now and then she noticed someone actually using a swipe card, but for the most part doors remained open.

She spotted Benny through the glass of a lab, its outer wall lined with comps and screens. He seemed to be executing some sort of martial arts kata, mouth grim, eyes shielded by VR goggles.

Good moves, she decided. Smooth, controlled, quick despite his human stickman build.

This one did more than sit in a cube and pretend.

She hooked her thumbs in her back pockets, watching until he made the ritual ending bow.

He jumped when she rapped her knuckles on the glass.

When he pulled off the goggles, his eyes looked dazed and glazed and made her wonder how long he'd been caught in the VR.

He fumbled a little with the lock code, then slid the door open.

"Lieutenant Dallas. I'm sorry, I didn't know you were out here."

"No problem. Good form. What level are you?"

"Oh, none." There was an awkwardness to his shrug that hadn't been there in the movements of the routine. "Not really. Virtually and in holo? I rock, but I don't actually compete or practice or anything."

"You should."

He said, "Well . . ." And shrugged jerkily again. "Is there something new about Bart? Did you find out who killed him?"

"We're working on it. Were you testing a new game?"

"Oh no. Not really. We're always adding new functions and levels to our VR instructional programs. But mostly I was just . . . going away for a while. We should've closed today." He looked over her shoulder, away. "I think we probably should have closed. But Var thought we'd all be better off here, doing something, being together. He's right, I guess. I don't know what I'd do at home." He shrugged again. "The same thing I'm doing here, probably. Sorry. Do you want to come in? Or go to the break room? Something."

"In's good." She stepped past him. "You do some of your testing here, some development?"

"Sure. Mostly VR and interactive screen in this lab. We've got others for straight comp, pocket games, and instructionals, holo. I use it for research, too, comparing on-the-market stuff with things we're working on."

"Must be fun."

"Yeah, mostly it is. Bart . . . He implemented this policy early on. Everybody plays. It's like part of the job description. Everybody who works here has to log in a certain number of hours on actual play. You can't create games if you don't play games—that's his philosophy."

"So, does everybody who works here get a shot at something that's still in the development stage?"

"No. That would depend on their level and specific involvement. But we have all our on-the-market games available for employees, and a lot of our competition's. Do you want to try something out? I can set you up."

"How about the holo-lab? I'll try out Fantastical."

He winced. "I really can't. I'm sorry. We don't test that with the staff here. Not yet. We do weekends and after-hours. In a few more weeks, we'll be ready. Bart's already talking about the launch, and how . . . I mean—God. Goddamn it."

Benny leaned back against a work counter as if his long legs wouldn't support him any longer. "I can't get it. I just can't pull it in and keep it there. He's gone. He's really gone."

"Bart had big plans for the new game."

"Mega. He had a way of seeing the whole picture, taking it down the line. Having Plan B and C in place just in case."

"You went back a long way. I stopped in your office, looking for you. I saw the pictures."

"Yeah. I can hardly remember a time when Cill and Bart weren't right there. Then Var." He etched a square in the air with his fingers. "We clicked the corners and boxed it in. Four square. Oh Jesus."

"It's a hard loss. A friend, a partner. You shared a lot. The picture in the costumes. *Star Wars,* right?"

"Yeah, *A New Hope.* Episode four." After heaving out a breath, he pressed the heels of his hands to his eyes, then dropped them. "Leia, Luke, and Han. The summer before college, at Worldcon."

"Bart must've been a big fan. The costume, his house droid."

"Arguably, *Star Wars* opened things up, and the CGI developed by Lucas . . ." He managed a ghost of a smile. "You don't want to get me started."

"He probably played it a lot, in fantasy games. Maybe favored versions of it in the new game."

"Not so much. I mean in the new game. We've got buckets of *Star Wars* and Jedi games. Really intense."

"But he knew how to use a light saber."

"Wicked frosted. He could holo or VR pilot any ship or transport, too. When Bart goes gaming, he's into it. He works at it."

"What did he favor in the new game?"

"Gosh, we mix it up a lot. You've got to when you're developing." But the question, the thinking it over, seemed to settle him. "He likes the battles. Save the girl or the village or the planet deal. Quests and wizardry, facing the Black Knight, slaying the dragon. The thing about the new game is you can do all that and more. You can build the world, the mythology."

As he spoke, excitement sparked in his voice, onto his face. "Bart's the undisputed champ at world building. He wrote the outlines and consulted on the scripts for the vid versions of Charrah and Third Star. Bart's a really good writer, and you combine that with the programming chops, you got something way up."

Benny wound down, sighed, seemed to deflate again. "I can't get it straight in my head that he's gone. Really gone. It's like it won't stick in my brain from one minute to the next. I don't know what we're going to do. When you find out who did it, when you put them away, will it get better? Will it?"

"I don't know. You'll know who and why, and you'll know Bart got justice."

"It matters." He nodded. "Justice mattered to Bart. It's why he liked to play the hero, I guess. But the thing is, Lieutenant Dallas, justice won't bring him back."

"No, it won't."

She left him, headed to the steps, started down. When she looked back she saw him, VR goggles in place again, hands fisted as he gave the opening salute.

Going away for a while again, she thought.

After the sticky, sweltering heat that seemed to bounce off the streets of East Washington into the faces of anyone with business out of doors, the chill of a hotel lobby felt like bliss.

Even better, Peabody felt completely uptown in her plum purple multi-zips—the cut and placement of zippers helped, she believed, made her ass look smaller. She'd married it with knee-high shine boots and a float tank—low scoop—that gave her tits a nice lift.

She'd added a temp tattoo on one of those nicely lifted tits of a winged dragon inside a heart, pumped up the facial enhancements, gone wild and curly with the hair, and draped on plenty of sparkles.

No possible way she looked like a cop.

She knew the outfit worked because McNab had taken one look at her, made that flattering *mmmmm* sound of his, and grabbed her ass.

Undercover meant blending, and she concluded they'd passed that test, she in her plum purple and candy pink, McNab in his spring-grass green and Son of Zark tee. Hand-in-hand they glided across the lobby in her heeled shines and his ankle skids toward con registration.

In his many pockets and inside her many zips, they carried weapons—which had required a stop and private ID scan at Security—as well as badges, restraints, 'links, and communicators.

Neither expected trouble, but both sort of hoped for it.

They collected their con passes, registration packs, and freebies—which included go-cups featuring characters from a new game, some free downloads, discount chits, and map discs.

"This is the frost on the ice," McNab decided as they moved into the first display area. "This is total. Did you see they have VR demos all day—and look, man, that's the new 3-Z system. It's got portable holo capabilities. Costs the earth and a couple satellites, and it's first generation, but you can play holo without a full holo-room."

Peabody stopped long enough to watch the demo. "The characters look like ghosts. Flat, jittery ghosts."

"Yeah, well, it's first generation. Give it a couple years. Tech rules, baby."

They wandered along with aliens and warriors, villains and heroes and geeks, while the air zipped and buzzed and crashed around them.

Lines snaked for demos, for meetings with game to vid or vid to game characters. Screens exploded with battles, space wars, air-to-ground chases, and magic quests.

"There's the U-Play booth." Peabody pointed. "We should go hang around there, get some dish."

"Yeah. Yeah." McNab craned his head to watch the screen as she dragged him along. "I could beat that score. I have beat that score. I should sign up to play. It's in character."

"Later. If Dallas tags me while you're screwing around, it'll be both our butts. We make contact, get the feel, get all juiced about weapons, see what we see. *Then* you can kick ass in Worm Hole."

"She-body." He gave her a little one-arm cuddle. "You're so efficient. They've got adults-only games one level down."

She slanted him a look under plum-tinted lashes. "Oh yeah?"

"I checked the map."

"Well . . . It would be in character. It's all for the cause."

"Abso. If we don't play a few games while we're here, somebody'll get suspicious."

"We'll work our way down." She leaned over, nipped his multi-ringed ear. "Then I'll take you down."

"Fighting words." He gave her ass a nice squeeze.

People crowded in and around the U-Play booth, a colorful throng against the streams of black crepe. A poster of Bart Minnock held center stage while on-screen he conducted a seminar on game play.

Some of the attendees wept openly, while others purchased mementoes, systems, games, and action figures. All reduced ten percent, in memorial.

They worked their way in, and Peabody widened her eyes at a woman manning a section of the booth. "Is he really dead? I heard it was just a publicity stunt to kick off a new game."

"He's gone." Her already red-rimmed eyes watered up. "We're all just flattened."

"Did you know him?" McNab asked. "Like, personally?"

"Not really. I work out of East Washington, mostly handle marketing for this region. I met him though. He was a great guy."

"But come on." Peabody pushed a little. "What they're saying can't be true. Getting his head cut off, in a holo-room. It sounds like a game to me."

The woman's teary eyes went cold. "He was murdered, and that's not a game."

"Well, Jeez, sorry. It just doesn't sound real. I mean, who'd do something like that?"

"I hope they find out soon, and make him pay. Gaming's lost a really bright light. And those of us with U-Play, well, we feel we lost the heart."

"It's really sad," Peabody said, and added a pat-pat on the woman's arm. "My guy here's the big fan. We hooked work and everything to come down because we heard about it."

"I told you it was real." McNab tried for scolding and sorrowful at the same time. "I just want to say I really related to Bart. You know, he was the face of my generation of gamers. I bought U-Play's first PS system, and I've never looked back. I got their PS-5, with the substation for Christmas last year. It really sings."

"We're very proud of it. Have you demo'd Excursion?"

"No, not yet."

"Let me give you a complimentary demo copy, in memory of Bart."

"Mag. I mean, thanks. I don't mean—"

"I got it." She offered the disc. "This'll give you ten plays before it wipes. I hope you enjoy it."

"No question. You know, some of my favorites?" McNab easily

rattled off a list of games, heavy on war and weapons. "We have a Dead of Knight tournament every couple months at our place."

"He was actually going to e-mail U-Play and invite Bart," Peabody added, inspired.

"Oh, you should have! He might've come."

"I'm thinking of having a big one next month—full costumes, props, the whole banana. Like kind of a tribute."

"If you do, let me know." She pulled out a card. "I might be able to get you some attention, and arrange for some freebies."

"Hey, that'd be total. I heard a lot about Bart's collection. I relate there, too."

"I'll say. My boy likes weapons, especially the phallic ones," Peabody added with a wink. "We've got our game room loaded with them. We're always on the lookout for something really tight. I like to find them and surprise him."

"They've got a terrific weapons display up a level."

"Yeah, we're heading up there."

"Ask for Razor, show him my card. I don't know a lot about weapon collecting, but he knows everything. If it exists, in any form, he can find it, get it, sell it."

"Frosty. Razor." McNab glanced at the poster again. "I sure hope they get whoever did it."

"We all do."

As they left the booth, Peabody unzipped a pocket for her beeping 'link. After a glance at the display, she switched to privacy mode. "Hi, Mom!"

"Cute," Eve said. "I'm—what the hell do you have on your face? And your hair's all screwy."

"Undercover, remember?" Peabody muttered. "I'm blending."

"Where? At the Geek Skank Parade?"

Peabody narrowed her eyes. "What do you know about geek skanks? And who's here because they *do* know?"

"Point taken, so never mind. I'm on my way back to Central. Report, Detective Skank."

"Ha-ha-ha." Peabody sniffed. "We haven't been here long, so we're still feeling our way. But we just had a nice talk with one of the reps at the U-Play booth. They've got it draped in black, got a big picture of Bart—and they're running a discount on for-sale merchandise due to death. Business is brisk."

"Death sale? Interesting. I wonder whose brainchild that was."

"We're heading up to Weapons now. The rep gave us a contact."

"Good. Let me know if you get a hit. How many times have you stopped to play games?"

"Not once. I swear."

"Well, play something, for Christ's sake. You're supposed to be players. You can't blend by skank alone."

"You know, I'm starting to take the skank as a compliment. Game play's on the slate."

"And get back here asap. Feeney's bitching about losing his boy."

"We're—" Peabody blew out a breath as Eve broke transmission. "Do I look like a skanky geek or a geeky skank?"

"If those are my only two choices, I abstain. I think you look like my one and only She-body, supreme."

"That's a really good answer." She grabbed his hand, and continued to the third level. "Anyway, we're supposed to get a hit, play games, and get back asap."

But McNab didn't respond. He stood, dazzled, circling slowly.

Blasters, battle-axes, peacemakers, swords, sabers, lightning discs, and more and more. Some shined, some glowed, some shimmered at the edges—and many did so behind security glass and lock.

Peabody snapped her fingers under his nose.

He blinked, grinned. "Just staying in character."

"You're a character all right. What is it about things that maim, hack, and kill?"

"I like things that blast better." He made a credible blasting noise and grinned again. "But today, I'm all about the sword. Let's find Razor."

It took nearly an hour, but Peabody didn't have the heart to rush him. Plus, he unquestionably looked like a geek mesmerized by weapons, which was part of the point. He talked the talk with any number of attendees, collectors, reps—and got points for remembering he was supposed to be a sword guy rather than a blaster guy.

She left him long enough to go to Vending for a couple of fizzies. When she came back he stood holding a mean three-bladed weapon that sizzled with zagging red lights as he turned it.

"Hey, baby, check it out! Master's tri-sword from Edge of Doom. It's one of the originals used in the vid."

"I thought you had that already?"

"No, no, you're thinking of the trident from Poseidon's Rage."

"Okay." She handed him the fizzy.

"This is my Dee-Light," he said with a wink at the short, stocky man with a gleaming head adorned with tattoos. "This is Razor."

"Right. The rep downstairs said you were the man."

"Weapons rule, and I rule the weapons." He gestured toward the tri-sword in a way that made the snake tattoo from his knuckles to elbow seem to slither. "Only four of those in existence, and only two still on the market. Plenty of replicas, sure, but this is the real deal. You get a certificate of authenticity with it."

"It's way tight." McNab moved into a warrior stance. "Way," he said again. "I'm going to keep it in reserve. What I'm really after is a single blade. Zapper broadsword. The real, real deal." He set the tri-sword down. "I'm licensed. I'm building a collection of blades, different levels, you get? Toys, props, and reals. I'm zeroed on reals today."

"I get, but you're still talking prop or toy with the zapper sword. I can get the Doom model, the Gezzo, Lord Wolf—like that, but the vid prop—and that'll run ya. Or I can get you a deal on a repro. But there ain't no real."

"Underground says different."

"Underground?" Razor snorted out a derisive laugh that made his silver nose ring shimmer. "You gotta wade through ten feet of bullshit just to see the underground."

"The word I got is it's a weapon featured in a new game, and they made reals so they could create the program." He leaned a little closer. "I've got this friend of a friend thing, who worked in R&D at U-Play. Something hot's coming, and this weapon features."

Razor's eyes tracked right and left. "Something hot's coming," he agreed. "I got friends of friends, too, and might be there'll be a new line of weapons coming, too. But if there was a zapper sword, a real, I'd be the first. You can ask anybody in the game who knows what there is to know. They'll say Razor."

McNab pursed his lips, shoved a hand in one of his many pockets. "I don't know why they'd string me on this. What's hot is supposed to be, you know, *fantastic*."

Razor held a hand up, lowered it. "Keep it down-low. Yeah, I got that word. But weapons are my thing, and there's no word on what you're talking about. Plenty of props, toys, models of that kind of thing, but no reals. It's fantasy, man."

McNab adjusted his face toward the dubious and disappointed. "How close are the models and props to reals?"

"I'll show you one so close you'd swear you could slice your opponent in two, and leave the two pieces smoking."

They spent another twenty minutes testing and discussing different swords. While all of them looked lethal, none of them could have caused more than a minor scratch, if that.

McNab ended up buying a toy replica of the three-bladed sword. "For my nephew," he claimed. "He'll get a charge. Listen, if you hear anything about what we were talking about before?" He scribbled down an e-mail contact. "Let me know."

"Will do, but you're chasing an urban legend, friend."

"Or the wild goose," McNab said to Peabody as they merged back into the crowd. "My gut says if anybody knows about this weapon, Razor knows."

"My gut's with yours. He figured you had the want and the means. If he could've brokered a sale, he'd've jumped. And if he knew about it, I think he'd have let it show. Ego, rep on the line. If it's out there, it hasn't hit the grapevine or the underground."

"Maybe it's military, top secret."

"Think about it. Why would the military need swords? Any kind?"

"Gotta point. We hit the egg of the wild goose on this, Peabody."

"Yeah, but we did the job. I say we continue in character and head down two levels." She wiggled her eyebrows. "Time to play like grown-ups."

"She-body, you are so my girl."

"You're about to prove it."

In New York, Eve wrote an updated report before running a new series of probabilities. Speculation, she thought, *feelings,* gut impressions. They were, to her mind, as much a part of police work as hard evidence.

She studied the results, let out a *huh,* then put her boots up on the desk, closed her eyes, and thought about it.

"Nice work if you can get it."

She didn't bother opening her eyes. She'd already heard the click of heels, the rhythm of them, and knew Nadine Furst, Channel 75's ace on-air, and host of the wildly popular *Now* stood in her doorway.

"I don't smell any doughnuts."

"It's middle of the afternoon. I used cookies." She rattled the little box in her hand. "And saved you three—and it wasn't easy."

"What kind of cookies?"

"Mega chocolate chunk. I know you, don't I?"

"And I know you. I'm not giving you anything on the investigation."

"I'm here for that—though I'd never turn it down." She dropped the box on the desk. "I had Bart Minnock on my show a couple of times. He was a sweet boy. I hope you roast the balls of his killer."

Eve opened her eyes, looked into Nadine's always camera-ready face. Those clever green eyes meant business. "Working on it."

Nadine gestured to the murder board. "So I see."

"Shit." Eve's boots hit the floor. "That's off record."

"How long have we been friends?"

"Not really all that long," she said and made Nadine laugh.

"God, you're a hard-ass, which is probably why you're my friend. I'm here to personally and in person remind you your presence is desired at my book launch party tomorrow night." She winged up her brows as Eve frowned. "And no, I don't expect you to remember, but Roarke will. It hits day after tomorrow. The book does. So . . ." She ran her fingers through her perfectly styled streaky blond hair—a sure sign of distress. "God, I'm so nervous. No, make that terrified."

"Why?"

"Why? *Why?* What if it bombs?"

"Why would it bomb?"

"Well, Jesus, because it sucks?"

"It doesn't suck. You made me read it. I mean, you asked me to read it," Eve amended, on the chance there was a friendship rule about "made me." "For accuracy since the Icove case was mine. Which I did. It didn't suck, and it was accurate."

"Great, it doesn't suck." Nadine tossed up her hands. "Fabulous. I wonder if I can get them to put that as a PR quote. 'Lieutenant Eve Dallas says this book doesn't suck.'"

"Do you need written permission?"

Nadine plopped down in a chair.

"Oh, make yourself the fuck at home. Can't you see I'm working on a murder here?"

"Can't you see I'm having a breakdown here?" Nadine snapped back, and gave Eve pause.

"Okay." Because it was rare to see Nadine so jittery, Eve rose and went to the AutoChef. "You can have coffee, pull yourself together, then you're out of here."

"Oh, thanks a bunch."

"Listen, I told you it was good when you made me"—shit—"asked me to read it." Eve pushed the coffee at Nadine. "The reviews say it's good."

Nadine blinked. "You've read the reviews?"

"I maybe saw one or two, somewhere. The point is, you did a solid job. More than, if it matters what I think. You made it human and important, and you didn't sentimentalize it—if that's a word. You got it accurate, and that matters, but you made it real. And that's probably just as important. So stop being a big baby about it."

"I knew I'd feel better if I came by here. You bitch." She grabbed Eve's hand. "I'd really like you to be there tomorrow night, even if you can't stay long. I might need you to kick me in the ass again."

"What're friends for? Look, I'll try. I'll plan on it, but if something breaks on this case—"

"Remember who you're talking to. I know the priorities of the job. Anyway, if you're roasting the balls of whoever did this instead of kicking my ass and drinking champagne, I'll be fine with it." She sat another minute, finishing the coffee. "Okay. All right. That should hold me for a couple hours."

"Go bother somebody else if you need a booster shot."

"I do have other friends, you know." She glanced at the board again. "Go get them, Dallas."

Eve sat again. After a moment, she opened the box and took out a cookie. She studied it a moment, then took a bite, sighed at the rush of sugar.

And she thought about friendships.

II STILL THINKING OF FRIENDSHIPS, SHE LEFT her office and stepped into the bullpen. There cops manned desks and cubes, worked the 'links and comps, followed up leads, pecked away at the never-ending paperwork.

The familiar sounds, beeps, clatters, voices, Reineke's off-key whistle, crisscrossed in the air.

There were friendships here, she knew, born out of the badge and nurtured in some cases by other shared interests or copacetic personalities. Competition, too, but she deemed that a good thing, a healthy and productive element of any group. The last thing she wanted was a bunch of easygoing, complacent cops.

Friction, an inevitable by-product, rubbed on personalities who worked long hours, and lived with the stress of the job. Only droids operated without friction, and she preferred men and women who sweated and bled and occasionally pissed each other off.

Her division ran smooth not only because she demanded it, but because—she felt—she trusted her people and didn't hover over every case or every step of an investigation.

They lived with murder. They didn't need her to remind them what she, the department, the victim expected of them.

Some were partners, and that ran deeper even than friendship, could be a more intense and more intimate relationship than lovers. A partner had your back, shared the risks, the work, spoke the language, knew your thoughts, kept your secrets.

If you were a cop, a partner trusted his life to you, and you did the same with yours. Every day, every minute.

Trust, she thought, was the foundation and the safety net of any partnership.

She started out—a second trip up to EDD in one day might implode her nervous system, but it had to be done. Before she reached the door, the whistling Reineke hailed her.

"Yo, LT." He hauled himself up and over. "We're on that pizza murder."

"Mugging off Greene." Just because she didn't hover didn't mean her detectives' caseloads were off her radar.

"Yeah. Guy goes to pick up a veggie pie and gets coshed with a pipe wrench. Mugger took his wallet, and the pie."

"No point wasting a pie."

"You got that. Wife's at home, see, waiting for him to bring it. Gets worried after he's gone, like, an hour. Tries his 'link, but he can't answer being dead and all. Tries the pizza joint, but they're closed by that time. Tries to tag him a couple more times, and finally calls it in. Respondings found him three blocks away, tossed down some steps."

"Okay. Where are you on it?"

"No prints on the pipe, no wits. He took the hit right in the face, then a second for luck that opened his head up. Take the wallet, kick him down the steps for good measure, and walk away. But how come you take a twenty-dollar pie and leave a seventy-five-dollar pipe wrench? And how come dead husband's out picking up the pie that time of night when they deliver? It smells."

She couldn't argue when she smelled it herself. "You're looking at the wife."

"Yeah. Neighbors say they never fought. Never." He shook his head, his eyes cynical, and all cop. "You know that ain't normal. And coincidentally, there's a call on the house 'link, about five minutes before she tried to tag the dead husband. Wrong number, the guy says, sorry about that. And it came from a clone 'link so we can't trace it back."

"Yeah, that smells pretty ripe. Insurance?"

"He upped it six months ago. It's not a bundle, but it's sweet enough. And for a couple months more than that, she's been going out two nights a week. Pottery class."

"With the thing." Eve made a vague outline of a wheel with her hands. "And the gunk."

"Yeah. You put the gunk on the thing and shape it up into something and put the something in the cooker. I don't know why the hell, because if you want a vase or some shit, they've got 'em right in the store."

"Feeney's wife took pottery classes. Maybe she still does. She makes stuff then gives it away. It's weird."

"Yeah, but they got classes for every damn thing. We checked it out, and the wife, she's registered. Never misses a class. But the thing is, it's an hour class, and a couple of the neighbors who pay attention say how she leaves those nights before the husband gets home and doesn't get back until ten, sometimes later. Class runs from seven to eight, but she's out of the house before six. So you ask yourself, what's she doing with those extra three hours when the class is a five-minute walk away? Instructor lives in the studio, and that's pretty handy."

"Sounds like they're doing more than making vases. Priors?"

"Both of them clean up to now."

"What's your play?"

"We're trying to track the pipe, and we could bring them in, sweat them, but at this point they gotta figure they got away clean, and she's used to making those vases a couple times a week, and maybe she'd get a little antsy for a lesson. Seems like she'd want to, you know, get her hands in the gunk again. No classes tonight—we checked. Seems like a good time for some personal instruction, if you get me."

"I've deciphered your complex code, Reineke. Go on and sit on her for a night, see if she's compelled to take a spin on the pottery wheel. Either way, bring them in tomorrow and work them."

"Will do."

She started out again, stopped again. "If he's got no priors, and he killed for her, he'll be harder to crack. She's at home, fully alibied while he does the dirty work. He's going to start off trying to protect her. She's the cheat. She'll roll first."

Marriage, she thought as she made her way up the glide, was a minefield.

Following hunch and hope she bypassed the chaos of the EDD bullpen and tried the lab. She wondered what compelled e-types to work in glass boxes. Were they innately claustrophobic? Closet exhibitionists? Was it a need to see out, or a need to be seen?

Whatever the reason, Feeney and his team manned the comps and stations inside the glass, movements and voices silenced by the clear barrier. It was a little like watching a strange species in their natural habitat.

Feeney, his hair sticking up in mad tufts, popped one of his favored candied almonds in his mouth. Callendar, hips jiggling, fingers snapping, paced in front of a screen that scrolled incomprehensible codes. Someone she didn't recognize—who could tell them apart?—rode a wheeled stool up and down a counter, his baggies and skin tank red and orange blurs, his ring-studded fingers flying over keys and controls.

And Roarke.

He'd shed his suit jacket and rolled the sleeves of his black shirt up to his elbows. The twist of leather restraining his hair at the nape indicated full work mode. He, too, sat on a stool, but unlike his companions remained almost preternaturally still but for the rapid movements of his fingers on controls.

She knew he was focused, utterly, on whatever task he worked on. If it gave him trouble he'd be thinking in Irish, and muttering curses in the same.

He'd filed away whatever business he'd done that day, whatever he would deal with that evening, or the next. Which would be considerable, she thought. He did that not just for the man—the boy as he thought of him—he'd enjoyed, nor for the pleasure he gained from the work, the puzzle of it. He did it for her.

Whether or not they always agreed on the ways and the means of the work, that single fact shone through the gray between them. In her life no one had ever put her so completely, so absolutely first.

And as she knew him, she knew the moment he sensed her. His fingers paused; he turned his head. Those brilliant eyes locked on hers as they had the very first time at a funeral for another of the dead they'd shared.

Her heart opened, and it lifted, weightless and free.

Marriage was a minefield, she thought again, but she'd risk every sweaty, breathless step for moments like this.

He rose, evading the orange and red blur, skirting around the pacing Callendar, and came out to her.

She didn't protest when he tilted up her chin and brushed his lips against hers.

"You had such a look in your eyes, *a ghrá*."

"I was thinking about people. Friends, lovers, partners. You get a check in the all-of-the-above column."

He took her hand, a light link of fingers. "Conclusions?"

"Sometimes you get lucky with who you let in your life. Sometimes you don't. I'm feeling lucky today."

His lips curved slowly as he brushed hers again.

Feeney shoved open the door. "If that's all the two of you can think about doing, go up to the crib and get it over with. Some of us are working."

If she'd been the blushing type, she'd have turned scarlet. Instead mortification hunched her shoulders even as Roarke laughed.

"I'd be up for a break."

"You'd be up for eternity if you could manage it," she muttered. "No sappy stuff on duty."

"You started it."

She couldn't argue so she said nothing and went inside the glass box. "Progress?" she said in a crisp cop's voice.

"We're peeling the layers off the vic's holo-system," Feeney said in the same tone. "Looking for any shadows, echoes, and signs of tampering. So far, it's coming up a hundred percent on all levels. Same with his droid. No sign of tampering, no breaks in time or programming."

"Holo-room security's clean as well," Roarke told her. "We're picking it apart, bit by byte, but there's no indication anyone left or entered that room after Bart and before the droid bypassed the lock the next morning."

"If I didn't know better, I'd say the kid's head just magically chopped itself off." Feeney puffed out his cheeks. "I sent a team over there this morning. Had them scan and manually search every inch of that room, looking for another access. It's tight."

"I've got some semi-good," Callendar told her. "I've done analysis on the logs from the office holo-room and the vic's. Serious player. He could easily put in ten–twelve hours on a series of games in a day, and pulled a few all-nighters. A lot of solo play in there, too, but he logs in with a variety of partners, home and office."

She took a swig from a tube of Orange Sweet. It made Eve's teeth ache.

"He logged in a lot of time on the new game over the last several months, again solo and office. And this isn't the first time he took a demo disc home to give it a whirl."

"Is that so? Always logged it before?"

"Always. Like a half-dozen home whirls before the last one. Crossing it with his home unit it was always solo play. The thing is, it's different stages and versions of the game."

"Improvements," Eve concluded. "He'd take it home to test it out with the tweaks, or maybe add some from there."

"That's how it reads. Early days, they called it Project Super X."

"You're kidding."

"No, seriously. Project Super X, or PSX. Playtimes after five or six on weekdays, and some long multi-player sessions on weekends. Anyone who worked on any section of it had to log in and know the passcode, then had a user code. The four user codes that had full access track back to the four partners, but if any of those who worked sections confabbed with any of the others who worked sections, they'd have most of it."

"Then it could be duplicated."

"Close." Callendar took another swig from the bright orange tube. "It would take a lot of time, trouble, skill, and cooperation, but you could get close."

"What about the scenario he was playing at TOD?"

"That's trickier. Passing to you," she said to Roarke.

"One of the security measures, what I'd call an on-the-fly sort of precaution, was to change user names and codes every few runs."

"So if anyone tried to hack from outside, or inside, they'd hit a new wall."

"Theoretically," Roarke agreed. "Still, even with the firewalls and fail-safes, you'd only have to get lucky once, access from that point. I've found some hack attempts, some attempts at infections from outside sources, typical stuff, and none of it successful. And there are several hack attempts from inside, but they coincide with basic security checks. To run the game in its holo form, the player would have to input his current name, code, and ID with thumb- and voiceprint. All of those are possible to bypass, of course."

Eve aimed a cool look. "Of course."

"But they had their additional security, which would have sent out alarms at an attempted hack. Assuming the hacker hadn't already bypassed those. The discs themselves, at least the one in Bart's home unit and the copy we have here, are imprinted to jam if any of these steps are missed or the ID process fails. An attempt to remove the disc, as we learned, results in self-destruct."

"I know all of this."

"Laying the groundwork, Lieutenant. They were careful, clever, vigilant. But certainly not absolutely hackproof as nothing is. In any case, those precautions make it tricky to ascertain absolutely who played what and when. So we have to extrapolate."

"Meaning guess."

"A reasoned and educated guess based on probability. Bart used a variety of user names and codes between his home and office, but as with most people, he has a pattern, and he repeats. To simplify, I've had the computer cull him out and label him User 1 in both locations."

He ordered the data on-screen. "Here you see the dates and times he logged in on their PSX, by location, and whether it was solo or multi-player. We've crossed that with the other players, going alpha last name, you have Cill Allen as User 2, Var Hoyt as User 3, and Benny Leman as User 4. We have a separate data run on every employee who worked on the game, when, how long, in what capacity. You'll want to run an analysis on those, I expect."

"Who's particular pals with who, sleeping with who, how long they've worked there. I know the drill."

Roarke smiled at her. "It's taken us this long to get here simply because the log-ins for this game alone are legion, and between the four of them they used several dozen user names and codes. Next problem."

"Would be?"

"The infinite variety of scenarios. They all have plenty of play on the defaults, but the bulk of the log-ins are off that menu. Some are saved either to play again with exactly the same elements, or discarded, or saved and replayed with alternate elements. Or two scenarios might be merged."

"Doesn't it keep a record? What's the fun of playing if you can't keep score?"

"It does, and the holo-unit would hard drive it. The problem is the data on Bart's holo doesn't match any of the scenario names or codes from prior uses."

"A new scenario?"

"Possibly. It's listed as K2BK—BM."

"Bart Minnock," Eve concluded. "His particular game? Or did they routinely label them with initials?"

"No, they didn't. There's no coordinating listing on the copy U-Play messengered over today. The scenario isn't on disc under that name or code. There's nothing on his holo-unit that shows him creating it on the day he was killed, or any other day. He put the other copy in, the one we're trying to reconstruct, and called for that game, with a request to begin at level four."

"You don't start on level four if you've never played it before. You want to start at the beginning."

"Yes, you would. Or certainly the probability is high."

"So he played it before, but on the copy he used it had been given a name or code not previously used." She walked and thought. "He had a date, so he had limited time. He didn't want to waste it on the early stages. He pushed it forward. A section he wanted to work on, or one he particularly enjoyed, or one he had trouble beating before. But he'd played it before. There's no question it was solo play?"

"None," Callendar told her.

"The killer might have started the game, logged it that way to cover."

"Then he should've been logged as observer or audience. The room only registered one player, one occupant. If someone else was in there, he found a way around it."

"Murder takes at least two players," Eve murmured. "He plays. He gets bruised up some, wrenches his shoulder. How?" She thought of Benny, smooth and graceful with his katas. "He knows how to fight, how to defend. He takes gaming seriously, so he's studied, practiced, but there's no sign he put up a fight. No trace, no blood, no fiber, no nothing from the killer in that room. And every reconstruct tells me he just stood there while the sword came down on him.

"Someone else's scenario," she considered. "The killer creates the disc, adding defaults or elements or openings, and recodes it. Something that could override the system long enough to pull this off. That's what these guys do, right? Find new ways. New ways to play the game. What did he play the most?"

"There are four scenarios he favored," Roarke told her. "He'd mix up and alter elements here and there, but usually stuck with the same basic story line and character grid. He named them Quest-1, Usurper, Crusader, and Showdown."

"Are they on the copy?"

"They are."

"Stats?"

"We're pulling and collating them now."

"Good. And when you run the games, prioritize anything with swords. It's pizza and a pipe wrench."

"What the hell does that mean?" Feeney demanded. "You're losing it, kid."

"No point in wasting a good pie. No point bringing a sword to a blaster battle. You want to make use of what you've got, and take what's useful with you. He took the sword, but he left the disc. The disc would be useless to us after self-destruct, and incriminating to him if found in his possession."

She stuck her hand in her pocket, nodded. "Sure. A woman says to the husband she wants dead, *Hey, honey, I've just got to have a pizza. Be a sweetheart and run down and get us a large veggie.* Now he'll probably say, *We'll just have it delivered,* but she's ready for that. *Oh, they take too long and I'm just starving for a pizza. Please, baby? I'll open some wine, and maybe I'll change into something you'll like. We'll have a little pizza party.*"

"What the hell does that have to do with this?"

She glanced at Feeney. Cynical and rough-edged he might be, but he was a blusher. "Working it out. The guy goes for pizza—going to get lucky, so hey, it's worth the walk. The wife who wants him dead has her lover waiting with the pipe wrench. Smack, bang. No need for a divorce and all that bother, no point losing the nice chunk of life insurance—and hey, there's a nice fresh pizza, too. It's mean, just a little mean, but efficient and practical, too, to take the pie, leave the wrench."

"'Leave the gun, take the cannoli,'" Roarke said, and Feeney grinned.

"Okay, that I get."

"It's mean," Roarke echoed Eve, "just a little mean, but efficient and practical, too, to murder Bart during a game he enjoys, and to do so by means that play into one of his fantasies. Mean, efficient, and practical to do it in his own home—and it's another game added to that. How will the cops figure it out? He'll have played that scenario, your killer, tried the elements out until he was confident of the win."

"I just bet he has," Eve agreed.

"But a good game always tosses in an unknown, a bigger challenge. That would be you."

"Crib's still up there," Feeney muttered and earned a sour look from Eve.

"Copy the copy. I'm going to want to work at home. They're not going to give us a search warrant for private residences with what we've got. Everybody's alibied, no clear motive, no physical evidence. Barely any circumstantial at this point. We need more."

"Whose residence?" Callendar asked her.

"Partnership's like marriage. It's a freaking minefield. And one of Bart's partners decided on that pizza and pipe wrench."

Back in her office, she deemed it time to dig deeper, a lot deeper on the three remaining partners of U-Play.

She needed something, just a little something she could turn, twist, or tweak to convince the PA to go after a search warrant.

The killer's home comps would certainly have been doctored by now. She wasn't dealing with an idiot. But EDD had its ways, as did her expert consultant, civilian.

While her own computer dug, she rearranged her murder board. Studied it, rearranged it again.

She thought she understood, at least partially, the why. It was small and it was shallow, but murder had been done for much, much less. Without Reineke's nose, a man's death might very well have been put down to the contents of his wallet and a veggie pizza.

There'd be bigger under the small, and deeper under the shallow, but it was enough for now. Enough to help her create her own scenario.

"I'm back! Did you miss me?" Peabody bounced in, then flopped in the visitor's chair. "Jeez, do you know what the shuttle's like this time of day? It's a zoo—animal ferocity and smells. Plus, the air unit fizzled twenty minutes out of the station. Add jungle heat to that. I want a two-hour shower."

"You had sex."

"What? What? Why do you say that? You can't have sex on the shuttle! You'd die of heat prostration, then be arrested."

"You had sex before you got on the shuttle. There better not be an expense chip for some cheap by-the-hour flop on my desk tomorrow."

"We didn't use some cheap by-the-hour flop. We . . ." Peabody cleared her throat as Eve simply kept up the long, steady stare. "Played games. As ordered."

"I don't want to know what kind of games."

"Really, really good games. Ones that call for excellent reflexes and superior physical stamina." She grinned, unrepentant. "We're going to save up and buy a new, juicy game system for each other for Christmas."

"Is this your report?"

"No, this is the shuttle-boiled-my-brain babble. Whew."

"What's on your tit? What the hell is that?"

"Oh." Peabody ducked her chin to glance down. "It's my love dragon. It's a temp."

"A love dragon? You're wearing a love dragon on your tit, most of which is spilling out of whatever that is you're not covered up with."

"It's a look—and it works. Trueheart nearly choked on his tongue when I walked through the bullpen." Peabody sighed. "It's pretty satisfying."

"It may be you confused undercover with undercovered. Either way, I don't want to see your love dragon tomorrow. Now if you've rested and recovered from your arduous assignment, I'd like that report."

"Sure. The contact, Razor, the King of All Weaponry, hasn't heard of a sword like we're after—not a real. Props, toys of a similar and non-lethal nature, but nothing that could decapitate or leave those burns."

"Could've been made custom."

"We thought of that after . . . after a little gaming inspired us. We went back, discussed. After a little persuasion he gave us the names of a couple of sources who might be able to make something along the lines, for a price. A really, really whopping-ass price. Out of those, there was maybe one who might do it off the grid, unregistered. But that ups the price to about double whopping-ass. I know we looked at the financials, and nobody on our radar had an expenditure that comes close."

"I'm doing deeper runs right now. Maybe it'll pop. Some people game for money," Eve considered. "Some game for money off the grid. So, we might have somebody who had a double whopping-ass pile of unreported cash."

"Well, meanwhile, we did some poking around on the underground game sites on the way back. Razor's already putting out feelers. We left it like we'd be willing to pay, and how we'd heard one of these swords was out there. Now he's looking, and we're watching him while he's looking. McNab's going to keep tabs. If Razor gets a hit, we'll get it, too."

"That's good thinking. Go home and take that shower. I can smell you from here."

"It's not my fault. Plus, with the sweating I think I might've lost a pound or two just sitting there trying not to breathe." She pushed herself up. "Oh, nearly forgot. We got you a present."

"Why?"

"Because." She unzipped one of her pockets and pulled out a very small gun.

"What is it?"

"It's a toy gun. A derringer—like cardsharps and saloon girls carry in western vids. It's like a clutch piece."

"Hmmm."

"And check it." Peabody cocked it, and a sultry female voice purred out of the barrel. *Put those hands where I can see them, cowboy.*

"It has all sorts of audio streams—male, female. I figured you'd want the female. Plus—"

She aimed it at Eve, pulled the trigger even as Eve said: "Hey!"

The little gun let out a brave little bang. *Next one goes lower, and you won't be poking a woman with that stick of yours for the rest of your miserable life.*

"Isn't it cute? You could play saloon girl and Roarke could be high-stakes gambler, then . . . and that's entirely none of my nevermind." Peabody offered a big smile.

"Yes, it's cute, no, it's none of your nevermind." Eve took the derringer, recocked it. *You'd better hightail it before that tail's sporting another hole.*

"It could use better dialogue, but it's apt enough. Hightail it."

"Yes, sir."

"Peabody? Thanks."

Eve studied the gun, shook her head. Unable to resist, she shot her computer, her AutoChef, amused by the lame insults that followed.

That was another thing about partners, she decided. They knew what would make you laugh, often before you did.

 **THERE'D BEEN A TIME, ROARKE THOUGHT, NOT** so long ago in the bigger scheme, when a few hours in a cop shop would've been something to be carefully and ruthlessly avoided. Now, he spent so much time in one he knew which Vending areas to avoid, which glides tended to drag or crowd up, and just how filthy cop coffee could be by the end of a tour.

His life had taken a sharp and strange turn the first instant he'd laid eyes on a cop, his cop, in an ill-fitting coat and a truly ugly gray suit.

He fingered the button from that suit, one he kept for luck and sentiment in his pocket.

She'd been a first for him at a time when he'd come to believe he'd done nearly everything worth doing at least once. Had he been bored? he wondered as he angled his way onto a down glide. No, not bored, but perhaps a bit unsettled, restless, certainly dissatisfied in ways he hadn't been able to put his finger on at the time.

Then, there she'd been, and everything shifted, everything sharpened. He couldn't say what fell into place. Nothing with Eve was quite that easy, but pieces had begun to fit together. Some of them, on both sides, had required a bit of reshaping, and likely still would as more and more of their picture emerged.

As he rode down, a pair of uniforms rode up. The rattail-thin man between them protested loudly and continually.

"Somebody musta planted that wallet on me. I got enemies. I was only running 'cause I had a bus to catch. Do I look like a pickpocket? Do I? Do I?"

You do indeed, Roarke thought, and if you can't lift a wallet without fumbling the snatch, you deserve your ninety-day stretch.

Eve wouldn't think quite that way, he mused. It wasn't the getting caught, but the act itself that earned the stretch. Most of the time he agreed with her, and in fact had edged over to her side of that line more and more as time went by. But a bit of quick fingers? Well, everyone had to make a living, didn't they? Even a street thief.

He ought to know.

He crossed into Homicide where the sounds, the sights, the smells had come to be as familiar to him as those in his own headquarters.

Detective Baxter stood by his desk, straightening his tie. He paused, tapped a finger to his temple in salute.

"LT's in her office. Trying to get a head."

Roarke acknowledged the black humor with a quirked brow. "You've had all day, and that's the best you've got?"

"Already used up all the good ones. Anyway, I've been off shift for, hey, look at that, an hour. So my brain's a little . . . detached."

"Better, marginally. Where's your boy?"

"Sent him home, and stayed back to finish the Fours and other crap. He's got a date."

"Is that so?"

"Yeah, our Trueheart's finally worked it up to ask out the little redheaded cutie in Records. He was seeing somebody else, but it fizzled. Civilians can have a harder time working it out with cops. Present company excepted."

"Understood."

"Anyway, he's trying out the dinner and a vid routine, after which, they'll likely exchange a friendly handshake. Kid moves like a glacier when it comes to the female persuasion. Otherwise, he's a quick study."

"You suit each other."

"Yeah, who'd've thought? Anyway, I'm gone. I've got a date myself, and I expect to be shaking more than her hand at the end of the night."

"Good luck with that."

"Friend, it ain't about luck." He gave Roarke another salute and sauntered off.

Amused, and considering the concept of dates, Roarke walked into Eve's office.

She stood in front of her murder board, hands on her hips. "Computer," she said, "save and copy all data to my home unit."

"This is good timing."

"I need some mulling time."

"I've your copy. Sealed and logged."

She took it from him. "Aren't you all official?"

"I certainly hope not. You can have your mulling time on the way."

"I've got a couple more things—"

"That can wait," he interrupted. "I want dinner."

She pulled a derringer out of her pocket. Obligingly, he lifted his hands in surrender. "Don't shoot. I'm unarmed."

"Bet you're not."

He only smiled. "You can search me later. Clever little thing there. Where'd you get it?"

"Souvenir from Peabody and McNab." She cocked it. *It's small, but it's mean. Just like me.*

He laughed and stepped forward to take a better look at it. "There was this screen show—television," he corrected, "as it was about a century ago. What was it? In any case, it was in the American West, and the hero was a mercenary—a gun for hire. He carried one of these."

"I hope he didn't charge much."

"He had the full-size as well, but this was his—"

"Clutch piece."

"There you are. We'll have to watch some of them the next time we're free. Now, Lieutenant, as Baxter would say, we're gone."

"Okay, okay." She gathered up files. "You drive. I'll mull."

"You're looking at his three friends, the partners," Roarke said as they worked their way down to garage level.

"Easiest access to his personal space, most to gain, and most intimately acquainted with the vic's habits, routines, the business itself, and the game at the center of it."

"You're leaning toward one." With a regret and grim acceptance he thought they shared, they wormed their way onto a jammed elevator. "One more than the others," he continued, jockeying for room in a space that smelled of boiled onions and stale sweat. "Which?"

"I'm still structuring the theory. Besides that's not how the game's played." She shoved her way off again. "Which would you pick?"

"It's difficult for me to think of any of them as capable of this. I don't know them especially well, but what I do know just rejects the idea."

"Why, particularly?"

"I suppose, in part, because of the way they came up together. Longtime mates."

"And you had yours," Eve commented. "In Dublin."

"I did, and while none of us would've been above a bit of a cheat, as that's a kind of game as well, we'd never have hurt each other, or caused hurt."

"Yeah, it's one of the things I've been thinking about today. Friendships, long-term, short-term, what clicks and why. Friendships can enhance, right, complete in a way. But they can also erode and scrape, and simmer under the surface. Add money or sex or ego to the mix, and it can boil right over."

"I'm hardly one to look at things through rose-colored glasses, or for that matter to doubt your instincts." Their footsteps echoed as they crossed the garage. "Still, I've watched the four of them together, listened to them, and listened to Bart speak of them."

"You know, I bet when the pizza lady first hooked up with the husband she wanted dead, she had really nice things to say about him, too."

He had to shake his head, half in amusement, half in resignation. "Back to that, are we?"

"I'm saying relationships change, people change, or sometimes an event, an action, or a series of them just pisses somebody off." She slid into the passenger's seat when they reached her vehicle, waited until he'd taken the wheel. "Play the game. Let's call it *Deduction*. If you had to choose which murdered or arranged to have murdered the friend and partner, which? And why?"

"All right." If nothing else, he thought, it might help him reach some level of objectivity. "First, if one of them did the murder, Cill doesn't have the muscle for it."

"Well, you might be wrong there. She, like the others, practices martial arts, combat fighting, street defense, weaponry, and so on regularly. In fact, she has a black belt in karate, and she's working on one in tae kwon do."

"Ah, well. It doesn't pay to underestimate small packages."

"She'd be agile, quick, stronger than she looks. And the weapon itself may have given her more heft. Being a female with a small build doesn't rule her out."

"The blow came from above, but I suppose it's possible she stood on something, or used a leap or jump to give her height and momentum."

"Now you're thinking."

He shot her a mild look. "I can't see it, but will agree for now she can't be ruled out. Var. The same stipulations apply on the physicality. He'd be as capable of it physically as the others—I assume."

"Correct."

"Otherwise, from my outside observer's view, Var and Bart were like two parts of the same whole."

"Some people get tired of being a part, and want the whole."

"Such a cop," he murmured. "They both enjoyed digging down into the business side of things, digging into the nuts and bolts of sales, distribution, marketing as much as the creative side. They enjoyed having each other for the checks and balances, fine-tuning each other's concepts when it came to promotion, expansion, that sort of thing. Bart told me once when they met Var, it was like the last piece clicked on. I know what that's like."

Eve stretched out her legs, comfortable with the way he wound through irritable traffic. "And if they disagreed?"

"I can't tell you how they worked things out as I wasn't involved. But I never heard Bart express any sort of frustration on that score."

"We'll agree the victim was loyal and content with the status quo. That doesn't mean Var, or any of the others were. Are."

"There are considerably less messy ways of dissolving a partnership or changing the status quo."

Her smile edged toward smirk. "Easier ways to get rid of a husband than cracking him open with a pipe wrench."

"I believe I'm going to see that any tools we might have around the house are locked away. On to Benny. He'd be, to my mind, the most intellectual of the four. He enjoys spending his hours in research, sifting through details, theorizing about the underlying meaning of a game, and the reasons they're played. He'll research myths, real crimes, historical figures, wars and battles and strategies to add other layers to a game."

"Good with details, strategy, and the art of combat."

"You don't seriously believe—"

"Just pointing out the facts." She pulled out her PPC, added something to her notes. "When it comes down to it, they all had the means and the motive, and all could easily have arranged the opportunity. In fact, they all, or any two of them, might have planned it out together."

"To what end, really?" Roarke asked. "U-Play will likely get a quick boost in sales from curiosity and the public's thirst for scandal. But without Bart, they're going to be set back on their heels, at least for a bit. He was, and this is from a business standpoint, essentially the glue that held those four parts together into a productive whole."

Nodding, she keyed in more, spared Roarke an absent glance. "I agree with that. But that doesn't account for ego, and again, that deep, passionate fury that only people who are intimate in some way can feel for one another. These four were intimate."

"Family."

"Yeah. And nobody kills more often than family."

"In fact I believe I'll have the tools taken out of the house altogether." He swung over to grab a parking spot, and watched her frown.

"What's this? I thought we were going home."

"I see for once you were caught up enough in a game not to pay attention to your surroundings. I didn't say home," he reminded her. "I said dinner."

"I haven't updated my reports, or finished with the analysis of the runs. I have to run a full series of—"

As he stepped out and shut the door of the car, that was all he heard. He came around, opened her door. "Come on, Lieutenant, put it away for an hour. It's a pretty night. Time for a little walk and a meal."

"See?" She poked a finger in his chest when she got out. "This is why people in intimate relationships bash each other over the head."

He took her hand, kissed it. "An hour shouldn't kill either one of us."

"I have to go through the game scenarios on the disc."

"I've eliminated half of them. You're looking for one that uses a sword. There's only the two. Quest-1 and Usurper. The others involve more modern weaponry."

"Still . . ." She trailed off, and he saw when her annoyance faded enough for her to make the neighborhood. Just as he saw her smile bloom with surprise, and with pleasure, when she stopped in front of the hole-in-the-wall pizza joint.

"Polumbi's. It's been a while since I've been here. It hasn't really changed at all."

"It's nice isn't it, when some things remain constant? You told me you came here when you first got to the city. You had your first slice of New York pizza, watched the people walking by. And you were happy. You were free."

"I felt like my life could finally begin when I sat at the counter at the window. Nobody knew me or cared. I had no friends, no lovers. Nobody but me. And it was incredible."

She looked at him, those gilded eyes warm, so for a moment it seemed no one else walked the sidewalk, no one else breathed the air. Only the two of them.

"Things are different now. It's good they changed. It's good this is the same." This time she took his hand, linked fingers firmly. "Let's go have some pizza."

They didn't take the counter, but grabbed a narrow two-top and sat on squat, stingily cushioned stools.

He could have chosen anywhere, Eve thought. Snapped his fingers and scored them a table for two at the most exclusive restaurant in the city. Somewhere with snooty waiters, a superior wine cellar, and a temperamental chef who created complex dishes with an artist's skill.

But he'd given her a crowded, noisy joint where the tables crammed so close together the patrons' elbows bumped, where the scents of spices and onions and cheap wine in squat carafes stung the air.

More, he'd given her a memory.

When they'd ordered, she propped her chin on her hand. Yes, things were different now, she thought. She was hardly embarrassed at all that she went gooey over him. "Did you buy this place?"

"No. Some things should remain constant. But we're keeping an eye on it, in the event the owners decide to retire or sell off."

So it could stay as it was, for her, she thought, even if years passed before she came back.

"It seems to be the day for people to give me presents. I've got one for you."

"Really? What would it be?"

"There's a cookie in my file bag—a really good cookie with your name on it. Figuratively."

"What kind of cookie?"

She grinned at him. "Mega chocolate chunk. Nadine came by. It's her own fault she got the bullpen used to being bribed with baked goods, but she comes through."

"She wanted info on the investigation?"

"Actually no." The beer came in bottles, which made it a much safer bet than the wine. Eve picked hers up when the waitress set it on the table. "She did say she'd had Bart on the show a couple times, and I think she might've pushed there if she hadn't been so whacked."

"Her book hits this week."

"Exactly. And when were you going to remind me about this party deal tomorrow night?"

"Tomorrow." He smiled, sipped his beer. "Giving you less time to fuss and fret about having to go to a party when you're deep into a case."

"I don't fuss and fret."

"No, you bitch and complain, but it's such a nice evening I used code."

She eyed him over a swig of beer. There was no point in denying what was truth. "I suppose you've already decided what I'm wearing."

"There would be suitable attire earmarked, though naturally you might decide you'd prefer something else." He brushed his hand lightly over the top of hers. "You could always go through your closet tonight and give it some thought."

"Yeah, that's going to happen. I have to go. I mean, if the case breaks I can work around it and put in an appearance."

"If the case breaks, assuming you're right about it being one of the three, you'd hardly be facing down a career criminal or fighting for your life. At the core of it, they're still geeks."

"One or more of them killed a fellow geek in a really creative and ugly way," she reminded him. "But yeah, I think I can handle him, her, or them."

"So tell me why you have to go, which is not your default statement when it comes to events like this."

She blew out a breath as the pizza landed in front of them. "Because I meant it when I said Nadine was whacked. She's got herself all wound up, wrapped up, twisted up about the book thing. How maybe it sucks and all that. Lack of confidence isn't what you call her default setting either."

"She put a lot into it, and it's, for her, a new area."

"I get it." Eve shrugged with another sip of beer. "So I've got to at least show my face, do the moral support deal. Which is one of the annoyances of friendships."

"There's my girl."

She laughed, picked up a slice, then took a bite. Closed her eyes. She could see herself, with absolute clarity, taking that first long-ago bite by the window while New York and all its possibilities rushed, pushed, and bitched along on the other side of the glass.

She opened them, smiled into the eyes of her friend, her lover, her partner. "It's still damn good pizza."

He'd been right, she thought as they walked outside again. The hour had cleared her head, settled her mood, geared her up for the next steps and stages.

"I want to go by U-Play before we head uptown."

"It would be closed by this time," he said, as his fingers linked with hers. "I can certainly get you in if you're after a bit of B&E."

"Nobody's breaking and entering. I don't want to go in anyway."

"Then?"

"I figure it's closed, sure, but I wonder if it's empty."

He indulged her, wound his way through traffic and farther downtown. The summer light lengthened the day, spun it out and gilded it. The heat of the day had given way, just a little, just enough, to a few fitful breezes.

Both tourists and those who made their home in the city took advantage, filling street and sidewalk with a throng of bare legs, bare arms. She watched a woman, blond hair flying, race along, long tanned legs scissoring with pretty feet balanced on towering needle heels.

"How do they do that?" She pointed to the blond as she watched her lope along. "How do women, or the occasional talented tranny or cross-dresser—walk on streets like this in those heels, much less run like a gazelle across . . . whatever gazelles run across."

"I imagine it's the result of considerable practice, perhaps even for the gazelle."

"And if they didn't? If women, trannies, and cross-dressers everywhere revolted and said, screw this, we're not wearing these ankle-breaking stilts anymore—and they didn't—wouldn't the sadists who design those bastards have to throw in the towel?"

"I'm sorry to tell you, your women, trannies, and cross-dressers will never revolt. Many of them actually appear to like the style and the lift."

"You just like them because they make the ass jiggle."

"Absolutely guilty."

"Men still rule the world. I don't get it."

"No comment as any would be misconstrued. Well, you were right about this." He eased onto the edge of the warehouse lot. "Closed, no doubt, but not empty."

She studied the faint glow of light against the glass, imagined the way the sun would slant through the windows this late in the day. The shadows cast, the glare tossed back at certain angles. Yes, they'd want the artificial light. For comfort, she thought, and for practicality.

Just as she imagined they'd want to be together, the three of them, in that space. For comfort, and maybe for practicality.

"Are you seriously imagining them in there discussing how they'd managed murder and what steps to take next?"

"Maybe." She titled her head, studied him. "You don't like it because you like them, and because you see something of yourself in all four of them. Just a little piece here and there. Because of that, because you'd never kill a friend, never kill an innocent or kill simply because killing was expedient, you don't like the idea one of them did."

"That may be true, all of it true enough. But you and I have both killed, Eve, and once you have you know taking a life isn't a game. Only the mad think otherwise. Do you believe one of them is mad?"

"No. I think they're all very sane. I'm not looking for a mad scientist or a geek gone psycho. This is something else." She watched as a shadow passed behind one of the windows. "Whoever did it may regret it now, may feel it's all a terrible mistake, a nightmare that won't let go. I may crack the killer open like an egg with that guilt and horror when we get that far."

She watched those windows, the lights and shadows, for another moment in silence.

"Or, and we both know this, too, sometimes the taking of a life hardens you, it . . . calcifies your conscience. He deserved it, I only did what I had to do. Or worse yet, it excites. It opens a door in you that was so secret, so small, so tightly locked no one, even you, knew it was there. And there's a kind of joy in that. Look what I did! Look at the power I have."

It could still make her sick, deep in the belly, if she let it.

"That's the type who can never go back," she said quietly, but her eyes were hard, almost fierce. "Who have to do it again because sooner or later, the power demands it. Some of the shrinks will claim that's a kind of madness, that compulsion to feel that power and excitement again. But it's not. It's greed, that's all."

She shifted to him. "I know this. I felt that power, even the excitement, when I killed my father."

"You can't toss self-defense in with murder. You can't equate murder with a child fighting for her life against a monster."

"It wasn't murder, but it was killing. It was ending a life. It was blood on my hands."

He took the hand she held out, shook his head, pressed his lips to the palm.

"Roarke, I know the power of that, the sick excitement. I know the horrible, tearing guilt, and even the hardening of the heart, the soul, because I felt all of that over time. All of it. I know, even though what I did wasn't murder, what the murdering can and does feel. It helps me find them. It's a tool."

She touched his cheek, understanding that the memories, the idea of what she'd been through until the night when she'd been eight, hurt him as much as they hurt her. Maybe more now, she realized. Maybe more.

"I was twenty-three the next time I took a life," she continued. "Fifteen years between. Feeney and I went after a suspect. He'd beaten two people to death, in front of witnesses, left DNA and trace all over the scene. Slam dunk, just have to find him. We followed a lead to this dive. Sex club where his girlfriend worked. We figured we'd shake her down a little, see if she knew where he was. Well, where he was happened to be the sex club. Idiot girlfriend screams for him to run, and runs with him. He's mowing people down right and left, and those who aren't mowed are stampeding. We chased him all the way up to the roof, and now he's got a ten-inch blade against the idiot girlfriend's throat, who is now singing another tune.

"It's summer." She could still feel it, smell it, see it. "Hot as a fuck in hell. Sweat's pouring down his face. Hers, too. He's screaming at us how he'll slice her open if we come any closer. And now there's blood trickling down with her sweat where he's given her a jab to show he means it. He's using her as a shield, and Feeney doesn't have the angle for a stun stream."

"But you do," Roarke murmured.

"Yeah, I do. Barely, but I've got it. And we're trying to talk him down, and it's not going to happen. He gives her a second jab. Feeney keeps talking, talking, pulling the guy's attention to him, and gives me the go signal."

And Roarke could see it, too. He could see it in her eyes as she spoke.

"I stun him—nice clean stream, and his body jerks the way it does with a hit. She shoves forward to get clear, pushes clear, bumps him back, and he's jerking. The son of a bitch went right over the edge. Momentum, gravity, bad luck, whatever, but he went over and hit the sidewalk eight stories down.

"I didn't feel excited when I looked down at him. I didn't feel guilty either. A little shaky, sure. Jesus, it was a straight stun, neither of us expected him to go over that way. I didn't even have to go through Testing. We'd turned on our recorders when we started the chase, and it was all on there, it showed the girlfriend's push and stumble caused the fall. Or basically. Bad luck for him, that's all."

She let out a breath. "But I'm the one who aimed and fired. Fifteen years between. It took me that long to be sure, absolutely sure, I wouldn't feel that excitement, or that guilt, or that hardening when I had to take another life."

She looked back toward the building. "One of those three, at least one of them, might be wondering if they'll feel that again. One of them may want to."

"I can't tell you how much I hope you're wrong."

Her eyes, flat and cool, met his. "I'm not."

"No. I very much doubt you're wrong."

13 SHE SPENT A GREAT DEAL OF TIME PICKING through data on the lives of three people, analyzing it, scraping away at tiny details of family background, education, finances, and communication.

She played each one against Mira's profile, and the computer matched each one of them with a reasonably high probability to the general outline.

Organized, detail-oriented, competitive, wide e-skills, known and trusted by victim.

But the violence—that face-to-face, blood-on-the-hands cruelty bottomed them out again.

Still, nowhere could she find any hint, much less any evidence, that any had bought a hit.

Money wasn't the only currency, she mused. A favor, sex, information—all those could stand in for dollars and cents and never show on any balance sheet. But that didn't account for the fact Bart had known his killer. There was simply no reason to believe he'd allowed a stranger into his apartment, into his holo-room, into his game.

One more time, she told herself, and rose to study and circle her board.

Vic comes home happy, whistling a tune. And comes in alone according to both the doorman and the security cameras. EDD verifies by all that's holy there'd been no tampering with the locks, and no entry before the vic's in any access into the apartment.

Still, she considered, we have three very skilled, very clever e-geeks. If there was a way to bypass without it showing, they'd find it.

Or, more realistically, one of them, or another party met the vic outside and entered with him.

Only the droid says otherwise—and once again EDD remained firm that no one tampered with or reprogrammed the Leia droid.

Eve shut her eyes.

"Maybe he doesn't secure the door immediately. He's excited, happy. The droid brings him a fizzy, he tells her to go ahead and shut down. The killer may have entered at that time, *after* the droid shut down, before the door was secured. It's possible."

The friendly face shows up, Eve thought, tells the vic, *I couldn't resist. I want in on the game, or want to observe.* One of the partners, she thought again. *You play, I'll document and observe.*

Also possible, she concluded. *Why wait until after-hours? It's almost ready. Let's run it.* The killer could've brought the disc, which explains why the vic didn't log it out, as was his routine. Or, the killer told the vic he or she would log it for him.

The weapon might have already been on the premises, or brought in by the killer.

And the game begins. System reads solo. Bart plays, killer observes—it's logical, it's efficient.

But at some point, the killer stops observing. Bruising, wrenched shoulder indicate a scuffle.

And that, Eve thought, was where it just didn't fit for her.

The weapon's there, the plan's in place, so why the scuffle? Bart's in good shape—superior shape for a geek—and he's studied combat moves. Why risk a fight, why risk him getting some licks in?

An argument? Passion of the moment? No, no, *dammit*, it wasn't impulse. Too many safeguards in place.

Ego? She studied the three faces on the board.

Yes, ego. I'm better than you are. It's about time you found out how much better. Tired of playing sidekick and loyal friend and partner. *Have a taste of this.*

She studied the autopsy photos, the data, rocked back and forth on her heels.

Considering, she opened the panel for the elevator and ordered Roarke's weapons room. She used the palm plate, keyed in her code, and stepped into a museum of combat. Display after display held what man had used again man, or beast, over centuries. To kill, to defend, for land, for money, for love, for country, for gods. It seemed people could always find some new way to end each other, and some handy excuse for the blood.

From ancient sharpened points, to silver swords with jeweled hilts, from crude and clumsy muskets that used powder and ball to rip steel into flesh, to the sleek, balanced automatics that could wage a storm of steel with a twitch of a finger. Lances, maces that looked like iron balls studded with dragon's teeth, the long-ranged blasters of the Urban Wars, the razor-thin stiletto and the two-headed axe all spoke of the violent history of her species, and very likely its future.

She found studying them, seeing so many killing tools in one space, both fascinating and disturbing.

She opened a case, selected a broadsword. Good weight, she decided, good grip. Satisfied, she stepped out and reengaged the security.

"Is there a problem?" Summerset demanded as he seemed to eke out of the shadows.

Eve gave herself points for not jolting, smiled instead as she leaned on the sword. "Why do you ask?"

"The weapons aren't to leave the display."

"Gee, maybe you should call a cop."

The long, cool stare he gave her was as derisive as a sniff. "What you have there is very valuable."

"Which is why I'm not poking you with it. I might hit the stick up your ass and break the tip. Don't worry. Roarke's the one who's going to be using it."

"I expect it to be returned to the display in the exact condition it was in when you removed it."

"Yeah, yeah, blah blah." She stepped back on the elevator, and couldn't resist tapping the flat of the blade to her forehead in a quick, sarcastic salute before the doors closed.

"I'd better not be stitching someone up tonight," Summerset muttered.

Eve stepped out in her office, walked over to Roarke's. "Hey."

He made a humming sound, and continued to work his comp.

"Can you come in here a minute?"

"In five," he said.

While she waited she went to her own comp, ran a reenactment of the murder using a figure representing each of the partners in height, weight, reach.

"What do you need?" Roarke asked her. "And why do you have that sword?"

"I'm trying to figure how it went down. So . . ." She stepped into the center of the room, and imagining Summerset's horror, tossed the sword to Roarke. "Come at me."

"You want me to attack you with a broadsword?"

"We'll start with that version."

"No."

"Why not?"

"I'm not going to go at you with a bloody sword."

"Well, for God's sake, I don't want you to whack me with it. I don't want it to be a *bloody* sword. Demonstration purposes only. You're the killer." She pointed at him. "I'm the vic." And tapped her chest. "Now you've got that big, sharp, shiny sword, and I've got some useless holo-weapon, so wouldn't you just—"

She broke off as he took one quick step forward, and had the flat of the blade an inch from her throat.

"Yeah, like that. And see, my instinctive reaction to that move would be to bring my useless weapon up like this." She moved slow, to block, shoving the sword aside. "The thing is, the gash was on his other arm. Vic's right-handed, so logic says he'd have the useless holo-weapon in his dominant hand. The wrenched shoulder's on that side, but Morris said it's the kind of injury you'd get from over-rotating."

"Maybe, in surprised defense, he brought his other arm up."

"Yeah, but, see, if he did, the gash is just wrong." She demonstrated again. "Logic again says the wound should go across, not up and down. Besides, if you had a big, long sword, and I didn't, wouldn't you just ram it into me? You've got the advantage of reach."

"I would, yes. Get it done."

"But it didn't just get done. Bruises on the arms and legs. See, if we're fighting. Put it down a minute." When he had she gave him a finger curl. "Come at me."

She blocked, pivoted. He blocked her side kick.

"See, we're fairly even here, and if we meant it, I'm going to get some bruises where I either land a blow or block, or you block me. But you're not going to block me with your arm when you've got that big sword."

She held up a hand for peace. "I ran some reenactment. They just don't play out logically."

"We argue, it gets physical," he suggested. "I lose my head, grab the sword, and take yours."

"If it went down that way, why is the sword there in the first place?" She paced away, frowned at her murder board again. "If it went down that way, why isn't the disc logged out? Why was it timed so the killer arrived after the droid shut down? And why did the killer evade building security on the way in?"

"Might be coincidence."

"One might be a coincidence." Hands on her hips, she turned back. "Put them together it's a pattern."

"Well, I'm forced to agree with you. So we've had our fight. What do you do when I pick up the sword?"

"I say, what the fuck are you doing?"

"Or words to that effect," Roarke agreed. "And when I come at you?"

"I run, or at least try to get the hell out of the way of the really sharp point."

"And, you'd run, one would think, for the door."

"If the game's still up, he might've been disoriented."

"True enough." As she did, Roarke tried to see it, to put himself into it. "Then wouldn't you do one of two things—use the game, the holo-features for cover? Attempt to hide. Or call for the game to end, then try for the door."

"Yeah. But the body was well inside the room, nearly center, and facing—so to speak—away from the door." She huffed out a breath. "It skirts all around the edges of logical. I can't make it work in my head.

I can't see the steps. Maybe there were two people. Mira believes there might've been."

She tilted her head at the reconstruction she'd paused on-screen. Maybe she needed to add another figure. "The killer and the planner. If so, he still had to know and trust both of them to let them into that room during game play. The game was too important for him to let anyone he didn't know, anyone who wasn't involved get a sneak peek."

"It depresses me to say it, but maybe it was the lot of them. All three."

"Possible." She'd circled around that herself. "I can't figure why all three of them would want him dead, but possible. Two to do the job, one to stay back and cover for the other two."

She paced away again. "I can't find anything in the business that indicates there was any trouble, anything that makes me think he might've been throwing his weight around or threatening to walk away, or anything else that relates specifically to the partnership that comes up motive."

"So it was personal."

"I think it was, yeah." That, she mused, was the one element that kept repeating for her. "Personal could've come out of the partnership, the business. They practically lived together in that place. Worked together, played together. The only one in a semi-serious outside relationship was Bart. Need to talk to her again. The girlfriend," Eve added.

She turned back to Roarke. "Are you up for a game?"

"Will I need my sword?"

"Ha." She gestured toward the broadsword. "Bring that one, too."

"Ha," he echoed.

"I want to run the two scenarios you culled out." She retrieved the disc. "From the level he started." They moved into the elevator. "Solo play," she decided when Roarke ordered the holo-room. "Let's replay as close as possible to what he might've done."

"Question. Why does what he was playing matter?"

"Because I can't see it." And that, she had to admit, was a pisser. "I can't make it work no matter how many ways I play it out. The injuries, the timing, the entry and exit by the killer. Every time I get one part of it solid, another part goes to goo in my fingers. Something's missing. I could bring the three of them in," she said as they stepped out again. "Pressure them some, try playing one against the other. Maybe I'd crack it. Or maybe I'd shore up whoever did it—because something's missing and I don't have it to use. Whoever did it would know that. Right now they think they're clear, and maybe, just maybe, the killer relaxes and makes a mistake. If I push when I can't see it, a mistake's more likely."

"You play the first one, Bart's character menu."

"All right."

"They could do it again."

He paused, looked back at her. "Why? If it was specific toward Bart, why again?"

"Because it worked. Gaming can be a kind of addiction. It's what they do—what the killer does—all day, one way or the other. It's what feeds them, what excites them, what gives them purpose and pleasure. Higher stakes once you've killed. A new level. Some gamers start skipping the lower levels—like Bart did—once they nail them. It's a little boring, right?"

"Yes. Yes, you're right."

"It's hard to go back to the simple stuff once you've proven yourself. Not just the kill, like we were talking about before. But the challenge. More, if it is one of them—say just one of them—they're close, they're tight. Day in and day out. One little slip, something said or done that makes the others wonder. Good excuse to do it again. You're just protecting yourself."

"The murder of another partner would increase your focus on the two remaining," Roarke pointed out.

"True gamers juice on the risk, the challenge. Right? They want the buzz. Maybe need that buzz."

"You believe the killer's playing against you now."

"Yeah, at least on one level. And the ego's saying hey, I'm better than she is."

"The ego would be wrong," Roarke commented.

She tucked her thumbs in her front pockets as he inserted the copy of the game into the holo-unit. "Since I feel like I'm spinning my wheels, I'll take the confidence booster."

"You're not spinning anything. A day ago, I wouldn't have believed one or more of his friends would plot his death. But you've picked it all apart and laid it back out so that there's simply no other answer. To my mind, that puts you well ahead in this game."

"I wish I was wrong."

"For my sake, or Bart's?"

"Both."

"Don't wish it," he told her. "Just win."

He programmed Quest-1, level four, and requested the last run by Bart on the copy.

"I'll take the sword," Eve said, and kept it by her side as the room shimmered into a forest glade where silver beams of sunlight streamed through tall trees in full leaf.

Roarke wore a brown tunic, rough trousers, knee boots. His sword was sheathed at his side, and on his back was a quiver of silver-tipped arrows and a golden bow.

She couldn't have said why the costume suited him, but understood he looked both heroic and dangerous.

Out of the shadows and into the gilded stream of light came a white buck.

"What's the play?" she asked him.

"This world is under the enchantment of a wicked sorceress who's imprisoned the king and his beautiful and tempestuous daughter."

As he spoke, he sidestepped into the cover of trees, but didn't approach the buck.

"I'm the apprentice of the wizard she killed to cast her evil spell. Before he died, he told me I must complete seven tasks of valor, collect seven treasures. Only then would I be ready to face the sorceress and free the king and his daughter."

He glanced back where she stood in the observation circle.

"The white hind is classic quest symbolism, and in this case how my master, the wizard is able to guide me."

"Okay then."

The hind leaped, began to race through the trees. Roarke followed.

She watched, and the sunlight died into dark and storm. The rain that pelted down was red as fire, and sizzled like flames on the ground.

And watched as the yellow eyes that peered out of the torrent became skulking black forms, and as the forms became a pack of huge wolves that circled him.

The sword hissed as he pulled it from its sheath, and whistled as he swung and struck. He battled fang and claw, spilled blood and shed it.

And to her surprise, shot flames from his hand.

"Fairly frosty," she murmured, when the wolves lay smoking on the ground.

"Every level you win awards you with a bit more magic," he explained.

An arrow whistled by his head. He said, "Bugger it," and dove for cover.

At the end of forty minutes, he'd completed the level and was well into the next where he was currently tasked with crossing a chasm to a cave guarded by a dragon.

"Okay, that's time."

"I'm just getting started."

"You can slay the dragon next time. You're past Bart's game time."

He gave the cave a glance of regret before ordering game end.

"No sword fights," she commented.

"What do you call that bit with the wolves?"

"Man against dog. The fireballs were interesting. Fire burns. He had burns, but . . . I'll take the second one. Usurper, right? What's the story?"

"You're the right-wise king—make that queen in your case— of Juno. When you were only a child your family was slaughtered by the machinations of your uncle, who desired the throne, and by the hand of his henchman, Lord Manx. Only you survived, and were secreted away by loyalists. You've been at war all your life, trained in that art. You fight to avenge your family, to regain your throne from the man who ordered their deaths and has for two decades raped the land, oppressed your people. At this level, you've taken back the castle, but the uncle, being a coward, of course, escaped. The castle is now under siege, and the man you love is defending it. To get to him, and bring your reinforcements, you must fight your way through, and at last meet Manx in battle."

"I bet we're outnumbered."

"Naturally, you'd have already given your St. Crispin's Day speech."

"My what?"

"We'll discuss *Henry V* later. You'd like it. Ready?"

"You bet."

She wore light battle armor and sturdy boots. And God help her, she was on a horse.

"Shouldn't I know how to ride this thing before I . . . ride this thing?"

Roarke grinned at her from the observation circle. "It'll come to you."

"Easy for you to say. Jesus, it's big. Okay, avenging warrior queen."

There were hills and valleys, forests and streams. She tried to see them as Bart would have. He'd think in character, she imagined, and noted the men she led were battle scarred and weary. Some carried fresh wounds. But she was the hero, the leader.

He liked playing the hero, liked being the leader. The good guy, always the good guy, fighting for a cause, searching for the answers.

The going was rough and rocky. She heard the creak of the saddle under her, the ring of the horse's hooves on the hard ground. She saw storm clouds gathering in the west.

And heard the sounds of battle.

The castle bore scars of its own, and people stood on its parapets shooting arrows that flashed and flamed. Others fought viciously with sword and axe on the burned and barren ground around it.

He would probably think of home, and about his lover, Eve decided. About vengeance.

She thought: *Shit, shit, I hope I don't fall off this thing.* And charged.

She drew the sword, instinctively squeezing her knees and thighs to keep her seat. Wind rushed through her hair, over her face, and the speed, the sheer power of motion lit a fire of excitement in her.

Then she stopped thinking, and fought.

Bloody and bitter, the battle raged. She *felt* her sword slice through flesh, hit bone. She smelled blood and smoke, felt the mild jolt from a glancing blow as the horse danced and pivoted under her.

She saw him, his armor black and stained with blood, sitting on a huge black horse with the castle—her castle—at his back. The sounds of the battle receded as she rode forward to face him.

"So, we meet at last. A pity for you, our acquaintance will be short."

"Yeah, yeah," she responded. "Let's go."

"This day my sword will wear your blood, and the blood of your lover."

"Yawn."

"You rush death? Then come meet it."

The programmers, she noted and quickly, had made Manx very big and very strong. Blocking his blows sent shocking aches up her arm, into her shoulder.

Wrenched shoulder.

Sweat ran down her back, down her face, into her eyes to sting. She'd never beat him on these terms, she realized. She had neither the skill nor the strength.

And when he slid past her guard, she felt the jolt as his sword drew blood.

Arm wound.

He lifted his sword, the dark light of death in his eyes; she ducked and plunged her sword into his horse.

It screamed. She had a moment to think the sound was eerily human before it stumbled. As it fell, she swung out, caught her opponent in the side. Not a death blow, she decided. Time to finish it off.

"Pause game. Save, and stop."

Breathing hard, she turned, looked at Roarke across the empty holoroom. "I don't get to kill the bad guy?"

"You're past Bart's time, by a minute or so. Interesting strategy, killing the horse."

"It worked. They built that bastard strong. He was going for the . . ." She swiped her finger across her throat.

"He certainly was. And if he'd landed the blow, game over. You'd have to repeat the level until you defeated him to move on to the next."

"This is the game he was playing when he died. It all fits. Bruises from fighting, the shoulder, the arm wound, and the loss with the decapitation. K2BK. King To Black Knight."

"Yes, I got that when he came into play."

"Obviously there weren't real horses and a bunch of dead guys littering the ground, but the killer reconstructed the game, using a real weapon. If he got in, programmed himself as the Black Knight, and used a real weapon. The right steps, the right angle."

"I'd agree, but it doesn't explain how he got in, and how he managed to delete a two-man competition from the unit without leaving a single shadow or echo anywhere in the system."

Screw logic, she thought. Sometimes facts weren't logical. "He figured it out because the Black Knight killed the king. Bart played that exact scenario before, that's why it's on this disc. But he didn't stab the horse, and he lost. He'd have been more prepared this time, may have avoided the loss, or that exact loss, but—"

"When his opponent's sword actually cut him—the pain, the shock, the blood—all real, he was too stunned to react."

"And the game ended for real the same way it ended in play before. This works. I need to fast-talk my way into search warrants. By their own statements only the three partners knew all the details of the game, only the three partners ever participated in play. Those three knew this program, this level, and the results of previous play, so they're the only ones who could have used it to kill him."

"While I hate knowing you're right, I don't see how it could be anything or anyone else. And shifting that to me, I'm considerably pissed off I could have made such an error in judgment. I'd never have believed any of them capable of this."

"Neither did he, and he knew them all a hell of a lot better than you. People can hide and hoard and stroke all kinds of nasty stuff no one else sees. You saved that play, right?"

"I did." He smiled now. "You were fairly magnificent. We'll have to go riding in real life sometime."

"I don't think so." But she remembered that sensation of speed, of power. "Maybe. Anyway, I want to view it, then do an analysis. He'd have saved the play, too, so he could study it, see his mistakes."

"Absolutely."

"The one he used the day he died is toast."

"We're getting some of it. A little some at this point."

She nodded as she called for the elevator. "And maybe that was his disc, where he'd saved his play, his levels. Or maybe, since it wasn't logged out, the killer gave it to him. You know, Hey, Bart, I did some *tweaking*—or whatever words you geeks use. You need to try it out."

"If so, there'd be another copy, Bart's copy. Which, if the killer has any sense, has been destroyed."

"Maybe. But people keep the damnedest things."

That night she dreamed of blood and battle, of castles and kings. She stood, observer now, her feet planted while the wind whipped the stench of death around her. Men, their wounds mortal, moaned and begged as they scattered the ground.

Those who turned their faces toward her she knew. Victims, so many victims, so many dead who lived inside her head whose ends she'd studied, evaluated, reconstructed to find the one who'd ended them.

Some who fought, who sliced with sword and axe, she knew as well. She'd helped lock the cage doors behind them. But here, in dreams, they'd found freedom. In dreams, in the games the mind played, they could and would kill again.

Only in dreams, she reminded herself. And if she shuddered as she saw her father, her eyes met his manic ones coolly.

Only in dreams.

She watched with pity and resignation as Bart fought a war he'd never win. Swords and sorcery, games and dreams. Life and death.

She watched his end. Studied and evaluated even as his head, eyes still wide in shock, rolled to her feet.

And the Black Knight wheeled his horse and grinned at her, fiercely. When he charged, she reached for her weapon, but all she had was a small knife, one already stained with her father's blood.

Only in dreams, she told herself, but knew a terrible fear as he came for her.

**14** SHE JERKED UP, SHOVING HERSELF FREE OF the dream. For an instant, just one beat of the heart, she swore she felt the keen edge slice at her throat.

Shaken, she reached up, half expecting to feel the warm wet of her own blood.

"Shh, now. It's all right."

His arms were there, drawing her in, closing around her like a shield. As her heart continued to bound, she leaned into them, into him.

"Just a dream. You're home. I'm right here."

"I'm okay." No blood. No death. "It wasn't a nightmare. Or not exactly. I knew it was a dream, but it was so real." She drew one breath, then another. Slow, she ordered herself. Slow and steady. "Like the games. You lose track of what is and what's not."

He tipped her face up, and in the glow of moon and stars through the sky window met her eyes. "We're real." He touched his lips to hers as if to prove it. "What did you dream?"

"The battlefield, the last game." Bart's last game, she thought, but not hers. "I wasn't playing. I was just watching. Observing the details." She sighed once, rubbed her hands over her face. "If you don't watch, if you don't see, you don't know. But it weirded on me, the way dreams do."

"How?"

"The dead, the dying, their faces. All those people I don't know until they're dead."

In those eyes, so blue in the starlight, came understanding. "Your victims."

"Yeah." The pang in her heart was pity, weighted down by resignation. "I can't help them, can't save them. And their killers are out there, free, killing more. It's a slaughter." And the simmer beneath it was an anger that bubbled up in her voice. "We put them away, but it doesn't stop it. We know that. We all know that. There's always more. He was there. You have to figure he'd be there."

"Your father."

"But he's just one of the many now."

Still she trembled, just a little, so he rubbed her arms to warm them.

"I'm not engaged. I'm not playing. I'm not one of them. Not one of the dead or dying, not one of the killers. Just an observer."

"It's how you stop them," he said quietly. "It's how you save those you can."

And some of the weight eased. "I guess it is. I watched Bart fight. I know what's going to happen, but I have to watch because I might have missed a detail. I might see something new. But it happens just the way I see it happen. Then the Black Knight, his killer, turned to me. Looks at me. It's just a dream, but I go for my weapon because he's coming for me. I can feel the ground shake and feel the wind. But all I have against that fucking sword is the little knife I used all those years ago, in that horrible room in Dallas."

She looked down at her hand, empty now. "That's all I have, and it won't be enough, not this time. The sword comes down, and I feel that, too. Just for a second before I wake up."

She let out a breath. "Sometimes they crowd me."

"Yes. I know."

"Killers and victims. They get in your head, and they never really leave." She cupped his face now. "They'll get in yours, because you can't just step aside, just watch me do the job. You can't just observe any more than I can. I'm in the game, always one of the players. Now, you are, too."

"Do you think I regret that?"

"One day you might. I wouldn't blame you."

"I knew you for a cop the minute I laid eyes on you. And I knew without understanding how or why, that you would change things. I'll never regret that moment, or any that followed." He gave her shoulders a little shake—as comforting as a kiss. "You have to understand you're not alone on the battlefield. And since that moment, that first moment? Neither am I."

"I used to think I was better off alone, that I needed to be. And maybe I did. But not anymore."

She touched her lips to his cheek, then the other. "And never again."

Then laid her lips warm and soft on his.

What they brought to each other closed all the rest outside. A touch, a taste, a promise renewed.

He enclosed her, brought her in, brought her close. He knew, she thought, simply knew she needed to be held, to have his arms around her. His hands warming her skin were gentle, so gentle after the blood and brutality of the dream. His lips, those slow, tender kisses offered her peace and solace, and love.

Passion would come, she knew. It was a low fire always kindled between them. But for now he gave her what she reached for, could always reach for with him. He gave her comfort.

Did she know, could she know what it meant to him when she turned to him, when she opened herself to him like this? In absolute trust.

Her strength, her valor remained a constant wonder to him, as did her unrelenting determination to defend those who could no longer defend themselves. These moments, when she allowed her vulnerabilities, her doubts, her fears to tremble to the surface compelled him to take care. In these moments he could show her it wasn't just the warrior he loved, he treasured, but the woman, the whole of her. The dark and the light.

Softly, softly, as if tending wounds, he stroked her skin, unknotted muscles tight from the day and the dream. And when she sighed, he laid his lips on her heart.

It beat for him.

In the blue wash of moonlight, she moved for him, rising up, another sigh, giving over. Giving.

Her fingers slid through his hair, glided down his back and up again. An easy rhythm even when her breath quickened and her sigh deepened to moan.

Lost in it, this quiet pleasure, she drew him closer, closer still. Body to body, mouth to mouth, thrilled with the weight of him, the shape of him. She drew in his scent like breath, and opened to take him in.

Smooth and slow and sweet, they moved together. As sensations shimmered through her like light, she cupped his face in the dark.

Not all magic was fantasy, she thought. There was magic here and she felt it glow in her body, in her mind and her heart.

"I love you. Roarke. I love you."

Magic, she thought, watching his heart rise into his eyes.

"*A grah.*" My love. And with the word he lifted her home.

In the morning, Eve drank the first half of the first cup of coffee with the concentration of a woman focused on simple survival. Then she sighed with nearly the same easy pleasure as she had the night before under Roarke's skilled hands.

No question, she admitted, and set the coffee aside long enough to jump in the shower: She'd gotten spoiled.

She didn't know how she'd managed to get her ass in gear every day before Roarke—and real, honest-to-God coffee, black and strong and rich. Or how she'd lived with the stingy piss-trickle of the shower in her own apartment before she'd discovered the sheer wonder of hot multi-jets, on full, pummeling her awake.

Good things, little things, really, that she'd lived without all of her life—like the warm, clean-scented swirl of air in the drying tube. She'd gotten used to those good things, those little things, she realized, so that she rarely thought of them.

She stepped out of the tube and noted the robe hanging on the door. Short, soft, and boldly red—and probably new. She couldn't be absolutely sure as her man had a habit of buying her pretty things—good things, little things—without mentioning it.

She put it on, picked up her coffee, and stepped back into the bedroom.

A typical morning scene in their household, she supposed. Roarke sipped his own coffee on the cushy sofa in the sitting area, stroking Galahad into a coma while he scanned the morning stock reports. Already dressed, she observed, and he'd probably dealt with at least one 'link conference or holo-meeting before she'd cracked her eyes open.

He'd nag her to eat breakfast, unless she came up with the idea on her own—and very likely let her know if whatever jacket she pulled out didn't go with whatever pants she pulled on.

Good things, she thought yet again. Little things.

Their things.

While she'd come to rely on the routine, sometimes, she decided, you needed to shake it up.

"What're you hungry for?" she asked him.

"Sorry?" He glanced over, obviously shifting his attention from screen to her.

"What do you want for breakfast?"

He cocked his head, lifted his eyebrows. "Have you seen my wife? She was here just a minute ago."

"Just for that, you'll eat what I give you."

"That sounds a bit more like the woman we know and love," he said to the cat. "And yet . . ." He rose, sauntered over to her. He gave her a spin and a dip, then a kiss more suited to steamy midnight than bright summer morning.

"Well, well, it is you after all. I know that mouth."

"Keep it up, ace, and that's all you'll be tasting."

"I could live with that."

She gave him a poke to nudge him back. "I've got no time to wrestle with you. I've got search warrants to secure, suspects to grill, killers to catch."

She programmed waffles and mixed berries, more coffee. She imagined Roarke had already fed the cat, but programmed a shallow bowl of milk. Galahad leaped on it like a puma.

"It'll keep him out of our hair," she said as she sat.

"And isn't this nice, our little family having breakfast together." He plucked a fat blackberry from his own plate, popped it in her mouth. "You look rested. No more dreams?"

"No. Something relaxed them right out of me." She picked up a raspberry, popped it in his. "But I was thinking about it. Dreams are subconscious whacka-whacka."

"A little known psychological term."

"Whatever. I can figure out most of it; it's just not that deep. But I have a lead suspect in my head, so why was it the fantasy figure that killed Bart in the dream? Maybe because my subconscious was just following the game, or maybe because it's telling me I'm wrong."

"You might run it by Mira."

"Maybe. If there's time. When the warrants come through, the searches are going to take a while. Hitting three places means extra time, extra men."

"Mira might back you up on the need for those warrants."

"Yeah, I'm holding her in reserve. The killer knew Bart's routine, that's part of the thing. His inside-his-own-place routine, and that takes a certain intimacy. It's like this, us," she explained wagging a finger between them. "The way I knew you'd be sitting here when I came out of the shower. Drinking coffee, petting the cat, checking the stocks and morning media. It's what you do. You deviate now and then, as necessary, but odds are it's like this."

"Mmm." Roarke cut a bite of waffle. "And the killer played the odds."

"They were good odds. Just like I favor the odds on whoever killed him making a move to take the leadership role at U-Play. Bart's death leaves a void, and part of the benefit of that death would be filling it."

"You're leaning away from more than one of them being involved now."

"It's still a good possibility, but killing a friend, a partner, it's an absolute betrayal of trust."

He nodded. "And anyone who's capable of that sort of betrayal wouldn't easily trust someone else."

She tapped her fork in the air. "You got it in one. These people live by creating scenarios, and calculating all the steps. Take this choice, get this result, and that leads to the next. I think the killer would have calculated the pros and cons of pulling someone into it with him."

"If the other weakens, makes a mistake, threatens, it's a new problem. Difficult to kill another partner," Roarke commented. "It would shine your light brightly on the remaining two. But . . ." He knew her, too. Her routine, her thought patterns. "You're concerned that might happen."

"It depends on what's to be gained, or lost—and how much ego and satisfaction were stoked by the first kill. When someone believes they're smarter, more talented, just plain more *right* than anyone else, and they harbor this kind of need, they're very, very dangerous."

E ve tried Cher Reo first. The APA was another friend, and Eve supposed in a broad sense, another partner. *I knock them down,* she thought as she pushed her way through morning traffic, *you put them away.*

When she contacted Reo's office she learned the APA was already at Central overseeing Reineke's case.

That didn't take long, she mused, and cut west, away from Broadway and the crowds that inevitably partied there.

The pizza would roll on the pipe wrench, she concluded—or vice versa. One would take a deal, and the other would do the full weight.

And that had to be enough.

She left a voice mail on Reo's 'link, requesting a meet as soon as she finished sealing the deal, but it surprised her to find Reo already waiting—with coffee, in her visitor's chair.

"Thought you'd take longer," Eve commented.

"They were at it since just after two this morning, which was when your boys decided the happy couple had had enough snuggle time." Reo stretched, rolled her shoulders. "She'd slipped into his place about eight. Lights went off at midnight. Or thereabouts. They have it documented."

She yawned, combed her fingers through her fluffy blond hair. "They got sloppy. Didn't even bother to pull the privacy screen. Your guys got quite a little show before and after the lights went out."

"I'm betting the wife rolled on the lover."

"Like a wheel down a steep road. Tried all the usual first, apparently. She was just looking for comfort after the loss." Reo widened her eyes, batted her lashes. "Oh my God, he killed my husband! Shock, dismay, tears. Anyway." She shrugged. "They got very detailed confessions out of both, and I saved the taxpayers a bundle. She'll do a solid dime, he'll do double that."

She held up a finger before Eve could speak. "Yeah, we probably could've gotten them both life in a trial, but this seals them up. It's not a bad way to start the middle of the night."

She might've argued, for form's sake, but Eve wanted Reo's good graces. "I need three search warrants."

"For what?"

Eve got her own coffee, sat, and spelled it out.

Frowning, Reo tapped a finger to the side of her mug. "No physical evidence on any of them?"

"That's why I need the warrants. To find some."

"You don't really know what you're looking for."

"But I'll know it when I find it. The weight's there, Reo. Motive, means, opportunity, e-skills—and an intimate knowledge of the vic's domicile, habits, and security. Add in by their own statements only those three had full knowledge of the game."

"They're alibied."

Eve shook her head, dismissing it. "The alibis are soft. They're so soft they're squishy. You haven't seen the place. I have. It's like a beehive, with the bees buzzing everywhere. It's a five-minute walk to the scene. Any one of them could have slipped out for an hour without anybody knowing. And if someone had, the killer would've had another alibi ready. It's the way they think—in cause and effect, action and reaction. Mira's profile adds more. He knew his killer."

Reo puffed out her cheeks. "I can work it. You say they've been cooperative so far?"

"Oh yeah."

"You could always request a search, see how each of them reacts."

"And that gives any of them time to ditch whatever it is I might find."

"I can work it," she said again. "And I sure hope you find something." She rose. "Do you know how uncomfortable that chair is?"

"Yeah."

Reo laughed, rubbed tired blue eyes. "Regardless, if you'd been another ten minutes, I'd've been asleep in it. I need a damn nap. See you tonight? Nadine's party?"

"I'll be there."

"I'm going to have to trowel on the enhancers to look half human. I'll get your warrants," she added as she headed out.

"Thanks."

One down, Eve thought, then walked out to pull Peabody away from her desk. "Let's go have another talk with CeeCee."

As they started for the glide, she spotted Reineke at one of the machines in Vending. "Good work, Detective."

"Thanks, Lieutenant. Jenkinson's walking them through processing." He drew a very sad-looking Danish out of the slot. "You know, turns out in the end they were just a couple of idiots. He still had the clone phone he used to tag her before he went out and bashed the dead husband, and the pizza box hadn't run through his recycler yet. And her? She bought fancy underwear online a couple hours after she's notified she's got a dead husband. Stupidity shoulda gotten them more than ten and twenty."

"I bet they don't come out any smarter. Good work," she said again. "And I don't want to find out you and Jenkinson shared the surveillance doc around the bullpen."

"It's too bad because they may be stupid, but they're damn flexible." She waited until she was on the glide to grin.

"We're not looking at the girlfriend? CeeCee?" Peabody asked.

"No. It's one of the partners, but she may know more than she thinks. She's had some time to settle. I want to poke at her memory, and impressions."

They found CeeCee at home, in a tidy little apartment she shared with a trio of goldfish in a glass bowl.

Eve wondered about people who kept fish. Did they like to watch them circle, circle, staring out with those weird eyes? What was the appeal?

"I took some time off work." CeeCee sat in a high-backed scoop chair. She'd pulled her hair back in a tail and hadn't bothered with enhancements. She looked pale and tired. "I just can't go back yet. It feels like if I do, it's saying Bart didn't matter enough for me to stay home. And he did."

"Have you called a counselor?"

"No. I guess . . . I guess I'm not ready to feel better. That sounds stupid."

"No, it doesn't," Peabody told her.

"I don't know if we'd have stuck. I mean, things were good, and I think maybe . . . But I don't know, and I keep thinking about that. Would we have moved in together, or even gotten married? I don't know."

"Did you ever talk about it?" Eve wondered. "Moving in together?"

CeeCee managed a little smile. "We sort of circled around it. I don't think either of us was ready for that. I think if we'd stayed together a few more months, we'd have talked about it, seriously. We weren't in a hurry, you know? We thought we had plenty of time."

"And you each had your own interests," Eve prompted. "Your own routines and your own friends."

"That's true. I had a boyfriend once, and he crowded me. It was like if we weren't together twenty-four/seven, I didn't care enough. It wasn't like that with Bart. We did a lot together, and he liked my friends, I liked his. But we didn't have to be together every minute."

"You got along well with his partners. His closest friends."

"Sure. They're great. Good thing," she added with a smile that warmed her tired eyes. "I don't think I'd've been Bart's girl if I hadn't liked his friends, and they hadn't liked me back."

"Oh?"

"Well, they're like family. Some people have trouble with family. I could tell you about my sister." She rolled her eyes now, and Eve began to see some of the charm and energy that must have attracted Bart eke through the grief. "But I guess, I don't know, when you *choose* your family it's different. You can still disagree or argue, but you're always going to stand up for each other, too. I guess that's true with my sister, even when I'm mad at her."

"It'd be natural for Bart to get mad at his partners sometimes."

"Maybe, but he really didn't. It was more like he'd shake his head and go, *Jeez, what's Cill thinking about this,* or *What's Benny doing that for,* or *Var's out of orbit on this one.*"

"He'd talk to you about them."

"Sure. I'd be a kind of decompression chamber for him, if they'd had a rough few days. I know they'd been working really hard on a new project. Long hours and lots of testing stuff. Maybe they argued a little, the way you do over stuff like that, especially when you're overdoing it."

"Anything specific? Every detail helps," Eve added when CeeCee bit her lip. "One thing can lead to another, give us a better picture."

"Oh. Well. I know he was miffed at Cill a couple weeks ago. Nothing big, but he was upset that she'd gone overbudget for a marketing campaign proposal. And she was miffed because she put a lot of time into it and thought it was worth the extra. And he didn't. She gets madder than he does. Did."

She sighed, then shook it off.

"He said they yelled at each other, but he doesn't—didn't—really yell, so I'd say she did that part. But they made up, like always. He bought her flowers. He liked giving flowers. And he and Var got into it about the direction of this new game. It was technical, so Bart didn't really say what. Just about how they weren't going off mission statement, and not everything should reach its full potential. That's a weird thing to say, isn't it?"

"Yeah. What did he mean?"

"I don't know. He just said U-Play was about play, and that was that. He could be a little stubborn. Not often, but when he was . . . It was kind of cute."

"How about Bart and Benny? Any tension?"

"They go back so far. They'd tease each other a lot—that kind of ragging guys do on each other. Like I was over there last week, because we were going to catch a vid after work. He and Benny were testing one of the games, going one-on-one, and Bart just slaughtered him. And Bart rubbed his face in it. They do that all the time, but I guess all the work they'd been putting in was starting to tell, because Benny got steamed. I could see it. Benny said maybe they'd try it IRL—in real life—next time and stalked off. Bart just laughed. I told him when we left he'd hurt Benny's feelings."

She shrugged. "It was just guy stuff. Stupid guy stuff."

She's a nice woman," Peabody commented when they got back in the car. "I know it's pointless to speculate, but I think they would've stuck. His history indicates he's the sticking kind."

"Yeah. And he feels a little more normal now. Gets irritated with friends, has some arguments."

"None of them seemed murderous."

"Not to him. We can't be sure about the friend. Cill—questioning her authority and creativity. Var—shutting down an idea for change. Benny—skewering his ego and e-skills. It tells us he's normal, that two of the partners wanted something he didn't and were overruled, and the third got his ass kicked in front of others. It's unlikely any of those incidents were the first of their kind, and very possible any of those incidents was, for one of them, a last straw."

"You and I argue, and you've been known to shut me down and kick my ass. I'm not plotting your murder. At this time."

"I bet you've imagined kicking my ass."

Peabody cast her gaze up to the roof of the vehicle. "Imagination is not against the law or any departmental regulations."

"That's the point. It takes a certain type, or a flashpoint incident to cause someone to turn imagination into reality." She drummed her fingers on the wheel, thinking it through as she drove. "They all fit the profile, in my opinion. And turning imagination into something as close as possible to reality is what they try to do every day. So, one step more, and it's absolutely real."

She glanced down at her dash 'link, smiled at the text on-screen. "Reo came through. Put three teams together," she ordered Peabody.

"Me?"

"Is someone else here?"

"No, but—"

"An e-man with each team. We'll circulate. I want all weapons confiscated, even the toys. I want all discs evaluated, all comps, all coms evaled on-site." She ran down the list briskly while Peabody scrambled to key tasks into her PPC. "Any question on any of them, they come in. I want all sinks, tubs, showers, and drains tested for blood. I want any and all droids on any of the premises also evaled."

"Okay." Peabody swallowed, then nodded. "I follow you."

"Good. Make it happen. You and I are going by U-Play to notify the partners. Tell the ranking officer on each team to secure the warrant for his or her area."

"Copy that. Dallas, do you really think, if one of the partners killed Bart, they'd leave evidence in their own space?"

She thought of a simple pizza box. "It happens."

 WHILE PEABODY PUT THE TEAMS TOGETHER via 'link, Eve contacted the commander with an update.

"Are you looking at all three partners, acting in concert?"

"No, sir. I don't believe they could've pulled it off, nor do I believe all three of them could or would have turned against the victim and toward murder. It's possible, and it's possible two of them conspired as Mira's profile indicates a strong probability for two killers. But . . ."

How to explain?

"It doesn't fit for two of them in a conspiracy. It's too off-balance. If half the whole goes bad, how can the other half not notice? I believe they've all been under a lot of pressure to complete the project, and that caused some friction in the group. But to plan a murder like this takes time and thought, and goes deeper than friction between friends and partners. It may have been the excuse, the catalyst for one to act, but it was always under there."

"Which one?"

She hesitated. "I'll be better able to answer that after we see what the searches turn up. Having their personal space searched also adds pressure. I want to see the reactions."

"Turn up the heat and see if one of them boils over?"

"Something like that, sir."

When she completed her update, Eve glanced over to see Peabody staring at her with cool, narrowed eyes. "What?"

"You know."

"Many things."

"You know which one."

Eve shook her head. "I lean toward one."

"Which one?"

"You tell me."

"That's not fair." The cool look edged into a pout. "We're partners. You're supposed to tell me."

"You're a detective. You're supposed to figure it out."

"Fine. Fine. Okay, I get the whole half of the whole, off-balance, how could two of them turn on their old pal. But I think it had to be two. Not just because of Mira's profile, which plays out for me, but because logistically it's more solid. One to slip out and do the job, the other to hang back and cover."

"You're right. It's more solid."

"And you still think it's just one of them?"

"Yeah, I do. They're a tight circle—square, whatever. A closely knit and tied group. One of them veers off on this. That individual could disguise the resentment, envy, hate, ambition. Whatever of those served as driving force or excuse. Bad mood, overwork, distracted. Now make the individual a pair, which first means the spearhead in this has to take on a partner, has to trust."

Off-balance, she thought again. Too much weight—or hate—on one side of the whole.

"Now you have two people trying to hide murderous intent," Eve continued, "and by and large people aren't that good at strapping down their more passionate feelings. And after the deed's done, both those people have to project shock and grief, not only to us but to the last remaining member of the group."

"If all three of them conspired?"

"Then Bart Minnock would have to have been completely oblivious to what was going on in his circle of close friends and partners. That's not how I read him, certainly not how I read him after this last interview with the girlfriend. He had a sensitivity, a read on his people. And at the base, there's just no motive, no sense in the three of them plotting to kill him. They'd be the majority. If they all wanted something from him, from the business, wanted a change or were just fucking sick of him, they vote him out or off, or push as a unit."

The murder and the method equaled more than business, Eve thought. More than a bigger share of the pie.

"In the legal sense, the partnership agreement, they went with majority rule. And he didn't have any more authority or power than any of the others. They *gave* him the authority and power, a tacit sort of deal. They let him run the show because he was best suited for it, and it was working."

"Okay, you're talking me into it," Peabody said. "And one of them didn't want him to run the show anymore, but that meant it was three against one, so, take him out and it's no longer a problem."

"That's part of it. It has to be deeper, but the method of murder says raging ego to me, and serious loathing. The loathing may have built over time. Bart got the majority of the media attention, and he was the go-to guy at U-Play. He said no, or let's go this way, they tended to go along."

"Now there's a void. And voids need to be filled."

"That's correct, Detective."

"Given their backgrounds, skills, and personalities, any one of them could fill it."

"I'm not convinced on the personalities." She pulled into the lot. "For now, let's go in and screw up their day."

The warehouse was busier than the day before. Machines beeped and buzzed, shapes and colors filled screens. People went about their business with black bands around bare arms or the sleeves of colorful tees.

Eve spotted Cill riding up a level in one of the glass-walled elevators. The long fall of black hair had been tamed into a single neat braid. She wore a black suit, and black dress shoes with short, squat heels.

Respectful, Eve mused. Sensible—and unless she missed her guess, new.

Out of curiosity, Eve tapped one of the techs. "Where can I find Cill?"

"Um. Her office? She's been in there all morning."

"Uh-huh. Thanks."

She glanced at Peabody, then jerked a head toward the stairs. "Most of these people are in their own bubble, or in a bubble with whoever they're working with. They don't pop it unless they're told to or need something. The alibis aren't going to hold."

They didn't find Cill in her office, but in the break room where she sat alone, rubbing her left temple and staring into a power drink. Her head snapped up, and her knuckles whitened on the tube.

"You're back. Does that mean—"

"No. Not yet."

Her body slumped. "I don't know why it matters so much. When you find out who killed Bart, he'll still be dead. I don't know why it matters."

"Don't you want to know who killed him?"

"Yeah. Yes. But . . . right now, it just doesn't seem to matter. Sorry." She waved a hand. "I'm just bottomed, I guess. Do you have more questions?"

"Actually, we're here to notify you that we've obtained search warrants for your residence, and those of Benny and Var. They'll be carried out this morning."

"I don't understand. You're going to search my apartment?"

"That's correct."

"But why? For what?"

Eve watched her face change, those sharp green eyes fire, her cheeks flush with furious color. "You think I did this to Bart? To *Bart*? What the hell is wrong with you? You're supposed to be ace-high at what you do, and you think I killed Bart?"

"No one's accusing you. It's necessary to explore all avenues."

"That's just bullshit. You're getting nowhere so you start hassling us. You waste time with us while whoever killed him gets away with it." Tears sparkled in her eyes for a moment, but the heat of temper burned them off.

"I thought it didn't matter, finding Bart's killer."

"Don't you even say his name to me." Her voice spiked up; her fists clenched. "I don't want you pawing through my things."

"We have a warrant to search, and that warrant will be executed. It's your right to be present during the search, and to have legal counsel or representation present."

"You're a stone bitch. I *loved* him. He was my family. We—Jesus God—we're having his memorial service this afternoon. His parents are coming. I've been dealing with all the details, and now you come at us with this? You think I can just leave and go watch you get your rocks off poking into my private space?"

"Your presence is a right, not an obligation."

"What's going on?" Var rushed in with Benny right behind him. "Cilly, we could hear you on Mars. What's going on?"

"Contact Felicity. We need to contact her right now. This excuse for a cop thinks we killed Bart."

"What? Come on. No, she doesn't."

Var reached her first, squeezed her arm. Once again, Benny followed. They flanked her. The three points of the triangle, Eve thought.

"What's going on, Lieutenant?" Var asked.

"She's going to search our apartments. This morning."

"What for?" Benny stared at Eve as his arm went around Cill's shaking shoulders.

"Is that legal?" Var looked from Eve to Peabody and back again. "I mean, don't you have to ask or get a warrant? Something?"

"We have warrants. As a courtesy, I'm notifying you that these searches will take place this morning. None of you is being accused. We're simply pursuing all avenues in the investigation."

"You could've just asked." Benny drew Cill closer, angled his long, skinny frame toward her. "We'd tell you anything you want to know. We have. It's not right what you're doing. It's not right that you'd upset Cill like this, today of all days."

"It's Bart's memorial." Var pressed his lips together. "Couldn't you just wait, one day? One day. His parents will be here. If they hear about this it's only going to make it harder on them. God, isn't it hard enough?" He turned away, stepped over to brace his hands on the counter. "We're trying to do what's right for Bart. What he'd want."

"Yeah," Eve said, "me, too."

"He wouldn't want you upsetting Cill," Benny cut in. "He wouldn't want you making us feel like suspects."

"I'm not responsible for how you feel," Eve said, deliberately harsh.

"I'm responsible for the investigation. It's within your rights to be present during the search, and to have a legal representative present."

"I want Felicity," Cill insisted.

"I'll take care of it. I will," Benny told her. "Don't worry. We can't all go, all be there." He glanced over to Var. "We can't all leave, especially today. You can go, Cill, if you'd feel better."

"I can't. I still have things to do for the memorial. I haven't put it all together yet."

"I can take care of that."

"No." She tipped her head to Benny's chest briefly. "I need to stay and finish it."

"You go, Benny." Var turned back, sighed. "One of us should. Cill and I can handle things here. It's just what they do, the police, I guess. Just what they have to do."

"So, what, it's not *personal?*" Cill snapped, then immediately closed her eyes. "Sorry. I'm sorry, Var."

"It's okay." Weariness more than anger reflected on his pleasant face. "We're all upset. Let's just get it over with. Benny, maybe you could check at each of our places."

"I can do that. I can do that, sure. I'll go to your place first," he told Cill. "I'll be there when they start. Don't worry about it."

"My place is a mess."

He smiled at her. "What else is new?"

"It doesn't matter, does it?" She reached out, took Var's hand so they were once again united.

"It's just what they have to do," Var said. "But I'll get in touch with Felicity. You're right, Cill, she should know."

"Okay, that's the plan." Cill lifted her chin. "If that's all, Lieutenant, we'd like you to go. We don't want you here."

"Your attorney can contact me directly if she wants to see a copy of the warrants." She started out, giving a quick shake of her head in case Peabody spoke before they were clear of the building.

"Impressions?" Eve asked when they were in the vehicle.

"Well, Cill's got a temper. A lot of heat there."

"Passionate, territorial."

"Yeah. Benny's protective. He was pissed, too, but he pulled it back, tried to smooth it over with Cill."

"He's stuck on her."

"Oh yeah, he is." Peabody nodded. "Which makes him—since there's no sign there's anything going on there—controlled, maybe repressed. Var seemed rocked back on his heels initially, but he recovered. Pretty seriously pissed, too. He had to take a minute to pull himself together. Insulted. They all were. A lot of people react that way to search warrants. Each of them took a role. Nobody stepped forward and said okay, you do this, you do that, I'll take care of the other thing. Nobody's established a clear leadership role yet."

"It's subtle, but it's there." Eve shrugged. "Then again, maybe I'm looking for it, projecting it."

"Something else. Insulted and pissed, yeah, but none of them seemed especially worried about what we might find."

"Tracks covered. Detail-oriented. But people never cover their tracks as well as they think. We're not going to walk in and find the murder weapon in the closet, or an e-diary of the plot. But I think it's going to be interesting, whatever we do find. We'll start at Cill's."

She pulled up at the nondescript three-story building. "You know, they all live within easy walking distance of work and each other. Bart, he goes for a little jazz. Doorman, penthouse, multi-level. Not so fancy inside, but the foundation is. Cill goes for the loft. A little more bohemian. Not as many people living inside the building."

"Good building security though," Peabody pointed out.

"Yeah. I bet she had a hand in that. Who's on this one?"

"I put Jenkinson and Reineke—they're pretty clear after closing a case this morning. I've got McNab with them. I'll check on their ETA."

"Do that," Eve said as her own 'link signaled. She lifted her brows as she scanned the readout. "That was quick," she commented. "It's the lawyer. Dallas," she said.

She did the dance, then signaled for Peabody to go ahead inside when the team arrived. Before she'd finished with the lawyer, Benny came down the sidewalk at a steady jog.

Changed his shoes, she noted. He'd been wearing dress shoes with his memorial suit, as had his partners. Now he bolted up the short steps to the entrance in black-and-white running shoes that showed some wear.

She slid her 'link back in her pocket as he keyed himself in.

He'd never even noticed her, she mused. Too focused on the mission at hand.

She went in, and up an elevator designed to resemble an old cage type. But its guts were fully 2060. She ordered Cill's third-floor loft, and obeyed the computer's request for her name, her business, then a badge scan.

The team had already begun their work when she stepped into a wide and open living area. Benny stood, hands in his pockets. Fists, she corrected. Seriously pissed.

"She's very private with outsiders," he said to Eve. "This has really spun her out. She's already down, and now this."

"We all do what we have to do. A lot of space," she added, glancing around at the bright, cheerful colors, the framed comp art, the triple screens, the cushy chairs.

"So what? It's not a crime to like space."

"Never said it was. You'll want to chill, Benny. It's going to be a long day."

She wandered through, glanced at the kitchen, which appeared to actually be used to cook. A few dishes scattered the counter, the sink.

Eve opened the fridge, noted some brews, some soft drinks—heavy on the power type—water, milk that had expired the day before, some sort of lettuce that seemed to be wilting.

Hasn't been shopping for a while, she thought.

"Do you expect to find a clue in the damn fridge?" Benny demanded.

Eve closed it, turned so they were face-to-face. She read passion on his, as bold and bright as his red dreads. "This is going to be harder on you if you try to pick a fight with me. I don't mind a fight, but you're going to end up losing, and potentially being hauled down to Central for interfering with a legal search."

She left him stewing to walk through the loft. Lots of space, she thought again, lots of comfort. No frills, but still subtly female. Plenty of toys, game systems.

At first glance the office appeared to belong to a disorganized teenager, but Eve saw the method under the clutter. She'd bet a month's pay Cill could put her hands on exactly what she wanted. On the far side of the office from the workstation was a screen and several game systems.

She could work on something, then try it out right here. Do her testing, her tweaking.

No guest room, she noted. Not much on company.

In the single bedroom, the sheets on the unmade bed were a tangle, projecting restless nights.

"She just bought the suit and shoes she had on." Peabody turned from the closet. "The bags are in here, with the receipt. Just yesterday. It's kind of sad. She doesn't have another black suit, or much black at all in here. So I guess she felt she needed to get something appropriate."

"Good-sized closet for a woman who didn't own a black suit until yesterday."

"A lot of costumes—con-wear—and work clothes if you're in e. Couple of formal things, a couple cocktail type things. But mostly it's work and play."

With a nod, Eve slid open a bedside drawer. She found what she thought of as basic female self-serve sex tools, a scatter of unused memo cubes, and an e-diary.

"She kept a journal."

"That's private." Benny stood in the doorway, fury vibrating off his skin. "If she wrote something in there, it's private."

"There's nothing private now. I don't care about her personal thoughts, unless they pertain to the investigation. And you're making me think I might find something here that does."

"That's off. That's so off. You don't know her. She's never hurt anyone in her life."

"Then she doesn't have to worry. Detective, log this in, and see that it's transported with the other electronics to Central."

"Yes, sir." Peabody took the diary, slipped out.

"You want to take me on, Benny?" Eve said quietly. "You've got the training, so it might be an interesting fight. Before you're charged with assaulting a police officer, with obstruction of justice, with interfering with a legal search. Do you want to spend Bart's memorial in a cage?"

"I'm never going to forget this. Never." He spun around, walked away.

"Bet you won't," Eve murmured.

She left the bedroom, crossed the length of the loft to Cill's holo-room. To satisfy herself, she tried the log. Was denied.

She went in search of McNab. "I want the data from the holo-log as soon as you can get it. I want to know when she last used it, and what she used it for."

"No problem. This place." He let out a low whistle. "These people know how to live."

"Yeah. Until they don't. Peabody," she called out. "With me."

She opted to walk, and though Benny's building was only a half a block away, chose to cover the three blocks to Var's.

"Who's on this one?"

"I put Carmichael, Foster, Callendar on this one. It's supposed to storm tonight. Do you think it's going to storm?"

"How do I know? Do I look like a forecaster?"

"I've got these great shoes to wear to Nadine's party, but if it rains and we get stuck getting a cab or have to walk to the subway, they'll get screwed." Peabody searched the sky for answers. "If it storms I need to wear these pretty mag boots, but they're not new. Plus the shoes are so totally uptown."

"Peabody? Your footwear is of absolutely no interest to me, and at the moment the source of mild annoyance."

"Since it's only mild, let me continue. I sprang for a new outfit, too. It seemed like a good excuse for one. Nadine's book, fancy deal. And the Icove case was ours. I'm in the book and all that. I want to look complete. What are you wearing?"

"I don't know. I don't care."

"You *have* to." To bring the point home, Peabody stabbed Eve's arm with her finger. "You're like the star of the book."

"I am *not* the star of the book." The idea was horrifying. "The case is the star of the book."

"Who was in charge of the case?"

"I'm going to show you my current footwear, Peabody, up close when my boot connects with your nose."

"It's usually my ass, so that's a nice change." She stopped, tipped down her shaded glasses to study Var's building. "Post-Urban. One of those temps that became permanent. It's in good shape, though. Good security again. He's on the top two floors, roof access. I bet it's a nice view from up on the roof."

Inside, they rode up to ten.

"I bet you guys are taking a limo tonight," Peabody said with some envy.

"I don't know. I don't care."

"Easy not to care when you have a limo just by snapping your fingers."

Eve sighed. She supposed it was. "Look, if I get you and McNab a limo will you stop whining, and say nothing more about your damn shoes or anything else about the damn party?"

Peabody let out a very uncoplike squeal and grabbed Eve in a hug before Eve could evade it. "Yes! Yes! Wow. Thanks, Dallas. Serious thanks. I can wear my new . . . I can stop having any concerns about the weather."

Eve shoved her back, struggled to realign her dignity as they stepped out.

Var didn't command the entire floor, but took the west side of it.

He went for more muted tones, she concluded. More masculine, and a style she found more restful than that of his other two partners. In furniture, he'd gone sleek leaning toward avant-garde, curved shapes, sharp angles.

Order, she mused, a certain style and clean to the point of shining. Unlike Cill he avoided clutter, but he shared her predilection for mega-e in comps, systems, screens, toys. A display held a collection of weapons—props, she noted, toys again. No reals.

She studied the contents of his fridge—all liquids. Wines, beers, soft and power drinks. He relied on the AutoChef for food and had that well-stocked. Like Bart's, she mused, heavy on the pizza, burgers, tacos, sweets. Steaks, she noted, potato sides, big on fried.

Guy food.

"His place is neater than hers," Peabody observed. "Seems more organized, and more stylish."

"She has her own organizational style, but yes, tidier."

She moved onto his office, where Callendar was already at work on the comps. She said, "Yo."

"Nice setup."

"Nice? Baby, it's rocket. Like total command center. From the main comp, he can control all the systems, the screens, even the ones in other rooms. He can multitask, no problem, but he adds to those capabilities with the aux. Workstation's equipped with built-in smart screen. Oh, he gets hungry? He can command the AutoChef here or in any of the rooms. Have one of the droids serve it up."

"How many droids?"

"He's got three, no human replicas, straight mechanical. I haven't gotten there yet, but my guess is cleaning, serving, security, that kind of deal."

"Get me everything there is to get."

Callendar wiggled her shoulders. "Good thing I'd be happy staying here all day."

Eve stepped out.

"You can see why they're friends." Peabody gestured toward the bedroom closet. "Lots of costumes, lots of work gear. He's got better clothes than the woman, but basically it's the same deal. And like hers, and the vic's for that matter, this room like the rest of them is set up for lots of play. Not bedroom type play, game play. Not bedroom game play, but—"

"I get it, Peabody."

The bed, a roomy platform with a padded headboard, was neatly made with a good all-weather duvet and a few plumped pillows.

"No sex toys," she announced. "Memo cubes, unused, a couple of handheld games, over-the-counter sleep aid."

"Bathroom kicks ass," Peabody called out. "Bubble tub, multi-jet steam shower, sauna deck, music, screen and VR systems built in, drying tube, the works."

"Check for meds and illegals."

She toured the rest, the second bedroom outfitted for games, a small, well-outfitted home gym, and as she'd expected, a holo-room.

She gave Callendar the same instructions as she had McNab, called Peabody, then headed out to check the last space.

"Baxter, Trueheart, and Feeney," Peabody told her before she asked. "Feeney wanted in."

"He just wants to play with the toys. Impressions so far?"

"They live and work as they please, and they live their work. She's busy, likes to have several things going at once, so she's got clutter because she doesn't necessarily finish one thing before going to the next. She does a little cooking and since she doesn't have to, she must like it. No droids, which is kind of odd given what she does. I think it's that privacy issue. When she's in her personal space, she wants to be alone. He's more streamlined, and pays more attention to style. The second bedroom's set up for gaming, but he's got a convertible sleep chair in there, just in case."

"Okay. There's our shadow." Eve jutted her chin.

Across the street, Benny stood on the steps of his building, watching them come. As they approached, he jammed his hands in his pockets, hunched his shoulders, then walked quickly in the direction of Var's apartment.

"He's mad, but he's sad, too. At least I think so," Peabody added.

"You can kill and be both."

Benny had gone for a loft, too, with a space that occupied the rear of the building, on two levels.

Peabody gaped as they entered. "Wow. It's Commander Black's quarters."

"Who the hell is that?"

"Commander Black. *Star Quest*. This is a reproduction of his living quarters aboard the *Intrepid*." Peabody ran her hand over the scrolled arm of a brown sofa. "It's even got the burn marks from when Black had the blaster fight with Voltar. And look! That's the old desk that was his great-grandfather's, the first commander of the *Intrepid*."

"He lives in a vid set?"

"Vid and game. And it's a really frosty set. It's got every detail. Plus some that aren't." She gestured to a pair of worn white socks, an open bag of soy chips, two empty brew bottles. "Still, tidier than the woman."

Eve repeated the routine, going room by room, absorbing.

Yes, she thought, she could see why they were friends. Though individual preferences came through, the overall focused on the same. Fun, games, and fantasy.

Like Bart, he kept a replica droid. Male, she noted.

"Name's Alfred," Feeney told her. "Butler to Bruce Wayne, confidant of the Dark Knight."

She spun around. "What? The Dark Knight."

"Batman, kid. Even you've heard of Batman."

"Yeah, yeah, vigilante with psychotic tendencies who dresses up in a weird bat costume. Rich playboy by day, right?" She turned, frowned at the droid. "Hmm."

"The Dark Knight's an icon." Feeney's jabbed finger matched his tone. Insult. "And he uses those so-called psycho tendencies for good. Anyway, old Alfred here's been shut down the last couple days. His basic programming is to clean the place, serve meals, greet guests. I'll fine-tooth his memory board, but at a quick once-over, I don't see anything hinky."

Eve opened the fridge. "He's out of beer."

"You thirsty?"

"He's been drinking. Sitting out there in his fantasy commander's quarters drinking his brews."

"Wouldn't mind doing the same myself. He was just here."

"Yeah, I saw him leave."

"He tried to slip something out."

"What?"

"A photograph. Had it in the bedroom, drawer by the bed. Trueheart caught it. The boy's got it. He's upstairs."

She went up to where Trueheart continued to work on the master bedroom. The bed was made—halfheartedly. Two more empty bottles stood empty on the nightstand.

"Lieutenant." In his uniform, the young, studly, and shy Trueheart looked fresh as spring grass in the crowded, cluttered room.

Eve glanced toward a large object draped in a colorful throw.

"It's Mongo," Trueheart told her. "A parrot. The subject covered his cage so he wouldn't get too excited."

Curious, Eve crossed over, lifted the throw. Inside, an enormous bird with wild feathers cocked his head and eyed her.

"Hi! How you doing? Want to play? Let me out of here. Want to play?"

"Jesus," Eve muttered.

"Ben-nee!" Mongo called.

Eve dropped the throw.

"Dammit," Mongo said clearly and with what sounded like true bitterness.

She turned away to see Trueheart grinning. "He was doing a lot of that when I came up. It's pretty chill. He even asked me my name. Benny said he's about thirty-five years old, and . . ." Trueheart paused, cleared his throat. "I agreed it was best to cover the cage so as not to excite the bird or distract from the search. The subject requested I un-cover it when we're done, as the bird enjoys the light. Sir."

"Right. Where's the photo he tried to get by you?"

"Here, sir." Trueheart opened the drawer, removed it. "I checked it. It's just a standard digital, standard frame. He was more embarrassed than mad when I caught him."

Cill looked out, half profile, face bright with laughter.

There were other photos around the room, around the loft, as in his office at U-Play. But those captured the group, or various parts of it. This was only Cill, and obviously his private memory, or fantasy.

"Do you want me to take it in, sir?"

"No." She handed it back. "Leave it."

She finished her tour, filed her impressions.

Unlike Cill, Benny wasn't a loner. He kept a replica droid, and a pet. A talking pet. Things for company and conversation. Not as tidy as either Var or Bart. A brooder, she concluded, thinking of the empty beer bottles.

Before she left, she walked to the window. From the angle she could see Cill's building, pick out her windows.

What was it like? she wondered. And what did it do to a man who could stand here and look out and see the woman he loved, night after night?

Both sad and mad, Peabody had said, and Eve thought, yes, that was just about right.

16 EVE SPLIT OFF FROM PEABODY, SENDING HER partner back to Cill's to work with the search team while she divided her time between the other two apartments.

The problem was, as she saw it, what they looked for and hoped to find would be buried in electronics. It put her at a disadvantage.

"There's something to find," Feeney told her, "we'll find it sooner or later."

"It's the later that sticks in me."

"You're not showing much faith in me and my boys."

"Feeney, I'm putting all my faith in you and your boys." Hands on her hips, she did a circle around Benny's home office. "These three live and breathe e-air. When it comes to outside interests they still wind back to it. And according to Roarke, they're exceptional."

"They ain't hacks."

She pointed a finger. "Why not? It's tempting, isn't it, almost irresistible *to* hack when you're just that good. It's another kind of game. You're not going to tell me you've never poked your finger in that pie."

He smiled. "I'm a duly authorized officer of the NYPSD. Hacking's a crime. Hypothetically, theoretically, and saying you ever say I did you're a lying SOS, it could be experimental-type hacking keeps the gears oiled."

"And a group of geeks, with exceptional skills, playing games all damn day and night, would likely experiment. If they, or one of them wanted to take it a little further—keep an eye on the innards of competitors say—unregistered equipment would be handy, and damn near essential."

"Adds a nice layer of control and security," he agreed. "It'll cost, but they could afford it. Hell, this lot could probably build their own with spare parts. Everything in this place, and everything at U-Play HQ is properly registered."

"Yeah, and I've been through each apartment twice now. If any of them have a hidden room it's in another dimension. Off-site maybe, but still in the area." Hands on hips, she turned another circle. "They keep everything close."

"If they, or one of them, has a hidey-hole for unregistered, that would be the place they'd do the hacking. Just follows."

"And where you'd work up the outline, the scenario for murder. Where you'd play the game."

Another angle, she thought, another line to tug. But first she drove back to U-Play and Bart Minnock's memorial.

Full house, she noted, and glanced at the screens where a montage of Bart's life played out. She heard his voice over the voices of those who'd come to pay respect, and to mourn. Media interviews, cons where he'd given seminars, holiday trips, parties. Moments, big and small, of his life, she thought, spliced together.

Food and flowers, as much staples of a memorial as the dead, spread out in careful and creative displays. Simple food, simple flowers, she noted, along with self-serve fizzy bars.

She heard as much laughter as tears as she wound her way through to offer condolences to her victim's parents.

"Mr. and Mrs. Minnock, I'm Lieutenant Dallas. I'm very sorry for your loss."

"Lieutenant Dallas." The woman who'd passed her eyes, the shape of her mouth, onto her son gripped Eve's hand. "Thank you for coming. Do you . . . this isn't the time to ask if . . ."

"Your son has all my attention, and the determination of the NYPSD to bring his killer to justice."

"His life was just beginning," Bart's father said.

"I've gotten to know him over the past couple of days. It seems to me he lived that life very well."

"Thank you for that. Thank you, Lieutenant."

She eased away, moving through the crowd, scanning faces, listening to bits of conversation. And searching for the partners.

She saw the Sing family, the two beautiful kids in dark suits she thought made them look eerily like mini-adults. Susan Sing had an arm around CeeCee's shoulders so the five of them formed their own intimate little unit. Connected, she thought, by Bart's life and by his death.

Eve started toward them when Cill spotted her. The outrage on her face held as much passion as a scream. Anticipating her, Eve crossed over, away from the main packs of people, forcing Cill to change direction to come after her.

"You're not welcome here. Do you think you can come here now, *now*, when we're remembering Bart? Do you think you can just grab some pizza bites and a fizzy and spy on us *now*?"

"You don't want to cause a scene here, Cill. You don't want to do this here."

"This is our place. This was Bart's place, and you—"

"Cill." Roarke laid a hand on her shoulder. "Your anger's misplaced."

"Don't tell me about my anger." She shrugged his hand away. "Bart's dead. He's dead, and she's trying to make it seem like we killed him. What kind of person does that? For all I know she's decided this is an opportunity, and she's passing our data onto you."

"Be careful," Eve said softly. "Be very careful."

Cill jutted up her chin, and her eyes sparked challenge. "What are you going to do? Arrest me?"

"Come, walk outside with me," Roarke told her. "Just you and I, and you can say whatever you need to say. But away from here. You'll upset Bart's parents if this keeps up."

"Fine. I've got plenty to say."

As Roarke took her out, Eve gave them a moment. It was just enough time for Benny to elbow his way through the crowd.

"What's going on? What did you say to her?"

"Very little. She needs to blow off some steam. It'll be better blown outside where it doesn't upset anyone else."

"God." He scrubbed his hands over his face, then watched, as Eve did as Cill paced and pointed, threw up her hands. And Roarke stood, listening. "She's better off mad," Benny said at length. "I'd rather see her pissed off at you, at everything, then so damn sad."

"Does she know you're in love with her?"

"We're friends." His shoulders stiffened.

"It would be hard working with someone every day, as closely as you work together, and having those feelings. It's a lot to hold in."

"We're friends," he repeated. "And that's my personal business."

"Lieutenant Dallas." Tight-lipped, Var strode up. "This isn't right.

You can't come here now and interrogate us, anyone. This is for Bart. His parents deserve . . . What's Cill doing out there with Roarke?"

"Blowing off some," Benny said. "No, come on." He took Var's arm as Var turned toward the door. "Let her work it out. Let's not do this today, okay? Let's just not do this today."

"You're right. Okay, you're right." Var closed his eyes, dragged both hands through his skullcap of hair. "Look, can't you leave us alone today?" he asked Eve. "Just leave us alone while we get through this. It's not like we're going anywhere."

"I'm not here to hassle you. I came to pay my respects to Bart's parents as I was the one who had to tell them he was dead."

"Oh hell." Benny let out a long breath. "Sorry. I guess . . . sorry."

"We're the ones who have to be here for them now, and for each other. We get you're doing what you have to do. Well, Benny and I do," Var corrected with another glance through the glass. "It's going to take Cill a little longer. It's personal for her. It's routine for you, we get that."

"Murder's never routine." She glanced back at the screen, at Bart. "It's always personal. He's mine now, every bit as much as he's yours. Believe me when I say I'll find who killed him. Whatever it takes."

She walked away thinking she'd planted the seeds. Now she'd see how long it took them to sprout.

She went out to her car, leaned against it and watched Roarke and Cill. He was doing the talking now. Or most of it. Cill shook her head, turned away with her hands pulling at her hair until the tidy plait frayed.

But she was winding down, Eve judged, and within a few moments was weeping against Roarke's chest.

Eve waited them out, wished fleetingly for coffee as she started a search for property using the warehouse and the four apartments to triangulate. She glanced up as Roarke walked to her.

"So, how's your day so far?" she asked him.

"Up and down. You're still a bitch, by the way. But she's decided I'm not a heartless fuck using Bart's death for my own gain."

"Good thing I pride myself on my bitchery. I don't know how many things light her fuse, but once it's lit, it's short."

"Yes. I should tell you I felt obliged to let her know we had a project nearly ready for marketing that's similar to theirs."

"I bet she loved hearing that."

"I always considered you champion of creative swearing, but I believe she'd give you a run." Like Eve, he studied the building, the shapes and movements behind the glass. "When I managed to cut through some of the blue, I gave her some details. You wouldn't understand," he added. "It's technical."

"And I don't speak geek. Why? Why did you tell her?"

"When I was in, we'll say, the habit of stealing, I didn't mind being accused of it. My people have worked very hard on this project, and don't deserve to have that work diminished. She's a very bright woman, and with the details I gave her understands full well we're ahead of their curve, not only on timing, but on certain elements. That doesn't diminish their project, or their work. I have more resources, more people, and she understands that as well. Just as she understands if it had been my goal, I could've swallowed U-Play long ago."

"And she's smart enough to remember who Bart sometimes went to for advice, and who sold them that building."

"Competition makes the game more fun, and more meaningful. In a few years, they'll give me plenty of game." He reached up, skimmed a finger down the dent in her chin. "And how is your day panning out?"

"Searches are still ongoing. It's a lot. I'm going back to Central to tug a new line. As pissed as they all were about the search, none of them actively tried to stop or stall it."

"Which makes you think whoever killed Bart already removed anything incriminating."

"Or thinks so." Movements behind glass, she thought, weren't always the same as those in the shadows. "But it made me wonder if there's another work area, a more private one. One where someone could hack and practice and plot and plan without sending up any flags."

"A place for unregistered. I thought of that as well. Then again, some people are inherently honest."

"Present company excepted."

He smiled at her. "Murder's the ultimate in dishonesty, isn't it? So yes, there may very well be another place. Well, good hunting." He flicked her chin again, kissed her mouth. "I've work of my own. Don't forget Nadine's party," he added as he walked to his own car.

"I can remember more than one thing at a time."

He uncoded his locks, smiling at her over the roof. "What time does it start?"

"Tonight."

"Eight. I'll see you at home."

"Wait. Shit. I promised Peabody a limo if she'd stop talking about her shoes."

"Naturally. I'll take care of it."

"It's your own fault," she called out. "You make it too easy."

"Darling Eve, there's enough hard in the world."

She couldn't argue. She glanced back at the warehouse, thought of flowers and food and tears. There was plenty of hard in the world.

She was deep into the search for a second space, playing with alternate names, anagrams, hidden meanings while running her own scenarios on secondary when Peabody tagged her.

"We finished up here, and I've checked in with the other teams. Flagged electronics are on their way in for analysis."

"I want that diary."

"McNab's working on it. He's decided it's his personal mission to get past her journal security. We're going to head home from here, if that's okay. We're already cutting it a little close."

"Cutting what?"

"Prep time for Nadine's party. Oh, and thanks again for the limo!" Peabody added as Eve thought, *Shit, damn, fuck*. "Summerset contacted me with all the info. So, we'll see you at the do."

"Yeah, right." Eve cut Peabody off, saved all current data, ordered the whole works copied to her home office unit.

And fled.

She wasn't late, she told herself as she slammed the brakes in front of the house. She had plenty of time since she didn't take hours to primp in front of a damn mirror. Besides, nobody got to one of these deals on time.

Which made no sense to her. Why have a time, then ignore it?

Social functions were unwieldy and strange, and had their own set of rules that were even more unwieldy and strange.

She burst into the house, started to curl her lip at Summerset, then stopped and stared. He wore black—big surprise—but not his usual gear. He wore formal black, tuxedo black with a white shirt that looked as stiff as his neck.

"You might save the excuses for another time," he began. "You'll need all you have left to transform yourself."

"Why are you wearing that monkey suit?"

"It's a formal affair."

"You're going?"

He inclined his head. "Yes, and as I'll be on time, I'll explain to your friend why you are, as usual, late. They're waiting for you."

"I'm going. I'm going." She dashed to the steps. "They?" she repeated, but Summerset had dematerialized.

"He can't be human," she muttered, and hurried up to the bedroom.

"I'm not late because everybody goes late, which is only another reason why—" She broke off in sheer horror. "What's she doing here?"

Trina, all slitty eyes and exploding red hair, lifted what sure as hell looked like a glass of champagne. She sipped, long and slow.

"If you think you're going to this shindig wearing that hair, somebody must've stunned you with your own weapon. We're set up in that palace you guys call a bathroom."

"I don't have time. We're going to be late."

Trina's smile sent a fast chill down Eve's spine. "Everybody goes late," she said, echoing Eve's initial excuse. "It'll take me about twenty minutes, because I'm a frigging genius." She pointed a silver-tipped finger before Eve could speak. "I've got a rep. I've got a salon. I do Nadine's hair for *Now*—and I finished her about an hour ago. Most who know anything know I have your hair."

"I have my hair." Eve tugged it. "It's attached to my head."

"You skated out before I could take care of it at Louise's deal—murder and all that," she added. "And it looks like somebody hacked it with an ice pick. Are you going to this mag deal with that hunk of superior man-flesh looking like you've been in a fight with a farm animal?"

"I thought it was an ice pick."

"A farm animal with an ice pick. Do you look better when I've worked you or not?"

Eve opened her mouth, tracked her gaze over to Roarke. Let it burn there.

"I have nothing to say, whatsoever."

"Superior man-flesh with a brain," Trina said approvingly. "You hit the jackpot squared, Dallas. Now get your skinny ass in that bathroom."

Trina flounced, on five-inch heels shaped like the heart Eve wasn't certain she had, into the bathroom.

"Traitor." The word was low, vibrating with dark.

"Completely out of my hands. You can turn your knife in Summerset, as you're wont to do in any case. He let her in."

"Dallas! You don't want me to come out there."

Eve's shoulders hunched. "I'll deal with you later," she promised and marched in to face the music. "Just make it fast," she told Trina. "And don't—"

"Do I tell you how to track down killers?"

"Crap." Eve dropped into the portable salon chair Trina couldn't have gotten up there by herself. One of them had helped her, Eve thought. And they would pay.

"It's a big night," Trina began as she swirled a protective cape over Eve. "Nadine looks abso fab, thanks to me. And so will you." She pulled a lock of Eve's hair between her fingers. "Nice and clean. Good."

She pulled it back, secured it, then lowered the chair to half recline.

"Wait a minute," Eve said as Trina pumped some foam from bottle to palm. "You said hair."

"Your hair's attached to your head, remember? Your face is part of your head. You're getting a lightning facial. That's all we have time for."

"What's wrong with my face?"

"You've got a good one, and we're going to keep it that way. Give it up, close your eyes and it'll go faster."

Stuck, Eve closed her eyes. She'd never be able to explain, she supposed, how weird and creepy it was to have somebody rubbing and stroking her face—unless it was Roarke. And he didn't put goop all over her while he was doing it.

"Wait till you see Mavis. Leonardo designed a killer outfit for her. I did them this afternoon, and got to play with Bella. She's the baby girl of all baby girls. Almost makes me want one. Mavis is going to help Peabody with her 'do since I'm up here."

Eve let the words slide in and out of her brain while she tried not to think about what gunk and goo was going on her face and hair.

The chair vibrated lightly under her, massaging muscles she hadn't realized were so tight, so tired. She didn't realize she'd dozed off until Trina brought the chair upright again.

The snipping and tugging and combing, and gunking began. It didn't seem to take long, but she couldn't check because her wrist unit was under the cape, and she was afraid to move while Trina's sharp tool clicked around her.

Trina stepped back, took the last sip of champagne. "Okay. Totally ult, low on the flash, up on the class." She put away her tools, then swirled the cape off. "Up, up. I've got to rock."

She set her cases on the seat of the chair Eve vacated. "See you there," she said, and rolled the chair away.

Cautious, Eve turned to the mirror.

Her hair lay sleek against her head instead of tousled, and whatever Trina had plastered on it to get it sleek brought out the lighter shades so it looked just a little streaky. She ran a hand over it, relieved when it felt like her regular hair.

Her eyes looked bigger—but that was all the crap Trina had smudged on. Her cheekbones looked a little sharper, her lips more defined.

"Still you under there," she murmured. "It's just a kind of illusion. Or . . . a costume."

"I trust she didn't knock you unconscious to . . ." Roarke paused in the doorway, then stepped in for a closer study. "She is very good at her work. It's a different look for you, but lovely and a bit elegant. Very suitable for the occasion. Here, I thought you'd need this after your ordeal."

He handed her a glass of champagne.

"I guess I'm now worthy of superior man-flesh."

"I feel so objectified," he said as she took the first sip.

"You ate it up with a spoon." She took another sip, and a long look when he laughed. "But you do look pretty superior. And since you're already dressed I'd better get my skinny ass moving."

"I adore your skinny ass." He gestured toward the bed when they went out. "If you don't care for the dress we'll find another."

She would have called it yellow, but it wasn't accurate. It was deeper, richer than yellow. Not brown, not that deep, but something that blended both into the tawny. It had light, she mused. Not sparkle or shine, just light. No fuss, no flounce—to her relief—just a column as sleek as her hair, and at a touch of her finger, as fluid as water.

"I'd be stupid not to care for it. I'm not stupid. And I'm also smart enough to know I'm lucky you think about things like this so I don't have to."

"I enjoy it; you don't. Leonardo does exceptional work, and he knows your body, your style, and your preferences."

She couldn't argue with that, especially after she'd put it on. The material simply slid down, light as air, leaving her shoulders bare and giving her breasts a bit more of a boost than she thought they deserved.

But the hidden pockets in the side seams distracted and pleased her. She could easily tuck her clutch piece in one, her badge in the other.

What else did a woman need?

"You'll want these." Roarke handed her earrings—canary diamonds in long teardrops—and a cuff that married yellow diamonds with white. She added the necklace herself, the Giant's Tear diamond he'd given her the day he'd told her he loved her.

"You're beautiful."

Sparkly, she thought, shimmery, and a little sleek. A costume, she thought again. Everyone wore them.

"It's hard not to look good with all this. What color is this thing?" She brushed a hand down the dress. "I can't figure it."

"It should be easy for you, as you look at it every day." He stepped behind her, laid his hands on her shoulders. "It's your eyes." He laid his cheek against hers for a moment while she frowned. "We'd better be off or we'll be more than fashionably late."

"Why is late fashionable?"

"I suppose because it gives the impression you have so many things to do you couldn't possibly be on time."

"Hah. Who knew? I'm almost always fashionable." She held out her hand. "Come on, man-flesh. We've got to rock."

Music rang from the rooftop and into the deepening skies. People glittered and gleamed and glided, bussing each other's cheeks, chattering happily over bubbling wine. Candles, already lighted, flickered. The wind was picking up, Eve noted.

They were likely to get that storm before it was done.

"They're going to want to close the dome before long," Eve said to Roarke.

"We might as well enjoy the night air while we can. You'll want to congratulate Nadine."

"She's surrounded." And Trina had been right. Nadine looked abso fab in siren red, her hair artfully tumbled and scattered with sparkling pins that caught the last light of the sun. "I'll wait until she's got some breathing room."

"You're here!" Peabody, her hand caught in McNab's, hurried over on the famous shoes. They were silver, opened at the toe to show off pale pink toenails, strapped multiple times at the ankles, and as sparkly as Nadine's pins.

"Isn't this mag? Total. Everybody's here, and Nadine's so happy. The music's completely hot, and Mavis said she's agreed to do a number later. Gosh," she said after she'd taken a moment to breathe. "You guys look beautiful. Seriously."

"You couldn't look lovelier." Roarke took Peabody's hand and kissed it. "You're a lucky man, Ian."

McNab grinned. "Damn right, and if things go my way I'll get luckier later."

Peabody giggled and elbowed him.

Eve heard the squeal and turned. No one squealed like Mavis Freestone squealed. Her hair, summer blond and cotton-candy pink, bounced down her back as she bulleted—on the towering toothpicks held on her feet by two skinny crisscrossing straps—toward Eve. Her pink gown, caught at the hip with an enormous jeweled pin, flowed and flared with a slit that showed her pretty leg right up to the hip.

"I knew that dress would be Triple T on you!" She danced into Eve's arms, then back again. "This is the juiciest party, and look at us! We're the juice. Moonpie! Come see what your dress does for Dallas."

Moonpie—or Leonardo—walked over in his version of a tux. The long, smoked silver coat suited his coppery skin and his considerable size. That same silver wound here and there through the rich copper curls that fell around his wide, fascinating face.

"It's what Dallas does for the dress. I hope you like it."

"It's terrific. Thanks for the pockets."

He smiled at her, kissed her cheek. "I thought you'd like having them. Let me get you all a drink."

"I'll help you with that," Roarke said, and after another Peabody elbow poke, McNab went with them.

"Hey, there's Trina. Be right back," Peabody said. "I need to ask her a hair question."

"You sicced Trina on me, didn't you?"

Mavis rounded midnight blue eyes in innocence. "Don't you have to read me my rights before you question me?"

"Another smartass. Speaking of reading you your rights, we go back."

"Yeah, to when you first arrested me on the grift. Now look at me. I'm a married woman and a mommy, and I've got a career. I didn't have to steal any of it. Life's twisty keen."

"At least. I've been friends with you longer than I've been friends with anyone."

"Double back at you."

"So, we're tight, and we know each other about as well as people ever do. You could say we love each other, in a nonlesbian lifestyle way."

"We might've done the les, if we'd gone a really long time without men. If we, like, washed up on a deserted island for months, or—"

"Yeah, yeah, you'd be the first I'd jump," Eve said and made Mavis snicker. "But what I'm wondering is, what would it take, what would I have to do to make you want to kill me. Literally kill, not think 'I could kill Dallas for that.'"

"Oh, easy. If you did the steamy pretzel with my honey bear, I'd stick the first sharp implement I could find in your heart, and in his balls. I'd probably be sorry after, but too late."

"That's it? Sex with Leonardo is the only reason you'd want me dead? Think about it," Eve insisted. "What if I stole from you, or insulted you, made fun of you on a regular basis."

"Okay." Mavis tipped her head side-to-side in thinking mode. "If you stole from me you'd need whatever you took really bad. If you insulted me you'd piss me off and I'd insult you back. If you made fun of me you'd hurt my feelings and I'd tell you to knock it off."

"So the only reason you'd stick a knife in me—"

"Or a really sharp nail file. Maybe a kebab skewer. That would be, like, inventive. See, you were doing the steamy with my cuddle-up in the kitchen, so I just grabbed what was there. Murder by kebab skewer, and I'd get off on the temporary whacked."

Fixing rage on her face, Mavis demonstrated by pumping a fist toward Eve's heart.

"It's a good one. Anyway, the only reason you'd plunge that kebab skewer in me is the blind passion of the moment?"

"Yeah, so remember that if you ever get ideas about my baby doll, 'cause I'd kebab your ass."

"So warned."

Mavis grinned her sparkling grin. "Speaking of babies. You've got to see this mini vid of Bellamia." Mavis opened a tiny bag the same pink as her hair and the shape of a tulip.

Eve laid a hand on hers. "You wouldn't do it even then. You might want to, even think it, and you'd hate me, but you wouldn't kill me."

"I'd *really* want to, but no. But you'd never go after my man because you'd never hurt me that way, ever, much less cheat on Roarke. Real friends, real lovers don't do that shit to each other. Not the reals."

"Exactly. You're exactly right. Okay. Let's see the vid."

 **EVE DIDN'T KNOW IF BELLA WAS THE BABY GIRL** of all baby girls as she didn't have much experience with babies of either variety. But the kid was ridiculously pretty, especially if you overlooked the drool.

Still, she was happy to be spared watching Bella clap her hands, blow kisses, and babble a second time as the men came back with drinks. She cornered McNab while Roarke was treated to Bella's goos and giggles and baby-spit kisses.

"What's the status on the journal?"

"She's tricky. I got through the first level, but she put another layer on. Paranoid—and really good."

"I could probably get a court order for her to open it."

"And suck out my fun? Give me a couple more hours."

"If you don't have it by eleven hundred, I'm going to see what Reo can do. A woman who lives alone in a secured apartment who keeps a journal with that kind of protection has something to hide."

"Everything in her place is locked down double, even her house 'link. Again, can you say paranoid? Callendar and Feeney said the other two were overcovered, but this one? It's like Global Security."

"We'll brief at eleven hundred," Eve decided. "That gives you and the rest of EDD time to comb through what we have while Peabody and I go over what the rest of the team brought in."

"Then we'd better party now, because we're going to kick it early tomorrow. There's Baxter. Looking tight."

"Baxter?" Glancing around, she spotted Baxter and a scatter of other cop faces. "What, did Nadine invite the entire NYPSD?"

"Looks like it. I spotted Tibble over at the bar. I guess you got to do the invite to the commissioner. He looked like he was in a good mood."

"Let's close this case and keep him that way."

"Cop talk? This is a party." Nadine hooked arms around McNab's and Eve's waists. "With all my favorite people."

"From the looks of it," Eve observed, "you have a lot of favorites. And a good chunk of them are cops."

"You work the crime beat, you make friends with cops—or you don't work it long."

"It's a total bash," McNab told her. "The music slays. I'm going to get Peabody out there and show them how it's done. Cha."

"He's a cutie." Nadine beamed after McNab. "It's the first time I've ever seen a man in an orange tux."

"It's the glow-in-the-dark bow tie that makes it."

"It does add a flare. Well, look at him go!" Nadine added with a laugh. "He's got some moves. They look so happy." She sighed. "I'm so happy. All those nerves are gone now. I guess it takes a party, and a few hundred of my closest friends, to flip them over to happy."

"Congratulations." Roarke stepped over, gave Nadine a kiss. "It's a wonderful party, and the centerpiece is stunning."

"Thank you. Both of you. I'm just so . . ."

"Happy," Eve finished. "She's very happy."

"Perilously close to giddy." After lifting her glass in toast, Nadine drank deep. "And buckets of this adds to it. I need to steal Dallas for a minute." She laid a hand on Roarke's arm. "I won't keep her long."

"You're not going to introduce me to a bunch of people I have to make conversation with—because that's the problem with parties. You have to get dressed up then talk to a bunch of people you'll probably never see again and you don't care about their opinions or life stories anyway."

"You're such a social butterfly, Dallas. I don't know how you get any work done." Nadine kept a hand on Eve's arm, steering her through.

Like a dance, Eve thought. Not like whatever Peabody and McNab were doing, which looked more like sexual calisthenics, but a kind of gliding ballet. A pause here for a word, a gesture there to acknowledge someone, a turn, a laugh, all while moving without any visible hurry.

They passed an enormous display of the cover of the book. On a background of icy blue, interlocking faces stared out. The same face over and over—female and striking, with a small, secret smile.

They shimmered against the ice, while those eyes seemed to glow with some inner life.

"It's creepy, and compelling," Eve decided.

"Exactly."

"You didn't use Avril, or any of the others we identified as clones."

"No. It didn't seem fair. Some of them were still children. They deserve a chance at some sort of normal life. Or at least a private one. You let Diana, the one from the school, go."

"She escaped during the confusion."

"That's the way I wrote it. But that's not what happened. I hope I would've done the same." She slid her hand down Eve's arm to link their fingers in a kind of silent solidarity. "In writing the book . . . I hope I would've done the human thing when given the choice. There's a room for me inside here," she continued, going through the glass doors. "For interviews, and in case I want to catch my breath."

She opened the door of a small lounge, filled with flowers. A bottle of champagne sat waiting in a silver bucket beside a tray of glossy fruit.

"Nice," Eve observed.

"Louise and Charles sent champagne, and flowers. And the publisher . . . They're treating me like a star. I hope I don't disappoint them."

"Knock it off."

Nadine waved a hand. "The book's good. Damn good—you're right about that. And I know what I'm doing when it comes to promotion. But you can never be sure what the public's going to like, or not. So, we'll see. Whatever, I accomplished something I'm proud of. So . . ."

Nadine walked over to a counter and picked up a copy of the book. "I want you to have this. You have an actual library, so I wanted you to have a print copy rather than the e."

"I'm pretty sick of all things e at the moment."

"I imagine you are. Anyway, seeing as Roarke has a liking for physical books, I thought I might find my way into your library."

"Guaranteed. Thanks. Really."

"You don't have to cart it around all night. I'll have it sent, but I wanted to give it to you personally."

Eve turned it over, studied the photo of Nadine in one of her sharp suits with the New York skyline behind her.

"Sexy and capable. It says 'I cover New York, and nothing gets by me.'"

Nadine laughed. "That was the general idea. There's another addition to the version you read." Nadine took the book back, opened it to the dedication page. "Here."

Eve read:

For Lieutenant Eve Dallas,

courageous, relentless, insightful,
who honors her badge every day as
she stands for the living and the dead.

"Well. Wow." Flustered, touched, and mildly embarrassed, Eve looked up at Nadine. "I'm . . . thanks. I'm just doing my job."

"Me, too. We're damn good at what we do, Dallas, you and me. And we're damn good not just because we have the chops, but because it matters. It matters to us, every day. What the Icoves did was obscene, and that story needs to be told. The book matters to me, and what's in it mattered to you. You risked your life for it."

"So did others. I didn't stop them alone."

"There's a lengthy acknowledgments page. Read it at your leisure," Nadine added with a smile. "Take the book, and the sentiment."

"I will. I do." Eve narrowed her eyes. "This isn't like a box of cookies, is it?"

On another laugh, Nadine fluttered her lashes. "A bribe? From me? What a thing to say. Here." She poured two glasses of champagne, passed one to Eve. "To two capable, sexy women who cover New York, and are damn good at what they do."

"I can get behind that."

They clinked glasses, sipped. "I'll have the book sent to you." Nadine set it back on the counter.

"Signed."

A new smile bloomed. "Yes, signed. And now we'd better get back out there. My assignment is to mingle, and yours is to have a good time, so I won't drag you around introducing you to a bunch of people."

"Now that's better than a box of cookies."

Lightning flashed, a lance of light across the sky as they stepped back onto the roof. Thunder chortled in its wake.

"Hell, we'll have to close the dome."

"Yeah." Eve looked up. "But it'll still be a hell of a show."

As the first bolt of lightning stuck, Cill let herself into her apartment. She almost hadn't come home. Knowing the police had been through her things, poked and turned over her personal possessions, invaded her private space had her dragging her feet every step.

Her mother and stepfather had done the same. Always looking for something that could incite a lecture, shame, blame, punishment. Nothing had ever been private, nothing had ever been *hers*, until she'd walked out of that house for the last time.

Now what was private, what was hers had been searched and studied, again.

But where else could she go but home? She couldn't make herself stay at the office either, not with all those flowers, all the faded echoes of the people who'd come for Bart.

He was too much there, she thought, and now, she felt exposed in her own home.

Maybe she'd move, she considered. Or just get the hell over it.

Var and Benny were right. It was routine, nothing personal. But it *was* personal to her—that was the problem.

They'd taken some of her things, she could see that immediately. Felicity had counseled them that the warrant allowed the police to confiscate and examine. But why did their rights have to smother hers? Wasn't there enough to be miserable about without adding this?

She wandered into the kitchen, finally settled on a power drink. She hadn't been able to eat at the memorial, and she couldn't find the desire or the energy to bother with food now.

She took the tube with her to the window to watch the dance of lightning. But she set it down again after the first sip. It was too cold. Everything seemed too cold.

She wanted heat and sun, not cold and rain. She wanted to sweat. A good fight, until she was exhausted enough to sleep without thinking about Bart, without imagining the strangers who'd walked through her bedroom, touching her things, judging them. Judging her.

In any case, she'd agreed to work on the program. She didn't know if the push was because she needed to be shaken out of her funk or if the game needed more tweaks. Either way, she'd do what she promised and accomplish both.

She drew the disc she'd logged out of U-Play from the right cup of her bra. Probably a silly and overly girly place to keep it, she thought, but she'd figured nobody could steal it unless they killed her first.

She kicked off the new shoes that hurt her feet, then walked barefoot to her holo-room.

She loved holo. She could go anywhere. She'd seen the world with holo—not to mention worlds that only existed there and in the imagination. Benny's research was so thorough. She'd wandered Piccadilly Circus, shivered by a loch in Scotland, explored the Amazon jungles.

She didn't need a crowded transport, the hassle of customs, the inconvenience of hotels where countless others had slept on the bed before you. She only needed holo.

Even as she slid the disc in, her mood lifted. She set the program, then took a long, calming breath.

The heat enveloped her, the heavy, wet heat of a tropical jungle. Instead of the black suit she never intended to wear again, she was clad in the thin, buff-colored cotton, the sturdy boots, the cocky, rolled brimmed hat of a treasure hunter.

She loved this game for the puzzle, the strategy, the twists and turns—and yes, especially now—for the upcoming battles—fists, weapons, and wits—with any who opposed her on her search for the Dragon's Egg.

She opted to start at the beginning of the first level, and her arrival at the ancient village of Mozana. It would take hours to run the entire game, but that was all good, she decided. She wanted nothing outside of this, wanted to think of nothing else, maybe forever.

She went through the steps and stages, the meets, the bartering, the purchase of supplies.

In one part of her mind she was Cill the treasure hunter—ruthless, brave, and cunning. In the other she remained Cill the programmer, observing the tiny details of the images, the movements, the audio, searching for any flaws.

She hiked through the heat, watched a snake coil itself on a limb and hiss. She waded through rivers, and raced to the mouth of a cave as the ground shook with an earthquake.

And there, by the light of a torch she found the cave drawings. Carefully, as she had countless times before in development, she copied them in her notebook by hand, and took photographs with her camera.

The simplicity of the first level would pull the gamer in, she thought. They want to move up, move on, face more challenges. As she did.

She gathered clues, racked up points, mopped the sweat off her brow, wetted her throat with water from her canteen.

It tasted sweet and clear, and the salt from the sweat stung her eyes.

It was perfect, she decided. So far.

On level three, an arrow whizzed by her head. She knew the path to take—which was maybe cheating a little. But it was fun! And work, too, she reminded herself as she charged up the steep path, her breath huffing out. Her boots skidded on mud from a recent storm, and when she went down, she felt the warm, wet dirt ooze between her fingers.

Up and running again, dodging left, right as muscle memory guided her.

Come on, she thought, *yeah, come on!* as her fingers reached for the Bowie in her belt.

The rival she'd named Delancy Queeg stood in the path, his knife already drawn.

"The henchmen you hired need more endurance," she said.

"They drove you where I wanted you. Go back now, and I'll let you live."

"Is that what you said to my father before you slit his throat, you bastard?"

He smiled—tanned, handsome, deadly. "Your father was a fool, and so is his daughter. The Dragon's Egg is mine. It's always been mine." He waved a hand, and she glanced behind long enough to see five barechested natives with bows ready.

"Not man enough to take me alone?" she demanded.

"Go," he ordered them. "You've done what you were paid to do."

Though they slipped away, she knew he was a liar. They would lie in wait. She would have to be quick.

She shifted her grip on the knife to combat stance, and began to circle on the narrow, muddy path.

Jabs, feints, and the scrape of blades. Perfect, she thought again, no tweaking necessary. She smelled blood where she'd nicked the bastard Queeg's arm, just above the wrist.

He'd cut her next, she thought, anticipating the next moves in the program as she played it. After he sliced her shoulder he'd smile, thinking he had the advantage.

Then she'd plunge it into his side, and leap from the cliff into the rock-strewn river below as arrows flew around her.

She considered dodging the slice since she knew when it was coming, and from where, but it was better to study the details, to look for flaws if she played it by rote rather than mixing it up.

His knife struck out fast, the tip ripping through cotton and flesh. But instead of the expected jolt, she felt the tear, the fire of it.

She stumbled back, dropping her knife as she brought her hand up, felt the blood as warm against her fingers as the mud had been. In disbelief, she watched the knife drip with it.

Real, she thought. Not holo. Real.

As Queeg's lips spread in a feral smile, as his knife began another downward arc, she slipped on the muddy path and tumbled over the cliff with a scream snapped off by the rocks and rushing water below.

The next morning, Benny paced Var's office. "I'm going to try her again."

"You tried her five minutes ago." Standing at his window, Var stared out in the direction of Cill's building. "She's not answering the 'link." He rubbed his hands over his hair. "Or e-mail, or text, or any damn thing."

Frustration in every line of his face, he turned back. "You're sure she didn't say anything to you about not coming in today?"

"No, I told you, just the opposite. She said she'd be in early. She didn't want to stay at her place any longer than she had to. I told her she could bunk at my place. You know how she is about her things, her space."

"Yeah, she said the same to me, and that if she didn't go back and stay the night, she'd probably never go back at all. Goddamn it." He looked at the time. "She's probably just overslept, that's all. Maybe she took a sleeper—"

"Maybe she took too many sleepers."

"Jesus. We should go over. We'll go over and check on her. Just in case . . . Probably just tuned out for a while, but we should check."

"Let's go now. Neither of us is going to get any work done until we do. She logged out her copy of Fantastical," Benny added as they caught an elevator down.

"She did? Well, that's good. That's good. Work's good for her, and it's probably why she's tuned out. Sure. She got caught up, worked late, took a sleeper. Probably didn't crash out until dawn or something."

"That's probably it. Yeah, that's probably it, but everything's so screwed up."

He looked at the flowers, thought of Bart.

"I know." Var laid a hand on Benny's shoulder. "Let me tell Stick we're going off-site for a few minutes."

When they got outside, they walked fast. "She'll probably be steamed supreme that we woke her up," Var commented and managed a smile.

"Yeah, I can hear her now. 'WTF! Can't I catch a few extra zees?' We'll cage some coffee off her."

"Now that's a plan. Hell of a storm last night, huh?"

"The sky was lit up like the raptor battle in Third Planet. Serious window-shaking storm. Cooled things off a little."

"Yeah." When they reached the building, Var punched in the code for Cill's visitor alert.

They waited, hands in pockets. Moments later, the comp announced no answer at the residence. When Var started to try again, Benny shook his head.

"Let's just go in. Let's go." He used the swipe Cill had given him, the palm plate, then the entry codes.

"Just tuned out," Var said under his breath as they headed to her apartment. "That's all it is; she's just tuned out."

Benny used the side of his fist, gave the door a good pounding.

"Jesus, Ben."

"I'm not waiting." Again he used the swipe, the palm, and the two sets of codes. He pushed the door open partway, called her name.

"Cill! Hey, Cill! It's Benny and Var."

"Yeah, don't pull out the pepper spray!"

"Cill?" Benny shoved the door open the rest of the way, hesitated a moment as he looked around the living area. He saw the shoes, the new ones, her bag. Pointed to the bag. "She's here. She never walks out the door without her sack full of stuff. I'm going to check the bedroom."

"I'll look in the office."

They separated.

"She's not in here," Benny hurried out again. "I can't tell if the bed's been slept in because it always looks like that."

"She's not in the office, the spare, the kitchen. She's—"

"The holo-room!" Spinning on his heels Benny ran for it. He started to enter the code.

"It's not locked, man." Var jerked a head up to the green light, opened the door.

Benny shoved by him. "God! Oh God, Cill!" He sprinted to where she lay crumpled and bloody, and very, very still. "Call nine-one-one!" he shouted. "Hurry. Hurry."

Var whipped out his 'link, hit the emergency key. "Is she alive? Benny, Benny, tell me she's alive."

"I don't know." He took her hand, stroked her cheek. And as Var's voice came from behind him, as if through a long, dark tunnel, he gathered the courage to press his fingers to the pulse in her throat.

In her office, Eve prepped for the briefing. She'd requested Mira's attendance. She needed a professional opinion of her conclusions after having seen and analyzed each partner's apartment. With any luck, EDD would give her something concrete to add to that, and they could pull in her lead suspect.

She looked up as McNab pranced in.

"She's good," he said as he offered Cill's journal to Eve. "I'm better. Thought you'd want it right away."

"You thought right. Did you read it?"

"No, I wasn't authorized to . . . maybe a couple pages," he admitted under Eve's cool stare. "It's just—or what I read was just stuff. Daily stuff, some work shit, that kind of thing. Maybe she wrote a little about this guy she went out with a couple months ago. She decided he was a loser. I have to agree."

"Just a couple pages."

"Maybe what you'd call a few. Just to make sure there weren't any glitches."

"I'm going to let you get away with that because you saved me from having to press her to open it. You've got over an hour before the briefing. Go away—and don't bother my partner."

"I wouldn't be a bother," he began, but her communicator signaled and he slipped out.

"Dallas."

Dispatch, Dallas, Lieutenant Eve. Report to 431 Spring Street, Apartment 3.

"Cilla Allen's residence. Is she dead?"

Negative. Allen, Cilla, is being transported to St. Ignatius Hospital by emergency unit. Condition critical, multiple injuries. Report to officers on-scene and secure.

"Copy that. Dallas out."

She swung into the bullpen. McNab, who was bothering her partner, started to grin. Then saw her face. He laid a hand on Peabody's shoulder briefly. "Shit."

"Cill's being transported to St. Ignatius, critical condition. Let's go."

"What happened?" Peabody asked as she shoved up to follow Eve's long stride.

"That's what we're going to find out." She shook her head as Peabody started to speak again. "Try U-Play. I want to know if Var and Benny are there, and if so, I want you to verify that by speaking to them."

Peabody followed orders as they rode down to the garage. "Not there. Both of them left, together, about a half hour ago."

"Together," Eve murmured, nodded. "Yeah, that's a good play. I want a guard on her—in the ER, the OR, ICU, whatever and wherever. She's under our watch as of now, twenty-four/seven. See if we can get any details on her injuries, her condition. I don't want to hear multiple injuries, critical. I want some fucking details."

"Yes, sir." Peabody slanted a glance toward Eve as they jumped into the vehicle.

She braced herself as Eve peeled out.

18

EVE IGNORED THE RETRO-STYLE ELEVATOR AND bounded up the steps. "Report," she ordered the officer on the door as she grabbed Seal-It from her field kit.

"Sir. Nine-one-one came in from Levar Hoyt at nine fifty-six from his 'link and from this location. My partner and I were dispatched as was a medi-unit. We arrived on-scene at ten-oh-two, ahead of the medi-unit by approximately two minutes."

Good response time, Eve thought, and gave him a go-ahead nod.

"We were met at the door by Mr. Hoyt, who immediately showed us into the holo-room at the east side of the unit. The victim, Ms. Cilla Allen of this address, was on the floor, unconscious, and appeared to be seriously injured. A Benny Leman was found in the room with her. He stated that he had not moved the victim in fear of adding to her injuries, but had checked her pulse, and attempted to ascertain the extent of said injuries. He was somewhat incoherent at the time. My partner and I re-moved the two men and placed them in what appears to be a viewing room where Officer Uttica remains with them. They became increasingly agitated and expressed strongly the desire to remain with the victim, who they identified as their business partner.

"I returned to speak to the MTs regarding the victim's injuries, which they described as critical and including a fractured skull, a shattered elbow, a broken leg, and at least two broken ribs as well as numerous lacerations and contusions. They transported her to St. Ignatius Hospital, departing at approximately ten-fifteen."

"That's some report, Officer Kobel."

"I like to be thorough."

"Stay on the door," she ordered.

"Yes, sir."

She moved directly to the holo-room where Cill's blood, she assumed, stained the floor.

"Let's get samples of that, make sure it's all hers."

She walked over to the control. "There's a disc in here, and it's going to be Fantastical."

"Same setup as Minnock," Peabody observed, "but from the description of her injuries it sounds like the killer decided to beat her to death."

"Then why didn't he finish the job? She's down, broken, unconscious. Why leave her breathing after you've gone to all that trouble?"

"Maybe he got spooked, or thought she was dead."

No, Eve thought. Just no. "He's too smart to leave her breathing. It's a really big mistake."

"Not if she doesn't make it."

Eve shook her head. "Go ahead and call the sweepers, and EDD. We'll see if the partners know her security code. Maybe we can get this disc out without frying it. Either way, I want to know when she started the game, how long she played it."

"On it. Do you want me to take one of them in another room to get his statement?"

"No. We'll take them together. Let's see how they play it. Come in when you finish up here. Then interrupt me, take me aside to give me some news. Keep it low, but I want them to hear you say *EDD, breakthrough, recovered data*."

"If they're—or one of them is guilty, it'll be bad news."

"Yeah. Sometimes you have to water the seeds."

"Huh?"

"Nothing." She left Peabody to go into the viewing room. Both men leapt to their feet and started talking at once.

"Stop! Officer, if you'll join your partner and keep the scene secured. Sweepers and EDD are being notified. No one else gets in."

She turned to the two men. "Sit."

"They wouldn't let us go with her. They won't even let us check with the hospital. Please. Please, Lieutenant." Benny's voice shook with the tears that swam in his eyes.

She pulled out her 'link. "This is Lieutenant Dallas," she began and gave her badge number. "I need to know the status of a patient, Cilla Allen, who was just brought in." She held up a finger before either man could speak again, and walked to the other side of the room. She listened, murmured back, then slipped the 'link back in her pocket before going back across the room.

"They're working on her. They have a team on her, and they're trying to stabilize her so they can move her to OR."

"Operate? She's going to need surgery?" Var asked as Benny simply stared at her.

"Her injuries are very severe, and they're doing everything they can. She's critical. You need to prepare yourselves."

"She's not going to die. She's not going to die. She's not going to die."

As he said it again and again, Benny rocked in the chair until Var put an arm around his shoulders.

"Come on, Benny. Come on, man. She's tough. Cilly's strong. We need to be there with her," he said to Eve.

"I need statements from both of you. I'll make it as quick as I can, and I'll have the officers who responded transport you to the hospital as soon as we're done. I need to know what happened."

"We don't know." Benny shook his head. "How could we know? She was . . . she was lying there when we got here."

"What time did you get here?"

Benny shook his head again, then dropped it into his hands.

"It was about ten or just before. I don't know exactly," Var told her. "We got worried when Cill didn't come in to work, and she didn't answer her 'link, or her e-mail. We should've come before. We should've checked on her earlier, then maybe . . ."

"I shouldn't have let her go home alone last night." Benny raked his fingers over his bold hair. "I should've made her stay at my place."

"What time did she go home?" she asked Benny.

"It wasn't late. Maybe nine or nine-thirty. We talked about going out and getting something to eat, or just getting blasted. But none of us much felt like either."

"Did she log out a game? Did she log out Fantastical?"

"Yeah. Yeah. We found out this morning she'd logged it out. Why is this happening?" Benny demanded. "Somebody tried to kill her. Somebody killed Bart. Why is this happening?"

"We're doing our best to find that out." Eve glanced over as Peabody came in, signaled her. "Give me a minute."

She crossed over, leaned in.

"That was a mag-ass party last night," Peabody whispered, modulating her voice to lift just enough on the key words. "My feet *EDD* are

killing me today. But *breakthrough* totally worth it because all that dancing, *recovered data* probably took a solid pound off my ass."

"You do understand you're obsessed with your own ass? Now, nod
like I've just given you an order, then pull your communicator out as
you step out. Wait a few minutes, come back in, give me a nod, and then
stay in for the interview."

"Got it." She nodded, added a "Yes, sir!" for good measure, and took
out her communicator as she left the room.

"Is that about Cill?" Benny demanded. "Is it something about Cill?"

"No. So, you last saw Cill at about nine-thirty last night?" She
glanced at Var for verification.

"About that."

"And what was her state of mind?"

"What do you think?" Anger leaked through as Benny fisted his
hands on his knees. "She was wrecked. We all were. It was hard enough
when she was putting the memorial together, editing the vid stream,
thinking about the food. But at least that gave her, all of us, something
solid to do, to work on. Now . . ."

"We were tired." Var sighed. "We were all just really tired."

"Where did you go after?"

"We went home." Now Var shrugged. "We all just went home."

"Did you walk together?"

"Yeah. Well, we walked together to Cill's, then I headed to my place.
Benny headed to his."

"Did you notice anyone hanging around? Anyone near her building?"

She glanced over as Peabody came back in, gave her a nod.

"I waited until she went in," Benny said. "We even talked for a couple more minutes. I wouldn't have left her alone if I'd seen anybody
hanging too close. I watched her go in before I went across to my place.

Her light was on when I looked out my window after I got inside. I know she got in okay."

"Do you always check like that?"

He shifted a little. "If we take off at the same time, I like to make sure she gets in okay. She can take care of herself, but it's just something you do."

"Did you talk to anyone, see anyone, have any contacts after nine-thirty?"

"God." Var rubbed his eyes. "I got something to eat, tried to watch some screen. I couldn't settle down so I went online for a few hours. Into a couple game rooms. I played some World Domination, tourney style. You know, elimination rounds. Maybe till about two. I didn't go out. I didn't want to go out."

"Benny?"

"I didn't talk to anybody. We'd talked to people all day. I did some personal e-mail, then some research on a couple of projects. I guess I went down about midnight. Her light was still on. I happened to notice. I almost tagged her, just to see if she wanted company, or just to talk, but I didn't. I figured she wanted to be left alone. I should've gone over." His voice trembled again. "I should've just gone over."

"Stop it." Var laid a hand on his shoulder. "Stop. It's not your fault. We need to go be with her," he told Eve.

"Nearly done. How did you get into the building, into her apartment?"

"I have a swipe and her codes," Benny said. "I live the closest, and if she's got to go somewhere for a few days, I water the plants. She's got a couple of nice plants. Plus, I just make sure her place is secure. It's important to Cill her place is secure."

"Why, especially?" Eve demanded. "Why is she so focused on security and privacy?"

"I . . ." Benny glanced over at Var.

"Go ahead. Maybe it'll help."

"It's just her mother and stepfather never gave her any privacy, any peace. They used to search her room all the time, pry into all her stuff. They even put a cam in there once, to spy on her. Like she was a freaking criminal. She just . . . she just wants her private space private. That's all. It's why she got so upset with the searches. I guess . . ." He let out a long breath. "I guess it's why I did, too. I know how it made her feel so it pissed me off."

"Okay. Was her security in place when you got here?"

"Yeah, it was." Var gave Benny's shoulder a bolstering rub, then nodded. "We thought she'd maybe taken a sleeper and was just conked. We checked the bedroom and the office, then we . . . we looked in the holo and found her. We—I—did the nine-one-one right off."

"And checked her pulse."

"I did." Benny pressed his lips together tight. "I couldn't find it at first, but it was there. Barely there. She was cut up and banged up. All torn and bloody. Can you at least check again? For God's sake."

"Peabody, check with the hospital. We're nearly done. Was the holo-room secured?"

Benny frowned a moment. "No. It wasn't locked. But we've holo'd here a lot of times. I don't think she usually secures the room. I don't in my place most of the time. That was Bart's thing. Super Spy Minnock," he murmured, then squeezed his eyes tight.

"Okay. There's a disc in the holo-program as I told you. Can you remove it?"

Benny shook his head. "I don't have the code or sequence." He glanced at Var.

"No, me neither. We could make a best guess, but if we're wrong, it'll hit destruct."

"All right. We'll deal with it."

"She's in surgery," Peabody announced. "Indications are she'll be several hours."

"Is there family who should be notified?" Eve asked.

"Just her mother." Var passed a weary hand over his face. "They're not close, as I guess you could figure, but I guess she should know."

"We're her family," Benny said fiercely. "We are."

"I'll have the officers take you to the hospital. Detective Peabody and I will be there shortly."

She gave the uniforms instructions, secured the door behind them. "We're going to want eyes on those two, softclothes."

"Their alibis are easy to check out. EDD can confirm or dispute the online activity. If they're in this together, they're both good at the masks, but it would slide in with Mira's two conspirators theory."

"How do you see it going down, if they're in it together?"

"They walk her home, just the way they said, but they come up, talk her into distracting herself with the holo-game. I don't get that because the place is pretty well soundproofed, but the holo-area would be the more secure and soundproofed section in the space. And, she would be distracted. They attack her, or one attacks, one keeps watch. They leave her for dead, go home. Pull the 'We were worried about her' this morning so they can be the ones to find her."

"Alive. Why not finish her off then?"

"We'd have TOD to coincide with their presence. They have to think fast, decide on calling it in, getting to the hospital. She's a mess, Dallas, and her chances aren't good. Either one of them could finish her there. Or could if we didn't have a man on her."

"It's not a bad theory. Run some probabilities on it."

"You don't like it."

"It's not in my top five." She gestured to the power drink tube. "That wasn't there yesterday, and she didn't come home until last night."

"Okay. And?"

"If she has company, why does she have an open drink—just one drink and one it doesn't look like she touched? We'll check the supply, and the recycler, but I don't think you're going to find a couple more drinks of any sort taken out last night. Just here, standing by the window, deciding she doesn't want the damn drink after all. She did the same thing the day we notified them Bart was dead. Got the drink, opened it, set it aside."

"Too upset from the memorial," Peabody concurred. "Yeah, that plays."

Eve gestured to the shoes. "What do you do when you get home and your new shoes hurt your feet?"

"Take them off."

"But if you've got company you're probably not going to leave them in the middle of the room, right in the traffic flow." She shrugged. "Neither may mean anything, but there are little details that give me a different picture."

"She doesn't secure the holo-room, so they could've come in while she was in game."

"How did they know she'd be in game?"

"Because . . . one or both of them knew she'd logged out the disc."

Now Eve nodded. "Yeah, and I'll go one up from that. One of them gave her the disc to take home. The game, under it all? That's the murder weapon. The killer likes the weapon."

She walked to the door herself to let the sweepers in. While Eve showed them the holo-room, gave them the setup, Peabody chewed over theories.

"They give her time to come up," Peabody said when Eve came back. "Time to settle in a little, to start the game. They come in. She's distracted, into the game. And the rest follows my previous theory."

"Also possible. You should run all variations."

"I'm asking why. Why Cill, why now? Right on top of Bart, it's absolute we're going to be looking at the last partners standing. So, did she become a threat? Find something out? Was she asking the wrong questions?"

"Could be. Yesterday Roarke told her his people have been working on a similar game, similar technology, and have been for months."

"That had to be crap news for them."

"Yeah. And she'd have passed it to the others. She'd have told them. Maybe somebody was pissed enough to kill the messenger. And that one's between you and me. I don't want Roarke going there."

"Understood."

"I've got other reasons that's not my number one. You play a game, you make decisions, and one leads to the next. You face off with different obstacles and opponents. It's a good strategy to throw a new problem at your current opponent."

"Which would be us. She was a ploy? Beating her half—and a good chance all the way—to death is a ploy?"

"And it ups the stakes. Yeah, we'll be looking at the last two standing. And isn't that exciting? Especially when you think you're so fucking smart, so much better than the rest of the field. And now? There's one less person who knows him, in and out. Intimately. Or thinks he does. It's a calculated risk, but a good move."

"If she comes out of it, she'll ID him."

"Yeah, that's the sticking point. I'm working on it." She went to the door again, this time for Feeney and McNab.

"Holo-room. I need whatever you can get me. But before you start, I want to talk to you about a setup I have in mind."

Cill was still in surgery when Eve arrived at the hospital. "Go check on the partners. Be sympathetic, and try to get them to talk."

Eve hunted down a floor nurse, badged her. "I'm on the Cilla Allen investigation. I need to know everything you know or can find out."

"I can tell you they worked on her down in ER, had to zap her, but got her back. She's lucky Doctor Pruit's on today. She's the neuro. The head wounds are severe and priority, but the other injuries are considerable. She's going to be in there awhile."

"Chances?"

"I can't tell you."

"Educated guess."

"She's lucky she made it in at all. She looks like she'd been thrown off a cliff."

Eve took the nurse's arm before she could move on. "A fall? Not a beating?"

"I can't tell you. If she beats the odds, she'll tell you herself."

She frowned as the nurse hurried away. And the frown deepened when she saw Roarke coming toward her.

"I heard. I thought I should come."

"Are the partners in there?"

"Yes. Peabody's with them now."

"Impressions?"

"Shocked, scared—as you'd expect. Propping each other up you could say."

"Did either of them ask you about your game in development?"

"No. I don't think that's on their scope at the moment."

Eve shifted her gaze toward the waiting area. "It is for at least one of them."

"You believe one of them beat that girl—from what I understand—to pieces?"

"No question about it. Not anymore. The only question is how to nail it down. Buy a little time, change the focus, tug the heartstrings. She was the short end of the triangle, hotheaded, impulsive, the weak spot. So she's a logical sacrifice in the game. She—"

"Christ Jesus, Eve. The girl's shattered like glass, and it'll take a bloody miracle to put her together again. And you're standing here talking about fucking games?"

She met fire with ice. "Obviously your heartstrings are playing a tune."

"It might be because I have them," he shot back. "Because I'm not so caught up trying to win some shagging *game* that I consider a young woman a logical sacrifice. She's still alive, Lieutenant. She's not on your side of the board yet."

"Why don't you go back to the waiting area. You can all join hands. Maybe hold a prayer meeting. You go ahead and do that while the one who put her in the OR is chuckling up his sleeve. I've got better things to do."

She strode away, steeling both her heart and her belly against the hurt. It wasn't just the body, she thought, that could shatter. And it wasn't only fists and pipes and bats that could shatter it.

She found an empty restroom, leaned against the wall, and gave herself a moment to settle. She checked in with Feeney, updated Whitney, consulted with Mira.

This is how it worked, she reminded herself. How *she* worked. Sitting around patting heads, stroking hands didn't get the job done. It wouldn't bring Bart's killer to justice or save Cill.

She'd be damned if she'd apologize for doing her job the way she saw fit to do it.

Calmer, she found another nurse, badged her, and arranged for a setup in a private observation room. She stood, alone, drinking hideous coffee, and watching as the medical team struggled to put that shattered glass back together again.

Even if she lived, Eve thought, those pieces would never fit quite the same way.

Not on her side of the board yet? Fuck that, she thought. Cill had moved to her side of the board the minute she fell to the floor.

She glanced back as the door opened, saw Roarke come in, then turned her attention back to the screen.

"I have no excuse for that," he began. "Absolutely no excuse for saying those things to you. I'm unspeakably sorry, Eve."

"Forget it."

"I can't. I won't." He walked to her, stood with her, but didn't touch. "And still I hope you'll forgive me."

"It's been a long few days."

"That's no excuse. It's not even a reason."

"Fine. Give me one."

"She wept in my arms yesterday. I knew you considered her a suspect, and a part of me wondered, even as she wept in my arms, if she'd had some part in what happened to Bart. More, from what I've gathered, she was very likely lying on the floor, alone, broken, bleeding while we were on a rooftop drinking champagne."

"You're too close to it."

"I am. You're quite right about that, and I can't fully explain, even to myself, why that is. But I can't step back. Those might be reasons, Eve, but they're still not excuses for slapping at you that way, for doing that because I knew you'd take it, could take it."

"You hurt me."

"Oh God. I know it." He took her arms then, lightly. "You know me. You'll have the satisfaction of being absolutely sure I'll suffer for knowing it."

"You weren't altogether wrong."

"I was, altogether and completely wrong."

"No. Whatever I think about that." She nodded toward the screen. "About any of it, all of it, I have to maintain. It's not a shagging game for me, but it is for him. I have to calculate how he thinks so I can stop him."

"I know how you think, and I know how much you care. I can only tell you again I'm sorry."

She looked into his eyes, felt some of the sickness in her belly recede. "I've said things before designed to hurt you. You forgave me."

"I did, yes. I will again, no doubt."

"So, let's put it aside. You get a big black mark on the asshole side of the column."

He smiled, pressed his lips to her brow. "What's the score so far?"

"We're neck-in-neck in that area."

"You'd best check those stats. I really think you're ahead."

"You want another big black mark?"

"I don't." He drew her in, letting out a breath when she relaxed against him. "This is better."

She turned her head so they watched the screen together.

"Why was she a target?" Roarke asked her.

"Because he doesn't consider anyone indispensable but himself. He's going to run the show now, and nobody's going to slip ahead of him, the way Bart did. It probably felt good to soak up all that sympathy over Bart, and exciting to have the cops taking a look at him. Part of the game, and he's racking up the points, anticipating the next moves."

She glanced at Roarke. "That's the way it is for him."

"Yes. I know it. You're right."

"He's a gamer, so he'd look at what was on the board. Players, scenarios, options. Cill? She was angry, depressed, taking it harder, at least on the outside, than anyone. It made her more vulnerable. She's the most in tune, it feels to me, with the other staff. And being an attractive female, may be the most logical next public face for the company. He wants that for himself. And he has a taste for it now. That human nature thing."

She eased back a little. "I've got some technical questions, and they may be way out of orbit, but—" She broke off as on-screen the medical team began to move quickly. "Something's wrong. Something's gone wrong."

Roarke ordered the screen to zoom in, enhance. "Her blood pressure's dropping. Look at the monitor. It's bottoming out. They're losing her."

"Goddamn it, goddamn it. She's got to fight! Does she want to stay alive or not?"

They watched in silence while Cill hovered between life and death.

 **19** WHEN EVE STEPPED INTO THE WAITING AREA, both men jerked to their feet, then seemed to deflate back into their chairs.

"We're waiting for the doctor, for one of the medical team." Var looked up at the clock. "It's been a long time."

"They said they'd update us. But nobody's been in for more than an hour now."

"I've been observing the surgery," Eve began, and held up a hand when both men rose again and began talking at once. "Hold it. They're working on her, hard. There was some trouble— Hold it!" she ordered again over the peppering questions. "I didn't bring my medical degree, but I can tell you it appears they're doing everything they can."

"You got to watch, to see her? Where?" Benny demanded. "We could go there, see her. It's got to be better than just sitting here."

"You're not allowed to observe. Only medical personnel, police in a criminal matter, or family."

"But we're—"

"You're not family," Eve interrupted as Benny protested.

"Not legally," Peabody said more gently. "I understand what you mean about family. I have friends who are family to me. But you're not legally her family, so they might be sticky about the technicalities right now. It sounds like it's going to be a while more," she continued. "You should go get some air, some food, take a walk. It'll make the time go faster," she added.

"Something might happen while we're not here."

"I've got your 'link numbers," Peabody told Benny. "If anything happens, anything changes, I'll let you know right away."

"Maybe we could get some air. And they probably have a chapel or meditation center. We could . . ." Var flushed a little, lifted his hands helplessly. "You know."

"Yeah. That's good. That's a good thing to do. Just for a few minutes. If anything happens—"

"I promise." Peabody watched them walk out together, nodded at Eve as she pulled out her communicator.

"Tell the shadows not too close," Eve said. "I don't want them to know we've got anyone on them yet." She turned to Roarke. "Look, I know you've got an interest in this, but if you're not going back to work to buy up the northern hemisphere, I think Feeney could really use you."

"Distracting me?"

"That's a side benefit. Either Peabody or I will be in here, keeping tabs on Cill, and watching the partners. I'm going to see if I can cop a room where I can set up shop and do some work while we switch off."

"Let me be liaison there. I'll see about getting you a work area, then I'll see if Feeney wants me."

"Good enough."

"You said you had technical questions, before."

"Yeah, and I do." Wrong place, wrong time, Eve thought. "Let me line them up a little better first."

"All right." He curled the tips of his fingers in hers briefly. "Stay in touch, will you?"

"Yeah." She turned back to Peabody. "Anything about the last ninety minutes I should know?"

"No. They're acting and reacting as you'd expect given the circumstances. I swear, I don't get any vibe off either of them."

"If I'm gone before they get back, I want you to get them to agree to having officers go in their apartments to check their alibis. Just getting it off the slate so we can focus on Cill and how this happened to her. You know how to play it."

"Can do."

"Get their agreement on record. Then get EDD to send somebody to each place. I want somebody who knows how to look for details that aren't on a comp. Just observe, note, report. We have the record from yesterday's search. Let's see what's different today, if anything."

"Yes, sir. How bad was it? Was she? When you were observing?"

"Jesus, Peabody, she's a mess." She jammed her hands in her pockets as memories of the dream snuck back in her head.

You couldn't save them all.

"They've got the brain doc messing around in her head, and another guy working on her arm. It must be bad, really bad if they started there instead of the leg. They've got that in a sterile cage—whatever they're called. Her face looks like somebody went at it with a bat. They're dealing with internal injuries on top of it, trying to tie off bleeders or whatever they do when things inside are bleeding out. It looked to me like she was busted up every-damn-where."

She did a short circuit of the room. "I've seen a lot of beatings. I'm not sure that's what this is."

"What else could it be?"

Eve shook her head. "We need to see the medical data, talk to the doctors, get a better look at her. Until then, it's just speculation."

"I got the report on the blood samples. It's all hers."

"Yeah, it would be."

"Lieutenant Dallas?" The floor nurse came to the doorway. "We have an office set up for you."

"What's the status on my victim?"

"There have been some complications, but she's holding her own."

"We'll take shifts," Eve said to Peabody. "I'll come back for you."

She followed the nurse down the long corridor, then to the right down another. "I got a look at her in observation," Eve commented. "She does look like she fell off a cliff."

"It's really just an expression."

"Maybe. You people took pictures. Bone and body and scans. I'd like to see them."

"I'm not authorized."

"You can get authorization. You got a look at her."

"Yes, I did."

"Your people are doing everything they can to save her. I'm doing everything I can to find the son of a bitch who did that to her. Her name's Cilla Allen, but they call her Cill. She had her twenty-ninth birthday six weeks ago. A couple days ago one of her closest friends was murdered, and yesterday she ordered food and flowers for his memorial. She cried for him. And last night or early this morning, the same person who killed her friend tried to kill her. The sooner I see what he did to her, the sooner I figure out how he did it, and who did it, the sooner I put the fucker away so he never hurts anyone else."

The nurse opened a door. "I'll get the authorization. This room is generally available for family members of surgical patients. You're free to use the equipment."

"Thanks."

It was a small office and still nearly twice the size of hers at Central. It boasted a sleep chair, an AutoChef and Friggie that took credit swipes. The desk held a comp, a 'link, and a small vase of yellow flowers.

A window let in the summer light, but was filtered so as not to toss glare on the wall screen.

She charged another cup of lousy coffee, sat, and got to work.

It was probably crazy, what she was considering. No, it *was* crazy, she corrected, and still she started a search on numerous underground e and game sites.

The weirder the better, she decided.

She popped into the chat rooms McNab had given her, the message boards, and noted that Razor was still putting out feelers for the weapon—with no results.

Or none that showed, she thought.

She tried Mira, and was told by her chilly-voiced admin that the doctor was in session. Eve requested a 'link consult as soon as Mira was free.

At the knock on the door, she called out, "Yeah, come in." She expected the floor nurse, hoped to have a file of medical data to comb through. Instead, a waiter walked in carrying a tray.

"Got your lunch order."

"I didn't order lunch. You've got the wrong room. Scram."

"Room 880, East Surgical Wing. You Dallas?"

Frowning, she gave him and his tray a closer look. "Yeah."

"Got your lunch order. Got one for Peabody, too. Waiting room A, East Surgical Wing."

"Who placed the orders?"

"Ordered up by Roarke."

"Of course they were. Well, what've I got?"

He set the tray on the desk, pulled off the insulated top. "Got your burger—that's moo-meat, too. Got your fries, got your small side salad. Got your coffee—real deal. A double, black."

"Never misses a trick." Eve dug into her pocket, came up with enough loose credits for a decent tip. "Thanks."

"Enjoy."

"I guess I will," she murmured as he went out. She sampled a fry as she tagged Feeney. "What've you got?"

"We're not going to try removing the disc. Working on some ideas first. We got your time frame. Vic set up the holo at—is that a burger?"

"No, it's a catcher's mitt. What does it look like?"

"It looks like a burger. Is it meat?"

"Mmmm." She took a huge bite, grinned around it.

"That's cold, kid." Genuine sorrow clouded his eyes. "Just cold."

"You get that disc out without blowing it up, I'll buy you ten pounds of cow meat. Time line?"

"Holo starts at twenty-one forty-six. The program ran until twenty-three fifty-two."

"Over two hours. Longer than Bart."

"Solo player, like him. We've got her starting off the jump. Level one."

"He started at four. So she ran whichever scenario she picked from the beginning, either because it was new to her—and I don't like that one. She started at square one because she wasn't playing so much as working. Working to shut out the grief. She's going to check the program, look for any flaws or glitches, or any place to improve it. Can you tell where she stopped?"

"She nearly finished level three."

"Nearly?"

"It reads ninety-one percent. She didn't make it to the end of the level."

"You play. What would make you stop that close to moving up a level?"

"Screwing up, getting shut out."

"Losing the level, okay. What else? If you got interrupted?"

"Nobody's going to stop me from moving up unless they're bleeding or on fire. And they'd have to be gushing blood or frying. And I'd have to like them. A lot."

She glanced up at the knock on the door, then nodded as the nurse stepped in. Held up a finger. "Can you tell if she messed up, got shut out?"

"Not from the program, but up to then, from the time frame, it looks like she was cruising right along. I got through some of her older logs. She hits levels ten, twelve and up consistent."

"But we don't know if any of those were this scenario."

"Can't tell you until I get this disc out and you hand over ten pounds of cow meat."

"But it's unlikely, given her skills and experience, she'd have crapped out that quick. Or have stopped voluntarily that close to completing a level. Got it. I'll get back to you."

She clicked off.

"I got authorization to put what we've got on disc. You have to sign for it."

"Thanks." Eve dashed her name on the form, noted the woman's wistful glance at her plate. "Do you want half?"

She smiled. "No, I'm watching my intake. But thanks. It's a nice offer. I went in to get an update on her. She's hanging in, but . . . she's got a long way to go."

She started for the door, stopped. "We see a lot of hard things in our professions."

"Yeah, we do."

"I hope she makes it."

"Me, too," Eve murmured when she was alone.

Eve inserted the disc then called for the data on-screen.

She studied it, side-by-side with the records of the first responders.

On the holo-room floor, Cill lay crumpled, broken as a china doll heaved against the wall by an angry child. Blood had pooled and congealed under her, while her arm and leg cocked at unnatural angles. Snapped bone speared through the skin of her shin. Jagged, Eve thought, ignoring the movements of the cops, the voices as she focused on the victim. Not a clean break there. Several gashes, including one on her shoulder that appeared straight and true rather than torn.

Bruising around the eyes, she noted, scrapes at the temples.

She switched off, studied the scans. Several internal injuries, bruised and damaged organs. But the external bruising . . .

She scrolled through, backtracked, scrolled again, studying the battered, torn body as she ate her lunch. She pulled out her beeping 'link, glanced at the readout.

"Doctor Mira."

"Eve. I heard about Cilla Allen. What's her status?"

"She's still in surgery. I'm looking through the records, the scans. It's bad. He used the victim's holo-room again, the same project—the Fantastical game. She logged it out, or it's been made to appear she did so. It's the same basic setup—she appears to have been playing the game solo. But the method of attack is markedly different. Why?"

"He'd already won the game, that scenario. He'd want a different challenge with this new player. Possibly a game that opponent favored. It adds to the challenge."

"Yeah, that's my take. And it's meaner than the first victim. That was quick and clean. He may be escalating, wants more bang for the buck. Except . . . Can you take a look? I'll send you the record from the first responders."

"Of course."

"Hang on just a minute." Eve ordered the transfer of data. "The two remaining partners discovered her this morning. The statement, from both, is they became concerned when she didn't come in, walked over to check on her. The nine-one-one went out immediately."

"She sustained severe trauma." Mira's toned remained even as her brows knit in study. "Blood loss. The leg . . . It would seem he spent considerable time and rage. I'm surprised her face isn't more badly damaged."

"Does it look like a beating to you?"

Mira's brows unknit and lifted. "What else?"

"Could these injuries have been the result of a fall?"

"A fall? Are you considering the holo-room a dump site rather than the attack site?"

Eve hesitated. Not yet, she thought. Not ready to share quite yet. "I'm considering all kinds of things."

"This isn't my area of expertise, and I hesitate to make a conclusion based on this, but I would say that yes, it certainly could be the result of a fall. What do her doctors say?"

"I haven't been able to interview any of them. They're pretty busy with her."

"I can try to make some time later today, come to the hospital and study her data, speak with her medical team."

"No, that's okay. I've got another angle on that. Why is she alive? That's the sticker. Why didn't he finish her?"

"He may have thought he had, but that kind of mistake isn't consistent. It's possible drawing it out adds to the enjoyment. It prolongs the game."

"If she lives, it would box him in. He could lose."

"Yes. It's possible that adds to his sense of competition. It doesn't fit well, but often the criminal mind doesn't follow a logical path. Still . . ." Mira frowned, slowly shook her head. "He didn't finish the game, and he should have."

"He's stuck on this level now, and can't advance unless, or until she dies."

"I'm sure you have her well protected."

"Yeah, I've got her covered."

"I'd like to think about this further, review my notes and this additional data."

"Thanks. I'll get back to you."

She clicked off, and contacted someone whose area of expertise might give her some answers—and more questions.

While she waited, she tried out her theory with a probability run, and got back a percentage she considered the computer equivalent of *Have you lost your freaking mind?*

"Yeah, that's what I thought you'd say."

Since she didn't have her murder board, she worked to create a facsimile of one on-screen. Then sat back, sipped excellent coffee, and studied it.

"Whacked theory," she murmured. "Way-out-of-orbit theory. But, didn't we just have a party last night to celebrate a book about mad scientists secretly creating generations of human clones? That's pretty whacked."

She adjusted the screen, putting her two victims side-by-side.

Partners, she thought. Friends. Those words, those concepts meant different things to different people.

History, shared interests, trust, emotion, passion. All shared.

Shared business, profits, work, risks.

Both attacked during play, in their own secured homes. One dead, one hanging on by the skill and efforts of medical science—and maybe her own grit.

No weapons, no signs of forced entry, no trace other than the victims'.

Add the timing, yeah, add the timing in there, too.

People were always finding new ways to create and destroy, weren't they? It's what humans did. Technology was a tool, a convenience, and a weapon.

She walked over to answer the knock on the door. "Thanks for coming, Morris."

"It's nice to get out of the house now and then."

He wore black, as he had every time she'd seen him since Coltraine's death, but Eve took hope from the flash of the shimmering red tie that the leading edge of his grief had dulled.

"I need you to look at these pictures and the medical data, and give me your opinion on the cause."

"I'd do better with the body."

"Well, she's not dead yet."

"That's fortunate for her. I might point out you're in a hospital, and there are likely doctors wandering around who tend to serve and assess those not dead yet."

"Yeah, the ones working on her are busy. And I don't know them." Trust, she thought again, the solid base of friendship. "What I'm looking for is your opinion on how this twenty-nine-year-old female incurred these injuries."

She turned to the screen, ordered the image of Cill on the holo-room floor.

"Ah, well. Ouch. You say she's alive?"

"So far."

He moved closer, tilting his head. "If she lives, I hope she has an exceptional orthopedic surgeon on that leg. Enhance that for me. A bit more," he said when she complied. "Hmm. Now down to the ankle, same leg," he told her after a moment.

"You can run it. Take your time."

As he went section by section, injury by injury, she swiped the Friggie for two tubes of Pepsi.

He grunted in thanks, and continued. "You have her scans?"

"Yeah." Eve ordered them on-screen, then rested a hip on the desk as he studied, as he worked.

"She'll need the god of all neuros," he murmured. "And even then I'm afraid I might see her on my table. The head injuries are the worst, and the rest is very nasty. If she gets her miracle, they'll have to replace that kidney at some point, and the spleen, and she'll require extensive PT for the leg, the arm, the shoulder. She's got a lot of work ahead of her. Brain damage is another risk she faces. She may live, but it may not be a blessing. Still, it's a wonder she didn't snap her spine in a fall like this."

"A fall." Eve all but leaped on it. "Not a beating."

"A fall," he repeated. "The contusions, the breaks, the lacerations aren't consistent with a beating, but a fall. She landed primarily on her back, with the impact shattering that elbow and twisting the leg with enough force to break the bone. A hard, uneven surface, I'd say from the type of injuries. Broken concrete, rocks, something on that order."

He glanced back at Eve. "I'm sorry. Where was she found again?"

"Here." Eve brought the image back on-screen, watched Morris frown.

"A smooth surface. She didn't incur those injuries by taking a tumble on that floor."

"Could she have been moved, and dumped here?"

He shook his head. "I don't see how she would have lived through it. Look at the blood pool. She certainly would have bled profusely at the point of impact. Moving her would mean more blood loss. Added to this? No, I don't see how that could be."

He took a drink from the tube, frowned again. "This is annoying. I feel I've let you down. Let me go through the scans and data again."

"No, you haven't let me down. Your findings mesh with mine."

"Do they?" He angled away from the screen, taking another sip as he looked at Eve. "Are we going to explain to each other how this twenty-nine-year-old female managed to fall onto a smooth surface and incur injuries consistent with a fall of—I'd say—at least twenty feet onto a rough and uneven one?"

"Sure. After I get someone to explain it to me."

"Well, I love a mystery. Still, I hope she lives so she can tell you herself. It's rare, if ever, you and I consult over someone with a pulse. Tell me more about her."

"She's one of the partners of my last victim."

"Ah. The head job. Holo-room." He gestured to the screen. "And this would be a holo-room as well."

"It would. Hers. In her apartment, which was secured. She was, by the evidence on-scene, playing the same game, though it may have been another scenario, as the first vic."

"Consistency is often an advantage. Burns? Does she have internal burns at the site of the injuries?"

"I don't know yet."

"Let me look at the scans again, enhanced. If we can get a strong enough picture, I might find them. I wasn't looking before."

"Help yourself. It used to be you had to do everything on a comp by hand, right? Fingers on keyboard only. No voice commands, no smart screens."

"When I was a medical student we keyboarded nearly everything, and had only just begun to use palm scans routinely for diagnostics. Holo wasn't yet considered reliable or cost-effective for teaching or diagnostics. I remember as a boy we—ah, look here. Do you see this?"

She moved closer to the screen. "What am I supposed to see?"

"Along the leg fracture—the shadows? Dots really. So small, so faint. But there."

"Burns."

"I'll give you five to ten. See, yes, see, there all over her. Every point of impact, every wound, difficult to separate as she's so badly damaged. This, here, yes, here, on this shoulder wound, they show more clearly."

"Where he cut her."

"I agree it could very well be a knife wound. Or, like your previous victim, a sword. I'd want to see it in the flesh, so to speak, take measurements, do an analysis, but from a visual like this, a sharp blade. And the burns—those minute internal singes. Fascinating."

"She'd have been armed, too. But she wouldn't have known it."

"Sorry? How would she not know?"

Eve shrugged, her eyes on the scan. "Just a whacked theory I'm working on."

The door opened. "Dallas. Oh, hey, Morris. Ah, you're a little early," Peabody said to him. "The vic's coming out of surgery. The doctor's coming out in a minute to give us the picture."

"I need to shut down here, then I'm on my way."

"I'm interested in your theory, whacked or not," Morris said when the door closed. "When you're ready to share."

"I need to run it by another expert. You've made it seem a little less whacked."

"Always happy to help." He glanced at the screen before Eve shut down. "I hope I don't have the pleasure of meeting her."

"The human body stays pretty much the same, right? Technology changes and science advances. This one? She started out tough, so that's her advantage. Now it's up to technology and science to pull it out."

"Not just the body, but the spirit. Technology and science don't hold a candle to the human spirit. If hers is strong enough, she may stay not dead yet."

20 THE PARTNERS PACED NOW, WEARING A GROOVE in opposite sides of the room. If she'd gone by visual alone, she'd have concluded both were utterly exhausted, holding on by those thin threads of hope, faith, and desperation.

"You should sit down," she said. She wanted them seated together, where she could watch and gauge faces, hands, bodies. "Sit," she repeated, putting enough authority in it to make it an order. "We'll hear from the medicals soon enough. Meanwhile, you should know we're making some headway on the investigation. Little steps," she said quickly, "and I can't be specific with you. But I wanted to be able to give you some positive news."

"I don't care about the investigation, not now." Benny sat, eyes trained on the doorway. "I can't think about that. Just about Cill."

"We just want to keep focused on her. Like—I know it sounds weak, but like pushing energy to her." Var shrugged. "It feels like something we can do."

"I think you're right." Peabody offered an understanding smile. "I believe in that kind of thing."

"Free-Ager," Eve said with the faintest—and very deliberate—tone of dismissal. She moved slightly to the side as a woman in surgical scrubs entered.

She was on the small side, but with broad shoulders. Her hair was as short as Caesar's and midnight black. Her almond eyes tracked the faces in the room, settled on Eve.

"You're the officer in charge?"

"Lieutenant Dallas."

"Doctor Pruit."

"Please." Var reached out a hand, dropped it again. "Is she okay? Is Cill okay?"

At Eve's nod, the doctor sat across from the two men.

"She came through surgery. You're family?"

"Yes," Benny said before Var could speak. "We're her family."

"Her injuries are very severe."

"But you fixed her," Benny insisted.

"We put together a team of doctors and performed several surgeries. She suffered massive trauma to the head, which required extensive repair."

Eve listened while Pruit explained the damage, the repair, the prognosis, and watched faces. But she'd already seen it—just that quick flash.

"I don't understand what you're saying." Benny looked at Var. "Do you? What does it mean?"

"Cilla's in a coma," Pruit explained. "This isn't unexpected, and it may give her body a chance to heal."

"Or she won't wake up at all," Var said, bitterly. "That's what you're saying."

"Yes. We've done everything we can do for her at this time, but we'll be monitoring her very closely. She survived surgery, and you can take hope from that. But you must be prepared. She remains critical, and should she come out of the coma, there is a possibility of brain damage."

"God. Oh God."

"Don't think about that." Var closed a hand over Benny's. "Not yet."

"You may want to speak to the other surgeons who worked on her. I can give you the basics. Her internal injuries were also severe. One of her kidneys was damaged too critically to save. We replaced her spleen, and can, should she wake and elect it, replace the lost kidney. She will need further surgery on her leg. We were unable to complete repairs without endangering her life."

Var took a ragged breath. "Are you telling us there's no hope?"

"There's always hope. Once she's settled in ICU, you'll be able to see her. Very briefly. You can rest assured that we'll continue to do everything we can for her. She'll get the very best of care." Pruit rose. "If you have any more questions, someone will page me. Or you can speak to her other surgeons. Someone will come get you when she's ready."

Eve followed Pruit out. "Give me her chances. Straight."

"Fifty-fifty is generous, but I'd have given her much less when she came into the OR. She has a strong constitution. She's young, healthy. You had an officer in my OR."

"That's right, and I'll have an officer in her room twenty-four/seven. Not just on the door. In the room. You're doing all you can to see that she survives. So am I."

"You're concerned with security, and another attempt on her life?"

"Not as long as I have an officer in the room."

"Fair enough. If she makes it through the next twenty-four hours, I'll consider that fifty-fifty more solid. For now, we'll go minute by minute."

"I need to be notified immediately of any change in her condition, one way or the other."

"I'll see that ICU has those instructions."

"I'd like a look at her before you let those two in."

"All right, go on up. I'll let them know you're coming."

Eve made her way up, noting the ways in and out, the basic security measures, the movements of staff, ID. Decent, she concluded, but there were always ways around security.

She badged the nurse at the desk, pleased when the man didn't merely glance at it, but gave it a good hard look before passing her through.

As in U-Play, the walls were glass. No privacy for patients, she thought. Cill wouldn't like it, Eve concluded, but for herself, she liked it just fine. Each room, each patient was monitored by cam and machine. She doubted any of the staff paid much attention to the room screens, but expected they'd hop if any of the monitors signaled a change in patient condition.

Still, she was pleased to see the uniformed officer sitting with his chair angled to the door. He rose when she walked in.

"Take five," she told him.

"Yes, sir."

Eve moved to the foot of the bed. They'd caged the leg, the arm, she noted, which made Eve think of a droid in mid-development. The limbs inside the cages showed the livid red and purple of insult and repair. Tubes snaked, hooking Cill to monitors that hummed and beeped in a slow, steady rhythm. The bruising around her eyes showed black against pasty white skin, and the lacework of bandages.

They'd shaved her head, Eve noted, and had it resting on a gel pillow that would ease the pressure. All that hair, Eve mused. That would probably be as much of a jolt as the glass walls and cams.

If she woke up.

"I've gotten messed up a few times, but I have to say, you win the prize. Coming back from being put together again's got to be almost as hard as being busted to pieces. We'll see how tough you are."

She walked over to the side of the bed, leaned down. "Don't you fucking give up. I know who did this to you. I know who killed Bart. I'm going after him, and I'm going to win. Then he's going to pay. You remember that, and don't you *fucking* give up. We're going to beat him, you by coming back from this, me by taking him down." She straightened. "He was never your friend. You remember that, too."

She stood watch until the guard came back.

And when the partners went in to see her, Eve stood watch a little longer, studying them on the monitor.

Do you think she'll make it?" Peabody asked when Eve got behind the wheel.

"She's not the giving-up type. That's in her favor. Reserve a conference room and set up a briefing with the EDD team. Thirty minutes. No, give me an hour." Eve used her in-dash 'link while Peabody made arrangements.

"Lieutenant," Roarke said.

"She's out of surgery, holding her own."

"That's good to hear. You spoke with her surgeon?"

"Yeah. They're doing what they do. Now we'll do what we do. Can you meet me in my office in twenty?"

"I can, yes."

"Bring an open mind."

He smiled a little. "I always carry it with me."

"You'll need it."

"We're set," Peabody told her. "Room B. You've got something." Peabody pointed a finger. "Something new."

"What I've got is a dead guy without a head, a woman in critical with injuries consistent with a fall who was found on a holo-room floor. No weapons, no trace, and no security breaches the aces at EDD can find. Logic it out."

"The weapons were removed, the killer sealed up. The victims knew and trusted the killer who has supreme e-skills that have so far baffled our e-team. They'll find the breaches."

"Assuming they're there to be found. He miscalculated with Cill. She wasn't supposed to fall."

"Fall where?"

"That's a question, and we may never have the full answer to that one unless she wakes up and tells us. Meanwhile, we think out of the box. Fuck. We burn the damn box."

She pulled into the garage at Central. "Set up everything we have, including the scans and data we got from the hospital."

"Okay, but—"

"Less talk, more work."

Eve double-timed it to her office and began to put her briefing together. She scowled at her computer and wished for better e-skills. She wanted to have at least the bones together before Roarke got there.

"Okay, you bastard, let's give this a try." She sat, and using the medical data began to build a reenactment.

Marginally pleased, she nodded at the screen as Roarke came in.

"Do you want the good news or the bad?" he asked her.

"Give me the bad. I like to end on an up note."

"We've scanned, dug, taken apart, and put back together Cill's security system, and used every test, idea, method known to man and machine going back over Bart's. We can't find a single abnormality. I'd stake my reputation, and yours for that matter, that no one entered those apartments after the victim secured the door."

"Good."

Irritation rippled over his wonderful face. "Well, I'm delighted you're pleased and we've lost countless brain cells on this."

"Fact: No one entered the scene after the victim. Facts are good. What's the rest?"

"We've made some progress on reconstructing the disc from Bart's holo-room. It's one painful nanochip at a time, but there's some progress."

"Even better."

"Aren't you the cheery one?" He stepped to the AutoChef, programmed coffee.

"I know who did it, and I have an idea how."

"All right, let's start with who."

"Var."

"Well, that's a fifty-fifty for most, but you being you, the odds are higher."

"It's nice to be so easily believed."

He waved that off. "You wouldn't say it so definitely unless you were bloody damn sure. So, it's Var. Because?"

"He's the odd man out. The other three go back to childhood. He comes along later in the game—you have to play catch-up. I bet he never liked playing catch-up. But he doesn't hook in with the already established group until college. Before that, if you look at his records, he was the best—by far—in his electronics, math, science, comp, theory classes. Nobody came close."

"Used to being the star—the champion, you could say."

Eve nodded. "Yeah, you could. Then, in college, he hooks up with the other three. Not only are they as good as he is, Bart's better. And he's popular. In a geeky kind of way. Supreme Wizard of the Gaming Club. Where do they come up with titles like that? TA for a couple of classes, dorm manager. Responsible guy, cheerful guy. Brilliant, skilled, and people tended to like him."

Roarke settled in the visitor's chair with his coffee. "And that's your motive?"

"It's the root. Who did you approach when you considered recruiting that group?"

"Bart. Yes. He was de facto leader, even then. Go on."

"And he turned you down, wanted to build his own company. His initial concept from all the statements, the data, the time lines. Equal partnership, sure, but Bart was the head, and the public face."

"True enough, but you could say both Cill and Benny had been competing with him even longer. Benny, for instance, always the side-kick."

"Yeah, I considered that. I had a moment in his apartment during the search with the droid. The Dark Knight connection."

Roarke lowered the coffee, obviously baffled. "What would Batman have to do with it?"

"How do you know that?" Baffled, she tossed up her hands. "How do I say 'Dark Knight' and you immediately click to Batman. How do you *know* this stuff?"

"The question might be how do you not know. Batman's been part of the popular culture lexicon for more than a century."

"Never mind. It's just weird. I could . . ." She narrowed her eyes. "Who murdered sixteen male prostitutes between the ages of eighteen and twenty-three over a three-year period and fed their remains to his prizewinning hogs?"

"Christ Jesus." Despite the image, Roarke had to laugh. "I'm delighted to say I have no idea."

"Hanson J. Flick, 2012–2015." She smirked. "You don't know everything."

"And your particular area of expertise is occasionally revolting."

"Yet handy. In any case, Benny's stuck on Cill, which could have been a motive on Bart, except there's zero going on there in the screwing around department. And Benny's happy with his place in the company. He likes his research. Cill's apartment was a mess—a kind of organized mess. Benny's was lived-in, and he's got Mongo and Alfred for company when he wants them. It's probably healthy in some weird way."

"Mongo?"

"A parrot. It talks. A lot, I'm betting. And you didn't ask who Alfred was."

"You said Benny, Dark Knight, so Alfred's the butler."

To that Eve could only heave out a breath. "Okay. Benny's place. There were signs of grieving and . . . simplicity," she decided. "Var's place was clean. Like he was expecting company. He knew we'd need to do a search—he'd anticipated the steps in the game, and he was ready for it. He stocks good wine, fancier food, spends more on clothes and furniture. He opened the door for the cops at Cill's."

"And that . . . ah. Benny was alone with her. He could have finished her easily. Simply closed off her airway. It wouldn't have taken much, wouldn't have taken long."

"He got to her first, and stayed with her. Var couldn't do anything about it. He expected to find her dead. It had to be a shock when Benny found a pulse, but he thinks on his feet—and he had to hope, to believe, she'd never make it through surgery. It surprised him, and pissed him off when she did. It showed, just for a second. He's good, a good actor. Most sociopaths are, and all that role-playing's worked for him over the years."

"And you believe he played the role of friend and partner, all these years."

"It may have even been true, as far as it goes, off and on. The business is successful, he's making a good living with potential for more. It'll be the more that pushed him, or gave him the excuse he wanted. And the fact Bart could and did overrule him. He's already edging himself into a leadership role at U-Play. Taking Cill out just cements it. Benny doesn't want to run that show. He wants to keep doing what he's doing, so he's not a threat but an asset. Cill could run it, and Benny would side with her. Remove her, and the field's clear."

"All right, say I'm convinced you're right. How? I'll agree he could easily have arranged to go in with Bart, it's trickier with Cill as Benny claims he watched her go in, and Var walked on. I suppose he could have circled around, entered another way, intercepted her before she went in the apartment, but—"

"He was never in either apartment, not at the time of the murder or the attack."

"Well then, how did he manage it? By remote control?"

"In a way. Okay, engaging that open mind you carry around with you, the hologram did it."

"Eve, even a flaw in the system—which we haven't found, couldn't decapitate a player."

"Not the system. The hologram. Bart fought the Black Knight, and the Black Knight won. It cut off Bart's head, and in whatever scenario Cill played, it pushed her, or caused her to fall."

Roarke took another sip of coffee. "Let me understand you. You're suggesting that a holographic image, which is essentially light and shadow, attempted murder and committed it."

"But it's not just light and shadows. Neuro- and nanotech have advanced, and the images produced in holo-programs act and react, according to that program. They appear three-dimensional, appear to have substance. The player's senses are involved and engaged."

"It's an illusion."

"Right. But with clarity. And, some hold the theory that the wave front could be enhanced further, and the beams increased in power, and remarried to complex VR—"

"Results in burnout and system failure," he finished. "You simply can't create actual substance in holo. It's replicated imagery."

"You wouldn't have to. But if you found a way to get around the system failure and increase those beams, the enhanced wave front, to channel that increase, you might also increase the power stream of that light. A kind of current that, okay, not actual substance, but an electronic replication of that substance. A kind of laser."

"It's . . . hmm." He set the coffee aside, rose to go over and edge a hip onto her desk. "Interesting."

"The jolts you get in the game. Tied in to that illusion of contact in, say, a sword fight with the Black Knight. But, if you've found a way to do this enhancement, to take a jump on the tech trampoline, the sword could, conceivably, cut, slash, sever. Or the current could—in the shape of the holo it's programmed to produce. Or in Cill's case, replicate an impact where those currents, or whatever the hell you'd call them, could inflict the same damage as what *they'd* been programmed to replicate."

When he said nothing, she shifted. "Listen, laser scalpels cut. Laser blasters, well, blast. Why can't light imagery—essentially—be manipulated to slice and bash?"

"It would run hot—should run hot enough to shut down the system. To fry it for that matter. But . . ."

"How come all your hotshot R&D people aren't all over this?"

"Oh, we have some toying with it. But the fact is, on a practical level it's not marketable. You can hardly produce games where the players can go around chopping pieces off each other, or other mayhem. You'd be shut down, and sued within an inch."

Her eyes narrowed. "Then why do you have anyone toying?"

And he gave her an easy smile. "You never know what you might find when you're looking for something else, do you? And under certain circumstances, such an application might interest the military. In any case, it's low priority. Or was," he corrected. "And this would explain—"

"A lot. I've eliminated everything else. This is what's left. And when you've eliminated everything else, what's left should be true."

"Yes," Roarke murmured. "It certainly should. There's nothing on this technology on any record or comp at U-Play, or on the partners' equipment. He'll have that private space you're looking for. He'd have to."

"And he'll take the bait there. He'll have to. We'll find it, and when we do, I think we're going to find a lot more than a game." She checked her wrist unit. "Shit. I spent more time laying it out for you than I should have. I need you to program a reenactment of both events, using this theory, so I can use it in the briefing."

"Oh well, then, no problem at all. I can just take that jump on the tech trampoline in the next ten minutes, then take my bows."

"Sarcasm noted. Look, I've got it started. It just needs to be re-fined some."

"It's not like twisting the top off a tube of bloody ketchup after you've loosened it."

"Too much for you?" She cocked her head. "No problem. I'll get McNab on it."

"That's bitchy. On here?"

"Yeah, I've just about got—"

"Go away." He sat, then glanced back at her scowling face. "Now."

"Fine. But don't spend the next century fiddling with it. I just need it clear enough to—"

"Close the door behind you, whether or not it hits you in the ass."

"No need to get pissy," she muttered, and closed the door behind her with a sharp snap.

Since she'd forgotten to get coffee before being kicked out of her own damn office, she stopped and snarled at Vending. Machine and technology, not her friends in the best of times, were currently on her short list. She fingered the loose credits in her pockets and considered her options.

"Hey, Dallas." McNab bounced up. "Great minds." He punched in his code, ordered up a Tango Fizzy—tangerine and mango, Eve thought as her stomach curdled. "Here, get me a Pepsi." She shoved credits at him.

"No prob."

"Any activity on the scan?"

"Not yet. We brought a portable down so I can keep my eye on it while we brief. Anybody takes a stab at hacking in, I'll know it. Here you go." He tossed her the tube. "Peabody says Cill Allen's hanging in so far. Hope she makes it, but I gotta say, I hate she might pop up and say, 'Hey, it was Colonel Mustard in the library with the candlestick' and make it easy after we put this much time in."

"Who the hell is Colonel Mustard?"

"You know, from the game. Clue. You should play it. You'd kill."

"I've had about enough of games that kill." She considered him as she cracked the tube. He was young, and as into gaming as anyone she knew. Plus, being a cop, violence was part of his life. "Would you want that? Want to play games where the stakes were real?"

"You mean where I could win a zillion dollars? Oh shit yeah."

"No. Well, okay, say there's a big cash prize." Because if this thing ever went public, somebody would figure a way to gamble on it. "But to win, even qualify, you had to face off against opponents with real weapons. Real blood, real pain—and potentially fatal."

"So I risk getting my ass kicked, maimed, or dead for money and/or glory? I do that anyway." He smiled, shrugged. "Why would I want to do it for game? Gaming's how you get away from the real for a while."

"Yeah. You're not as stupid as you look."

"Thanks." He lifted his fizzy as she walked away, then clicked in. "Hey!"

She strode into the conference room, nodded as the efficient Peabody finished the setup. She gestured toward the components and screens. "That's the monitor on the dummy files?"

"Yeah. If anyone tries to hack in, access the case files, read, scan copy, infect, EDD will know and trace. I'm keeping my eye on it for a minute while McNab grabs some fluids. The others are on their way."

"Roarke might be late. He's working on something for me."

"Wouldn't mind him working on something for me."

"Excuse me?"

"Hmm? Oh, just talking to myself," Peabody sang. "You know how it is."

Eve strolled over, clipped the back of Peabody's head with the flat of her hand.

"Ow."

"Oh, sorry, just an involuntary reflex. You know how it is." She shifted Var's ID photo from the group on the murder board and set it dead center.

"Him?"

"Him."

"Good. I just won a fifty-dollar bet with myself."

"First, how do you win a bet with yourself?"

"See, I bet myself fifty it was Var. I win, so I put it in my investment kitty. When I get a decent chunk in the kitty, Roarke's going to invest it for me."

"What if you'd lost?"

"Then I'd put it in the investment kitty, but it's more satisfying to win."

"Okay. Why'd you bet for—against—forget that. Why Var?"

"A couple things. His apartment was perfect, both times a team went in. Okay, a lot of people are neat freaks, but he'd be the first serious gamer I know who doesn't have a few stray discs sitting around, or some crumbs where he grabbed a snack while he was playing. And he said he'd been playing the night Cill was attacked. Maybe I just didn't want it to be Benny because he really loves her, and if I was wrong about that, it'd be depressing. Who wants to be depressed?"

"Poets," Eve decided. "You have to think they must."

"Okay, other than poets. Plus, Benny strikes me as more of a follower. You have to be a self-starter to pull this off. I think. So if it came down between the two of them, I bet on Var."

"I may need a tissue, my pride waters me right up."

She looked over as the EDD team came in. "All right. Let's get started. Roarke's working on something for me, so we won't wait for him. I've already briefed him."

She called the first images on-screen while the team settled. "Victim One, Minnock, Bart, decapitated while engaged in play of Fantastical in his holo-room, secured, in his apartment, also secured. Thus far we've found nothing to indicate another entry, invited or forced."

"Nothing to find," Feeney stated. "We have to conclude the killer came in with him, and there's some malfunction with the droid. We're going to take her apart again."

"Maybe not." Eve left it at that until she finished laying the ground-work. "The victim engaged in solo play for just over thirty minutes, starting at level four. We've concluded he gamed K2BK, which through process of elimination would be Usurper. We'll come back to the details of that scenario.

"Victim Two," she continued, "Allen, Cilla, attacked and critically injured while engaged in play of the same game, in her holo-room, unsecured, in her apartment, which was secured. No indications of another entry, invited or forced until her partners, Leman and Hoyt, entered this morning and discovered her on the holo-room floor. After questioning, her partners state her preferred game is Dragon's Egg—a treasure hunt. We'll go into those details shortly."

She glanced at her wrist unit. If Roarke ever finished.

"Victim Two began at level one, engaged in play for just over two hours. We have her just shy of completing level three. Expert medical opinion based on her injuries, the scans, concludes she suffered those injuries in a fall from perhaps twenty feet onto a hard, rough, and uneven surface."

"Can't be," Feeney disagreed. Absently, he took a cube of gum McNab offered him. "Screws the time line and the entry, and hell, the physical evidence on-scene. The attack went down in the holo-room."

"I agree." Eve stepped to the side of the wall screen to give the team an unobstructed view of the crime scene record. "So how does a woman incur injuries from a fall such as I've described on the smooth, flat surface of her holo-room? How does a man get his head cut off when all evidence concludes he was alone? The only logical explanation is Bart was killed and Cill attacked by their opponent in the game."

"If they were alone, Dallas, they didn't have a damn opponent."

Eve shifted her glance toward Feeney. "But they did. Each would have to defeat or outwit that opponent to reach the next level. For Bart, the Black Knight. For Cill, the rival treasure hunter."

"You're saying some holo jumped out of a game and sliced off the vic's head?" Feeney shook his own. "You've been working too hard, kid."

"I'm saying the killer used the game," Eve corrected. "I'm saying he used a new technology programmed into the game as the weapon. Enhanced wave fronts, increased power to beams and the haptic system, a refocus of laser angles and light, forming electrons and light source in the shape of the programmed images—replicating substance."

Callendar tilted her head. "Wicked. Wicked freaky."

21

"THAT'S SCIENCE FICTION SHIT."

"It's fiction until science catches up." Eve rocked back on her heels. "Feeney, you work with science every day. Go back to your rookie days and compare them with now. This isn't my area, so maybe it's easier for me to consider the possibility. Nothing else fits. And this? Figuring the evidence, the time lines, the circumstances, the personalities, and the areas of interest? It fits like a fucking glove."

"There's always some rumbling and mumbling on the under-ground sites," McNab commented. His eyes shone bright with the possibilities—what Eve thought of as a geek beam. "Way-out theories and applications."

"We got sightings of Bigfoot and little green men on-sites, too," Feeney countered, but he was frowning in a way that made Eve sure he was considering.

"Both vics had minute burns, internal burns, at the site of injuries.

We've gone around chasing some charged-up sword. I think we weren't far off. But it only exists within the program. I believe Levar Hoyt killed one partner and attempted to kill another through his programming. Let's take him for a minute."

She shifted gears, back to the comfortable, and outlined her reasons and conclusions on the suspect.

"He looks good for it," Feeney agreed. "You've got a nice pile of circumstantial. But say I came over to this idea of yours, how the hell do we prove it?"

"He's going to tell me. He's going to want to tell me." She paused as Roarke walked in. "Got it?"

"It's rough considering I was pressed for time—and your equipment is hardly cutting-edge—but I have it, yes."

"Load it up. Display on screen two. What we're going to see are reconstructions of the crimes, using the available data, images, medical findings, and applying the theory. The running time's bottom right. For both, we've utilized the victims' game pattern from records of their sessions."

She watched as Roarke set the program, displayed it on-screen. "Bart Minnock enters his apartment," she continued as the computerized images moved over the screen. "Interacts with the droid. He drinks the fizzy she serves him, orders her to shut down for the night. He leaves the glass on the table, goes to the third floor, and enters the holo-room, secures it."

She watched it play out, keeping an eye on the elapsed time. It fit, she thought again. The image moved through the steps, the pattern previously established. Maybe he'd done something different this time, but it didn't matter. He'd ended up, as he did now, facing off with the figure of the Black Knight.

Swords clashed, horses reared, smoke plumed. Then the tip of the blade scored Bart's arm, and the knight followed through with the coup de grace.

"You'll note the positions, the height, reach of the victim and the holo-image, the blow result in the exact positioning of the victim, head and body, as we have on record at the time of discovery. For the second victim, we'll move straight to level three."

"I put considerable time into the lead up," Roarke complained.

"Which is appreciated, and will be of interest to the PA's office. But for now, let's save time. Her character's after this artifact, and up against obstacles, puzzles, and opponents. She needs to reach the top of this rise, gain entrance to a cave in order to complete the level. Note the path is muddy."

Arrows flew. Cill's image dodged, weaved, slipped, scrambled up. Then came face-to-face with her opponent.

"The time line, considering her average pace and movements, indicates she found the holo-image here, on the muddy path, leading up the rise to the cave, with the cliff dropping on to the rocks and water at her right. There! Pause program."

The images froze as the knife sliced Cill's arm.

"She sustained this injury—one Morris states was the result of insult with a smooth, sharp object. Knife or sword. Resume program. She's shocked, hurt, and off balance on the slippery path, falls before her opponent can follow through. Or, he gives her a nice shove. She hits the rocks, and is knocked unconscious. Game over. Since she loses consciousness, the program no longer reads her, and ends."

She turned away from the screen. "Meanwhile the son of a bitch who arranged it is sitting at home with his fucking feet up entertaining himself, establishing his alibi, probably practicing his shock and grief. He eliminates two of his partners—two of his obstacles—and never gets his hands bloody."

Feeney scratched his chin. "I'll give you the timing works, and I'm not going to argue with Morris if he says that girl fell. But if this bastard figured out how to manipulate holo to this level, I'd sure like a look inside his head. Running that hot, hot enough to do this should've toasted the system."

"Maybe not the first time," Roarke put in. "He may have found a way to shield it. I don't think a standard system would hold up to multiple plays."

"He only needed one." Eve pointed out.

"That's what's so screwy about the disc, the one we've been working to reconstruct." McNab shifted to Callendar. "The high intensity of focused light, the concentration of nanos."

"Cloak that in tri-gees to keep the system from snapping."

"I'd use bluetone."

"That'd gunk it inside of six UPH."

"Not if you layered it with a wave filter." Feeney joined in, and Eve turned back to her board as the geek team argued and theorized.

Peabody came over to join her. "I speak some basic geek, but I don't understand a word they're saying. I guess I'll go back to Callendar's first comment. It's wicked freaky."

"It's science. People have been using science to kill since some cave guy set some other poor bastard's hair on fire."

She turned again, studied Cill's broken body on the holo-room floor.

"The underlying's the same, but sometimes the methods get fancier. He's a cold, egotistical son of a bitch. He used friendship, partnership, trust, relationships, and affection built over years to kill a man who would never have done him any harm. He put another friend into the hospital where one more friend has to suffer, has to watch her fight to live. And he's enjoyed every minute of it. Every minute of being the focus of our attention, absolutely confident in his ability to beat us.

And that's how we'll bring him down. Hang him with his own ego, his need to win."

She glanced over as the monitor began to beep.

"McNab!" The snap in her voice cut McNab off in the middle of a passionate argument over hard versus soft light.

"Sir."

She jabbed a finger at the equipment. He sprang up, rushed over. "We got a breach on the outer layer. He's testing it."

"Track the signal."

"Working on it. He's got shields up, and feelers out. See that? See that?"

Eve saw a bunch of lights and lines.

"Two can play," McNab muttered.

"Three." Callendar put on a headset, began to snap her fingers, shift her hips. "He bounced."

"Yeah yeah, he's careful. There, that's . . . No, no, that's a fish."

"I'll run a line on it anyway. Maybe he'll wiggle it back."

"Try a lateral, Ian," Roarke suggested. "Then go under. He's just skimming now."

"Let that fish swim," Feeney told Callendar. "It's not . . . There, see, there, he's sent out a ghost. Go hunting."

Eve paced away, circled, paced back as for the next twenty minutes the e-team followed squiggles and wiggles, flashes and bursts.

"He's nipped through the next layer," Roarke pointed out. "He's taking his time about it."

"Maybe we made it too easy for him." Feeney puffed out his cheeks. "We're scaring him off."

"I don't care how many layers he gets through. What he's going to find is bogus anyway. I want his location."

McNab glanced back at Eve. "He's a pogo stick on Zeus, Dallas. He's bouncing, then switching off, banking back. The bastard's good."

"Better than you?"

"I didn't say that. We've got echoes, we've got cross and junctions, so he's in New York. Probably."

"I know he's in New York."

"I'm verifying it," he said, testy now.

Roarke laid a hand on McNab's shoulder. "I doubt you want chapter and verse here, Lieutenant. But imagine you were in a foot chase with a suspect who could, at any given time, pop ten blocks over, or take a jump to London, zip over to the Ukraine, then land again a block behind you. It might take you some time to catch the bloody bastard."

"Okay, all right. How much time?"

"If he keeps at this pace, and we're able to track those echoes, extrapolate the junctions, it shouldn't take more than a couple hours. Maybe three."

She didn't curse. Var might have been bouncing all over hell and back in cyberspace, but as long as they had him on the monitor, he was in one place in reality.

"Can you run one of these at home?" she asked Roarke.

"I can, yes."

"Do you have any problems with that?"

Feeney gave her an absent wave. "A secondary setup at another source might help flank the bastard."

"Okay then, I'm going to work from home. In the quiet. I need to put this all down in a way that Whitney doesn't have me committed when I report to him tomorrow. You can save me a lot of trouble by locating the murdering fuckhead."

"If he keeps up the hack, we'll have him. Yeah, yeah, he's in New York. See there. Now let's start scraping away sectors."

"I'll hang here," Peabody said. "Keep them supplied with liquids."

"Be ready for a go tonight." Eve looked back at the team. It came down to trust again. If they said they'd pin him, they'd pin him.

"Maybe I should just take it to my office," Eve considered as they headed out.

"Feeney's right about the value of a secondary source. I can do more at home, and I have better equipment. Added to that, I'd like my hands in it, and here I'd just step on Ian's toes."

"All right. Set up at home, and I'll spend the next hour or two trying to find a way to write a report that doesn't make me sound like a lunatic."

"You came off quite sane when you ran it by me, and then the rest. Push the science. I'll help you with it," he added when she didn't quite muffle the groan. "We'll dazzle the commander with your in-depth knowledge of advance holonetics."

"I feel a headache coming on."

He brushed his lips over the top of her head as they stepped into the garage. "There now."

"One way or the other, he's in the box with me tomorrow. My turf, my area. And then we'll see who . . . Shit, *shit*, could it be that simple?"

"Could what?"

"Turf. Area." *Shit!* she thought again and pulled up short. "I have to figure he's got his hole within the basic parameters of his place, the partners, the warehouse. He's efficient, careful, meticulous. Why would he risk being seen—and maybe even by his so-called friends—going in or out of another building?"

Roarke uncoded the doors, pulled hers open, then leaned on it. "His own building. He'd want his special equipment close, wouldn't he? Easier to secure, to monitor that security, to use whenever he has the whim."

"Not his apartment. There's nothing in there. But there are other spaces in that building. Including the other half of his floor."

"Let's go have a look."

"My thoughts exactly. I'll run the address while you drive, see who rents or owns it."

He got behind the wheel. "Backup?"

"I'll let them know we're taking the detour, but I don't want to call out the troops then have this turn out to be a bust. Anyway, I think we can handle a cybergeek who kills by remote control. He's a coward on top of . . . Stuben, Harry and Tilda, ages eighty-six and eighty-five respectively. Owners, in residence for eighteen years. Three children, five grandchildren, two great-grandchildren."

"It could be a blind."

"Yeah." She drummed her fingers on her thigh. "There was good security on that apartment. Two doors, both with monitors, cams, palm plates. The inside setup is probably a mirror image of Var's. It's worth a knock. I'll run the other units. Maybe something will pop, but this one feels right."

When he parked, she pulled out her communicator. "Peabody, we're going to take a look at Var's across-the-hall neighbors. Following a hunch."

"Do you want me to meet you?"

"No. We'll take our look-see. If I don't tag you back in fifteen, send backup."

"Copy that. Across the hall from his own place. That would be smart, now that I think of it. Dallas, why don't you just leave the com open? I can monitor, and if I hear any trouble, I'll release the hounds."

"All right. While you're babysitting us, go ahead and run the other occupants of the building. And put your com on mute. I don't want to hear your voice coming out of my ass." She stuck the communicator in her back pocket as Roarke chuckled.

"Let's make this official. Record on. Dallas, Lieutenant Eve, and Roarke, expert consultant, civilian, entering Var Hoyt's building to interview suspect's neighbor."

She used her master to gain entry.

"You know, if I were him, I'd have the outer security rigged to alert me if anyone bypassed the normal entry procedure."

"Maybe. Still, he'd have to scramble to shut down operations in one space, secure it, get across the hall, unlock, get in, resecure. And when I push for another warrant, the security logs will show exactly that if so. Or we could just be interrupting an old couple's quiet evening."

"Maybe they're out doing the tango and drinking tequila shots." He sent Eve a grin. "As we will be when we reach their age. After which we'll come home and have mad sex."

"For God's sake. This is on the record."

"Yes, I know." He stepped off with her on Var's floor. "I wanted those future plans to be official as well."

She aimed a smoldering look before stopping outside the entrance to the apartment across from Var's. "He's locked up over there. Full red. Here, too," she noted.

She knocked, waited, with a hand resting on the butt of her weapon. She poised to knock again when the speaker clicked.

"Hello?"

The voice was female and a bit wary.

"Mrs. Stuben?"

"That's right. Who are you?"

"Lieutenant Dallas, NYPSD." She held up her badge so the camera could see it. "We'd like to speak with you."

"Is there a problem? Is there something wrong? Oh my goodness! Is it one of the kids?"

"No, ma'am," Eve began even as the locks opened, and the security went to green. "No, ma'am," she repeated when the door opened. "This is just a routine inquiry related to an ongoing investigation."

"An investigation?" The woman was small and slim in lounging pants and a flowered shirt. Her hair, tidy and ashy blond rode on her head like a helmet. "Harry! Harry! The police are at the door. I guess you should come in."

She stepped back, revealing a large, comfortable living area, crowded with dust catchers and photographs. The air smelled of lavender.

"I'm sorry, I didn't mean to be rude. I'm just so flustered." She patted a hand to her heart. "You can come right in, sit down. I was about to make some tea for Harry and me. A nice pot of tea while we watch our shows. Harry!" she called again, then sighed. "He's got that screen on so loud he can't hear me. I'm going to go get him. You just sit right down, and I'll go get Harry."

"Mrs. Stuben, do you know your neighbor across the hall? Levar Hoyt?"

"Var? Sure we do. Such a nice young man," she said as she started up the stairs. "Smart as they come. We couldn't ask for a better neighbor. Harry!"

"Tea and flowers," Eve murmured, "everything's just so homey."

"Which, of course, automatically raises your suspicions. Still, some people . . ." He stopped in his turn around the room. "Eve," he said, just as the locks on the door snapped shut, and the room shimmered away.

"It's a goddamn holo." Eve reached for her weapon, and drew a sword. "Oh, fuck me!"

"We'll have to wait on that. To your left."

She barely had time to pivot, to block before the blade sliced down. She looked into a scarred face mottled with tattoos. It grinned while twin red suns turned the sky to the color of blood.

She came up with her left elbow, rammed him in the throat. When he stumbled back she took a fraction of a second to glance toward Roarke. He fought a bare-chested mountain of a man armed with sword and dagger. Beyond him, in the blue observer's circle, stood Var.

Frightened, she thought as she met the next thrust. Scared, desperate, but excited, too.

"They'll come looking for us, Var!" she shouted. "Stop the game."

"It's got to play out."

She felt the boggy ground under her feet, and part of her mind registered the heavy, wet heat, the scream of birds, the wildly improbable green of thick trees. Swords crashed, deadly cymbals, as she fought for any advantage.

To play the game, she thought, you had to know the rules.

"What the hell are we fighting about?" she demanded. She leaped when her opponent swung the sword at her knees, then struck back at his sword arm. "We've got no beef with you."

"You invade our world, enslave us. We will fight you to the last breath."

"I don't want your damn world." She saved her breath, spun away from his sword, and reared up in a kick that caught him in the side. When she followed through to finish him, he feinted, fooled her, and ran a line of pain down her hip with the tip of his sword.

She leaped back. "I'm a New York City cop, you son of a bitch. And I'm going to kick your ass."

Riding on fury, she came in hard, her sword flying right, left, slashing through his guard to rip his side. She pushed in, slamming her fist in his face. Blood erupted from his nose.

"That's how we do it in New York!"

Rage burned in his eyes. He let out a war cry, charged in. She rammed her sword into his belly, to the hilt, yanking it free as he fell, then whirling toward Roarke.

Blood stained the black body armor he wore and smeared the gleaming chest of his opponent. Beside them a river raged in eerie, murky red while enormous tri-winged birds swooped.

As she ran toward him, she took the drumbeats she heard for her racing heart.

"I've got this," he snapped out.

"Oh, for Christ's sake." She swung her sword up, but before she could land the blow, Roarke sliced his across his opponent's throat.

"I said I had it."

"Great. Points for you. Now—"

She turned with every intention of rushing Var and holding the point of the sword to his throat. Another warrior leaped into her path, then another, and more.

Men, women, tattooed, armed. And as the drumbeat came from the bones more of them rapped rhythmically on the trees.

"We can't take them all," Eve murmured as she and Roarke moved instinctively to guard each other's backs.

"No." He reached back, took her free hand in his, squeezed. "But we can give them a hell of a fight."

"We can hold them off." She circled with them as the first group moved in slowly. "Hold them off until the backup gets here. If you can get to the controls—if you can find the damn controls, can you end it?"

"Possibly. If you could get through to that little bastard over there."

"Solid line between us and him. A goddamn sword's not enough to . . . Wait a minute, wait a damn minute."

It wasn't real, she thought. Deadly, murderous, but still not real. But her weapon was. She couldn't see it, couldn't feel it through the program, but it was *there*.

Muscle memory, habit, ingrained instinct. She shifted her sword to her left hand, drew a breath. She slapped her hand to her side, and her hand remembered. The shape, the feel, the weight.

She fired, and watched the warrior struck by the beam fall.

She fired again, again, scattering the field.

"Clutch piece. Right ankle. Can you get it?"

"No time." Roarke whirled to strike at the man who came at her left. "Hit the controls. Blast the bloody controls."

"Where the hell are they?"

She took out another before he landed his sword on Roarke's unguarded side.

"Right side of the door!" he shouted, grabbing a second sword from a fallen warrior. "About five feet up."

"Where's the fucking door?" She sent out streams, shooting wild and blind. Those unearthly green trees fired and smoked, screams ripped the air while she struggled to orient herself.

They just kept coming, she realized as she fired again and again in a desperate attempt to keep the charging warriors off Roarke.

Var had rigged the game, programmed it for only one outcome.

"Well, *fuck* that!"

Across the damn river, she thought, and east. She concentrated her fire. Five feet up, she thought again, and plowed a stream in a wide swath at five feet.

She caught movement out of the corner of her eye, started to pivot, to lift her left arm and the sword as she continued to fire with her right.

Roarke struck in between her and the oncoming warrior, knocking the sword clear of her.

She watched in shock and horror as the dagger in the warrior's other hand slid into Roarke's side.

In the same instant tongues of flames spurted with a harsh electric crackle and snap. The images shimmered away. She grabbed Roarke, taking his weight when he swayed. "Hold on. Hold on."

"You cheated." Var stood, stunned outrage on his face, in a room filling with smoke. He made a run for the door.

Eve didn't spare him a word, simply dropped him.

As Var's body jolted and jittered, she eased Roarke to the floor.

"Let me see. Let me see."

"Not that bad." He took a labored breath, reached up. "You took a few hits yourself."

"Be quiet." She ripped open his already ruined shirt, shoved his jacket aside. "Why do you always wear so many clothes?"

She didn't know she was weeping, he thought, his cop, his cool-headed warrior. When she shed her own jacket, ruthlessly ripped off the sleeve, he winced. "That was a nice one, once."

She folded the sleeve, pressed the cushion of material to the wound in his side.

"It's not bad." Well, he hoped to Christ it wasn't, and concentrated on her face. Eve's face. Just Eve. "Hurts like the bloody fires of hell, but it's not that bad. I've been stabbed before."

"Shut up, just shut up." She yanked out her communicator. "Officer needs assistance. Officer down. Officer down."

"I'm an officer now, am I? That's insult to injury." As she shouted out the address, he turned his head at the violent thumping at the door. "Ah, well, there's the backup. Wipe your face, baby. You'd hate them to see the tears."

"Screw that." But she swiped the back of one bloody hand over her cheeks. She pressed his hand to the makeshift bandage. "Hold that?

Can you hold that?" She ripped off the second sleeve. "You're not leaving me."

"Darling Eve. I'm not going anywhere." Her face, he thought again as the pain seared up his side. "I had worse than this when I was twelve."

She added the second pad, laid her hand over his. "You're okay. You're going to be okay."

"That's what I'm telling you," he said as the door burst open. The entry team came in loaded, with Peabody behind them.

"Get a medic!" Eve demanded. "Get a damn medic in here. We're clear. We're clear."

"Sweep the place," Peabody ordered. "Secure that asshole." She dropped to her knees beside Eve. "MT's on the way. How bad?" She reached out, stroked Roarke's hair back from his face.

"Stabbed him in the side. He's lost blood. I think we've slowed it down, but—"

"Let's have a look." Feeney crouched down. "Ease back, Dallas. Come on now, kid, ease back." Feeney elbowed her aside, gently lifted the field dressing. "That's a good hole you've got there." He looked into Roarke's eyes. "I expect you've had worse."

"I have. She's some of her own."

"We'll take care of it."

"It's clear." McNab shot his weapon away, knelt down beside Peabody. "How you doing?" he asked Roarke.

"Been better, but, hell, we won."

"That's what counts. Callendar's grabbing towels out of the bathroom. We'll fix you up."

"No doubt." As he started to sit up, Eve shoved in again.

"Don't move. You'll start up the bleeding again. Wait—"

"Now you shut up," he suggested, and tugged her to him, pressed his lips firmly to hers.

22

EVE SAT IN THE CONFERENCE ROOM WITH THE
team, her commander, Mira, and Cher Reo.

She watched, with the others, while her recording
played on-screen, and tried to ignore the fact that on it she fought for
her life wearing a black skin-suit and copper breastplate.

If she couldn't still feel the memory of Roarke's blood on her hands,
and the aches and burns in her own body, it would've been ridiculous.

Again, she watched Roarke block her from attack while she fired at
holo-images. Why hadn't she hit the controls sooner, she thought? Why
hadn't she found them sooner? Seconds sooner and he wouldn't have
taken the knife. Only seconds.

She saw it happen again, the pivot and block to save her, the fierce-
ness of his face. And the slide of the knife into his vulnerable side.

Then the scene changed—like a flipped channel—and they stood in
a room ruined by her blasts and streams, smoke thick, the controls
crackling flame, and Roarke's blood staining the floor.

"It's bizarre," Reo murmured. "I've watched it twice now, listened to your report, and I still have a hard time believing it."

"We'll need to keep as many of the details as possible out of the media." Whitney scanned the faces in the room. "As many as possible inside this room. All of his records and equipment were confiscated?"

"Everything in the place," Eve confirmed. "He may have another hole, but I believe that's unlikely. He kept it all close to home. We'll take him into Interview shortly." She turned to Mira. "Ego, competition, pride of accomplishment?"

"Yes, all those areas are vulnerable points. He's become not only addicted to the game, but may have lived inside it for some time. It's a more exciting reality, one where he controls all—but stands aloof. He didn't engage in play with you."

"He's a coward."

"Yes, but one who believes himself superior. You only won because you cheated. He believes that, too."

"The game was the weapon, he controlled the game. Can we charge him with First Degree on Minnock?" Eve asked Reo.

"Tricky. It could be argued he only intended Minnock to play, and that the victim could have won. And we have no proof Minnock wasn't fully aware of the technology when he himself started the game."

"That's bullshit."

"I agree, but I can't prove it beyond a reasonable doubt in court. We go for Man One—just hear me out," she said before Eve could object. "Man One on Minnock, Reckless Endangerment on Allen, the same on both you and Roarke, adding Assault on a police officer, and the stack of Cyber Crimes, the unregistered equipment, false statements, and so on. We wrap him up, Dallas, make the deal, avoid the trial that could drag on for months—and sensationalize the technology and the crimes in the media. He'll do a solid fifty or more in a cage. A cage, due to the cyber-charges, without access to the e-toys he knows and loves. It's harsh, and it's apt."

"I want Attempted Murder on Cill and Roarke. I want him charged, goddamn it." She pulled herself back, pulled it in. "I'm going in on Murder One on Bart Minnock. If you deal it down later, I'll accept that, but I want him charged, and I want to start the deal at the high mark."

Reo studied Eve's face. Whatever she saw there had her easing back. "Let's see what happens in Interview, and go from there."

"Then let's get started."

Whitney pulled her aside. "He can sweat until morning. Until you've had a little more recovery time."

"I'm fine, sir." Going now, she thought, and going hot. "He's already had a couple hours to regroup. I don't want to give him any more."

"Your choice. Dallas? Don't make it personal."

"No, sir."

But it was. It was, she thought as she walked over to Roarke.

He wore a shirt copped from Baxter's locker, and under it, she knew his wound was still fresh, still raw. His color was back, his eyes clear. Not pale, so pale, as he'd been when his blood had seeped through her fingers.

"I know you want to see this through," she began. "I get it. But I'll arrange for you to view the record. You need to go home, take those damn drugs you refused, and let Summerset hover over you."

"I will if you will."

"Roarke."

"Eve. We understand each other, don't we? Let's finish this."

"There's going to be a chair in Observation. Use it."

She walked away, found Mira. "I'm going to ask you for a favor. I need you to keep your eye on Roarke. If he looks like he needs it, jab him with a damn pressure syringe full of tranqs. I'll take the rap."

"Don't worry." Mira slipped her arm around Eve's waist, just for a moment. "We'll have him outnumbered."

She nodded, then ordered herself to shake it off. Just shake it off and do the job. "Peabody." She paused, pushed a hand through her hair. "You're sympathetic, even a little impressed. Not too soft, nobody would buy it. But you're younger than he is, and he'll read that as naive. If he's done any digging, and he would have, he knows you're cohabbed with an e-man."

"Got it. Suggestion? I'd lose the jacket you got out of your locker. Go in bare-armed so he can see the hits you took. It'll give him a little rush."

"That's good." She tugged it off, setting her teeth when her arm twinged. She tossed the jacket to McNab. "Hang onto it."

Then she nodded to Peabody and opened the door of Interview A.

He sat at the table, hands folded, head down. He lifted it as they entered, gave Eve a sorrowful look. "I don't know what happened. I—"

"Quiet," she snapped. "Record on. Dallas, Lieutenant Eve, and Peabody, Detective Delia, entering Interview with Hoyt, Levar. Mr. Hoyt, have you been read your rights?"

"Yeah, when they—"

"Do you understand your rights and obligations?"

"Okay, yeah, but the thing is—"

"Look, asshole, I'm not wasting time on your lame explanations and bullshit. I was there, remember? Had a ringside seat to your sick game."

"That's what I'm trying to *tell* you." His shackles clattered when he lifted his hands. "The whole thing got away from me. Some sort of glitch, and I was trying to fix it when—"

She slammed both hands on the table, made him jump. But she saw his gaze slide over, and up to the wound on her arm. "You stood there, you bastard, watching that vicious world you created go for us. You stood there."

"I was trying to make it stop, but—"

"Stood there, observing. Too much of a coward to actually play." She reached out, grabbed his shirtfront. "Too weak to take me on?"

"Easy, Dallas. Easy." Peabody laid a hand on Eve's shoulder in warning. "The guy created something pretty amazing. He's a scientist. He probably doesn't do much combat."

"I can hold my own."

Eve snorted in disgust, paced away.

"Well, sure." Peabody sat now. "But I'm just saying, up against somebody trained like Dallas, or in the shape Roarke's in, you'd be at a disadvantage. Physically. When it comes to e? You're off the scale."

"Maybe you two would like a moment alone," Eve said coolly.

"Come on, Dallas, credit where it's due. How long did it take you to develop the program? The tech's beyond the ult. I can't get my head around it."

"It's an entirely new level. It took years, but I could only put so much time into it. It'll open up a whole new world, not just for gaming, but, well, for training you guys, and military. That kind of thing." Eager now, he leaned forward. "I wanted to create something, to *give* something to society. I tried dozens of theories, applications, programs, before I was able to refine it. The realism offers the player true risk and reward. And that's . . ." He drew back, as if realizing he was digging a hole.

"I never expected it would cause actual harm. That's why I've been working to retool, to offer that same realism but without the potential to cause injury."

"You knew it could harm, could even kill," Peabody said, still wide-eyed. "So you've been trying to fix it."

"Yes, yes. I'd never want anyone to be hurt."

"Then why didn't you tell Bart? Why didn't you tell him the program was fatally flawed?"

"I . . . didn't know he was going to take the disc. He didn't log it out, he didn't say anything."

"But what was it doing there, at U-Play, if you were working on it outside the office?"

"I wanted to run it for him, to brainstorm with him, but he must've taken the disc to try it for himself." Var lowered his head into his hands again. "I don't know why he did that. Why he took a chance like that."

"You're stating that you told Bart about your work, about the program, and the risks?"

"Absolutely."

"Just Bart?"

"That's right. I didn't realize he'd taken the experimental disc until—"

"Then why is Cill in the hospital?" Peabody persisted. "How did she get her hands on a second program disc if you only took one in to Bart?"

"After Bart I told her about it." He widened his eyes, all sorrowful innocence. "I had to tell someone."

"And she just got some wild hair and repeated Bart's mistake?"

He sat back, set his jaw. "She must have. She didn't say a thing about it. You can ask Benny."

"We'll be asking her. She's out of the coma," Eve lied and turned back. "The doctors said she's going to make a full recovery, and she'll be able to talk to us tomorrow." She glanced at her watch. "Make that later today."

"Thank God. Thank God for that. But you have to understand, she's really pissed. She's really wrecked and totally pissed at me about Bart. She blames me."

"Imagine that. And imagine, Var, who we're going to believe when she tells us you gave her that disc, told her to work on it."

"I never did any such thing. You'll never be able to prove that. My word against Cill's, and she's right out of brain surgery. Maybe I should get a lawyer. I bet a lawyer would tell you the same thing."

"You want a lawyer? Fine. We'll end the interview now while you make those arrangements. And while you are, the e-team will be dissecting your precious program, your logs and records, your unregistered, and destroying same."

"Wait! Wait!" His restraints rattled again as he came halfway out of his chair. "You can't do that. That's my work. My property. You've got no right to do that."

"Tell it to your lawyer."

"Let's just hold off. Let's just wait."

"Are you saying you don't want legal representation at this time?"

"Yes. Let's just talk this through." He folded his hands again, but this time, Eve noted, his knuckles had whitened. "That work is valuable and complex. Your e-people aren't going to get it. It's years in the making. It's mine."

"Yours? Not U-Play's? You have a contract, Var. Share and share alike. Any of you develops something, it goes in the kitty."

"That doesn't seem altogether fair," Peabody added. "Not when you did this on your own. Something this brilliant."

"I would've shared it, but Bart . . . Look, I discussed all this with Bart and he didn't want any part of it. So it's mine. Exclusively."

"You told Bart about the work, the concept for the program?"

"He's the marketing genius. We could've revolutionized the market."

"But he was shortsighted."

"Games are games, that was Bart's line. He couldn't see expanding beyond that, couldn't see the possibilities. He was all about the risks. So it's mine. I did all the work, put in all the time—my *own* time."

"And melded it with the concept and technology in Fantastical," Eve finished. "Not yours exclusively." She pointed a finger. "You cheated."

"I did not!" Color rose, hot and bright, on his cheeks. "Look, he had a choice, and he made it. It's all about choices, isn't it? Every gamer decides what action to take, then plays it out."

"And Bart was a better gamer than you."

"Bullshit."

"He had a better focus, and looked at long-range strategy. You're the detail man, and you tend to miss the big picture."

"He's the one who's dead," Var snapped back.

"Yeah, got me there. You set him up, and you took him out."

"Facts." Var punched a finger on the table. "Bart took the disc. Bart plugged it. Bart played the game. I wasn't there. Nobody forced him to play. He had a bad game, a terrible accident, but I'm not responsible. I created the program, worked the tech, but that's like saying the guy who built that weapon you're carrying is responsible when you zap somebody."

"He's got a point." Peabody nodded. "You're just the brains behind it."

"That's right."

"I guess you're the smartest one of the four, too. None of them came up with anything close to what you did."

"They never think outside their box." He drew four connecting lines in the air. "Four square."

"Frustrating for you, to be able to see so much more than they could." Peabody sighed a little in sympathy. "Why didn't you ever cut loose, just go out on your own? You didn't need them."

He shrugged.

"Or maybe you did," Peabody continued. "I mean, a smart man knows he needs to use other people, pick their brains, let them handle some of the work so he can focus on what's most important. You've known them a long time, worked with them, so you know their strengths and weaknesses, and how to use them for, you know, that big picture."

"You've got to make a living so you can do the work."

"Right. They supplied that. I get it. So when you gave Bart the disc, it was really just an experiment. You needed to see what would happen. To test it out with an actual human player."

"That's right. He gives good game. I thought he'd last longer than . . . I couldn't know," he said, backtracking. "I wasn't there."

"You couldn't know when you gave Cill the disc either," Peabody agreed. "You couldn't know she'd fall. Plus, their weapons were as lethal as their opponents'. It wasn't like you sent them in unarmed."

"It had to be fair." Var leaned forward, focusing on Peabody. "Look, Bart played that scenario a million times. If he hadn't figured out how to take out the Black Knight, it's not my fault."

"How could it be? And if you'd told them they were plugging in *your* program, your new technology, it wouldn't have been a valid experiment. A true gamer is supposed to believe it's real, right?"

"Exactly." He gave the table a quick slap. "There's no point otherwise."

"You had no responsibility to tell them about the program when you gave them the discs."

"No, I didn't. What happened after that was on them."

Eve started to speak, then hooked her thumbs in her pockets to let Peabody play him out.

"But those can't have been your first experiments. Not for a scientist as meticulous and involved as you. You must have played the game yourself."

"I used droids, once I figured out the tech, and what was possible, I used droids against the holos. It's all in my logs. I documented everything. I didn't do anything wrong. It's not my fault anyone got hurt."

"Droids and holos." On a low whistle, Peabody shook her head in admiration. "Man, I'd love to watch that play out."

"Holos took it eighty-nine-point-two percent of the time. But they could run it for hours. Wicked frosty."

"You knew they weren't coming out," Eve murmured. "When you sent your *friends*, your *partners* into those holo-rooms, you knew they had almost no chance of surviving the game."

"I couldn't know." He folded his arms, smiled a little.

"You've got us there." Eve nodded. "They walked in on their own. You weren't there. It's not like you forced them to play."

He shot out a finger. "Bingo."

"Wanting Bart gone, that's not a crime either. And you did want him gone, didn't you, Var? You'd done with them. You had what you'd worked for, and here's Bart, who's not nearly as smart, as inventive, as visionary as you are, refusing to play. All the resources of the business, all the tools available—that you'd helped build. And he said no, no dice, not going there. What gave him the right to deny you?"

"He didn't have the right. I'm just as much a part of U-Play as he was. Just as important. But if Bart said no, everybody went along."

"That's a pisser. But if Bart's not around, you go up a level. You have more control, more power, more say."

"Like you said, wanting him gone's not a crime."

"And you had a way, where you wouldn't be responsible, and he'd be gone. It's brilliant."

"It's what I do. I build the scenario, create the tech, and the player decides. Win some, lose some."

"He loses, you win." Eve studied his smug, satisfied face as she rocked slowly back and forth on her heels. "And you've tied our hands on it. You always knew we couldn't come at you for murder, even if we figured it out."

"I have to say, I didn't think you'd figure it out. Not for a while, not at least until I had the program on the market. Going military and security with that, by the way. It's not for the kiddies. You can see right in my logs and notes that I never intended the tech for the open market. You just can't come at me on this."

"You gave them the discs, and didn't tell them about the augmentation."

"Yeah, I gave them the discs. So what? And Bart should've figured out the augmentation after five minutes if he was paying attention. It's not like I *forced* him to play the game."

"Cill didn't know about the new tech. She knew nothing about it."

He shrugged. "Okay, so what? She should've figured it, too. She's so freaking smart. Benny's already making noises about having her take Bart's meetings, the interviews."

"Pushing her in front of you." Eve nodded. "Too bad she fell, instead of getting a knife in the heart."

"The program shuts down if the player's unconscious. I didn't realize that until it happened. That's the problem with droids. Now, I know, so I can adjust. Oh, and I wanted to say, you held up good out there. You and Roarke really showed some skill. But you can't bring in alternate weapons—that's not play. And, like I said, I was trying to shut it down, but hit some glitch. These things happen." He smiled again. "I saw Roarke took a hard one. I hope he's okay."

She leaned in. "Fuck you."

"There's no need to get steamed." He smiled broadly. "You happened to come in, and I was in the middle of an experimental game—and that's not against the law either. Listen, you can get me on the unregistered. I'll pay the fine, do the community service, whatever. I won't even sue you for zapping me—in my own place. Now I should really get to the hospital and see Cill. I can't even imagine how scrambled her brain is after what she went through. So, can I go now?"

"Yeah. Yeah, Var, you can go. To hell, via a cage. You're under arrest."

"Arrest?" He rolled his eyes. "Come on, come on, we've been through this."

"That's right, and you've admitted to creating the program, to giving both Bart and Cilla the discs without informing them of the augmentation or the risks."

"I didn't *make* them play. I didn't—"

"You keep going down that road," Eve advised. "It's going to dead-end on you. The PA's going to have a field day on charges. We'll say Murder One on Bart, then the Assault with Intent on a police officer and a duly authorized expert consultant, civilian, Attempted Murder on Cilla, various and sundry cyber crimes."

"I didn't kill anybody!" he shouted. "They lost the game."

"Your game," Eve said. "Your rules. Your play. You're going to be a very, very old man if and when you get out of that cage, Var—a cage where you'll be banned from the use of any electronics. No more games for you, you fucker."

"This is whack." He looked at Peabody. "You know this is whack. You get it."

"Yeah, I get it. So let me put it this way, just to play the same theme as my partner. Game over, fucker. You lose."

Face cold, eyes flat, Peabody got to her feet. "I'll take him through, Dallas. McNab and I will take him through."

"Okay." She sat now, suddenly and completely exhausted. "Okay. Peabody? Good work."

"This isn't fair," Var protested. "It's just another cheat. You can't put me away for this," he continued as Peabody hauled him up. "I didn't *do* anything. I wasn't there. It's their own fault."

Eve closed her eyes as his voice, and the tears in it, faded away.

He believed it, she thought, at least in some small part of his mind. He'd done nothing more than provide, so couldn't be held responsible for the results. And maybe his lawyers, when he got them, would play that one, but she had faith in Reo, and the system.

She had to.

She opened her eyes when Roarke came in and closed the door. He sat across from her, kept those wild blue eyes on hers.

"Been a while since I've been in the box with a cop."

"Do you want me to read you your rights?"

"I'll waive that. You let Peabody lead him along. She did well."

"He believes some of that bullshit, enough of it to convince himself it's Bart's own fault he's dead, Cill's problem she's in a coma." Her heart squeezed, hard, before she finished the thought. "If that knife had gone into you a couple inches over, it'd be your own fault."

"Going by that logic, it would be my own agility and skill that has me sitting here now, looking at you. You're tired, Lieutenant, and you're sad, and a bit beaten up as well."

"I want to be pissed, and satisfied. I'll get around to it. They thought he was their friend, and they were his. He used them, sucked what he wanted from them, and gave back only what he wanted to spare, that was—in turn—useful to him. They never really meant anything to him, in all those years they worked together, spent together."

She drew a breath, let it out. "No, worse, they were just a means to an end, just levels to get through to the win. It made me think about what's involved in friendships and partnerships. Relationships. I could try to be a better friend, a better partner, but I'll probably forget."

"From where I sit you do quite well enough, but I'm happy to remind you if you like."

"Roarke." She reached over the table, took his hands. "I thought I understood, when Coltraine went down, I thought I understood what you deal with because of what I do. What I am. But I was wrong. And tonight . . . It was so fast. Blasting that damn room to pieces trying to find the controls. And I did. I did, but seconds too late. In seconds I saw that knife go into you, and the world just stopped. It just ended."

"But it didn't." He squeezed her hands. "And here we are."

"I did okay before you—without you. I was doing just fine. Christ knows you were doing just fine before me."

"I don't want just fine. Do you?"

She shook her head. "I mean, it was okay. When you don't know what you can have, you do okay with what you've got. But now I know, and I don't think I can get through without you. I wouldn't be just fine, or okay, or anywhere close to it. I don't know how people get through. All the people left behind, the ones I have to look in the eye and say he's gone or she's gone. I don't know how they take the next breath."

"Isn't that why, in a very real sense, you do what you do? You are what you are?"

"Maybe. You can't think about it or it makes you crazy. Or sad and tired." She closed her eyes for a moment, then opened them to look straight into his. "When we were in there, and it looked like we wouldn't walk out again, I could deal with it. Because . . . I know it's stupid."

"We'd die together," he finished.

She let out a half-laugh at the beauty, and the oddity, of being understood so well. "Which is probably sick and selfish, and a bunch of other neurotic shit Mira could pick at. But, yeah. Going down together's one thing. Taking the next breath without you? That's not possible. But you have that . . . possibility to cope with every day. Roarke, I wish—"

"Don't." His fingers tightened on hers, and his tone sharpened. "Don't sit there and tell me you wish it could be different. That you could be. I don't want different. I fell for a cop, didn't I? I married a cop, though she discouraged me. We're not easy people, either of us."

"Really not."

His arched his eyebrow. "Do you want easy?"

"No. Hell, no. I want you."

"Well, aren't we the lucky ones to have exactly what we want?"

"Yeah. We should go home." She let out a long breath. "Get a little sleep," she added as she rose. She saw Roarke's body stiffen, saw the wince as he got to his feet. "After Summerset takes a look at your side."

"I don't need him fussing over me. It'll do."

It might be small, it might be petty, she thought, but it was both a relief and just a little satisfying to reverse their usual routine.

"The MTs said you could use a follow-up at the hospital," she reminded him. "So it's that or Summerset."

"It's literally a flesh wound as the knife didn't get anything but meat."

"It's your meat, pal, which makes it mine. In this case, I'll go with Summerset, a soother, and some sleep. And before you argue, think back to the number of times you've hauled my ass to a hospital when I didn't want to go, or poured a tranq down my throat. Being you're just a consultant, I outrank you. You were injured on my watch."

"You're enjoying this."

"Maybe a little. Probably more when we get home and Summerset gives you grief. But for right now?" She looked up at him as she guided his arm around her waist. "Lean on me. I know it hurts."

"It bloody well does," he admitted, and leaned on her, a little, as they walked out together.

EPILOGUE

EVE LOOKED THROUGH THE GLASS WHERE BENNY SAT AT Cill's bedside, his hand over her still one. She could see his lips move, and imagined he read her something as his gaze tracked from his handheld to her face.

Her eyes remained closed, as they had since the attack.

"Word is he's here every day all day," she told Roarke. "Most of the night—all if he can talk the medical staff into it."

"Still no change."

"No. No change." She walked in. Benny stopped in midsentence.

"We're reading the latest issue of *Whirlwind*." But he set the handheld aside. "Got company, Cill."

"We can sit with her awhile if you'd like to get some air," Roarke said.

"No, but thanks."

"I wanted to let you know," Eve began, "Var's lawyers and the PA's office have reached a plea agreement. I can break it all down for you if you want, but the short version is he'll do fifty years, hard time, off-planet."

"It doesn't matter. What happens to him doesn't matter. She's all that matters. Three days now. The doctors, they say that every day she . . . that every day's good. That she could wake up in five minutes. Or five years. Or never."

"You believe she'll wake up." Roarke laid a hand on Benny's shoulder.

"And I think when she does, it'll matter to her that Var pays. For what he did to her, to Bart, to all of you," Eve added.

"We thought he was one of us, but he wasn't. Four square—but it was all a lie. I don't understand it. I can't. We were together all these years, every day. We worked together, studied, played, ate, laughed, cried. I don't know how he could do what he did. I'll never understand it, so he doesn't matter to me. He won't ever matter to me again."

But he drew in a ragged breath. "Why didn't he go for me instead of her? Why?"

"Do you want the truth or do you want it easy?"

He looked at Eve. "The truth."

"You were more useful, and she more dangerous. In his mind, in his plan. She's more of a leader, and you prefer the solo, the research. He could use you, and when he'd used you enough, or when he just couldn't resist, he'd have set you up, too."

"If I'd gone in with her. If I'd just—"

"She'd be dead without you," Roarke said. "He meant to kill her, Benny, and if you hadn't been there, if you hadn't stayed with her every second when you found her, he'd have finished her. You saved her life."

Roarke pulled a chair over, sat beside Benny. "What will you do now, with U-Play?"

"I don't care about that."

"She will. She helped build it as you did, as Bart did."

"If we hadn't, Bart would be alive. She wouldn't be here."

"No. Var's responsible," Eve corrected. "Not a company, not a game, not technology. A man. He put her here."

"I know that." His tone weary, Benny rubbed his hands over his eyes. "I know it, but . . . You could buy it," he said to Roarke. "We have good people, and—"

"I could, but I won't. Bart wouldn't want that, and neither would she."

"She'd hate it. But she's hurt so bad. Even if . . . when, even when she comes out of it, she'll have so much to go through."

"But not alone," Roarke murmured.

"No, not alone." With his eyes on Cill's face again, Benny stroked the back of her hand with his thumb. "I keep sitting here, thinking about all the times I had a chance to tell her I love her. I've loved her since we were kids, but I never have the guts to tell her or show her. I was afraid I'd screw up what we had. And now—"

"You'll stop wasting time," Roarke finished.

"You don't understand."

"Don't I?" Roarke looked at Eve. "I know love, and what it does to you, for you. I know that it can bloom out of friendship, or that friendship can open out of love. Both are precious. And when you have both, there's little that can't be done."

"You need to stop feeling sorry for yourself," Eve told him. "And start doing what can be done."

Anger flashed over Benny's face, then died. "You're right. I'm not helping her by thinking about what I can't do, what I don't want. Fuck Var. We're not going to let him win. Dammit, Cill, we can't let him win. Fifty years? Think of all *we* can do in fifty years. We've barely started."

He started to bring her hand to his cheek, stopped. "Her fingers moved." His voice trembled as he squeezed her hand tighter. "Her fingers moved." He shoved out of his chair to touch her face. "Cill. Cill. Come on, Cilly, *please*."

"Keep talking to her," Eve ordered when Cill's lashes fluttered.

"Wake up. Please, Cilly, wake up and look at me. Can't you just look at me? I need you to wake up. I need you so much, Cill." He touched his lips to her cheek, then gently, gently brushed them over her lips. "Wake up, Cill."

"Benny." The word was raw and weak, her eyes dull and unfocused—but open. "Benny."

Roarke rose, nodded at Eve. "I'll have them page the doctor."

"Hey, Cill." Benny's tears dripped onto her face. "Hey."

"Benny. I had a terrible dream. Can you stay with me?"

"Right here." He shoved down the bed guard, sat beside her. "Right here. I'm not going anywhere."

Eve backed out of the room, stepped aside as one of the nurses hurried in. She walked to Roarke. "We'll give them some time. Peabody and I will come back tomorrow and get her statement." She glanced back. "She's in for a long, painful haul."

"She'll make it. They will."

"Yeah, I think so."

Friendship to love—maybe it would work for them.

Then there was the other choice. Love to friendship, she thought as they took the elevator down. She supposed she and Roarke had taken that route.

It seemed to be working out just fine.